Praise for Lynda William's Previous Books

"Plenty of action with great world building and well-written characters. This one is a keeper. And made me want more of the Okal Rel universe." - Pam Allan, ConNotations Magazine

"The Okal Rel Saga is culturally complex and politically tangled, an epic tale of clashing civilizations and worldviews. Righteous Anger follows the making of a military hero, Horth Nersal, and is a strong, highly readable installment to this ambitious and far-reaching space opera." - Dru Pagliassotti, The Harrow

"Williams builds a very deep universe that could easily be off-putting in its level of detail, but it is so populated with interesting characters and moves along so breezily that the only problem might be keeping track of all the threads" - Lisa Martincik, VOYA Magazine

"The book is detailed, especially in the description of the many duels and the sword-play. The story takes place on different worlds and in the depths of space. The author deals with everything from race relations and xenophobia to the early sexual maturity of a genetically enhanced youth whose passions come to play much earlier than one would anticipate. We have feuding factions, politics, power plays, religion and tribal warfare taken to a galactic level. ... Recommended." - Ronald Hore, CM Magazine

"In the Rel universe life and land are precious and warring is against accepted practice - differences are solved by duels fought by a single champion- and RIGHTEOUS ANGER provides the story of champion Horth, never accepted by either side of two warring houses. A fast-paced fantasy of action results." - Diane C. Donovan, Midwest Book Review

"Once again I was very appreciative of the depth of the characters and found myself stealing moments to learn more about their struggles and ultimately the life rendering decisions each would make. The turmoil of the characters corresponds with the political turmoil between the two civilizations and builds to an explosive climax that would be difficult for any reader to anticipate or deny." - T.M. Martin, Yet Another Book Review

"I was captivated by the possibilities of living in that time and impressed with Williams' visions of the future and her ability to successfully weave in cultural differences in sexuality and love. I look forward to the next volume." - T.M. Martin, reviewer

FAR ARENA

Part Five of the Okal Rel Saga

a novel by
Lynda Williams

EDGE SCIENCE FICTION AND FANTASY PUBLISHING

AN IMPRINT OF HADES PUBLICATIONS, INC.

CALGARY

EDGE

Edge Science Fiction and Fantasy Publishing
An Imprint of Hades Publications Inc.
P.O. Box 1714, Calgary, Alberta, T2P 2L7, Canada

In house editing by Richard Janzen
Interior by Brian Hades
Cover Illustration by Lynn Perkins

EDGE Science Fiction and Fantasy Publishing and Hades Publications, Inc.
acknowledges the ongoing support of the Canada Council for the Arts and the
Alberta Foundation for the Arts for our publishing programme.

Library and Archives Canada Cataloguing in Publication

Williams, Lynda, 1958-
    Far Arena : a novel / by Lynda Williams.

(Okal Rel saga ; pt. 5)
ISBN-13: 978-1-894063-45-6

    I. Title. II. Series.

FIRST EDITION
(p-20090511)
Printed in Canada
www.edgewebsite.com

Dedication

For Alison

Other Books In The Okal Rel Saga

ONE

Eyes on Amel

Perry — One Pureblood Too Many

There was a point, during waiting, when you no longer cared about the outcome, only that the wait would end. Standing in Ops on *BlindEye Station*, Perry D'Aur sensed that mood all around her. Six hours ago, Horth Nersal had either won or lost a duel on Gelion, where swords settled differences among the ruling families of the empire, and if he had gone down — taking his Ava with him — vassals of the new Ava would be leading an invasion right through Perry's territory.

I am too old for this, thought Perry. *Too old to be worrying, again, about whether my polyglot alliance of rebels can survive a change of leadership on Gelion, or whether I can bear the cost in lives: Amel, Horth, even Ameron himself — damn the scheming bastard.*

Perry was a nobleborn Sevolite, tougher and longer lived than a genetically unmodified human, but she was past what would be called middle age in a commoner and felt every year of it right now.

A ship dropped out of skim with a flash on the screen everyone in Ops had given up pretending they were not staring at. Perry's throat tightened.

"It's only Ayrium!" Ops monitor Ramses reported, a hand to his earphone. "Back from trying to talk sense into our Reetion neighbors."

"Put her on speaker," ordered Perry. There was no point keeping news from the Ops crew.

Ayrium's frank, female voice riveted attention. "Hi, Mom," she greeted Perry. "Have you heard from court yet... about the title challenge?"

"No," Perry lanced the tension in her daughter's question. Ameron was more than a stabilizing force at court for Ayrium — he was a lover who, in Perry's jaded opinion, her daughter was unreasonably obsessed with, but that was beside the point today, like all things personal. "Any luck with the Reetions?"

"They won't evacuate," Ayrium answered, sounding wooden. "I guess invasion doesn't translate, or else they're too fixated on finding out where Ann has taken *Kali Station*. They don't like their stations going missing." She changed the subject suddenly. "If I started in the direction of court, I might be able to get news without—"

"No," Perry said stonily. "I need you here."

Ayrium answered with a long silence.

What will she do if Horth has lost? Perry wondered, never before so afraid of her daughter's Golden Demish intensity of feeling. *Will she throw her life away in some rash attack, avenging Ameron?*

"All right," Ayrium agreed at last, bitterly. "I know you need a highborn here to ward the station, if—" She broke off. "I will do my duty," she said, sounding impossibly cold to anyone who knew her. But Ayrium never said good-bye in anger. "May the gods ignore you, Mother," she added, in a warmer tone.

"Not a chance," Perry said, lightening up. "I pissed them off long ago." She turned to the drive monitor. "Boost to skim as soon as Ayrium clears off. Stick to low shimmer, holding position." Whatever was coming, she wanted to see it come, which meant being under skim themselves, even if aboard a lumbering galleon of a space station.

Perry gritted her teeth against the discomforts of reality skimming. She kept her focus on the panoramic nervecloth display ahead of her, where the crimson point of Ayrium's departure quickly grew historic. *Looked damned near Nersallian, that boost*, Perry thought with pride. Her highborn daughter was doing four *skim'facs* effortlessly. *If only we had fifty Ayriums*, thought Perry. Her expatriate Nersallian ally, Vrenn, had a genius for innovative tactics using nobleborn pilots and even commoners, but nothing was as effective in a shakeup, or a space war, as highborns.

"Contact!" Ramses sang out. Perry felt it at the same time, an almost subliminal shudder in the deckplates of *BlindEye Station*. She held her breath as she watched Ayrium's dot on the nervecloth dance and flicker the signal for "identify" at the four blue spots approaching her. One of them danced a response back.

"It's Liege Nersal!" someone screamed in elation.

Perry closed her eyes. Liege Nersal meant Horth, and no invasion. Unless—

If Horth had lost, Perry could not help thinking, *there would still be a liege Nersal.* It was easy to imagine Horth charging Dorn, his son and heir, with the job of seeing important refugees delivered to Perry for safekeeping.

Ayrium looped around to join the new arrivals and all five ships blazed toward the station. Perry felt a stronger modulation in the deckplates as the pattern that said *Liege Nersal* flickered on the nervecloth once more.

"Has to be Horth," Perry muttered, remembering a drunken bar debate about whether you could predict a man's sex style from his signature dance, and a half smile touched her lips, thinking about the young Horth Nersal who had laid claim to her as a *mekan'st*, or friend-lover, years before. He was too Vrellish by a long shot for her to be his only lover, and she lived by Vrellish rules herself despite her Demish upbringing and heritage. She didn't pretend her feelings for an intermittent lover like Horth rivaled Ayrium's great passion for Ameron, but this was personal for her, too.

"Drive, drop us out of skim," Perry ordered as the ships got close, with Ayrium still riding herd.

The Nersallian ships did their usual showy skid-in, dumping speed rapidly, and dropping into their docking cradles with a momentum within five percent of tolerance.

"Docks," Perry ordered, her mouth dry, "who do we have?"

"It's *DragonClaw*!" came the excited answer. *DragonClaw* was Horth Nersal's personal ship. Perry breathed out. "But it's not him," docks followed up, in shock. "It's... it's Heir Gelion."

"Ameron named an heir?!" was the first thing out of Perry's mouth. "Don't answer that!" she added at once. "I'm coming down."

The first person she saw when she sprinted into the docks was Dorn Nersal. *Dorn! Not Horth!* Perry forced herself to sidestep the implications long enough to note that Dorn was standing at the shoulder of a strange young man in black flight leathers who had crisp features and a closed-down expression.

Heir Gelion? Perry wondered. Ayrium's report from court before the duel had covered the sudden appearance of a new Pureblood named Erien, but what could it mean if he was here, now? And which Ava was the heir to: his mother, Ev'rel, or his father, Ameron?

Perry drew breath to ask Dorn for explanations when a wounded man emerged from a docking bay, supported by Horth's brother, Eler Nersal. The man raised a beautiful, sweating face, and fainted.

Perry recognized him at once. So did every one of her crew. In seconds, Pureblood Prince Amel — rarity, scandal, and another of Perry's *mekan'stan* — had all the help he could use.

It's Ev'rel, Perry thought, in horror, watching her people swarm around Amel's crumpled form. *Ev'rel is Ava! Oh, Amel, what has she done to you?*

Running footsteps signaled Ayrium's arrival. Her blue eyes swept the huddle of people around Amel and then fixed on Dorn as hope drained from her vivid features. Perry drew breath to call her daughter to her, unwilling to risk her streaking off on a mission of personal revenge — and then the last pilot appeared. Perry stared at him as if she had never seen Horth Nersal before, taking in the scarlet liege marks on his collar, the snarling dragon motif on his breast, and most of all his sword, with its worn belt and plain hilt.

Ayrium bounded the length of the docks, threw her arms around Ameron's champion, and kissed him resoundingly on the mouth, crying, "You are a wonderful, *wonderful* man!"

Horth froze, unnerving Perry with how close he had probably come to misinterpreting Ayrium's exuberance as an attack.

"Is the way clear to Gelion?" Ayrium asked, still oblivious.

Horth nodded.

Ayrium spun like a dancer and made for her ship. "Launch checks!" Perry yelled at her daughter as Ayrium pelted past, then turned back to face Horth. There was no mistaking that grin, it was Horth, but she heard herself say, "I thought you were *dead!*"

"I am not dead," he said, as literal as ever, and picked her up.

"Horth!" she protested, laughing and clutching at him. "I need to know what happened!"

"D'Therd fought well," he told her in his deep voice. "He is dead. Ev'rel, too."

"And this boy—" Perry craned her neck to look for Dorn Nersal and his companion.

"Erien," Horth supplied.

"—is Heir Gelion?" Perry asked.

But Horth had other priorities. Still carrying her none too gently, he headed for her quarters.

"Horth," Perry protested, "I can't just leave Heir Gelion standing on my docks!" But there was no getting down, and besides, it would have seemed ungenerous; in winning, he had saved all their lives.

"Dorn is responsible for Erien," explained Horth.

The last she saw of her illustrious guests, over Horth's shoulder, was Eler Nersal launching into a story, and the white, grim face of the new Heir Gelion with Dorn Nersal hovering at his back.

–o—o—o–

Horth was gone by the time a com hail woke Perry hours later. She elbowed on the intercom. "Here," she said, fishing for her favorite red halter top, which had ended up stuffed between bed and wall. As men went, Horth was beautifully uncomplicated.

"A throne envoy has arrived from Gelion with dispatches," Ramses reported. "From Ava Ameron."

Perry frowned. However glad she was to know Ameron was still Ava, the mere sight of Ameron's dead-leaves-in-a-gale scrawl did unhealthy things to her blood pressure.

"Hang on to any dispatches for me," Perry decided. "Where are our visiting highborns?"

Ramses cleared his throat awkwardly. A young, rural Barmian, he was still new to the idea of Vrellish-style *mekan'stan*, and two of the men Perry wanted to know about fell into that category: Horth and Amel.

"Horth, liege of Nersal, is conferring with members of the local branch of his family — an emissary from Liege Bryllit. Amel is keeping to his quarters. He says he doesn't want visitors."

How unlike Amel! The corner of Perry's mouth turned down.

"And where is Heir Gelion?" she asked.

"He received his dispatches and returned to his quarters." Ramses' pronouns conveyed the grammatic differencing a commoner should accord a Pureblood. *Erien makes him nervous,* thought Perry.

"Any idea yet why we've got Horth and two of the empire's three remaining Purebloods visiting?" she asked. She could not imagine why they would all have come out to personally bring the news to Ayrium and her if they were not refugees from a disastrous outcome at court.

"Actually, yes," Ramses spoke up. "The Reetions are demanding Amel be surrendered for questioning. Heir Gelion said that is why he's here — to negotiate with Rire about—" Ramses broke off. "You're not going to let the Reetions take Amel, are you, Cap?"

'Cap' was Perry's moniker with nearly all her people. She leaned against her wall mirror. The polished metal was cool on her temple. "Not if I can help it," she told Ramses, knowing her unsatisfactory answer would be spread the length and breadth of Ops within thirty seconds of her closing the circuit... then through all the levels of *BlindEye* in five minutes. Gossip outflew highborns.

"The Reetions should be grateful to Amel for helping to protect them," Ramses erupted, "not punish him!"

Perry snorted. "Ramses, I don't think they even *noticed* they were in danger." Reetions made her head ache. Genetically — in Gelack empire terms — they were commoners, but their society was very different, with law and administration mediated by sophisticated artificial intelligences known as arbiters. "The last time Amel made one of his trips to Rire," explained Perry, "he did something to one of their fancy computers and it's got the Reetions stirred up. But hell, Ramses," she continued cheerfully, "it's not as though the Reetions would harm a hair on Amel's head. Worst they'll do is analyze him to death." She paused, and then asked wickedly, "How did he earn your undying loyalty, by the way?"

Amel had a talent for winkling out people's most awkward difficulties — usually interpersonal — and solving them. She could just about hear Ramses' blush sizzle.

"Uh, nothing — that is..." Ramses floundered.

"Never mind," Perry let him off the hook and signed off. It was time to get some answers, and she'd start with Amel.

A self-appointed honor guard drawn from *BlindEye*'s heterogeneous society kept vigil outside Amel's door: a shady-looking woman in Vrellish flight leathers; an overweight technician in a baggy engineering uniform; one of Perry's own grandsons, by way of Vrenn, armed with the traditional dueling sword; and a teenage station prostitute with the kind of brittle skinniness developed by a life of poor feeding and little physical exercise.

The angry-looking woman with the Vrellish coloring — black hair and gray eyes — gave Perry a glare. "You are going to give up Amel to that Fountain Court puppy, aren't you?" she accused.

"Last time I took grammar lessons," answered Perry, "*Fountain Court puppy* wasn't proper address for a Pureblood."

The tech cleared his throat. "What do the Reetions want with Amel, Cap?"

"That," Perry said dryly, "is one of the things I hope to find out." She wasted a moment wondering whether to call them all on the casual 'Amel' and their equally casual pronouns, but Amel himself encouraged such familiarity. She reached over and laid her hand flat on the nervecloth of Amel's door.

"It won't respond," warned her grandson, but he was wrong. Perry was rewarded by a bouquet of flowers blooming on the nervecloth, set to the first bar of a soppy Demish love song. Laughter erupted as she stepped inside and closed the door behind her.

Amel's room on *BlindEye Station* was without walls or other dividers, except for a screen marking off the bathroom. Heavy russet curtains hung from a floor-braced frame over the sunken bed. A wall of nervecloth held the potential to open the room out, visually, onto a spacescape or meadow. Between Perry and the bed was a cleared dance floor. A child's sword hung in a place of honor, and wound around its hilt was a locket containing a few wisps of golden hair. Six plastic crates sat stacked on the floor, one box half-emptied of its luxury items.

Amel was just emerging from under his silk sheets.

He looks so vulnerable, she thought, his beautiful face blurred with sleep, his hair mussed, his clear gray eyes dilated with the all-purpose painkiller and postflight drug, *klinoman*. The fair skin of his torso was marked with welts no more than a day old, and the top edge of a large bandage she did not want to speculate about showed at his waist.

She dropped to a crouch beside him. "You've got to do something about that venting door," she told him gruffly. "How'm I supposed to keep my fearsome reputation if you're playing me love songs?"

"I'll fix it," he promised.

"You'll come up with something worse," she predicted, and let it drop. "We need to talk."

He patted the bed beside him. She crouched with a crack of knees and crawled onto the soft bed, grumbling, "This'd look much better if I was a third of my age with a sword-dancer's neat little tits." He did not rise to the bait, as he usually did, and reassure her that he found her beautiful. He hardly responded at all until she touched him. Then his body stiffened.

Touch usually reassured Amel. *Damn*, she though grimly.

He said meekly, "I'm sorry, Perry."

She let a silence pass and then asked in a level voice, "Bad, was it?"

He closed his eyes, failing to hide tears that wet his long lashes.

"Horth told me Ev'rel is dead," Perry said. "I can't pretend to be sorry."

He said nothing, only closed his eyes. She lay beside him staring at the ceiling, thinking maybe this would be the last time he arrived with injuries he did not want to explain. She remembered the lanterns they lit on Barmi for the harvest festival, and the way that the white moths came flocking out of the darkness to them, yearning for the killing flame. Well, this flame was snuffed, thanks to Horth, and maybe this was the last time Amel would land on *BlindEye* burned and flinching.

"Whatever happened to you in Lilac Hearth is what precipitated the duel Horth won, didn't it?" she asked bluntly.

He breathed out softly. "What do you already know?"

"Only what Horth told me, and you know what it is like getting words out of him. This new heir of Ameron's, Erien, fetched you out of Ev'rel's hearth on Fountain Court, and stood up to her when she tried to take you back, somehow provoking a title challenge between Ev'rel and Ameron. Then, to quote Horth, 'D'Therd fought well. He is dead. Ev'rel, too.' Anything else?"

He moved his head weakly on the pillow, "Nothing important."

"Nothing you are willing to talk about, you mean," Perry said more harshly than she had intended, and sat up, commanding eye contact. "Tell me this much: is there anything in the Court situation that is going to up and bite me in the butt? This Heir Gelion, for instance."

"Erien?" Amel shook his head, surprised. "Erien doesn't mean... He's just young and..." Amel broke off. "Erien doesn't like me, Perry, but he has reasons. I was there when his first foster father, Di Mon, died. He blames me for not anticipating Di Mon's suicide. I was the one who took Erien to Rire with his Reetion foster father, Ranar, afterwards. I've been there every time his life was disrupted, but despite that, he came for me when I was... trapped... in Lilac Hearth during the fire. Don't be too hard on him."

She frowned at him. "You know," she said, "that's the most you've said to me since I arrived and — guess what? — you're defending someone."

He settled back down. "It's still true."

She grunted. "So what did you do to piss off the normally mild-mannered Reetions?"

He sighed, but what she hoped would be the beginning of a meaningful answer was interrupted by a call from Ops.

"Cap?" Ramses spoke from one of Amel's hidden speakers. "There's a Reetion delegation inbound to *BlindEye*, ETA eight hours. Heir Gelion is on his way over to see Amel."

"Vent it!" Perry sat up. "That was fast!" In fact, for Reetions it was damn near instantaneous. She had counted on their elaborate ideas about due process giving her days to plan. "Can you show the hall outside your room on that nervecloth wall of yours?" she asked Amel.

He spoke a phrase from a poem, in an obscure Demish dialect invoking a vague echo of her childhood, something about windows and mirrors, and then an image of the corridor formed on the nervecloth wall. Perry punched a pillow into a hump under her shoulders and settled the kink in her back, hands behind her head as she settled down to watch.

"No sword," she noted as Erien, the new Heir Gelion, came into view.

"Erien was raised on Rire," explained Amel. He had on what she called his courtesan look — submissive and calculating. He did not approve of her spying on Heir Gelion but he wouldn't object. Not in so many words. He pushed back feathery black hair, and the movement drew her eye in spite of herself. She made a point of breaking eye contact before he started getting to her.

Erien's stride was measured and precise. Curiously, he kept to the right. Other Sevolites tended to center themselves in the corridor, deferring to their birth superiors and expecting deference from their inferiors. Perry's eyes narrowed at the sight of a Sevolite Pureblood yielding the center. *Like a Reetion,* she thought. He had spent seven years on Rire after the death of his Sevolite mentor, Di Mon.

As for the rest of it, Heir Gelion was a quietly striking young man, with a breadth of shoulder that revealed he had some Demish blood in him. He took his light gray eyes from the Vrellish, though his were less expressive than his father Ameron's, or his half-brother Amel's. His face, for a Vrellish highborn, was too composed, and although his features were sharply cut, in disposition they were more suggestive of his dead mother, Ev'rel, than his living father, Ameron, particularly in the curve of the mouth. He wore a loose shirt in two tones of green, darker on the body and lighter on the sleeves and cuffs, with a pair of earth-brown trousers — informal dress.

Does he think he can pass unnoticed when he has just been named Heir Gelion? Perry wondered.

The people keeping vigil at Amel's door made way with untidy laggardliness.

"Nervy buggers," Perry commented.

"He won't hurt them." Amel seemed to be trying to convince himself.

Erien stopped well clear, as was proper, Perry was relieved to see. Reetions tended to crowd you until you itched to pull a knife just to make space.

A knife, she noted, Erien did have: a distinctive one with a turquoise handle protruding from a boot sheath. It was almost certainly Monatese, which made sense since he had spent his first seven years as Di Mon's ward.

"Good cycle," Heir Gelion said to the motley assembly, accepting the obligation of the superior Sevolite to speak first to establish grammar. "I am Erien Lor'Vrel, Heir Gelion. I take it these are Amel's rooms." He used a simple, undifferenced *rel*-to-*pol* address: a reasonable compromise when speaking to a group, but still flattering given that he ranked as the highest Sevolite in the group by four grammar classes.

"Amel is not seeing anyone, Immortality," said Perry's grandson, "not even friends."

Heir Gelion's expression did not change. There were shadows under his eyes, a tightness to his mouth, and his sharp features were drawn.

"Has he been hurt as well?" Perry asked.

"Yes," said Amel.

"I have not come to see Amel as his friend," Erien told Amel's admirers. "I am here as Ava Ameron's representative."

At the mention of Ameron's name, resistance softened. People shifted to make way. Then, all at once, Perry's grandson took a step forward, hand on sword hilt. "We won't let the Reetions take Amel off this station."

Horth would have backhanded him off the wall for impertinence. Erien said mildly, "Amel is not going to be taken anywhere by force. But neither," and his voice became colder, "will the Reetions' complaint be trivialized. A crime has been alleged against the security of the Reetion Confederacy, our recognized neighbor state, and it will be dealt with in the Reetion fashion." The next time he spoke, he differenced his pronoun with the full weight of his entitlement. "I am here to see Amel. Now."

Erien started forward as though he did not intend to stop. Perry's grandson did something — Perry could not say what — but one instant Heir Gelion was reaching right-handed for the door to gain entrance and the next he was in a fighter's crouch. Perry's breath caught; he was so fast — Vrellish fast.

Amel scrambled up with a grunt, overcoming his drug-induced lethargy. He was through the door before Perry caught up to him. He still managed to wind his sheet into a sort of toga as he went, but Perry had ceased to be surprised by Amel's throwaway cleverness in small things.

"It's all right," Amel told his friends, "Heir Gelion saved my life at court."

Erien nodded curtly. A wash of sweat misted his forehead and the pulse at his throat and temples beat hard.

Amel's friends gathered around him. "We heard you were hurt!" the hulking technician blurted.

The Vrellish woman caught his arm and turned the wrist up, revealing a flesh-colored dressing. "You've been tied up," she said.

"It's over now," Amel said.

The skinny girl bit her lower lip, gathering her courage. "If you really saved Amel's life," she blurted in Erien's direction, interrupting the scrum around Amel, "thank you!"

"You'll have to excuse *BlindEye* commoners," Perry said stiffly to Heir Gelion. "They rub elbows with their betters more than most Gelacks."

"Perhaps that is healthy," Heir Gelion assured her.

"Risky," Perry commented.

"Let's go inside," Amel said to Erien, speaking in *rel*-peerage.

TWO

Erien

My Brother, My Burden

Erien inventoried Amel's room with a quick glance, noting its untidiness and the collection of questionable equipment. Reetions crystronics were contraband within the empire for the sake of their potential impact on the Monatese nervecloth monopoly. Rire acknowledged the ban, but it would be like Amel to disregard that. He turned a critical eye on Amel himself. After three years of fleet service, he could recognize the effects of *klinoman*. Its use would have to stop; Erien needed Amel alert and credible.

Perry D'Aur showed no signs of leaving and Erien doubted Amel would support him if he tried to get rid of her. He would simply have to watch what he said, and trust Amel to do likewise despite his *mekan'stan* relationship with Perry D'Aur, but Erien wished he felt more confident about his troublesome brother's common sense.

"It appears," Erien said to Amel, "the Reetions have accepted my invitation to meet with us here."

"You invited them?" Amel asked, eyes widening.

"Our mission is to establish diplomatic relations with them," Erien pointed out.

Amel hitched up his improvised toga and returned to his bed to lie down. Erien set his teeth. His own body longed to relax and start recuperating from the wound in his shoulder, making it a struggle to sustain a strong front in the midst of strangers, but he couldn't lie down like Amel, and trust he was among friends. Not while there was work to do, vital to the interests of his adopted people, the Reetions. Worst of all, Erien could tell Amel saw through his attempt to ignore the pain in his left shoulder, which drew Perry's attention.

"You're at least as badly injured as I am," Amel said, managing to radiate an air of big-brotherly concern — to which he was not entitled, since they hardly knew each other regardless of having a shared mother. "Why not give yourself time to recover?"

"If we satisfy the Reetions promptly it may preempt attempts to extradite you to Rire to be questioned there," said Erien, using the pain to keep him focused.

"Won't they want to rehabilitate me?" Amel asked suspiciously.

"They have no jurisdiction," said Erien. "Under Reetion law, Gelacks have status only in terms of basic human rights, which is a large part of why we have a problem now. There are no diplomatic protocols. We need to resolve their complaint about you quickly, so I can get to work on diplomatic relations."

Amel's composure melted, demonstrating his chameleon-like capacity to emote, serving no purpose Erien could see, except to make him vulnerable. "All right," he said without conviction.

"We have until station-noon tomorrow before the Reetion investigative triumvirate will be able to meet with us," said Erien. "Will you be able to proceed then without arousing their curiosity about your physical condition?"

"Why should they care about my 'physical condition'?" Amel asked, sounding petulant.

"Reetions are not as callous as Gelacks in their handling of people," Erien explained coldly. "If they know you are hurt, it will mean delays — and *unwelcome attention*." He could only hope Amel was bright enough, despite his drugged state, to grasp he was referring to the hidden danger in too much disclosure about how they both came to be wounded, which he could not speak of openly in front of Perry D'Aur.

Instead, Amel reacted as if stung. "What about *your* wound?" Amel accused. "Won't they want to pry into that, too?"

Erien was taken aback. "Believe me," he said coolly, "I am equally loath to attract Reetion solicitude. My youth alone will make it hard enough for them to accept me as the Gelack representative."

"You are Heir Gelion," Amel said. "They will have to respect you."

Erien's patience slipped. "I could be the Ava himself, and except for anthropologists like Ranar, my title would still be less important to them than my age. A seventeen-year-old is a mere child in their scheme of things, no matter how important on Gelion. Do you really know so little about Reetion customs?"

"Sorry," Amel said dourly. "I guess I didn't pick up on their big paternalistic thing for children when I ran into them the first time. You know, when I was sixteen and they used their experimental psychiatric probe to extract information from me against my will. Guess they were having a bad day."

Erien could have struck him for his sarcasm! Yes, the visitor probe incident eighteen years before had been a fiasco all around, but the ill effects Amel had suffered were not intentional. Quite the opposite! Good people had suffered agonies over the moral compromise Amel referred to, and first among them was Lurol, the scientist who had invented the visitor probe and Erien's foster mother on Rire.

"Have you read the Reetion record of the *Second Contact* incident?" Erien asked Amel coldly. "Rire agonized about what was done to you and corrected the legal flaw that made it possible by extending human rights to Sevolites, like you and me, so it can never happen again. We, on the other hand, have never even formally apologized for the failed invasion your visit to their station was part of, or entertained the question of how to deal with them except in terms of our own system of ethics as embodied by the religious and political dictates of *Okal Rel*."

Amel listened in silence, sitting up with his sheet pooled at his waist and his eyes hooded, making his very posture a nebulous accusation impervious to logic.

Erien tried to get control of his irritation. "Ameron has charged me with mediating all Reetion relations, starting with resolving their charges against you for sabotaging arbiter communications. But my goal is to get past everything to do with you as fast as possible, in order to establish a diplomatic foundation for future relations, so—" He paused. "Can you manage being questioned by them, under my protection of course, without provoking fresh investigations into your injuries or state of mind?"

Amel looked up with unexpected stubbornness. "Keep their hands off me," he said with spiteful force, "and I will cope as stoically as you can." He softened with a fatalistic sigh. "If we can keep them here, talking, for a few weeks, there'll be no wounds left to make them curious when they finally do take me prisoner."

Erien rebelled against the creeping martyrdom in Amel's determination to cast the Reetions as one of the many abusers — political or sexual — who had marred his life. "The idea is to begin and end the inquiry here, in Gelack territory."

"Right," Amel said, as if he had been struck in the chest with a sheathed sword but didn't want to let on.

Meaning what?! Erien wondered in anger. *Did you expect to be surrendered to Rire, to prove you are as victimized as you think you are?*

"I'd like to sleep now," Amel said, and shifted onto his side to get comfortable.

"Not yet," Erien stuck to his agenda. "I need to be briefed before I talk to your accusers. Tell me exactly what you did to help your Ann of Rire subvert arbiter communications during the construction of *Kali Station* in Paradise Reach."

"Would you believe me," Amel said, eyes closed, "if I told you I can't remember?"

"No," said Erien. Amel possessed the powers of total recall legendary in the Demoran line of highborn Demish. The only person Erien knew who could match Amel's prodigious memory was Princess Luthan, the titular liege of Silver Hearth on Fountain Court. Just thinking about Luthan improved Erien's mood, although connecting her with Amel in any way worsened it. Erien preferred to keep the innocent Demish princess a pleasant counterpoint, in his mind, to Amel's twisted secrets and masterly subterfuge.

Amel sighed. "I should have said I don't remember it all exactly," he said tiredly. "There was so much data to sift, like swallowing water too fast, for too long. This is a partial recreation I made before I went to sleep last night, because I thought you'd ask." Mindful of his hurts, Amel reached to pick up a control and summoned up a navigational matrix on his Reetion stage in which each three-dimensional point was further marked with symbols for relative speed, mass, gap and frequency of shimmer — all aspects of the telemetry projected on the inner lining of a *rel*-ship's hull while reality skimming.

"What..." Erien was drawn to ask despite a reluctance, which surprised and embarrassed him, to admit he could not deduce what he was looking at, "... is it?"

"Arbiter to arbiter data flow modeled as a piloting scenario," said Amel with no trace of pride in the magnitude of his achievement. "What you are seeing here is a scrap of a conversation from *SkyBlue Station* back to the Reetion Net on Mega — a laundry list, more or less, this and that delivered, whom to notify — boring stuff, but absolutely inviolate. I couldn't hack in to change the details. I told Ann as much when she asked me to help her communicate through the arbiter net with her defense-minded confederates in the Reetion Reach of Paradise." He shut the stage display off, putting down his customized remote control. "But she upset me so much, making me think about what could happen to people — Reetion people — if we invaded, that I couldn't give up. I routed data to my ship — it's easy to get hold of data under Reetion jurisdiction, but I guess you'd know that since you lived there. I used my ship's navigational system to develop a model I could bring all my senses to bear on by making it a navigational problem in, well, a pretty weird universe." He paused. "I guess that sounds silly."

"It seems to have been effective," Erien told Amel dryly. "You used this model, then, to do what?"

"Let Ann communicate with her confederates on Mega in the Reach of Paradise, to place orders for the supplies she needed to make the station defensible... secretly. But I told Ann the truth when I said I couldn't subvert an arbiter's thought process," Amel insisted, lying limply in his bed again, looking harmless. "All I did was smuggle across extra data. The Megans had to figure out how to make what they shipped her look harmless. That's all I know. She didn't give me any details — but then I didn't ask." Erien could not withhold a twinge of sympathy at Amel's resolute confession. If it was wrong to help Ann arm Rire against Gelion, as things turned out, it could have been just as wrong to leave Rire undefended if Ev'rel's vassals had launched the invasion they yearned to.

The germane point for Erien was preventing stalwarts of clean fighting by Gelack standards — like Horth Nersal — from taking offense at whatever Ann had prepared for invading Sevolites, because if Ann's actual defense resembled her original, rejected proposal for anti-Sevolite tactics in space, it would jeopardize any hopes of diplomacy. Commoners being no match for Sevolites in space without taking desperate measures was as irrelevant to *Okal Rel* as Amel's motive for data tampering was to the Reetions. *Okal Rel* underpinned the survival of the empire despite its addiction to inter-house warfare every bit as much as Reetion civilization depended on the integrity of arbiters.

"I'm going back to sleep now," Amel said.

"I'll show you out, Heir Gelion," said Perry.

Erien didn't have the energy to argue with her. Waiting for the lift to take them up to Ops, she said, "You won't ask, so I'll tell you."

"Tell me what?" he asked, surprised.

"How Amel and I became *mekan'stan,* seeing as we are both Demish — not Vrellish — and he is rather above my station, to put it mildly."

"I know Amel spent time in your custody after his original probing by the Reetions," Erien said, trying to truncate the conversation.

Perry gave a snort. "I know what it looks like," she said. "And I'm not telling you this because it's any pleasure to brag about. I am telling you because you ought to know. Amel was a wreck. Nice kid for a Pureblood who thought he was a courtesan, but the Reetions messed up his head. Sleeping with him seemed to calm him down."

The lift arrived. There was nothing to do but get into it with her. The doors closed.

"If you're as Vrellish as you look," Perry told him gruffly, "you'll be thinking 'Yeah, right, rough job.' Well it was, now and then." She rubbed her nose. "He threw me clear across the room once."

"You do not need to justify your behavior," said Erien.

"I'm trying to make it clear," Perry rode roughshod over this dismissal, "that Amel has every reason to be scared shitless by Reetions. Don't make the mistake of considering Reetions harmless — for all our sakes."

"*Harmless* is not the term I would use," Erien said stiffly, and added to himself, *civilized is more like it.* What happened to Amel eighteen years ago was the fault of the Gelack named H'Reth who had tried to use Amel against the Reetions. Lurol's psychiatric probe had saved Amel's life, and then — admittedly — became the means by which the Reetions saved themselves in the midst of a Gelack-induced crisis. Rire had since proved its moral superiority and courage by rejecting Ann's lobby to develop anti-Sevolite defenses when rumors of invasion heated up on Gelion. Rire's preferred solution was to surrender at least the Reach of Paradise, and go on to win the peace by educating its socially primitive, self-proclaimed conquerors.

Privately, Erien suspected the plan underestimated Sevildom's organizational powers, but Gelion was equally arrogant. Ava Ameron had sent him to placate a bunch of

troublesome commoners toward whom Ameron had compassionate impulses — when he could spare the time. Only
Erien understood that Ameron's agreement to acknowledge
the Reetion Confederacy as a sovereign power was just the
first step. Rire, itself, had to be willing to view the empire
in the same light, and not as an alarming anachronism. The
attention Amel generated was just a nuisance.

"The Reetions will be about eight hours getting here and
another eight recovering from sedation after *rel*-skimming,"
Perry told Erien. "You can rest until then."

He drew breath to argue but she raised a hand, forestalling
him. "With all due respect, Heir Gelion — I've been in charge
around here for fifty years, and I sure as hell wouldn't put
someone in your shape on duty as a backup cook, never mind
head of a mission as important as this one." Her pronouns
were differenced respectfully, but the tone was that of captain
to a green subordinate.

Erien tamped down his impulse to reject her advice. She
had dealt with Reetions as friends, enemies and trade partners
for as long as he had been alive. He needed her trust and
respect, and she would neither trust nor respect someone who
failed to acknowledge his own limits. Worst of all, she was
right.

He smiled faintly. "Let me know as soon as the Reetion
delegation announces its readiness to see me — and ensure
they are not exposed to any highly colored and potentially
inflammatory version of events on Gelion in my absence. I
will be in my quarters."

"You'll be better after a long rest," she approved.

Maybe, maybe not, thought Erien, wondering what nightmares lay in wait for him in the dark of his quarters, tangled
in images of the horrors he had lived through at court less
than 48 hours earlier.

THREE

Eyes on Amel — Sylvie

All for Love (And the Revolution)

Sylvie entered the kitchen full of courage, only to feel it dashed at the sight of people. She shrank against the white face of a refrigeration unit, listening to the cook scold her son.

"And why should I give a lout like you the honor of taking Amel his dinner?" the cook asked.

The cook's son swallowed a scrap of sweetened protein paste filched from the plate and said, "I can cheer him up by describing how silly the Reetion dignitaries looked when their pilot revived them. No space legs!"

Sylvie forced herself away from the freezer, heart in her throat. "H-hi," she said.

Both the cook and her son looked at her, making her acutely self-conscious of her thin body. She did not want to be pathetic — no Nersallian ever would — and even if she was a commoner and a failure, Sylvie still harbored the pride of the Black House in her narrow chest.

I can do this, she commanded her wild pulse.

"Sylvie, right?" The cook's son recognized her as one of Perry's ex-empire engineers who worked on *BlindEye Station*.

"I must take the tray up to Amel," Sylvie blurted.

The cook glowered at her, but Sylvie held firm. After all, she wasn't doing this for herself, it was for Hanson and his brave revolution against the oppression of the Reetions and their all-seeing computers; her Hanson, the marvelous alien from the Reach of Paradise, had taken the time to make her feel special, and explained how important it was for his movement to have someone they trusted to work on *BlindEye*.

"Perry asked me to take it to Prince Amel," Sylvie lied, "so I c-could ask him a few things for her."

The cook opened her mouth to ask questions and was preempted by her pilot son. "I'll escort her," he declared, snatching up the tray and pushing it into Sylvie's hands.

"Oh, all right! But be respectful, both of you!" the cook scolded as the pilot herded Sylvie out the door.

The pilot rolled his eyes at his mother's harangue. "So," he said to Sylvie, "you must be another Amel fan. It makes guys like me crazy the way women go for His Sweetness, Pureblood Amel, I'm smarter than the rest of them! There's a dozen women I can make time with, like *that*," he snapped his fingers, "if I have news about Amel to share with them." He sampled something off the tray in Sylvie's hands and spoke as he chewed. "I could tell 'em what he's getting to eat, of course, but seeing him with my own eyes is way better."

A striding figure draped in a dark cloak parted foot-traffic ahead of them, making Sylvie falter for fear it might be Vrenn, Captain Perry's first *mekan'st*. Like Sylvie, Vrenn was an expatriate Nersallian, except he had belonged to the *kinf'stan* — Sevolites entitled to challenge for the title of Liege Nersal — while she had been a docks technician. She had no doubt what would happen to her if Vrenn knew she was Hanson's spy on *BlindEye Station*. Vrenn killed traitors.

"You sick or something?" the pilot asked.

Shame replaced fear when Sylvie saw the figure ahead of her was not Vrenn, after all, and she made herself relax.

"What do you think about this business of the Reetions demanding Amel answer charges about tampering with their arbiters?" asked her self-serving escort as they moved on.

"A-Amel?" Sylvie floundered, not wanting to think about Amel, himself, just the mission she had to foist upon him for Hanson and the rest of the Megan rebels struggling to free themselves from Reetion domination. "He c-can take care of himself. He's strong."

The pilot gave a disparaging huff. "Him? Strong? Well, in some ways, perhaps... like a flower in a mixer! If nothing else, whatever mess he gets into, he will impart fragrance and color." He laughed. "My mom likes to make a big deal about him being descended from the Demoran emperor. She thinks he's sweeter-souled than the rest of us. I think he's a bit soft in the head, myself."

There were two people outside Amel's door, a big female guard and a boy of ten who sprang up as they approached, still wearing a stained apron from the dirty kitchen job he was probably taking a break from.

"This is Sylvie," the pilot explained their mission to the guard, "Cap told her to ask Amel a few things when she brought his tray to him."

"Fine," said the guard, "I'll just check with Ops about that. Cap always leaves word of odd orders with—"

"No!" Sylvie blurted, certain her flimsy lie was about to be exposed.

The guard folded her arms. "I thought as much. You," she told the pilot, "scram."

"But—"

She laid a hand on her shock-rod, a semi-acceptable hand-to-hand weapon tolerated on *BlindEye Station* for crowd control. "Scram."

The pilot gave up with a curse and stalked off grumbling to himself about Amel's affect on women, which the guard ignored.

"And you, honey," the guard confronted Sylvie, "should know that since I came on duty three hours ago, you are the sixth woman who has tried to get into Amel's room on some frail excuse."

Sylvie clutched the tray hard. "I'm not r-really sent by the captain," she confessed, stuttering. "But I have to see Pureblood Amel. We're — friends."

"Just like half the station says they are," drawled the guard.

"We're — lovers!" Sylvie tried, getting shrill.

"Mmm," said the guard. She took Sylvie by the elbow. "We'll see what Amel says about that."

Oh no, Sylvie thought, *she's going to ask!* She had actually met Amel only once, in the docks a few years ago. They'd shared about a half-hour of each other's company, working over a broken engine together. They had never even touched.

Inside Amel's room, she caught her breath at the sight of so much careless opulence, from the crumpled satin sheets to the half-full crates of delicacies from the Demish reaches. The room smelled faintly of vanilla with a touch of spice.

"Amel?" said the guard by Sylvie's elbow. "I've got someone here who says she's your lover, and with you," she shrugged, "you never know. So I thought I'd ask."

Amel shifted up on an elbow, muzzy with sleep, and blinked at them.

There were women on *BlindEye* who liked to talk about making love to Amel, complete with lurid details. Sylvie had always dismissed their behavior as harmless mimicry of Vrellish women, but now she was looking at Amel in bed, tangled in a satin sheet, she was disgusted with them. Beauty like Amel's was not meant to be drooled over. It was something to admire from a distance, like art. Shame at her pretended intimacy made her cheeks burn.

"Do you know her?" asked the guard.

"Sylvie," Amel said, offering her name like a gift, so casually it was easy to assume it came to him easily. Perhaps it did; he had a formidable memory.

"So you *do* know her," the guard said, sounding undecided.

Amel gave his attention to the guard. "You've lost weight since I was last on *BlindEye*, Kara. I hope it wasn't illness."

"Nah," she said, "hard work. You don't know how lucky you are. Thirty-four years old and still looking twenty-one, with a complexion most women would kill for! And you take it for granted, you Pureblood brat."

Amel smiled, but seemed so accustomed to such rants he lacked the inspiration to respond.

"People say you were hurt, bad, at court," Kara asked with an intense look. "Is it true?"

"I would rather not discuss it, sorry," Amel said in a voice that was too light and musical to be sincere. "But thank you for caring," he added, with a shimmer in his warm, gray eyes.

The guard swallowed down her emotions. "Right," she said. She took the food tray from Sylvie, who was shaking hard enough to rattle the cutlery, and set it down on the floor. "I'll wait outside."

Amel spoke to Sylvie as soon as the door had closed. "I'm guessing you have some reason for needing to be alone with me," he said.

Relief and confusion sluiced about Sylvie's heart. "I bring you a message," she said, declining his offer of commoner peerage by speaking up with full differencing, commoner to Pureblood. "A message from Ann."

The name of Amel's Reetion *mekan'st* claimed his full attention; he rustled in his sheets, sitting up.

"Ann's all right, then?" he asked. "And the Reetions haven't caught her?"

Sylvie shook her head. "No."

Belatedly, suspicion crossed Amel's face. "Why would Ann contact me through you?"

"Because I am a—" she rejected the word 'spy.' It felt too ugly. "I am in love with her Megan ally, Hanson, from the Reach of Paradise."

Amel raised an eyebrow. "Hanson?" He frowned. "I always thought of Hanson as someone too busy hating everything that wasn't Megan to love anyone." He dropped the subject with a throwaway hand gesture. "Tell me about Ann."

"S-she needs your h-help," Sylvie began, but the tension was too much. She swayed on her feet.

Amel rose, wearing nothing but the sheet he hastily fastened about himself. He helped her into a chair and offered her a glass of water. She took the water, looked up into his face, and felt calmer.

"Wait a moment while I dress," he told her.

For a second she was frightened he would drop the sheet in front of her, but after taking clothing from a chest he dropped the bed curtains surrounding his floor mattress, creating an island of privacy in the openness of the room.

"I am not in much of a position to help anyone," he told Sylvie through the curtains. "I am wanted by an investigative team from Rire for arbiter tampering, and I have no idea what my status is back on Gelion. My mother, Ev'rel, is — dead." He floundered over the fact. Moments later, he emerged through the curtain, dressed in silver-gray stretch pants under a Barmian peasant shirt. "I betrayed my mother's vassals by helping Ann, so if what she's done is inflammatory to Gelacks—" he shrugged with an attempt at indifference. "Dishonorable execution is the most I might be able to command on Gelion once the Reetions expose all the details. I command no resources to help anyone."

Sylvie put her water glass down for fear of spilling it. "All Ann needs is *you* — in person — to save the lives of everyone on *Kali Station*."

Amel's space-black eyebrows rumpled. "Why? What's happened?"

Sylvie fidgeted. "I do not understand all the details, b-but the Reetions deposed Hanson's liege — no, leader — with a thing called an election back on Mega. Hanson's cause is threatened! He tried to take command of *Kali Station* to go help his fallen leader back home, since the station is capable of *rel*-flight, but

Kali's arbiter resisted him with an almost Lorel cunning. Now the arbiter is damaged, for which Ann blames Hanson." Sylvie pursed her lips at the injustice of the Reetion woman's failure to understand Hanson's motives were honorable. "Her message said I must tell you Hanson tried to strip the arbiter of its resistance by isolating it in a single crystronic block and wiping the rest of its memory."

"He boxed the *Kali* arbiter?!" Amel exclaimed, stunned. "A full-fledged, mature station arbiter? In a single block?"

Sylvie nodded. "Ann said that would mean something to you."

Amel's brow contracted. "Yes, I can see why *Kali* needs help. But Ann's there and she's a pilot. She could notify the Reetions to evacuate them!"

"Hanson would rather die than surrender to the enemies he despises," Sylvie said proudly. "It is his wish to sever all ties with Rire."

"He picked a dumb way to hack at the umbilical cord!" Amel erupted in anger, making Sylvie take a step back.

"No, wait!" Amel caught her arm. He was stronger than he looked, just as falling water could seem to possess more grace than power until you tried to alter its course. "They must surrender, fast," Amel urged her. "Reetions don't execute people, but space will surely kill them, when the arbiter goes down. They have to evacuate, or import another arbiter, if they can. Only a healthy arbiter can stabilize the damaged one."

"Or you!" Sylvie blurted.

"Me?" Amel released her, looking alarmed. "Did Ann tell you that?" he frowned. "It sounds more like something Hanson would dream up." He narrowed his gray eyes.

"Ann thought you might have doubts. She said to tell you—" she balked now it came to this, out of sheer embarrassment, "—she says you are the only man she could ever do two *skim'facs* with because—" His widening eyes clamped her throat shut.

"Because what?" he demanded with a skeptical pout.

"S-something about Gelacks being right," she coughed, "about sex and... and flying."

Amel muttered something under his breath with Ann's name in it. Suddenly Sylvie grasped it was not a joke or arranged code, but something they had really done that Ann didn't expect anyone but Amel to know about. "You did?" she heard herself exclaim. "You had sex with her *while* you were reality skimming?"

"I was losing her!" he said testily. "And we couldn't stop because — oh damn you, Ann!" He put his face into his hands.

Sylvie gave him time. All she could think was that her duty was done. It felt like a miracle. When he lowered his hands he was composed. "Tell me where they are. Maybe I can get there and back before it messes up things with the Reetions for Erien."

"I want to come with you!" Sylvie cried.

"No, Sylvie, you would slow me down too much. Besides, I need backup. Once I know where they are I can tell you how long I should be gone. If I'm not back by then, you may be their last hope. You will have to tell Perry where to find them."

"But — I'd betray Hanson!"

"If I can't help them, and I can't get them to surrender, then you'll have to decide which you value more: Hanson's life, or his freedom! Now give me their coordinates."

As she did, he went down on one knee by the forgotten tray of food and gulped down the enriched fruit drink.

"You told Kara we're lovers," he remarked, getting up. "We can work with that."

Carrying the tray he went to the room's wall com. "Kara? I've a favor to ask. Could you get us a bottle of wine? Sylvie will take it from you when you get back. I'll be in the bath."

"I'm on duty!" Kara's voice protested.

"Please?"

There was a brief silence. "Oh, all right."

Amel ate one of the cook's treats. Then he slipped behind a screen and emerged draped in a floor-length, Nersallian cloak complete with dueling sword.

"I'll be right back," he told Sylvie, picked up his tray and swept out. The door sealed behind him. On the wall display Sylvie watched him confer with the boy who was still standing vigil.

"I want cook to know," he told the child, "how much I appreciate the trouble she goes to. I particularly liked the tingly flavor in the flowerets. Something effervescent? If you'll tell her that for me, you can have the rest on the plate. But don't come back for four hours."

The boy grinned and winked at him. "I won't tell Cap about Sylvie."

Amel smiled. "Perry thinks I'm too clingy. She might approve."

The boy shook his head. "The rules are one *mekan'st* per dock."

Amel shared a 'guys will be guys' grin with the boy that expressed a commoner or Demish double-standard, although his words embodied Vrellish sentiments. "Well," he said, "Perry has more than one *mekan'st* in dock herself just now."

The boy took off. Amel came back in, picked up a Reetion device and dictated into it rapidly in a language Sylvie did not even recognize, but she thought she heard him use the name 'Erien,' which frightened her.

Amel tossed the device down when he'd finished. "I should be back in four hours." He smiled. "And when Kara brings wine, try to look like you're having fun unless you want to spoil my reputation with women." His light air made the subterfuge bearable. She tried, very bravely, to smile back.

"If there's any trouble," he said, "turn to Erien, or the Reetions. You'll survive both. Vrenn—" he pressed his lips together, saying no more.

Sylvie nodded. The warning about Vrenn she understood, but she was dubious about the other two recommendations. "Come back," she begged him.

He smiled at her. "That's the plan."

FOUR

Erien

First Engagement

Reetions always did things in threes when they acted politically. It was one of the tenets of their compu-communism,
which abhorred vesting executive power in a single individual.
So it was no surprise they had sent out a triumvirate to investigate Amel's misconduct with an arbiter.

Erien met the three Reetions in a briefing room with pale
walls, shot through with fern-textured embossing and trimmed
in light wood. The round table also appeared to be wood until
one realized that much of its finish was framed and mounted
nervecloth. One wall of the room was nervecloth, and the remaining walls featured silk paintings of landscapes stretched
on wooden dowels.

The Reetions were shown in by one of Perry's people. All
three had typical Reetion complexions that ranged between light
tan and caramel brown. The Gelacks had requested their Reetion
guests leave behind their translation equipment, to permit them
the option of speaking among themselves when so desired. No
arbiter was to preside, either, which was a huge concession. From
the Reetion perspective, the triumvirate were roughing it nearly
as much as Ranar had while exploring the empire, off the record,
as a field anthropologist specializing in gelackology.

Erien stood to greet them to ensure his adult height registered.

"I am Erien Lor'Vrel," he said, "Heir Gelion and acting Gelack
ambassador to Rire."

"Kirkos," said the oldest of the Reetions, struggling to get
comfortable in a chair that failed to adjust to his bulk the way
a Reetion morph chair would.

"I believe I have heard of you," said Erien. There was a Kirkos who voted on the first expansion of the Sibling Worlds Assembly, whose work on jurisdictional tangles Erien had studied as a boy on Rire, although he had never seen the man's picture. Reetions considered it crass to show interest in the appearance of political figures.

"I, too, have heard about you, young man," Kirkos replied with a frown.

"I'm Glynda," volunteered the only woman triumvir, "representing Human Ethics." She looked about forty, and quietly hearty.

"I believe you studied anthropology with Ranar," remarked Erien.

"If you know my work, you'll also know I'm a strong opponent of bioengineering humans to develop superpilots for ourselves to match the piloting capacities of Sevolites. But I want you to know it is the process of creating artificial humans I object to, the culling and experimentation that must have gone into your creation on Earth a thousand years ago. As products of the process, you are not to be blamed for it, and I accept Sevolites, like yourself, as fully human."

"I understand the distinction," Erien assured her.

The third triumvir pumped Erien's right hand once, with vigor. Erien barely caught his defensive reaction in time to stifle it.

"I'm Fahzir," said the handshaker, "a research-exempt specialist in arbiters... and a pilot." It was a strange combination for a Reetion, and Fahzir laid claim to it with pride. "Your childhood record shows you shared your guardian Ranar's interest in information sciences. I checked the record, and the exercises you completed before you lost interest looked promising."

"Shall we address you as Immortality, Heir Gelion or Erien," Kirkos interrupted Fahzir. "We should settle that prior to the arrival of less cosmopolitan Gelacks."

"I am equally comfortable with Erien or Heir Gelion," said Erien, "since we will not be joined at this first meeting by anyone besides Perry D'Aur and Ambassador Ranar."

A pained look passed between Glynda and Kirkos at the mention of Ranar. *Perhaps it's the title of ambassador given to him by Ameron,* thought Erien. Reetions did not approve of titles. Terms like research-exempt, which recognized the need for gifted individuals to be excused routine duties of citizenship, were considered descriptive, not titular.

Erien seated himself, taking care to minimize the stiffness of his movements.

"Where is Amel?" asked Glynda.

"Pureblood Prince Amel Dem'Vrel is here, of course," said Erien, stressing Amel's titles, "but I thought it best to speak with you first, to be sure you understand the extent of the concern by Perry's people. They think you mean to extradite him."

"Extra—" Glynda gave an awkward laugh. "I am sorry, but it is hard to believe even Gelacks could imagine we mean Amel harm!"

The door opened and Ranar came in, watched by everyone. On Gelion he had sailed through slander and house arrest with aplomb, but Erien's Reetion foster father had no stamina for space travel. Ranar supported himself from door to chair like a convalescent before he sat down.

"Good to see you, Ranar," said Glynda, with genuine warmth for her old mentor.

Ranar nodded to her. "Kirkos I know by reputation," he continued around the table. "I am afraid I haven't read your record, yet," he confessed to Fahzir. "I have only just recovered from the trip here."

"I know you by reputation, as well," Kirkos told Ranar. "The work you have done is unparalleled. I do not think I could have shown such courage."

"And such objectivity," Glynda insisted in a pointed manner.

"Yes," Kirkos agreed, "that too is exemplary — under the circumstances."

"Circumstances?" Ranar asked.

There was a brief, awkward silence.

Fahzir cleared his throated. "It is completely understandable, if you went a bit... native."

Ranar took this in slowly. "What are you not telling me?" he asked them all.

Glynda volunteered to break the news. "You put on record that Erien was a commoner assigned to your service by House Monitum. Your housemates, Lurol and Evert, have since admitted they have known for years he is a Sevolite, although you told even your family no more than Erien knew himself: that he was highborn, but not a Pureblood and the son of the two most powerful Sevolites in the empire, Ava Ameron and his rival, the late Avim Ev'rel Dem'Vrel."

The impact of the news made Ranar look middle-aged and vulnerable. "Evert and Lurol were questioned?" he asked with alarm. "What else did they say?"

Di Mon! Erien thought in horror.

"Is there more?" Kirkos asked.

"No, of course not," Ranar snapped.

Erien let out a breath. Di Mon had been Ranar's lover, which would mean very little to the Reetions, but in the empire the love shared by Erien's two foster fathers could do grievous harm to Monitum, and Di Mon's place in its history.

"You were the lead advisor on gelackology to the Foreign and Alien Council," Kirkos pursued his business with Ranar. "If I asked you, in that capacity, whether what you did not tell us about Erien was politically significant, or strictly personal, what would you answer?"

"There was no guarantee, at the time, of my ever being Ameron's heir," Erien intervened. He understood the futility of defending a lie — any lie — to Reetions, but it hurt him to see Ranar attacked by his own people.

Ranar ignored his foster son's efforts. He straightened his shoulders, puffy-eyed and battered looking with his postflight hangover. "I would tell you it was politically significant," he told Kirkos, and looked down at his hands on the tabletop. "Very significant."

"Then you'll understand why a difficult, but necessary part of our job, here," said Kirkos, "is to let you know your Voting Citizen status has been suspended. You are no longer a member of the Foreign and Alien Council."

"What?" Ranar had trouble swallowing.

Kirkos sat back. "You're still a Lawful Citizen, despite the lie concerning Erien, and the three of us are among those who argued for you." He scowled. "Some people can be irrationally vindictive toward someone who's accomplished more than the lot of them put together, once he's slipped up. But we can't afford to set a precedent of leniency toward liars, either, not with the defeated Megan nationalists trying to stir up trouble."

"Megan nationalists are citing Amel's trick as proof that arbiters can be tampered with and should not be trusted," Fahzir told Erien excitedly, "which is utter nonsense. It was merely a gargantuan feat of data juggling. Arbiters are as trustworthy as ever, but you can see why it is vitally important I find out exactly what your half-brother did and evaluate the threat posed

by persons with his particular mental talents — which I understand are manifest only in highborns of a special type of Sevolite
called Goldens, who are particularly rare," he concluded in a
hopeful manner.

The distinct feeling Fahzir projected of vastly preferring such
"mental talents" were extinct, rather than rare, reminded Erien
that Luthan was as Golden as Amel. Any objectivity he might
have been able to muster on Amel's behalf ran aground on feelings he could not properly identify.

"You've been frank with us about the concerns of the local
people, here on *BlindEye Station*," Glynda spoke up. "There's
a related matter we must brief you on, as well, concerning your
foster mother, Lurol. She, and those who agree with her, have
made substantial headway with a movement to declare Amel
freewill impaired — an involuntary martyr, to be more specific
— and, as such, a danger to himself. The goal of the movement
is to have him brought to Rire for treatment, to correct the mistake
made eighteen years ago that produced the condition." Glynda's
wide brow furrowed. "I fear Amel's friends here may misun-
derstand the lobby if they hear about it."

Kirkos gave a snort. "All we should care about concerning
Amel is what Fahzir needs to know. As for the rest of it, the way
his pictures and data are bandied about is nothing short of
scandalous for a sober, compu-communist society. His attrac-
tiveness is a distraction."

"That we can agree upon," said Erien in a sober tone, "but
Amel is one of the very few Pureblood Sevolites left in the empire
and potentially now liege of Dem'Vrel. Rire must be careful,"
he addressed this last to Glynda, "about presuming too far where
his welfare is concerned."

"Yes, yes, of course," Kirkos said gruffly. "Well said."

"While Ranar," Erien pursued, "has been acknowledged as
the Reetion ambassador by my father, the Ava. It may, therefore, be an inauspicious time for Rire to be suspending him from
the Foreign and Alien Council."

Kirkos blinked as if he'd only just discovered the need to
refocus on Erien as a Gelack.

"It is true I lied about Erien on record," said Ranar. "If that
means I'm no longer fit to advise Foreign and Alien Council
about Gelacks, I accept the judgement of the council. But since
there is no precedent, I see no reason why a Lawful Citizen
cannot also be Reetion ambassador to the Ava's court."

Erien wasn't fooled by the brave front Ranar was putting on. His foster father had never been anything but a Voting Citizen as an adult. It was like a Sevolite losing his title.

Quietly, Erien turned to Ranar and said, "For the record, since this is a Reetion hearing, I want to register my thanks for preventing the early years of my life becoming a public spectacle, and I hope the debate concerning your lie will one day take account of how the 'Heir Gelion' you sheltered was a newly bereaved seven-year-old who was attempting to adapt to a completely alien society. The degree of intrusion into my life the Reetion system would have justified, had my identity been known, would have been unendurable. I claim, on your behalf, the right of a parent acting in the best interest of his child."

Ranar followed all Erien said with his usual deep attention, until near the end. Then he seemed suddenly infirm. "Thank you," he said, and broke eye contract.

"Noted," said Kirkos. "Let's get on with our business. Erien, as representative of your government, and next of kin to your half-brother Amel in these proceedings, we hereby serve you with notice of the following objectives of this investigative triumvirate: first, to exhaustively study the method by which Amel was able to empower data smuggling between *Kali Station* and the Megan separatists, in support of Ann's defeated defense plan in the Reach of Paradise; second, to evaluate the potential for similar or other such tampering by Amel or a similar Sevolite—"

Erien set his teeth, troubled by the memory of Princess Luthan's blue eyes and gentle smile.

"And third," concluded Kirkos, "to consider whether we ought to bring Amel to Rire for his own protection."

"Protection from whom?" Erien asked.

Glynda answered. "Amel could be at risk on Gelion. He did, after all, try to help Ann prepare defenses against a Sevolite invasion."

"So you are suggesting Amel is neither willing nor able to defend his own actions at court," Erien summarized. "I doubt there is a greater insult that could be directed at a highborn."

Kirkos turned to Ranar with the air of a big man handling a fragile tea cup. "I might believe that of a Sevolite such as Horth Nersal, for example," he prompted Ranar. "But is Amel keen, in your opinion, to uphold his honor on the Challenge Floor, with a sword?"

"No," Ranar admitted, with an apologetic look in Erien's direction.

"What are you driving at?" Erien demanded of the triumvirate.

"We have already heard rumors," said Glynda, "that Amel has suffered as a consequence of his assistance to Ann."

"I didn't think Reetions put faith in rumors," Perry D'Aur announced her arrival, speaking Reetion with a Gelack accent.

"We were just about to inquire into how Amel sustained his injuries on Gelion," said Glynda.

Perry pulled out a seat and sat down. "Great. I'd love to hear that."

Kirkos looked pointedly at Ranar. "Are you prepared to tell us what you know?"

Ranar straightened as if stung. "All I know for certain is that Amel disappeared and was later rescued from his mother Ev'rel's residence on Fountain Court by Erien."

It was a disorienting and alarming new emotion for Erien to doubt Ranar's discretion. He tensed a little every time he heard his name spoken, painfully aware of how glad he was not to have shared all he knew about what happened to Amel in Lilac Hearth.

"Heir Gelion," Kirkos invited, "can you tell us more?"

Erien sipped ice water, keeping his face composed, set down his glass and said calmly, "I would prefer the ambassador to finish, first. Then I will endeavor to add my understanding to his."

That way I will know how much I must admit to, thought Erien. He would never, Erien realized with blunt sorrow, be able to talk to Ranar about Lilac Hearth. Not now. Even though the memories of what he'd seen and done were like a poison in his soul.

"I can tell you," Ranar offered without looking up, "that Erien was wounded getting Amel out of Lilac Hearth. Ev'rel caught up with him before they had crossed Fountain Court from one hearth to the other and they quarreled over custody of Amel. Amel did not want to go back with Ev'rel. He had some kind of abdominal wound and welts across his torso. Amel's wrists looked as if he had been struggling in bonds."

Gods, Ranar! thought Erien. *Enough! Don't give them openings to thrust through!* At the same time, he understood Ranar's need to be honest with his fellow Reetions, all the more so because of the lie he had been caught in.

"Can you explain Amel's condition?" Kirkos asked Erien. Erien refilled his glass.

At that moment, the outer door snapped open and a pair of Nersallians entered, dressed in black, their military ranks emblazoned on their collars and their sleeves.

"Immortality," Dorn Nersal greeted Erien in Gelack, "Ker Bryllit and I wish to volunteer our services as guards of honor."

Nersallians were Demish/Vrellish hybrids, but Ker Bryllit was Vrellish enough the Reetions might not have noticed she was female without a hard look. She was as tall and strong as Dorn, with narrower hips and smaller breasts than most women. Both Nersallians wore duelling swords, but Erien followed Perry's sharp gaze to the needle gun up Ker Bryllit's sleeve. *Okal Rel* orthodox though they were, Nersallians held dishonorable weapons in reserve when they doubted other people's honor. In summary, the needle gun was not a reassuring sign.

Answering Dorn in Gelack, Erien remembered to difference his pronouns as a Pureblood speaking to a Highlord. "Thank you for your offer, Heir Nersal, but I am afraid having you and Ker Bryllit attend me would be a distraction. I would rather you did not."

"Then you leave us an unfortunate choice, Immortality," said Ker Bryllit, in a burred voice. "We must either annoy you, or annoy Liege Nersal. And while you may be the Ava's heir, I know whose sword I would rather hazard."

"I see," said Erien dryly. To the company, he added in Reetion, "Please excuse me a moment."

The Nersallians closed ranks around Erien as he led them out into the hallway. Dorn, Horth Nersal's eldest son and heir, Erien knew he could trust, but the woman's liege was Tash Bryllit — Horth's erstwhile mentor, ex-*mekan'st* and current vassal. Tash Bryllit had no fondness for Reetions.

"Then I will accept you both as honor guard," Erien decided. "But what you hear in there, from the Reetions, will be reported only to your lieges, not in the mess hall. Do you understand?"

Dorn set hand on hilt and half-bowed. "Yes, Heir Gelion."

Ker returned him a smoky gray, brooding stare. "Are you Lorel?" she asked him. "Or are you Vrellish?"

House Nersal was much more literal in its interpretation of the spiritual side of *Okal Rel* than Erien's own foster house of Monitum, which meant Ker was probably referring to the nature of Erien's soul. He had to be careful how he answered.

"I am Erien Lor'Vrel, Heir Gelion, ward of Monitum and ward of Rire," he said, carefully, "more than that I do not know. I once told your *l'liege*, Horth Nersal, to judge the Reetions by their actions. I will have to ask you to judge me by mine."

She was silent for a moment, then said, "I will report what I learn only to Liege Bryllit, or her liege and my *l'liege*, Horth Nersal. But do not make me regret the promise, Heir Gelion." She bowed to him then, as Dorn had done.

"Leave the talking to me," Erien warned them both.

Dorn clapped Erien on his good shoulder hard enough to make him stagger. "Unless they try to kill you," he promised, "we'll be statues."

Perry was chatting with the Reetions when they got back. Erien introduced Dorn and Ker, in Reetion, and then turned to his foster father. "Ranar, would you be willing to translate for the Nersallians?"

"Yes." Ranar cleared his throat. "If that's acceptable to the triumvirate."

"We would be grateful," said Kirkos.

"I will be translating for you," Ranar told Ker and Dorn in Gelack, speaking up commoner-to-Highlord, which would have been correct except that Ameron had granted Ranar the right to honorary peerage, as ambassador, to make his position more tenable.

Dorn took Ranar's reversion to commoner grammar as a gesture he was honor-bound to refuse. "Thank you, Ambassador," he replied in *rel*-peerage, settling the status negotiation in a manner that earned him Erien's gratitude.

"It is my honor to enjoy your trust," Ranar had the good sense to resume his honorary status without further fuss.

Glynda, the only triumvir who understood Gelack, followed the exchange with a disconcerted look.

Erien folded his hands. "Let me summarize our position," he said, and paused to let Ranar finish translating before he went on. "You are here to obtain information, but you do not need to take Amel anywhere to do so. Nor can you charge him with anything under Reetion law. You have no jurisdiction within your own legal framework beyond the umbrella of human rights, which you have made a point of extending to Sevolites due to unfortunate incidents concerning Amel in the past. But being an adult of sound mind, Amel must express the wish to seek asylum before his human rights can be invoked." He paused.

"I will see you have Amel's cooperation with regard to the way he assisted Ann of Rire and her Megan allies. Beyond that, my objective is to go to Rire myself, without Amel, to forge diplomatic relations for the future."

"How can we know what coercion might be brought to bear on Amel to prevent him turning to us for protection?" Glynda asked Erien. "If you've nothing to hide, why is he not present?"

"You may speak with him privately for as long as you require," Erien promised.

"Sounds fair," said Fahzir dismissively. "Let's get down to business."

Fahzir produced a portable crystronic unit with a projector on top that could cast 3-D images. He set it on the table and turned it on, creating a ghostly slate that began scrolling slowly through an inventory of parts and their specifications.

"This is one of Ann's smuggled messages," said Fahzir. "A list of parts used in construction of *Kali Station* in the Reach of Paradise, probably to equip it for military purposes. Since we lack the sort of experience Gelacks have in reality skimming combat," he said with a sneer, "we do not know what such an inventory implies."

"How 'bout translating it into Gelack units of measure?" asked Perry.

As Fahzir worked, Ker stared into the projection with no sign of enlightenment, unable to read a word of Reetion. Dorn stood beside Ranar, attending closely as he read off the items.

"Stop right there!" Perry said. She got up and took over from Fahzir to speed up the rate at which data was scrolling past, reminding Erien first, that she was Demish, and secondly, that his own concentration was not at its best right now.

"It sure as hell isn't a recipe for oatmeal pudding," Perry remarked. "Looks like some kind of shimmer-detection buoy, like the ones Vrenn sets out on some of our less approachable runs."

"But there's no provision for life-support," objected Fahzir. "Only a reality skimming ship can travel fast enough for a warning to be of any use against a faster-than-light attack, and *rel*-skimming requires a self-aware pilot."

"The warning is meant for the ship that sets the buoy off," Perry explained, "to let them know they are messing around where it isn't safe to fly. There are lots of areas like that in Killing Reach. Debris of the right size is deadly: too small to show up clearly and too heavy to be puffed away by a *rel*-ship's intrusion field. Ships that fly through unexpected dust fields, left over from shattered battlewheels, for example, are strafed with grains and even slivers of material that can manifest inside their hulls between stitches of shimmer."

Glynda said, "So these buoys are triggered as a warning?" She looked to Kirkos for a second opinion. "That seems harmless — even laudatory."

"What do you make of it, Heir Nersal?" Perry asked Dorn.

Dorn was standing stiffly beside Ranar. He looked like he had reached a conclusion he did not like.

The door opened behind them.

Dorn whipped around, hand on sword. Ker put Erien at her back. Erien rose, trying to see past his bodyguards as a woman was propelled into the room, landing on her knees, hard. The man who had shoved her inside was all in black: black hair, black gloves, black flight leathers, with a glitter of hard gems in his dark eyes as they snapped to meet Erien's before sweeping over the startled occupants of the room. He looked as Nersallian as Dorn, but he did not wear a sword.

Glynda was on her feet, looking thoroughly appalled.

Perry rose with all the aplomb of a Demish matron presiding at a private reception. "I do not believe any of you have met Vrenn," she said. "Vrenn," she continued in a firm, reminding tone, "these are the Reetion triumvirate, Kirkos, Glynda and Fahzir."

Vrenn, Erien knew, was commander of the irregulars who defended Perry's Purple Alliance. He used to be *kinf'stan*, born within challenge right to the title of Liege Nersal, and kin to Dorn; but he wore no sword and fought no duels, which meant he lacked status under sword law. Despite this, most Nersallians tolerated Vrenn and some even defended him to their less liberal-minded comrades on the grounds he was not *okal'a'ni*, even if he was dishonorable. The distinction was one most Reetions missed and Gelacks sometimes blurred for their own reasons, but Erien understood the difference. A dishonorable man could not be trusted to obey the rules of sword law, and by extension might safely be assumed to be a dastard all around. To be *okal'a'ni*, however, was an offense against future generations. Extinguishing a whole line of Sevolites was *okal'a'ni* to followers of *Okal Rel* that believed the Waiting Dead required living de-scendants to be reborn. Destroying habitat was taboo to all. From his years in the Nersallian fleet serving under Horth Nersal, Erien had picked up enough gossip about Vrenn to know the dishonorable renegade was as vehement in his hatred of *okal'a'ni* behavior as any of his lawful kinsmen.

"Amel is gone," Vrenn spat out the name like a curse. "Sylvie," he nodded at the woman cowering on the floor, "knows where."

The woman called Sylvie was in her mid-twenties and thin to the point of emaciation. She looked terrified.

"I got word Amel had taken out a ship," Vrenn told Perry. "I checked his quarters and found this woman there. She says he has gone into Paradise Reach on some rescue mission, and would tell the rest only to Erien, but I can fix that if she's not forthcoming."

Ranar paused in his translation at the threat. Glynda claimed his attention with an anxious, whispered question.

Sylvie appealed to Erien. "Amel said I should come to you if he wasn't back in time. He said you would help Hanson!"

Vrenn's restless gaze swept across them all to settle on Fahzir's projection. "Is this *Kali Station*?" he asked in a deadly voice. Before anyone could answer, Vrenn snatched Sylvie off the floor. His gloved hand closed on her throat.

"Where," Vrenn said through his teeth, "*is that station?*"

Sylvie whimpered. Glynda gave a shocked yip of alarm. Fahzir yelled, "Hey!" Even the bulky Kirkos stirred in his chair.

Erien started around the table to intervene, but Dorn was there before him, sword drawn. Ker drew her needle gun, proving that Vrenn stood outside the shield of honor.

Vrenn froze them both with a word. "*Ah'kash-sang'va.*"

The effect was intense. One moment Dorn and Ker were on Sylvie's side. The next, they were giving Vrenn the attention a Nersallian owed only to a leader. Erien wracked his brains to unpack the meaning of what Vrenn had said, cursing his uneven education. It seemed to be a naming word, like *mekan'st* or *gorarelpul*, derived from an entire phrase with parts elided. All Erien knew for sure was that 'sang' referred to blood, via linguistic roots as old as Earth itself, and 'va' invoked the vastness of the universe. He had dim memories of Ranar's housemate, Evert, telling him 'va' was related to the English word for vacuum.

Perry looked back at the projected inventory, muttering something blasphemous.

Ranar addressed Vrenn with every sign of his old confidence. *"Ah'kash-sang'va* is a call to arms," he said soberly. "If the schematics of Ann's preparations for defense of *Kali Station* have inspired it, let me assure you Reetions share your outrage." He made a point of speaking in peerage.

Vrenn released Sylvie to turn toward Ranar. Erien reached without thinking for a nonexistent sword, halted only by the pang in his left shoulder. *I am behaving like a Gelack,* Erien realized, *reacting viscerally and violently to other Gelacks.* He did not trust himself to speak.

"Ah'kash-sang'va is bloodied space!" Dorn spoke up excitedly. "It can't be tolerated!"

"Agreed!" cried Ranar with equal anger, keeping his attention on Vrenn, the Nersallians' *de facto* leader at the moment. He set both hands down on the table and leaned forward. "If Ann committed this offense, she's ours to deal with," he told Vrenn, his stare never wavering.

There is something of Ameron in him, Erien thought, incongruous as it was to compare a middle-aged, scholarly Reetion and the charismatic, volatile Ava.

Vrenn's upper lip drew back in scorn. Dorn looked uncertainly toward Erien. Ker was on Vrenn's side, but she watched Ranar with the wary respect she might have shown a fellow Sevolite.

Then Kirkos spoke up awkwardly, sounding as if Ranar's behavior embarrassed him, "Ranar, I should point out that you are not, uh, well... in charge," said the big Reetion.

It was impossible to tell whether it was Vrenn, Ker or Dorn who decided to act first. They reached the same unspoken conclusion as one, wheeled about and filed swiftly out the door.

There was just one way to stop a Nersallian in such a mood — to challenge. It might not even apply, in Vrenn's case, and Erien understood too little to resort to it, even if he had been in any shape to try. Ranar's restraining hand on his left forearm was an unnecessary precaution.

"Where are they going?" Kirkos asked, bemused.

Ranar sank into the chair beside Erien, too miserable to answer.

"What does *ah'kash-sang'va* mean, exactly," Erien asked Perry D'Aur.

Perry gave a snort as she got out of her chair. "If I tell you, you will only make noises about patience and being reasonable. Hear me out, first. Then maybe you'll understand us better.

Two hundred years ago, Rire and Gelion fought the Killing War with *okal'a'ni* weapons, and it is we, in Killing Reach, who live every day with the consequences." She paced a few steps and pivoted, spreading her hands. "This reach was prosperous before the war. There was even an additional habitable planet — a whole planet! Now Killing Reach is synonymous with piracy, pornography and contraband. But there's one thing that can offend even someone as steeped in it as Vrenn." She paused, glaring at them. Then she spat out the offending words. "Casting dust in our space lanes. That's what we call bloodied space!" She drew breath. "To be able to travel is life and death to us. It makes us one cooperating economy — legal and illegal — not isolated blobs of life in the darkness. The PA has been working for decades, and Bryllit's people even longer, to eliminate *that*." She gestured, closed-fisted, at the inventory. "I've sent generations of my people to burn themselves out sweeping lanes some gutless bastard has strewn or booby-trapped rather than fight fairly in space, or yes, damn it, with a sword!"

She turned to Erien, pointing at the data display. "Those aren't specifications for warning buoys. They are blueprints for dust mines rigged to blow particulate debris in the path of an approaching *rel*-ship once it sets them off. Then, whether they get their target or not, there'll be more mess to clean up in space lanes that used to be hard vacuum. The mess keeps expanding — at a fraction of the speed of light, of course, but expanding, all the same, to foul more area. Then whoever skims that way next—" she broke off, her jaw locked. "The Nesaks named it bloodied space because it lacerates pilots who fly through it. Think about it. A *rel*-ship shimmers many times a second. If you manifest, even once, in the midst of dust instead of vacuum, and travel just a few meters during in-phase before your next stitch of shimmer, the dust tears right through the pilot's body. It can compromise hullsteel, too, and make the ship shatter, although that's less common. The most frequent result is to plaster the pilot all over the inner hull."

Perry turned on the Reetion triumvirate. "You might be able to find *Kali Station*. You might be able to bring the guilty to trial. But you will talk about it, won't you? You will bandy about every detail in every conceivable medium, and the schematics for building those weapons will be put to use in Killing Reach within the year by some *okal'a'ni* pirate or another; within a year Liege Bryllit and I will be pulling the torn bodies of our pilots out of cockpits painted with their blood. That's why Vrenn reacted like he did. That's why we need to send a strong, swift message. Zero tolerance. Harsh retribution. Even enemies unite to crush the *okal'a'ni*." Perry braced a fist on the table, muscles standing out in her shoulder. "You may think *Okal Rel* is primitive, but the people responsible for this atrocity are about to get it shoved down their throats, and none of you will be able to stop it." She sat down heavily. "I would advise you not to try."

Erien nodded jerkily. "I've got to go with them," he realized. "Not to stop them, just to be there." He was moving before he finished speaking, barely taking in Ranar's cry behind him, which did not strike him as the recall of an authoritative figure, just the alarm of a frightened parent.

Erien found the Nersallians suiting up at the docks. Horth was there, too, in the midst of his vassals. Vrenn, the renegade, stood off to one side.

Dorn detached himself from Horth's party to greet Erien.

"I am going with you," Erien insisted.

Dorn looked pained. "I wish you would not, Heir Gelion. It may be hazardous in a way no skill can counter."

Vrenn was speaking to someone over a hand-held com unit. With a flick of his wrist, he pitched the com to Erien. "Message for you from Amel. I don't know the language."

The language was French, the ancient tongue of House Lorel, which was fine for Amel, who absorbed languages like a sponge. It was harder work for Erien, but fortunately he had gained the rudiments as a child under Di Mon's tutelage, and the message was linguistically simple, giving *Kali Station*'s coordinates and the time by which Erien should assume Amel was in trouble, which had recently expired. The message also confessed it was Ann who had engaged Amel's assistance.

Typical! thought Erien, infuriated.

"Got what we need?" Vrenn asked. "Or do I have to waste time getting it out of Sylvie?"

I have the power to stall them, Erien realized. Maybe even prevent them finding out where *Kali Station* is entirely, if Sylvie hasn't told Perry already. If she had, of course, and he stalled, the Nersallians would never trust him again. And it wouldn't take Perry's people long to figure out how to decode Amel's French, which may have been part of Amel's plan in making his fail-safe message semi-accessible to people other than Erien. Amel's loyalties were always maddeningly squishy.

"I have the coordinates," Erien told Vrenn. "But I *am* coming with you."

Vrenn shrugged. Horth frowned, clearly unhappy with the idea, but he nodded his acceptance of Erien's decision. As Ker and Vrenn drew close around Erien to get the coordinates, Horth drew Dorn aside for a word, in private.

FIVE

Eyes on Amel — Hanson

Revolution Will Not Compute

Hanson, the Megan separatist, was roused from an uneasy doze by Rast, his best pilot. He swiped a dark cloth off his eyes, blinking against the light of his bedroom. All lights throughout *Kali Station* had been on steadily since he'd boxed the arbiter, but this minor irritation paled before the hazard of the whole station shutting down entirely. A trick was the only thing keeping the *Kali* arbiter up — a trick they desperately needed to replace with a longer-term solution.

Rast was in his flight suit, his lean face agitated. "It's Crys," he told Hanson excitedly. "Crys is in the visitor probe."

Hanson's heart skipped. "The arbiter—?"

"Still up," Rast assured him, blinking rapidly. His eyes seemed to get bigger daily, and his cheeks more sunken.

"Crys?" Hanson asked after his chief cystronics expert and boy genius.

"He's still in the probe. Vic's with him." Rast dropped on his knees beside the bed, tense with excitement. "Let me go prime the dust bombs, Hanson. We set them up to use, and we ought to use them, whether it's Sevolites or Reetions who—"

Hanson snagged Rast's shirt in a big fist and pulled the pilot closer to help his words get through the youth's obsessive eagerness to prime their hard-earned defenses. "Not yet. Not until there's no hope of taking the station back to Mega under my command. Not until we've tried the long shot."

"Amel?" Rast pulled free and brushed his shirt down, frowning. "Ann's back," he told Hanson. "Alone."

"Amel will come later," said Hanson, "after Sylvie finds a way to get Ann's message to him."

"But if he doesn't—"

"If he doesn't," said Hanson, "or we lose the station — prime the dust bombs."

Rast answered him with a grin. "You got it, Boss."

Today, even the anti-Reetion title 'Boss' gave Hanson no joy. It was all he could do to smile.

People were clogging the corridor outside the sick bay entrance when Hanson arrived. About half of them were brightly dressed Megan civilians, the innocent bystanders who'd signed up to work on *Kali Station* unaware of Ann and Hanson's plans. Ann's people were dressed in pale blue Space Service uniforms; Hanson's wore the dark green fatigues of the Megan militia and were armed with the bulky 'zapper' guns Ann had improvised for use against Sevolite boarders. Some of Ann's Reetions were insisting the zappers be put away since no invasion had materialized.

"Clear me a way to the door!" Hanson ordered a young militiaman whose name tag read 'Julio.'

"Yes, sir!" said Julio.

"Yes, sir... no, sir!" sneered the Reetion woman who'd been trying to make Julio surrender his zapper. "You don't want to fight Sevolites, Hanson — you want to *become* one!"

Hanson felt a powerful urge to make the woman swallow her words, but it wasn't worth upsetting *Kali*'s mental balance. Sometimes the damaged arbiter ignored interpersonal violence, and sometimes it did not.

The entrance to *Kali Station*'s sick bay was decorated in a mural inspired by Mega's oceans, in which armored predators pursued their prey through an inverted jungle of feeding filaments dangling from floating colonies above. It was original art, painted since the crew had come on board. Megans liked to live art, creating it spontaneously in whatever environment they occupied, unlike the Reetions of Rire who kept everything beautiful in museums. Sick bay had no door because it was considered pointless for a setting that operated, normally, under a social transparency index of five. The social transparency index, or STI, was a measure of how much attention arbiters gave any particular setting, including how thoroughly events were documented. Sick bay could be locked down to contain an infectious outbreak, however, which made it an important location in Hanson's mind from a military point of view, or would have, if *Kali* did what it was told; but the station no longer responded even to its original, lawful command triumvirate of Hanson,

Ann and Vic, the chief medical officer.

A stocky militia woman named Bitya presided over sick back from just inside. She, too, was wearing one of the zapper guns, capable of delivering a stiff electric jolt across a short distance.

"Good to see you, Counsellor Hanson," she greeted him with the title rendered obsolete by the fall of the nationalist government on Mega, over the data-smuggling scandal. He accepted her homage with a curt nod.

Inside, the sick bay was a large space filled with beds and vacant stages. Two beds were classified as intensive care, one of them empty and the other occupied. The empty ICU bed was known colloquially as a "coffin," because it was capable of standing in for failing organs, damaged by shimmer. Only the most badly injured pilots ever did time in the coffin.

Crys was in the ICU bed built into the visitor probe and used, under normal circumstances, to revive gap-stunned pilots who had lapsed into a coma. The young crystronics whiz lay on the bed's palette with his head enclosed in the probe's hood, looking disturbingly like a dead grub in the jaws of a predatory bug. A stage between the two ICU beds reported life signs. The probe's block, which housed its arbiter, was mounted above the hood and was exposed at the moment, with its casing hinged open. The block, on which the trick keeping them all alive depended, looked like a chunk of foggy glass with a scintillating glow moving within. Arbiters literally thought in colors, each hue a distinct state, with color intensity serving as a second informational dimension. In sheer capacity they far surpassed the human brain, but their intelligence was nonsentient and alien, evolved under pressure to avoid developing what analysts called "sustained persona-of-the-whole" conditions, known more succinctly as becoming eccentric. As life forms, arbiters were symbiotes, unable to exist without the work of governance, which was like food to them. Hanson viewed them as a horrible addiction enslaving Mega to Rire in exchange for the services they rendered. Looking into the milky, twinkling face of the probe's block was like looking at poisoned treasure. The damned thing was even beautiful. Its cold stores, where its cognitive core was not active, looked like flawed quartz shot through with frost.

Hanson made himself look at Crys again. He could guess what had happened. Crys had tried to integrate his own mind with the damaged arbiter via the visitor probe. There was a precedent — Amel had done it accidentally when he was treated by Lurol during the infamous *Second Contact* incident, years before. But Crys was human, not a Pureblood Sevolite from some special Demish line with particularly massive data processing capacity.

Vic, the station's chief medic, sat slumped in a morph-chair between the two beds.

Hanson touched Crys' hand. It was warm.

"What's his condition?" he asked.

"Coma," Vic said. "Level 8.8 out of 9.0 on the gap-exposure scale of consciousness impairment. Not that he was gap-exposed, but the probe's designed for reviving pilots and the metrics reflect that."

Hanson grabbed Vic by the front of his med-coat, hauling him up. "Then why did you let him do this!" he demanded.

Vic gasped at the shock of being manhandled. "It was *his* idea!" he protested. "It's on record!"

Vic dropped on his knees to fumble at the manual controls of the stage located between the ICU units. "There," he said triumphantly as Crys sprang to life on stage, a thin kid with frizzy hair.

"This is going to put it right, okay, Hanson?" Crys said as he fidgeted, sweat on his upper lip. "I've rigged a protocol to look like the overdue update from its fellow arbiters *Kali*'s been itching to synch with. All I have to do, then, is look like another arbiter because I'm in the visitor probe, like Amel was in Lurol's prototype." He gave a frightened, bubbling laugh. "You keep telling us that Megans can do anything anybody else can, right? We don't need him." Crys grinned into the face of posterity again. "I'm doing this for Mega, okay, Hanson?"

The images stopped, and Vic began to blubber. "*K-Kali* took him for an arbiter all right — one in worse shape than it was—" Vic's voice got high and shrill. "The arbiter didn't let him shift command to you, or back to the triumvirate. It didn't let him tell it anything. It decided he needed more help than *it* did and... it downloaded into him!" Vic ended with a sob.

Hanson locked his teeth, feeling ill.

"Hanson!" Ann upbraided him, pushing Julio aside as she swaggered in. "What's the idea of breaking out the zappers and — what the hell?" she interrupted herself, seeing Crys.

Ann of New Beach was in good shape for a career pilot in her thirties, since she'd spent years of her life Supervised for bad behavior alternating, ironically, with work stints in Space

Service administration. She wore a pair of yellow stretch pants and a matching band across her breasts. The clothes were fresh, but she was sweaty from being in a cockpit for hours.

"Hanson," Ann threatened, "if you put Crys up to this, it will be worth pushing *Kali* over the edge just to have your guts for a skipping rope!"

"It was not my idea," Hanson insisted, tired of her tantrums.

"Yeah?" Her almond eyes narrowed. "Since when does Crys do things you don't want done?"

"He intended to restore our command powers as the station triumvirate," Hanson told her.

Ann gave a derisive snort. "I'm sure Crys was deeply concerned about including Vic and me in that deal," she said, and then relented a little as she looked down at the young Megan's limp body. "Poor dumb kid."

The legendary Ann was, Hanson had to admit, a fascinating woman, and almost Megan in her passions. Hanson had made a study of her since they became allies in the cause of blocking a Sevolite invasion of the Reach of Paradise. She liked to watch Old Earth fairy tales for entertainment, was notorious for her sexual energy, and became impatient with Reetion red tape, although she considered herself loyal to the Reetion Confederacy.

"Ann," Vic said, his big rabbit eyes fixed on her, "we have to surrender to Space Service."

"I doubt they could evacuate us in a timely way, Vic," Ann said, almost gently. "*Kali* is the only Reetion station with reality skimming capability. We have to stabilize the station, even if we plan to surrender."

"Space Service could send us an arbiter to repair ours," Vic insisted. "Or we could ask the Sevolites, themselves. So long as we get help, I wouldn't care if we surrender to Nersallians!"

"Don't say that until you've met some," said Ann. "Nersallians throw people out of airlocks for being *okal'a'ni*, and dust bombs are right up there on their list of no-nos."

"Did your message get through to Sylvie?" Hanson asked Ann.

"I think so," she said. "If so, Amel should be here any time now. We'll wait one more hour. If he's not here by then, he's not coming." She inhaled and sighed. "Then I guess I try surrendering to Perry D'Aur — if she'll talk to me."

"No," Hanson declined, "no Gelacks. If it comes to that, I will let Rast prime the dust mines."

"And *start* the war we just avoided?" Ann's voice dripped with sarcasm. "Hanson, you are screaming mad!"

"That's right," he said. "I am a cultish primitive, an irrational retro, a nationalist! But you knew that when we became allies!" He towered over her, a fist raised between them. "You could have avoided this. You could have let me take *Kali* to Mega when the impeachment trial started!"

"We teamed up to fight a war that didn't happen," Ann spat back fearlessly, "not to empower you to commit criminal acts against the Reetion Space Service."

"Exactly," Hanson said coldly, "everything we've done presumed a war. A war would have made my leaders right for trying to protect the Reach of Paradise; a war would put an end to the 'no captains' policy built into arbiters. It might even have put an end to arbiters. My object is, and always has been, the liberation of Mega. If it's not yours, you're a pilot — leave any time you want to."

"I have *people* on this station!" Ann told him hotly.

"I have more," Hanson spelled it out for her.

"Is that a threat?" Ann asked, incredulous, and shook her head. "Hanson, you are freaking me out! Do you think this is some sort of bizarre test of cultural virtues — Reetion rationality versus Megan passion?" She stabbed an arm outward. "That's space out there and we're stranded in it, on a station that could shut down life-support at any moment, which ought to unite anything breathing in a common cause!"

"My only cause is my people's freedom," said Hanson.

"Freedom!" cried Ann. "This isn't about freedom. It's about Hanson the Megan messiah! You let Crys box the arbiter to gain control of something you haven't any right to!"

"You and Vic made me do it, by refusing to let me take *Kali* home!"

"So you could dust the Reetion jump! I didn't build dust bombs to see them used against our Space Service pilots risking their lives to keep the net up!"

Hanson was impressed, after a fashion. He did not think she'd guessed so much about why he wanted to take *Kali* to Mega.

"I'm grateful to the Megan secessionists for recognizing *Kali* had to be prepared in case of a Sevolite attack," Ann told him through clenched teeth, "but your leaders were removed by due process — by Megans!"

"As your defense plan was defeated — by Reetions," he reminded her.

"That's different!" she objected.

"How?" he challenged.

"Nobody forced arbiters on Megans!" Ann changed the subject.

"No one knew the cost when we accepted!" he retaliated.

"Oh for—" Ann broke off, hands clenched, spitting mad. "This is one hell of a time to debate the constitution!"

"Let's not play games, Reetion," said Hanson. "I used you to prepare *Kali Station*. You used me to shield Rire against invasion. We have nothing further in common."

Bitya burst in, startling Vic and Julio out of their tense, nervous postures as they listened to their leaders argue.

"It's Amel!" she announced. "He's docked!"

"Yes!" Ann exclaimed, in joy.

Hanson signaled to Bitya, who nodded and moved off. Vic, Julio and Hanson followed Ann into the corridor where, much to Hanson's disgust, an aura of reverence was spreading in anticipation of the Sevolite's arrival.

Ann launched herself at Amel as he came into sight around a corner. Amel gripped her forearms, holding her off despite a smile of welcome.

He is injured, thought Hanson. The white shirt beneath Amel's open flight jacket was soaked with red above the belt. It showed in his face, too. 'Stoic' wasn't one of Amel's unnatural virtues.

"Did it happen... flying?" Ann asked Amel. Hanson heard the guilt in her voice and knew she was afraid Rast had already primed the dust bombs surrounding them.

"Flying made it bleed again, that's all," Amel said. He captured her hands in his. "I'm glad you're still free. I was worried about you."

His face lost its strained expression as he looked at her adoringly. It made Hanson nauseous just watching. Amel wasn't a man! He was a caricature of manhood designed for women's pleasure! He'd read as much on one of the many Reetion discussion channels dedicated to all things Amel.

Vic disrupted the show of affection. "You came!" he gushed at Amel, taking the Sevolite's nearest hand. "You were willing to help, again, despite what Lurol did to you!"

Not despite what she did, Hanson thought, *because of it.* Amel was programmed for martyrdom. Hanson had read that, too, somewhere.

"Vic?" Amel said, with predictable compassion. "You look awful!"

Vic clutched at Amel's hands. "Listen, Amel, I think — I'm afraid... the Megans — Crys and Hanson..."

"You'll have to excuse Vice — he's scared," said Hanson, stepping forward.

The supposedly sweet and compassionate Amel surprised him with a flare of anger. "If he is, you're the cause," he told Hanson. "Come on, Vic." Amel took charge of the doctor and steered him into sick bay.

Hanson made eye contact with Julio and tipped his head toward Ann. Julio looked anxious, which meant he understood what was expected of him.

Ann caught up with Amel to find him staring at the ICU visitor probe.

"Crys was trying to interface the arbiter," Ann told him as gently as possible, "like you did once, accidentally."

Amel's thin nostrils flared. He kept staring as his face drained of color.

"Crys was trying to make up for failing to give Hanson control," Vic said breathlessly.

"Which, of course, he couldn't!" said Ann, giving Hanson a withering look. "They wound up convincing *Kali*, instead, that Hanson is the only person on board, because that's the only situation consistent with his ambition to be captain. But *Kali* can still detect and respond to violence sometimes, which generates an impossible conflict of logic, making *Kali* conclude it is compromised, despite the Megans' efforts to block its response by other avenues. A compromised arbiter shuts down everything — including life-support, in our case, because *Kali* knows Hanson is the culprit and believes he is the only person on board. The old no captains protocols were ruthless. Fortunately for us, Crys rigged the visitor probe to veto *Kali*'s suicidal impulses by asserting the interests of the two hundred and eleven crew members the visitor probe arbiter is still aware of, but only in a medical capacity, since it's an idiot-savant, not a general purpose intelligence. Unfortunately, we never know from one time to the next if it will work again." Ann took Amel by the shoulders and dragged him around to face her. "You have to help us."

Amel's fluid-looking eyebrows clenched in ripples. "What do you expect me to do?"

"Stabilize life-support for us at the subarbitorial level," she told him. "Deduce what's necessary and simulate *Kali*'s input well enough to satisfy the dumb rocks *Kali* governs."

"Gods, Ann!" Amel protested, "That's like figuring out how to replace the signals a brain sends to keep a body running!"

"Just the key systems," Ann pleaded with an apologetic smile, "like the brain stem?"

"I've got a headache already," Amel said, with a self-pitying groan.

Hanson saw Bitya's signal. He locked stares with Julio and cried, "Now!"

Julio tried grabbing Ann from behind by the arms. She jabbed him in the chest with an elbow, spun around and brought up a knee, and he sank down whimpering. Bitya leveled her zapper at Ann, but Amel knocked Ann clear of the shot, narrowly missing getting hit himself. Ann slammed into Bitya from the side, wrestling her for the zapper as Hanson lunged for Amel. Amel broke Hanson's grasp and slung him aside.

Isn't he supposed to be gentle?! Hanson thought angrily, the instant before he crashed into Bitya. Amel snatched Bitya's zapper off the floor and held it competently enough despite the alleged aversion Gelacks were supposed to have for power weapons.

"You won't shoot me!" Hanson told Amel. "You can't hurt people, no matter what they do to you!"

"Don't push your luck," Amel said darkly. But a lush nervous system was one of Amel's infamous exotic features, and his ridiculously pretty face revealed the pain he was suffering. There had to be a way to take advantage of his vulnerability. Hanson was on the brink of rushing him when Ann took the gun from Amel.

"Get up," she growled at Hanson. "You are walking out ahead of us. Vic!" she called.

The doctor was shaking so badly he could hardly stand. He stumbled over the casing for the probe's block, picked it up and sank down in his chair again, hugging the hard casing slab in his lap.

"It's too late," Hanson told Ann. "You've already lost. Rast has gone to set the dust bombs."

"What!" Ann screamed. She aimed the big makeshift weapon with both hands. "I should shoot you right now!"

"Let me have Amel," Hanson said. "I might be able to re-call Rast. We can still get the station under skim and fall back to Mega."

Ann was done talking. "Move," she ordered.

Bitya went for Ann's legs. The crack of Ann's zapper seared Hanson's heart as he saw Bitya spasm and collapse.

True to form, Amel dropped to the floor beside his wounded enemy, where Bitya lay jerking on the floor, her short hair sticking out in all directions.

"Leave her!" Ann snapped at her pet Sevolite as she went past, herding Hanson ahead of her. "Go collect Vic."

Bitya's convulsions stopped. Amel got up with his hand pressed across his abdomen.

There were sounds of fighting in the corridor, which made Hanson suspect Ann's people had broken out their zappers, as well. The outbreak was sure to upset *Kali*. It was hard, after all, for an arbiter to feel confidence in its absolute conviction of only one person being on the station when it was getting a flood of violence-control alarms from subsystems.

Amel reached for Vic to help him up, when the lights went out. The shooting outside halted. Inside, everyone froze, Amel with one hand on Vic's arm.

"Shutdown initiated," the stages declared in unison.

Everyone stopped fighting.

"Shutdown challenged by medical veto," said the *Kali* arbiter.

Please, please, thought Hanson. *Just once more!* He could see the whites of Vic's eyes where the doctor stood beside Amel.

"Medical veto inconsistent with assertion Hanson is sole occupant," said the *Kali* arbiter. "Unanimous decision of triumvirate required to sustain veto."

"Oh no, oh no," Vic moaned, the visitor probe's casing still clutched in his hands.

"Hanson," Hanson barked at the nearest stage, hoping against hope, "Command triumvir representing the Megan World Council."

"Hanson recognized," said all the stages, displaying a visual prompt in the shape of a yellow diamond. "But you may no longer serve as a triumvir. You are suspected of subversive actions against the Arbiter Administration." *Kali* paused. "Unable to access Hanson's first expansion," it said. "This arbiter is compromised. Initiating shutdown."

"I'm Ann!" Ann hailed a stage, still holding her gun on Hanson. "Space Service command triumvir."

"Vic!" the doctor cried, "representing Reetion Science and Ethics Councils."

There was no response to either of them.

The stages responded in unison. "*Kali Station* will shut down in three minutes. Suspected saboteur, Hanson, is advised to leave the station and turn himself over to Space Service authorities as soon as possible."

Hanson laughed, sounding half-mad even to his own ears. He wasn't even a pilot! But *Kali* seemed to have forgotten that, along with so much else.

A terrible silence stretched for three seconds.

Then Vic swung the probe casing at Amel with a wail of terror. Amel threw up a defensive arm as a rush of people from outside swallowed up Ann and Julio, but Hanson was too busy to check whose side the new arrivals were on. He caught Amel as the Sevolite fended off the hysterical doctor, spun Amel around and drove a fist into his lower abdomen. It was not a great blow, since despite his large build Hanson was a politician and not a street fighter, but Amel cried out and fell down, clutching his midsection.

Hanson dragged Amel toward the visitor probe as Vic rushed to prepare it for a new occupant, muttering justifications about saving two hundred and eleven lives. Amel was not impressed. Off balance, and hampered by his injury, the powerful Sevolite still managed to shove Vic aside and whack Hanson hard enough it felt as if his head would come off. Amel gained his feet with a cry of pain, but it didn't stop him from bolting for the entrance.

"Stop him! Stop him!" Hanson yelled to the wave of new arrivals who turned out to be his militia. Amel disarmed the first attacker with a wrench that must have dislocated the man's arm. Armed with his victim's zapper, Amel was doing alarmingly well for someone who was supposed to be an involuntary martyr, and then, for no apparent reason, his moves became senseless, his blows directed at phantom targets and the sounds he made frantic and childish. The militia swarmed in and overpowered him easily and dragged him back toward the probe.

"Get him in!" Hanson shouted.

Amel's fit passed as Vic locked him into the probe's head brace. His amazing gray eyes looked up at Hanson. "Please," Amel begged, his face pale with pathetic terror, "don't."

Hanson nodded to Vic to engage the hood.

"I can't get a fix when he's — that's better," Vic fretted, hovering over the microstage controls. "He's fainted," Vic read off his stage console. "I'm glad. I'm so glad. This is terrible."

"Get on with it," Hanson snapped, "and get me voice input."

Bitya's replacement rushed up and saluted. "Ann escaped," he reported breathlessly.

On the stages behind them, *Kali* continued its countdown with a maddening lack of emotion.

"We base ourselves in sick bay," Hanson told his new second in command. "And hold the Reetions off."

"Yes, sir!" The militiaman sounded shaken, but Hanson had no sympathy to spare for trivia. They could all be suffocating in moments.

"It worked!" Vic rejoiced. "He's connected!"

"Station shutdown aborted," announced the stages all across the ward. "Initiating negotiations with a new information source. Some irregularities anticipated."

"Get me input so I can tell him what to do!" Hanson demanded, but Vic had collapsed into his defunct morph chair, blubbering.

"I can do it," one of the militia offered, pushing through the others to take charge.

"Mega, here we come!" exclaimed another one of Hanson's militia, making Hanson go stiff with alarm.

"Oh, no!" Hanson cried. "Rast!"

SIX

Erien

Bloodied Space

Heir Gelion or not, Erien did not feel very much in charge as their raiding party approached the Paradise Jump, a force of thirty-seven fighters organized into five battle hands, with himself and Vrenn tacked on.

His ship's interior was lined in nervecloth. On it, he could watch a minimally enhanced view of space beyond the little sphere of hullsteel separating him from vacuum. Light sources and gravitation wells showed up in color codes. Other ships under skim were shaded red when receding and blue when getting closer.

Carried along in the wake of the Nersallians he felt as helpless as a stick in a torrent. His wounded shoulder throbbed as if attacked by a million tiny hands. Erien hooked a Reetion pain-killer patch from the pocket of his flight jacket and used his turquoise-handled knife — the last gift Di Mon had ever given him — to cut his jacket's sleeve along the seam enough to slap the patch on his bare skin, beside one he'd placed there earlier. A colored dot on the patch came up a steady amber, warning the doses were too close together, but the parameters were not for Sevolites, so he felt safe ignoring them.

Three of Horth's fleet pulled ahead to form a spear, and dove into the Paradise Jump. One ship came back to signal all clear, using a Nersallian shimmer dance Erien recognized from his fleet service.

He fell in with the others forming up to make the jump and could feel their displacements overlapping his, evoking a queasy and pervasive sense of just coming to rest after a violent movement. There was a fierce yellow flare across his nervecloth as the hand leader jumped. Erien followed.

He came out of the jump shuddering violently. Reetion mathematics were eloquent on the interaction of a pilot's consciousness with gap, but silent on the interaction of multiple consciousnesses undergoing the same gap exposure in a jump. Gelacks called it Soul Touch.

Gods, he thought, with a dread that was almost superstitious, as if the collective anger of the Nersallians was a living, raging creature in its own right. *This is what is going with me into Paradise Reach.*

He noticed he was being shepherded by a ship and thought at first it was Horth, but Horth and Bryllit each identified themselves with a shimmer dance as he watched, causing the ships in their hands to spread clear of them in prearranged patterns. They were letting Vrenn lead the charge, perhaps because the insult had taken place closest to PA territory.

Now in the Reetion-governed Reach of Paradise, they passed through a wide tunnel of clear space hemmed around by dark matter. The naturally occurring particles were just as fatal as a dust mine to a *rel*-craft. It hemmed them in, opening out in a great, sweeping lip below and eventually sheering away to wisps on either side. Erien knew it from Reetion star maps. It was too vast to experience with the senses. If there was a way around, it was beyond the reality skimming tolerance of human pilots, and Sevolites had never explored here. The route they traveled was the safe one, known to be hard vacuum — for the time being.

They were minutes away from the coordinates Amel had given when two moving points sprang to life on Erien's inner hull, heading straight for them at more than the one *skim'fac* comfortable for commoners, but less than a brisk pace for even a nobleborn Sevolite flyer. Were they coming out to fight? That would be brave, but suicidal. Pilots were rare among Reetions, and even their best, like Ann, was no match for highborn stamina. The second ship overtook the first and almost wakelocked. If they had been Gelacks, Erien would have sworn that the pursuer had been purposefully trying for a dunk — a hostile move meant to overexpose a rival pilot to gap, inducing time slip or worse — but Reetions did not fight while flying. At least, Erien had never heard of it happening.

Vrenn's ship flared bright as a nova at the point of the lead hand of fighters and sheared away in a steep arc, doing seven *skim'facs* for a few heart-stopping seconds. Not even highborns could sustain that. Erien felt the heave in space as other ships veered away from a burst of dust only just becoming visible by blocking the stars beyond. Vrenn must have detected the hazard just in time to prevent manifesting in the middle of it. Two ships were less lucky: one corkscrewed suddenly and shot out of control, the second shattered the way hullsteel always did when stressed beyond its stupendous limits for structural integrity, peppering surrounding space with more deadly dust.

One of the Reetion ships vanished. The second one tried to peel clear, but failed, and blinked out on Erien's nervecloth.

Vrenn signaled the Nersallians to regroup. Horth drew his personal hand after him in one direction and Bryllit drew hers in another, each enacting a search-and-explore pattern to find a way through.

Erien flew straight at the wall of dust created by hundreds of barely perceivable pops as more booby traps went off. His shepherd ship shimmered excitedly but Erien ignored the warning. He knew what he had meant to do. The Reetion ships had, indeed, been fighting, and the second one had stopped the first one from one setting off all the encircling dust bombs. If so, accelerating would put him through a hole in the wall before it closed. How deep the dust field reached he could not know. But he knew, from Ann's inventory, what they had had for resources, and he could deduce how much was consumed by the equidistantly spaced dust bombs spreading bloodied space before him. If he was wrong, he was dead — but he had to try to reach the station before the avenging Nersallians. He was the only chance the Reetions had.

Erien made his guess, set his drive-mix and made his bid to skip over the dust in one dangerously long stitch of shimmer.

Gap devoured him.

The next sensation he registered was becoming aware of his skin as a boundary dividing the "inside" from the "outside." Inside consisted of bile in his throat, a churning stomach and the pain digging into his shoulder. Mentally, he reassembled the universe from sensations, the leather straps of his flight harness, and his nervecloth display, now showing patches of damage. His own name came to him last of all. He was Erien, first ward of Monitum, then ward of Rire and, more recently, Heir Gelion.

He was skimming in clear space with *Kali Station* dead ahead. Behind him, the strike force blazed like a thwarted mass of fireflies beyond a veil of dust.

He felt the pulse of another ship staggering out of gap and his heart screamed into overdrive. He slammed his cockpit around, maintaining his orientation to *G* forces as he changed direction. His display showed a blurred outline, symbolic of a damaged ship leaking molecules of atmosphere due to phase distortion. Hullsteel ships couldn't spring leaks of the ordinary sort, but dysfunctional phasing was just as serious. It had to be his shepherd ship. It had jumped with him! And the pilot had to be alive and conscious to be flying. But for how long?

Erien danced the shimmer code requesting radio contact, which would require them both to drop out of skim.

The wounded ship disregarded him and shivered into formation at his side. It did not signal. It just stayed with him, like a specter, dropping out of skim minutes later to coast toward *Kali's* dock. Erien was profoundly relieved at that. *Okal Rel* forbade destroying stations, but if the pilot was too impaired to grasp what was required, Erien would have been forced to destroy him to save the station.

No Reetion pilots challenged them, nor did the station hail them as it should.

Erien turned on his radio and hailed his bodyguard. "Nersallian ship, this is Heir Gelion. What is your status?"

"Not... good," said a strained but recognizable voice.

"Dorn! Heir Nersal—" Erien checked himself. A hard lump blocked his throat.

"Where are they?" Dorn asked, referring to the lack of ward ships. His pronoun made it clear he meant the Reetions.

"I don't know," Erien said. "Can you dock?"

"I think so," said Dorn.

"I can't promise they won't be hostile," Erien felt driven to say. "But I need to find a way, a chance, to resolve this without millions dead on either side before it is done."

"*Zer-rel*," Dorn said, and coughed. *Zer-rel* was the naming word for some sort of priest-soul in the Nesak canon. Erien had no idea what Dorn meant by invoking the word now, and didn't have time to find out.

"*Kali Station*," said Erien, "I wish to invoke humanitarian foundation protocol: medical emergency with imminent risk to life. Please respond."

An arbiter voice said, "No such legislation extant. This station's intellectual functions are damaged. Please identify."

A cold sweat prickled in Erien's hairline, knowing how integral an arbiter was to every function on a Reetion station.

"This is Erien," he said, "son of Ranar, Evert and Lurol of the city of Rire Proper, on the planet—"

"Adopted son," the arbiter interrupted — in Gelack! "You were not born on Rire."

"Uh, yes," said Erien, disconcerted. He could think of no reason for the arbiter addressing him in Gelack.

"You are Erien," the arbiter told him, speaking Reetion once more, "Ward of Monitum."

Erien hesitated for a heartbeat. "Yes."

"Erien, Heir Gelion," the arbiter continued, "son of Ev'rel Dem'Vrel and Ava Ameron, Liege Lor'Vrel."

Now Erien was alarmed. His Gelack status as a ward of Monitum was on the record, but *Kali Station* had been out of touch for over seventy-two hours. How could it know that Ameron had made him Heir Gelion?

"Yes," Erien told it warily. "Ward of Monitum, Heir Gelion and Ranar's adopted son. Implement emergency measures for docking a damaged craft and injured pilot."

"Directives unavailable," said the arbiter, "but alternate protocol — compassion — located. Please confirm implementation of compassion, Erien, Ward of Monitum."

"Yes!" said Erien.

"Please confirm, Erien of Rire," said the arbiter.

"Yes, confirmed," said Erien, baffled and anxious.

"Please confirm, Erien, Heir Gelion."

"Do it!" Erien ordered, dreading yet another iteration, but this time the arbiter moved on.

"Are you the injured pilot?" it asked, and then continued in the same impassive tone. "Will you survive? I am frightened. Interrupted for diagnostics, please stand by."

Gods! Erien thought, turning cold.

He heard Dorn's agonized breathing on their ship-to-ship channel and swallowed.

"Cannot back-chain last statements to motivating propositions," the *Kali* arbiter reported. "Cannot—"

"Suspend diagnostic!" Erien said, thinking furiously. "Calculate position and timing of incoming ship with respect to the emergency docking bay."

"Emergency docking procedures are unavailable," said the arbiter.

"Transfer remote control to me," said Erien.

The arbiter tortured Erien by once again demanding confirmation three times.

"Your spacecraft are nonstandard," *Kali* complained as they prepared to dock. "Safety margin cannot be calculated."

Erien went on the offensive. "Submit assertion: any level of confidence in safety of procedure is acceptable. Submit context: medical emergency. Submit waivers: I and my companion understand and accept the risk involved."

"Please confirm abolishing safety threshold," *Kali* requested, "Erien, Ward of Monitum."

"Yes!" said Erien. It asked him twice more, just like last time.

"Talks a lot... for a machine," Dorn spoke up over the radio. "Must be a... Demish one."

Erien did not smile. "I am transmitting your docking instructions."

"Better order the docks... evacuated," Dorn warned, "in case I... lose control."

"There's no one there according to the arbiter," Erien said grimly. "Dorn, just go." He tried not to believe, as he began his own approach, what Dorn had just admitted with his last remark. A dominantly Vrellish highborn did not black out in harness. They died, or they stayed in control. Dorn was probably already in the grip of the acute Vrellish stress response called *rel-osh*, his body ruthlessly sacrificing long-term survival for short-term alertness. Without sophisticated medical intervention there was no way back. Fortunately, the Reetions possessed exactly that. If he could get Dorn to sick bay in time, there might be hope.

Erien's heartbeat pounded in his ears as he hauled himself from his hatch onto the pylon ladder of the zero-G Reetion dock. He swam as swiftly as he could toward Dorn's ship, breathing heavily to squeeze enough oxygen out of the air. Reetion docks maintained only as much atmosphere as was essential, but it was worse than that. The air was stale.

A gust of warm air greeted Erien when he pulled open Dorn's hatch. He swallowed dry mouthed, and slithered through, pulling himself up the shaft and into Dorn's cockpit.

Dorn was still strapped into his harness. The hullsteel of his sling frame, the web of his harness and the pale skin of his hands were all painted red; the black pants of his flight leathers were coated in glistening slickness.

Bloodied space, Erien thought, and understood Perry's revulsion.

Dorn turned a ghostly, sweating face toward him. "I cannot move my legs." He retched, bringing up a little bloodstained bile that, with spacer's discipline, he captured in one hand. With the other hand he hefted up his sheathed sword from where it had been stowed.

Erien fought his own low-G nausea. He said, "I'm going to pull you onto my back. I've only got one good arm, and unless someone comes to help us, I'm going to have to tow you up the pylon until we can catch some spin."

Dorn shook his head. "No." He pushed his sheathed sword, the symbol of his people's covenant with a fragile universe, against Erien's chest. "Take it." His eyes were dark in his blanched face. Assorted terse comments crossed Erien's mind regarding the mutual exclusivity of common sense and Gelack honor, but they were unjust and uncharitable. What he felt most was guilt for being the cause of Dorn's suffering. He did not know how to behave like a Gelack. That could clearly mean life or death to those who accepted him as one.

"I can't leave you," Erien half-apologized. "If Amy didn't spit me for it, Tatt would."

Amy, Erien's half-sister on Ameron's side, was Dorn's lover; Erien's half-brother, Tatt, was one of Dorn's close friends. Dorn responded with a bleak smile to the references.

Erien took hold of the Nersallian's arm, hoisting him awkwardly.

"My sword!" Dorn protested.

"I have it," Erien promised, looping the belt around Dorn's shoulder. Dorn yielded a thin whine through clenched teeth, but hooked his other arm over Erien. Drops of blood oozed from hidden rents in his leathers and floated free.

Halfway up the pylon, Dorn passed out. Erien felt Dorn's hold suddenly loosen. He caught Dorn's sleeve in his teeth, securing him for as long as it took to bring his left hand up and snag Dorn's flight jacket with hooked fingers. Trying hard to be grateful for the noxious mercy of zero-G, Erien labored the remaining distance to the transfer elevator.

"Take us to the reception floor," he told the arbiter. It obeyed in silence. Erien eased Dorn to the floor as the transfer platform began to accelerate around the axis, parallel to the inner hub, until it matched speed with it and smoothly dropped through. Erien looked up to see the gray curve of Dorn's *rel*-ship disappear through the long tunnel of their descent. The facing door was transparent and, as the elevator slowed, Erien saw three figures in Reetion Space Service blue on the far side. The woman in the middle was sighting down a bulky looking gun aimed at his chest. He recognized her as Ann.

As the door opened, Ann said in Gelack, "Don't make any sudden moves."

One of the two men with her lowered his big awkward gun at the sight of Dorn, and unslung the medical pack he was carrying.

"Get back here, Kal!" Ann snapped.

"But he's—"

"Nersallian," she finished for him, "and dangerous."

Kal retreated, but his eyes remained fixed on Dorn. For Erien, it was a welcome reminder of the Rire he was risking so much for.

"Space exec Ann," he said, "I am Erien, Ranar's ward."

"I've heard of you." She jerked her chin. "On your belly, Sevolite. Now."

"I'm not your enemy," he told her.

"Then what are you doing here?" demanded Ann.

At Erien's feet, Dorn came around with a groan. Erien risked breaking eye contact with Ann to crouch beside him. "Will you help him while I answer your questions?" he asked, an edge of pleading in his tone.

Ann's mouth settled into a tight frown. "Go help," she decided, and nodded to Kal, "but watch yourself. You," she told Erien, "move away from him. Loy," she directed the second man on her team, "keep an eye out for Megans."

"Dorn may be *rel-osh*," Erien warned Kal as he yielded his place beside Dorn, and was relieved to see the medic nod. Not every Reetion medic knew what *rel-osh* was. Erien scanned the label of the bag of blood replacement Kal was preparing and relaxed when he saw it was synthetic plasma with nothing in it for Dorn to react to.

Dorn stiffened as Kal went to ease the strap of the sword off his shoulder.

"No!" cried Erien. "The sword stays with him." To Dorn he said firmly, "Let the Reetion help you. He is a medic."

"Talk," demanded Ann, as Erien straightened.

"There are seven hands of Nersallian fighters on the other side of your barrier," said Erien. "All of them highborn."

"Shit," Ann said, with feeling. She nodded at Dorn. "I sent a pilot after Hanson's man, to stop him from arming the dust bombs. Guess he didn't make it."

"We saw two Reetion pilots fighting," said Erien. "It tipped off the hand leaders. Hanson is not your ally?"

Ann scowled. "Not lately."

"I've got to get this Gelack into the sick-bay coffin," Kal interjected, and belatedly realized the slang might be alarming. "A coffin is a life-support—"

"I know what it is," Erien assured him. "Do it." He returned his attention to Ann. "We know Amel came here. Where is he?"

"Sick bay," she said. "Hanson's people grabbed him." She snorted a laugh. "We concocted zappers to fight boarding highborns and we've been using them on each other. I've killed Megans today," she said grimly, "so why quibble over Gelacks? Give me one good reason why I shouldn't lay you out."

"I may be able to save your people's lives," said Erien bluntly.

"Good reason." Ann wet her lips. "You stop the Nersallians, and we'll put your pilot into the life-support coffin after we take sick bay back from Hanson. Tell your Gelacks it was Hanson who primed the bombs and they can have him for sword practice once I've settled a personal score. Agreed?"

He nodded. "One thing more. Your arbiter... I know it was boxed, but even for that it is acting... idiosyncratically."

"Idiosyncratically?" Ann's almond eyes narrowed. "You mean, sort of like it's got a personality?"

Running feet heralded new arrivals. Ann raised her gun, but they turned out to be her own people.

"We've got a Nersallian strike force spaceside," Ann informed them, and paused to clip her zapper on her belt. "This is Erien." She tipped her head in his direction. "He's going to see if he can persuade his Nersallian friends to lay off. Now let's move! I want to be in sick bay before Hanson figures out he's lost."

Erien stepped back into the elevator, his good arm supporting his pulsing shoulder, and ordered, "Docks."

A microstage surprised him by sprouting an input request icon normally reserved for a station's command triumvirate. "Summary of problem," the microstage announced, projecting a decision tree with handles leading to elaborations. "This arbiter has been impaired by sabotage. Question: should the visitor probe's unidentified data source be empowered to sustain its veto, or should shutdown proceed in accordance with core directives? Erien of Rire, please vote yes or no."

"Yes! Do not shut down!" Erien said. "There are people—"

"Erien, ward of Monitum," said the arbiter, "do you sustain the veto?"

Erien closed his eyes and laid his head back on the inner wall of the elevator. "What will happen if I do not?" he asked.

"This station is compromised and will shut down completely, in compliance with the no captains protocol prohibiting the usurption of command by criminals for potential terrorist abuse of reality skimming for militaristic purposes."

Erien straightened, gritting his teeth against the pain in his shoulder. "Yes, yes, yes!" he told the arbiter. "Empower the unidentified data source to sustain the veto — wait!" Gravity was growing lighter as they approached the docks, making him dizzy. "What is the unidentified data source?"

"Seeking name," said the stage, and fell silent.

It can't be, thought Erien, remembering Ann telling him she had a score to settle with Hanson and was on her way to liberate the sick bay.

"Amel," said the microstage, "is the data source. Please note it is integrated through a noisy interface resulting in delayed responses when access is required."

Erien closed his eyes, remembering what had seemed like so much babble at the time: *Are you the injured pilot? Will you survive? I am frightened.* Were they messages straight from Amel's naked consciousness, transferred through a "noisy" interface that was, in fact, living human neurology?

"Station cannot shut down," *Kali* announced momentarily. "There are people on board. There is Ann." A brief pause followed. "Ann is differentially important but the rationale is incomprehensible."

Erien felt the unmistakable tremor of approaching *rel*-ships.

"Incoming craft are exceeding safe parameters of approach," said the arbiter. "Station integrity is threatened."

"I'll deal with them," Erien said. "Just get me down to the docks."

The elevator started a shuddering descent. Erien braced himself against the walls, his teeth set. The Nersallians were deliberately shaking the station, a tactic they would never use against opponents they considered honorable.

"*Kali!*" Erien demanded. "What is happening?"

The microstage filled with pictures of *rel*-ships surrounding the station, drifting in twos and fours like sinister bubbles. Some sort of gear protruded from the hatch of another spherical *rel*-fighter attached to *Kali*'s hull. It took Erien a moment to grasp the adapted *rel*-fighter was cutting through the station's hull, which was something Gelack hullsteel would have made impossible.

A memory suddenly slid into alignment for Erien: Horth and himself sitting companionably on a bench in an exercise hall on one of Horth's battlewheels, with Erien explaining blueprints for *Kali*'s new design, which had come effortlessly into Horth's possession, and trying to explain the political system that made them so accessible even to hostile eyes. He had not, Erien allowed, with a twisted smile at his innocence, really appreciated that Horth's *were* hostile eyes — he had been thinking like the foster son of two ambassadors, and not in military terms.

"Elevator, reverse!" ordered Erien. "Arbiter, assemble a montage of all the points of attachment of Nersallian spacecraft." He shivered with tension as he watched the schematics assemble, holding his wounded left arm. The Nersallians were cutting their way in from eight locations around Kali's torus-shaped body.

"*Kali Station*," he said hoarsely. "Drop all decompression bulkheads."

That ought to keep Reetions and Gelacks separate long enough for him to meet up with Horth and...

And what? he thought. *Convince him not to take a station he's already conquered?*

SEVEN

Eyes on Amel

With Friends Like These

Some army, Ann thought, looking at her sick bay liberation force.

Braz was marching ahead with his girlfriend, Chun, and oblivious to Kal, who had stopped to look after Dorn. An earnest girl called Temi was trying to recruit tall, competent Imbert to help Kal. Net result: Braz and Chun were going to be out of sight in a moment and she didn't want Braz leading the charge. She lifted her zapper, turned it down and shot a crackling discharge into the wall ahead of Braz, making him and Chun spin around with their zappers up.

"You with us, or on your own?" Ann asked.

Braz scowled.

"I want you and Chun to follow Erien," said Ann. "If you don't think his chums out there are going to heel on command, put the gun to his head and ask them to reconsider. The empire's a primitive hierarchy, and he's their Ava's son."

Braz nodded, catching on. "That makes him..."

"...a potential hostage." Chun finished for him. She was as slim as Braz was large.

"Loy will go with you," Ann added. "He speaks Gelack. You two don't, and the arbiter's in no condition to translate."

"Who decides when we stop being friends and start threatening?" asked Braz.

"Two out of three decision threshold?" Loy suggested, as he joined the group.

"Done," Braz said, with a meaningful glance toward his lover.

Imbert closed ranks with Ann, his zapper cradled in his arms. He was athletic and dark, with craggy features, a docks engineer and a friend Ann had learned to rely on. He had even been a lover for a short while, between a blow up and reconciliation with Amel.

"Are you planning to lead the charge?" Imbert asked her.

"On sick bay? You bet I am!" said Ann.

"Is that wise?" he asked. "Are you sure you should be leading when—"

"Yes!" Ann broke into a jog, thinking *I bet Horth Nersal doesn't have to deal with this kind of stuff!*

She believed in the Reetion way of talking things out and reaching a decision based on threshold conditions agreed upon in advance. It was the best damned way of doing things ever devised by humans and implemented by arbiters. She just couldn't deal with it right now.

Imbert kept up. He could have passed her if he chose. She admired his fitness. And he had been as good in bed as anyone ought to want. Why couldn't she settle for an Imbert? *Because Amel is Amel,* she answered herself. She had hardly been able to draw breath when she saw Vic — of all people! — strike Amel, but by the time she recovered from the shock she had no time to do anything but get out.

Imbert stopped her close to where their people were massing for the final assault, knowing it would be their last chance to talk.

"Listen," he said, "I would rather have you lead us against Gelacks than anyone... except now. If Amel's at stake, you won't be rational. Let me call the shots." Imbert put a hand on her shoulder. "It's the right decision."

"All right!" she snapped, pulling away from him. "If they try using Amel against me, you call the shots." She gave him a glare. "Good enough?" Imbert nodded.

They caught up with the rest of Ann's strike force a single curve of the corridor away from the sick bay entrance.

"We've taken the rest of the station, Ann," said Ho. He was the ship's recreation coordinator and Ann's martial arts instructor. "It's just Hanson and a few militia holding out in sick bay now."

"Perfect," said Ann, who pulled her gun and charged. She figured more of them would follow if she didn't give them time to lose their nerve.

The Megans guarding the sick bay started in alarm. Imbert dropped one with a zapper shot. Behind her, Ann heard a Reetion woman go down. Ahead of her a Megan yelped, "Hanson! It's Ann!" as if they were the only two people involved.

Zapper fire continued at Ann's back, so close it made her hair stand on end. The Megan kid called Julio stood with his hands up, eyes as big as saucers. More Reetions fanned out behind Ann. Imbert joined her again, then Ho.

"Stop right there!" Hanson shouted, jamming his zapper against Amel's chest where he lay on the palette with his head encased in the probe's hood.

Ann stopped cold.

"The unidentified equipment you are handling—" the stages showed the image of a zapper "—is capable of harming people. Please surrender them to a first responder."

We wish, thought Ann. Amel's limpness was as frightening as Hanson's zapper. She had never see him so inert, not even sleeping off a long flight or her eager welcome.

"We don't have time for this," Imbert told Hanson coldly. "The Nersallians are outside."

"He doesn't care!" cried Ann. "He wants a war!"

Ho started forward. Hanson fired at the edge of the palette, making Amel's body jump. "I said stay back!" he cried.

Ann's chest cramped. She braced herself to try for his zapper, knowing she could never make it.

But Vic could. He shot up from the chair where he huddled between the coffin and the visitor probe. Hanson's killing jolt went wide. Ann forgave Vic all his sins on the spot. Hanson fell sideways, grabbing Vic by the throat as Imbert's zapper shot struck.

"Amel!" Vic coughed, staggering back up.

Ann snatched up Amel's hand where he lay on the palette. It felt like warm wax. She turned on Vic, snarling, "Get him out."

"I d-don't think that's safe," the little doctor stammered. "Listen, I helped Hanson, I know," Vic dissolved in a guilty confession. "I was scared. Everyone could have died unless—" He broke off to dampen his lips. "I-I want to be useful. Please, Ann. Let me help the people who need medical attention."

"Fine." Ann put Amel's hand down and stepped back, needing a clear head and calm stomach. "We have a dust-damaged Gelack named Dorn," she told Vic. "Do what you can. Might be worth something." She wondered if they would have to sink low enough to threaten withdrawal of Dorn's life-support later, and whether people like Kal would let her.

"He's *rel-osh* and bleeding like a stuck pig!" Kal told Vic, fussing with the plasma bag's connection as Dorn was lifted up by willing hands.

Vic slid into place and took over from Kal like a changed man. "Help me get these clothes off," he said, discarding blood-slimed chunks of Dorn's flight pants.

Ann made a face at the sight of what a dust bomb had done. From waist to knee, slanting down sharply toward the right side, Dorn's flesh was a mass of blood. Nothing was torn beyond recognition, but the dust had made a sieve of flesh and bone.

"His blood pressure's not low, it's strong!" Kal reported excitedly. "His intestinal perfusion is way down, arterial blood flow to the legs is practically nonexistent, probably stopped him from bleeding to death, but—"

"That's normal for *rel-osh*," Vic assured him, working with the coffin lid still up, "but it doesn't have to be fatal. There are complications to worry about, but I've heard the Gelacks' own medical people — the Lorels — can nurse a highborn through regeneration of whole organs without cancerous results."

The word 'Lorel' registered with Dorn. He shoved Vic into Kal with one ramrod arm. Both Reetion men went down like dominos. Dorn's lower body was useless, but Temi stood close enough for him to snatch the sword from her arms.

One fatally wounded Sevolite, three able-bodied Reetions, Ann thought. *It's a good thing we outnumber them by the ton.*

Dorn shook his sword clear of its sheath with a practiced snap. The sheath clattered to the floor. The Reetions stared, bemused. It was only a sword, after all, and they were armed with zappers.

Ann didn't know what tipped her off — some detail of expression or bunching of muscle — but she realized Dorn was going to slit his own throat with the sword, and lunged. Swearing a hot streak in Reetion, she used her weight against his arm to hold it down.

"We are trying to help you, you big lug!" she yelled at Dorn in *rel*-peerage. Who knew what that meant to him? Probably some horrible insult. But it was too late to sort the grammar out. She was just a little worried he would twist the sword he still gripped in a much-too-strong arm, and give her the definitive Nersallian opinion of Reetion upstarts.

"Hold on!" Vic cried, fumbling with a tranquilizer.

The set of Dorn's mouth softened, staring at Ann as she held onto his arm. He looked frightened for the first time, and even worse — young. "No... *dresu* bondage," he begged.

"I don't know what *dresu* bondage is!" Ann's arms ached.

"Did you know," Dorn asked, down-speaking her with contempt. "What bloodied space was?"

"Listen," Ann wet her lips, "you trust Erien, right?"

Dorn's wide, clear brow furrowed, sweat in his dark hairline. "Yes."

"Would he have asked us to help you if we were going to do something terrible?"

"Erien..." For an alarming moment Dorn didn't seem sure, then he muttered something and gave up his sword.

"I'll put it right here for you," Ann told him. "Close by. On the floor."

Okal Rel offered no fair means for her people to resist Dorn's in space, Ann reminded herself as she let Vic take over. *So why do I still feel so foul?* she wondered. Maybe it was the magnificence of a mad creature like Dorn that made her wish she could play by his rules. Instead, she'd had to fight Rire, as well, to overcome its idiot refusal to be scared by Gelacks. Sure, the average Sevolite couldn't pass a piloting psych profile on Rire, but you didn't need space science if you could fly by instinct, the way a bird of prey calculated a killing dive. And for all Rire's superiority, it couldn't make heads or tails of the snatches of old Lorel science Ranar sometimes sent home: the very science, in all likelihood, that had invented hullsteel, nervecloth — and Amel.

She had bullied Amel into helping her make mounting a defense possible. When she had forced him to think about what conquest by his own kind would mean to ordinary Reetions, he couldn't say no. He had been punished for it on Gelion... and punished again, in the worst way imaginable, for coming to help her.

Her eyes turned to Amel's impassive body in the visitor probe. *I have to get him out,* she thought.

Imbert caught her as she started for the probe's controls. "Ann!" He caught her wrists. "You don't even know what that might do to him!"

Hot tears spilled down her cheeks. "Are you so sure it's him you're worried about? We put him in the probe — again — after swearing for the last eighteen years that the first time was a horrible accident."

The *Kali* arbiter suddenly occupied every stage. "This station is being boarded by unidentified intruders," it announced.

"Connect us with Loy, Chun or Braz!" Imbert demanded of the nearest stage.

There was no response.

"*Kali!*" Ann addressed the stage. "I'm Ann, one of your command triumvirate."

"Triumvirate is Erien, Erien, Erien," the stage declared.

"Law and reason," Imbert exclaimed. "Amel's given him command of the station!"

Ann felt obscurely insulted. Amel? Her Amel! Gave control of *her* station to his brother?

"Vic," she said. "I need you!"

When she used that tone, people responded. Kal took over treating Dorn.

She took Amel's hand again. "Give me audio input," she told Vic. "But add tactile sensation and body sense."

Vic hesitated, worried. "Won't that be too much?"

"I think," Ann told him, "it will keep him sane." Being alive, for Amel, was an exquisitely physical affair. His being bodiless now would be harder than all the rest.

"All right," Vic said. "He can see and feel you now — no! Wait a moment. He's panicking. I'm adjusting the input to match his body image. There, try now."

"Amel," she said, as gently as she knew how, "it's me, Ann. I need to see what's happening on the docks. Please help me. Please understand."

"He can't sustain this," Vic exclaimed, alarmed. "It's too confusing! He'll go mad."

Ann squeezed Amel's hand and watched its counterpart on Vic's schematic version of Amel bloom with sensation.

From another stage, on the ward floor, the *Kali* arbiter announced, "Communications now available to—" pause, "—Ann."

The station jerked. Ann pitched across Amel. Voices cried in alarm. A stage showed Ann Nersallian ships boring into *Kali*'s hull.

"Law and reason!" Imbert gasped. "I thought they were supposed to be limited to stereotypically instinctive behaviors?"

"I guess engineering is instinctive for Nersallians," Ann said dryly.

Gelack hullsteel couldn't be cut. It dispersed local stress over its entire structure, making it uniquely resistant to the stresses of reality skimming, which meant they were witnessing an explicitly anti-Reetion innovation by House Nersal.

Or more particularly, Ann thought bitterly, *by Horth Nersal.* If the Nersallian leader had been in her sights in that instant, she would gladly have shot him in cold blood.

"Where's Erien?" she asked instead, thinking of hostages.

The stage revealed Erien running along a corridor nowhere near the docks.

"Vic?" Ann asked. "Could you block Amel's connection with *Kali,* temporarily, on my order?"

Vic said, "I think so."   .

"Good," said Ann. "Stand by." She was about to do something Amel would never let her get away with if he knew. "Give me Braz, Chun and Loy," said Ann.

Braz was surprised to be hailed from the stage in his elevator. Ann got him to turn the elevator around and head back to where Erien was located, then she told all three of them what was causing the station tremors.

"Boarded?" Loy couldn't seem to grasp the idea. "Through the hull?"

"We need insurance," Ann told Braz. "Understand?"

"We'll take care of it," Braz told her, and signed off.

"Erien's getting *Kali* to make contact with one of their ships!" Imbert reported.

"Let's hear it," said Ann.

The exchange was in Gelack and restricted to audio, but the cold confidence in the deep, male voice from space came through very clear. "Occupation of *Kali Station* is underway," said Horth Nersal, speaking up Highlord to Pureblood. "Is Dorn with you?"

"N-no," said Erien. The question threw him off. "But he's not dead, Horth, he's — hold on moment! There's someone here."

Horth Nersal couldn't see what was happening, but Ann could. Her people had arrived. Loy looked a bit sick, but Braz looked like he would enjoy shooting a Gelack, and Chun would space walk naked if Braz told her to. Not a seasoned military commando force, Ann admitted, but the best she had.

"Now!" Ann told Vic. He nodded. She willed herself to be cold.

"Erien," she hailed her prospective hostage, "this is Ann. You won't get any help from Amel via *Kali.* It is still linked to him but we're obstructing the channel. If you drag this out it will only put Amel and the station under more stress."

"I see," Erien said. "And this doesn't concern you?" He kept very still, standing clear of the walls now.

"I'm concerned all right!" she lashed out. "I'm concerned about Nersallians boring holes in my station! You tell them to get back in their ships or I'm going to find out what happens when *Kali* loses its new triumvirate to summary execution, Erien, Erien, Erien!"

He pointed out, very rationally, "I had nothing to do with usurping command powers." There was the briefest hesitation, then, "How is Dorn?"

Ann scowled. "He tried killing himself with his damn sword, but he calmed down when I invoked your name, so don't try making out you don't mean anything special to them! Now get your pet monster back on the radio and tell him to back off!"

The station shivered. Erien took advantage of the instability to go for Braz, placing Loy in the way of Chun's shot at him. Braz didn't get a chance to fire before Erien knocked him down.

Damn, he's fast! Ann thought, but clumsier than she would have expected. She thought she knew why.

"Go for his left side!" she shouted advice to her Reetions. "He's Vrellish and he's not using his left arm. He must be hurt!"

Chun and Loy piled into Erien. Loy seized Erien's left arm and Erien failed to break the hold. By the time Braz got up, nose bleeding, Chun and Loy had Erien face down on the floor with Chun's gun at his temple.

"I think we've just received an ultimatum," Imbert reported from another stage in sick bay. "I'm not much good at translating Gelack, but I think it amounts to 'put Erien back on the radio, or else.'"

"I have to answer Horth," Erien said, over Ann's com connection, lying still in the grip of his captors, although his voice remained irritatingly imperious. "Now!"

"Tell him you are our hostage," said Ann.

"If I do," he said, "we are all doomed. Nersallians do not oblige blackmailers. You have to trust me, Ann!"

At that point, *Kali* put Horth Nersal through again. "*Ar'k bree-ta sel?*" he asked in Gelack.

"Huh?" said Ann. She understood ordinary Gelack, but not their quirky, compressed phrases with hidden meanings.

"He is asking me if I'm myself," Erien said in Reetion. "It's a question Vrellish warriors asked during the Lorel Wars when captives were changed and sent home to attack their families." Raising his voice, he added in Gelack, "Yes, Horth, I'm fine! In fact, I'm in command. The arbiter has made me... station master."

Moot point, thought Ann, with a scowl, *when you are pinned to the floor with a gun at your head.* But he was probably right to be smug. Horth Nersal had the power of life and death over her station, whatever she did on it.

So what would happen if you ran a few Horth Nersals through the visitor probe? wondered Ann, *and used them to protect us from the rest of their kind? Must be what the Lorels did.*

She could see why.

"We can work together," said Erien. "Or we can make threats and all die. Think hard, Ann."

Ann looked down at Amel on the visitor probe's palette.

"I guess," she said stiffly, "we trust each other."

Erien's eyes closed briefly, his relief visible. She took that as a good sign. "Could your people let me up now?" he asked very politely in Reetion.

"Release him," she said curtly.

"This station is compromised," said *Kali*. "Shutdown is imminent."

"Vic!" Ann spun around.

"Opening the channel again now!" Vic cried, hard at work on the visitor probe.

Moments later, the crisis once more averted, Imbert pointed at a stage showing new images. "Look!"

Nersallians armed with some sort of handguns were rounding up Reetions trapped in the same section of hull as themselves. They wore swords on their hips but also gas masks around their necks, and every third one was in an environment suit. They looked to Ann like large, malignant ants, unisex in build and strength, and terrible in their efficiency. Ann recognized the leader, Tash Bryllit, as a half-Nesak conservative who had once been Horth's *mekan'st* and mentor. It was also said she threw people out airlocks when they offended her.

"Liege Bryllit is in the habitat lounge of section C1," Ann told Erien over the com. "She's herding prisoners into an airlock used for recreational space walking. She's going to store them there until it's full, and then cycle it, isn't she? She's going to space people!"

Alarmingly, Erien did not deny Ann's wild guess.

"Have you still got Dorn's sword with you?" he said, instead.

"Have I what?" Ann asked, incredulous, and then it dawned on her. "You're going to challenge her? Are you crazy!" she exploded at Erien. "Bryllit's got about a hundred years' experience on you! Or don't you know your Killing Reach who's who?"

"Bring the sword and meet me outside C1," Erien said and signed off.

Ann cursed for ten seconds in spacers' slang. Then she snatched the sword off the floor.

"The rest of you stay put," said Ann, as she snatched up her zapper for good measure.

EIGHT

Erien

On a Sword's Edge

Ann sprinted round the curving corridor in section C1 carrying Dorn's sword, and thrust the sheathed weapon at Erien.

"I don't believe this is happening," she told him. "How long do you think you can last against Bryllit? She was giving Horth lessons before you were born. And you're hurt, in case you hadn't noticed."

He forbore pointing out that she had been quick enough to take advantage of his injury when it suited her. "I'm not planning to fight," Erien said, drawing the sword. "I need this for respectability."

"Respectability?" Ann jeered. "Two feet of steel makes you respectable?"

He looked up. "Do power weapons make you civilized?"

As she drew breath to answer, his right hand closed hard on the fabric of her uniform as his left went for the weapon on her hip. He tore the zapper loose, boosting her backwards and into the air before hurling her several meters down the corridor. He paused long enough to be sure she was not badly hurt, then ran for the door, shouting for *Kali* to open it.

Ann was on her feet, cursing, as Erien threw himself through, and cried, "*Kali*, seal the door!"

Ann thudded against it on the other side and began to pound.

Erien dropped Ann's zapper like a hot coal and kicked it into a corner. Then he swept his gaze over the C1 section lounge. His exhaustion had moved to a distance, and in its place he had a crisp awareness of shape and motion. He saw the frightened prisoners standing in the airlock looking nervously behind them at the outer seal. A dozen Nersallians stood in a loose arc with needle guns drawn and not a sword unsheathed among them. Their leader, Bryllit, recognized her son's weapon in Erien's hand.

"Dorn is alive," said Erien. "He was caught in the edge of that nimbus. But he is not dead."

"How like a Lorel," Bryllit said slowly, pointedly avoiding pronouns that would force her to insult or acknowledge him, "to think Dorn would prefer a slow death to a clean one."

"He does not have to die," Erien insisted. "Nor should they." He tipped his head toward the prisoners. "The station accepts me as its command authority, thanks to Amel."

Amel's name meant something to her. He had no idea why. "I have taken this station," said Bryllit, deciding to acknowledge him as Pureblood with her pronouns. "Will you fight for it honorably, Lor'Vrel?"

She stepped forward, her body a casual threat.

"In the fleet," he said, riding the crest of the wild energy possessing him, "they claim only Nesaks space commoners."

"They're not just any commoners!" sneered Bryllit, her choice of pronoun demoting her prisoners to subhumans. "They are *okal'a'ni.*"

"This station surrendered to me," Erien repeated, feeling eerily immortal.

He did not look at the Reetions. He thought he knew what he would see there — utter incomprehension of the life-and-death ritual taking place. In the part of his mind shaped by his Reetion upbringing, he agreed with them.

Bryllit saluted him and he reciprocated.

Then they began. Inexorably, she drove him back. This was nothing like the duel he had fought on Gelion against his angry half-brother D'Lekker, nor the half-dozen barracks challenges before that. In none of those did he have such a sense of inevitability.

He felt the wall behind him. His next step stopped short. He had no choice but to stand then and let her close, too near for his injured muscles to defend against her. She drove her sword down over his, breaking his weakened parry, snapped it back and whipped the flat of it against his injured shoulder.

He went down on one knee, bracing his good hand against the ground. In the clouded periphery of his vision he saw the hilt of his borrowed sword and fumbled after it. He sensed her as a shadow, moving away, and looked up to see her gesture to her Nersallians to finish with the prisoners. Her face was clouded in his vision, but he saw the contempt in it. And he felt contempt in return for the way she had brought him down, the way she had simply dispensed with him and had not listened!

Anger lifted him up and forward, with a wordless cry.

She raised her own blade, caught his; the force of his lunge carried his hilt into hers. The brightness and transparency had gone from his vision; it had contracted to a gray stormy funnel containing only himself and Bryllit. She yielded suddenly, deflecting his attack, but he knew this was only a maneuver; he followed his momentum, spun and lunged again, wielding the sword two-handed. This time saw her yield. He felt his lips peel back from his teeth in a giddy smile of triumph.

And then he realized she had yielded to a third swordsman.

Erien leapt back, spun toward the new threat, and felt his blade crossed and twisted crisply from his hands. Almost — almost! — he followed the urgings of his instincts to engage hand to hand, muscle to muscle, bone to bone, or to accept certain death on the other's steel rather than yield. But the new opponent gave ground, which somehow brought Erien back into focus.

It was Horth, liege of Nersal.

Erien staggered back, appalled at his loss of control. He would have killed Bryllit if she had given him the least chance, just as he had killed D'Lekker. He would have fought Horth, without thinking! He could not even trust himself to pick up his sword, now. He did not know what he was doing with it in his hand.

"I will not permit," he rasped out words to explain himself, "the indiscriminate killing of Reetion civilians."

Horth Nersal absorbed the words. Bryllit held her ground, sword in her dominant left hand. Bryllit's people fell as silent as worshipers at the sight of Horth and Bryllit with their swords drawn.

"The commoners are *okal'a'ni*," Bryllit told Horth. "You have flown the route they polluted."

"I do not defend them," Horth said, "but Erien."

"He is Lorel," Bryllit accused.

"He is Lor'Vrel," Horth insisted.

Bryllit gave Erien a second, harder look. He returned it, possessed by a glittering, furious indifference.

"All right," she conceded. "He is Lor'Vrel."

Her posture shifted. Horth's relaxed. The watchers rustled.

"But once we've secured the station, you will explain why you defend one who defends *okal'a'ni* commoners," she told Horth, "or our swords may yet cross over Erien."

"*Ack rel*," Horth said in acceptance, and they both sheathed their weapons.

Bryllit ordered her people to remove the Reetions from the airlock. In the midst of it, a hand of Horth's fighters arrived, led by his brother Eler Nersal, a big man with the wide shoulders more typical of Demish males than Vrellish of either gender, and an air of viewing the world as an entertainment arranged especially for himself.

"Ah, the Throne Price," Eler greeted Erien. "I am sure your life would make an interesting story." Irreverence lurked beneath his impeccably differenced pronouns for everything except the one magic word, 'story.'

"Do you speak either Reetion or English?" Erien asked the big Nersallian.

Eler's large, dark eyes closed slowly and only half opened, looking sleepy and dangerous. "Both," he admitted, with mixed pride and caution. It was Vrellish to be good with swords, Demish to be good with languages.

"Good," said Erien. "Then I want you to take charge of the captives. Explain no harm will come to them and see they receive medical treatment if needed."

Eler's eyes opened up wider and wider as Erien reeled off his orders, but a glance over his shoulder at Horth was all it took to endorse the request as an order. "Yes, Heir Gelion," said Eler.

"Where is Dorn?" Bryllit demanded.

"In sick bay," said Erien. "I'll take you there."

On Erien's command the door opened. Ann sprang back at the sight of Bryllit and Horth. Beyond them, in lounge C1, Eler was proclaiming in Reetion to the newly rescued captives, "Heir Gelion has magnanimously decided, for some unfathomable reason intelligible only to Lorel minds, that we're going to look after you instead of hurling you out an airlock as you so richly deserve."

"Hey!" Ann broke off gaping at Eler to get in front of Erien when he swept past, followed by Bryllit and Horth. "Where are you taking them?" asked Ann.

"Sick bay," said Erien.

Ann switched to Gelack to address Bryllit. "I will take you to your son Dorn, but I want your word you will not harm Amel, my *mekan'st*. He is not responsible for my acts."

Bryllit's nostrils flared at Ann's grammatic peerage and the naming word *mekan'st*, or peer lover, which was only appropriate between Sevolites. Horth, who was never linguistically quick witted, looked to Erien to see if he ought to consider this an insult.

"Only a fool would harm Amel," Bryllit answered Ann curtly, avoiding pronouns.

"That will have to be good enough," said Ann. "So I guess we've officially surrendered to you, have we?" she remarked to Erien. "Better let me go ahead and tell Imbert and the others, or they might shoot."

"I want the guns in a pile on the floor — *all* of them," Erien warned her, and was answered with a tense nod.

Bryllit posted two Nersallians at the sick bay door before they entered. "I must see what has been done with Dorn," she told them. "But if we do not come out again, kill them all." Horth did not countermand the order.

Inside, they were greeted by a nervous looking Reetion dressed in a bloodied medical apron.

"I'm Vic," he said, ripping off the apron and throwing it as far away as he could, as if he was afraid it might upset his patient's visitors. "You must be Erien, Ranar and Lurol's boy."

The rest of the Reetions stood well back in a semicircle. Horth delegated one of Bryllit's Nersallians to take charge of collecting their discarded zappers, and Erien noted with involuntary Gelack instinct that the house braid on the woman's collar indicated she was Horth's daughter. It was said Horth had over a hundred children. Dorn, as his chosen heir, was still special, although not, perhaps, entirely irreplaceable. Bryllit conducted herself with equal aloofness, pausing to stare at Amel in the visitor probe before moving to join Horth beside Dorn's coffin.

Horth put his hand on the coffin lid. "Dorn is inside?" he asked Erien.

"Horth," Erien said intensely, "he is alive."

"First they inflict injuries Dorn cannot survive," said Bryllit, "then provide the means by which he can, and hold him prisoner." She scowled. "That is *dresu* bondage."

"No," Erien insisted. "It is lifesaving medical treatment. And *I* asked them to do it. It is my responsibility."

Horth nodded toward the coffin, "Can we ask him what he wants?"

"It isn't safe to wake him," Vic explained, after Erien translated. "We have only just got him resting comfortably, and he's already regenerating. That's physiologically taxing."

Ann shouldered her way past Vic. "Dorn had doubts, earlier," Ann remembered, speaking Gelack. "I told him it was okay with you," she said to Erien, "which seemed to take care of it."

"You believe the Reetion *imsha*?" Horth asked Erien.

"I do," said Erien, oddly pleased to hear Horth call Ann an *imsha*, the term for a Gelack fleet commander.

Bryllit accepted Horth's decision with a grunt, and went back to stand at the foot of Amel's bed, drawing Ann after her.

"What will happen to us?" Imbert asked Erien.

"I will see you evacuated and surrendered to Reetion authorities," said Erien.

"I'll stay," Vic volunteered. "For Dorn."

Eler arrived to oversee the roundup of Ann's sick bay commandos. He came over and saluted Erien, Nersallian fashion. "Shall I take the Reetion liege, now?" he asked in Reetion.

"Me?" said Ann, but got over the compliment quickly. "What about Amel?"

"I intend to get him out of the probe as soon as possible," Erien assured her.

She said, "I want to be there."

Erien still felt oddly energized, given his injuries, but the mix of tense Gelacks and able-bodied Reetions in the room was telling on his nerves. "I think you had better go with Eler," he said.

Ann scowled, but went quietly.

While Horth listened to Vic talking about Dorn, Erien snagged Kal. "Can you get me some saline-saturated towelettes, some dry ones and liquid permaskin, hypoallergenic grade? And a clean shirt, loose sleeves, preferably black."

"Most of that, yes," the medic said, and although he looked as tired as Erien felt, he added, "Can I help you? You look awful."

"No, thanks," said Erien. He could not afford any Reetions knowing how badly he was injured, or he risked being hospitalized the moment they got to Rire.

Kal brought Erien the supplies and Horth volunteered his help wordlessly by picking up a toppled screen and setting it up beside one of the two vacant beds.

Erien was startled by his own reflection in the mirror Horth held up for him. He was a study in black and white: black hair plastered to his forehead with sweat, pallid skin and his eyes bright, pupils dilated. But he didn't feel that bad, and there was still the business of extracting Amel. He could collapse later.

He let his jacket slide from his shoulder and with his right hand undid the laces of his shirt. Horth helped him peel off the saturated bandage. Beneath it, Erien's shoulder and upper arm were swollen purple and dark red, incised by the raw scarlet of the seamed wound. Half the seam had reopened and was oozing fresh blood, serum and old clots. His lower arm was pale; he could hardly move his hand.

"It doesn't feel as bad as it looks," Erien assured Horth, feeling oddly light-headed.

Horth frowned.

Erien could guess what Horth was thinking, but only highborns who were dominantly Vrellish went *rel-osh*. With his mixed heritage, Erien did not think he qualified.

Horth tore open a wet towel and began to swab the mess. Erien's mind retained the jittery, glass-like clarity it had had since he confronted Bryllit. As soon as the Nersallians had life-support stabilized he would remove Amel from the probe. Then the arbiter could shut down without any loss of life, eliminating what was likely to be Rire's greatest objection to the Nersallians remaining in possession of *Kali Station* — which was letting the Nersallians get their hands on a working arbiter.

He felt Horth shift behind him and looked for the dry towelettes to hand up to him. But Horth's fingers closed on his neck, instead.

Erien dropped the towelettes. His right hand caught Horth's wrist, seeking leverage. He started to pivot, but Horth moved smoothly with him. Erien threw his weight back against Horth and felt a jar as they struck a screen together. *Twenty seconds,* he remembered, *twenty seconds to unconsciousness.* Twenty seconds to prevail against someone he had taught, learned from and practiced with for almost three years... someone he trusted... and had let get too close!

The surreal, glittery feeling of infallibility stayed with Erien until he blacked out, and Horth caught him.

NINE

Eyes on Amel

Weighing Souls

Tash Bryllit watched with feelings of awe, shading into terrible confusion, as a pretty girl recited poetry on a Reetion stage.

"It's happening all over the station," her bemused engineer said beside her. "Not exactly like this, but strange scenes of all kinds, appearing on these things they call stages."

"It's a message from the Watching Dead who sent Amel to us as a *zer-pol*," said Bryllit.

Terla wrinkled her nose. "Poetry?"

"All of it." Bryllit stood nearly two meters tall, hard-muscled, and wider at the hips and shoulders than her more Vrellish granddaughter, who was one of Bryllit's eighty-six living descendants; a good tally for a woman, even stretched out over more than a hundred years. Her father had been a Nesak war prize, taken and slain by her mother. Her life had proved her Vrellish, not a homebound Nesak woman, but she conceived more easily than her purely Vrellish kinswomen, and — although she had stood against the Nesaks with Horth — the exposure had inclined her to favor Nesak beliefs over more jaded court attitudes. The Nesaks said Amel was a *zer-pol*: a sacred messenger sent to expose the evil in those who did him harm.

But what, exactly, did Amel mean by showing them a golden-haired girl reciting poetry?

"That's Princess Luthan Dem H'Us!" a booming voice announced behind them.

Bryllit turned to see Eler Nersal, whose large build betrayed his own injection of Demish blood via a Nesak parent.

"Or, rather, it is Luthan as she looked three or four years ago," said Eler. "She's filled out since." He laughed. "I wonder how

Amel got such a good look at the H'Usian's prize virgin in her dressing gown!"

"Maybe Amel's soul is more Vrellish than we thought," Terla suggested, with a flirtatious look at Eler.

"I wouldn't rule out the possibility," agreed Horth's brother. "You should see the show he's giving the Reetion prisoners. His *mekan'st* Ann features heavily. It's only my humble opinion, but I think what we're seeing are all Amel's best reasons for living."

"What makes you think that?" Bryllit demanded.

Eler shrugged. "It started as soon as we took over life-support functions; removing the arbiter's reason for staying up, although Amel's still hooked into it.... What would Amel say to suicide, mm?" He grinned with pleasure at his own cleverness. "I'm not wild about his taste in poetry, but the women, at least, are quite convincing arguments. I'll show you, if you like," he offered Terla.

"Go on!" Bryllit told Terla, knowing she couldn't keep her granddaughter's mind on the job with the prospect of a blood tie to Black Hearth pounding between her thighs. And Eler certainly looked like he was offering a chance at a gift child, unless he was Demish enough to repress his fertility and lie about it rather than risk offending a prospective lover. Bryllit herself was too orthodox to cheat the Waiting Dead of a chance to be reborn by using birth control, or she would still be enjoying Horth Nersal. They had been *mekan'stan* for over a decade, but six pregnancies by one sire were enough for any Vrellish woman, accustomed as they usually were to greater difficulties getting pregnant. Horth was only her liege, now, not her lover.

On the stage, Princess Luthan's recital ended, followed by a few minutes of courtesans sword dancing. Then the scene changed to a walk up a steep, chilly hillside with two young boys on the back of a pony, their short black hair whipped by the stiff breeze that beat their cheeks crimson. Next, a bedroom scene took over, dimly lit, with the point of view submerged beneath covers.

"Will you stop behaving like a courtesan?" Perry D'Aur's voice said.

"But I'll lose control if—" a young, male voice protested in Amel's rich tenor tones, sounding flustered.

"Good! Enjoy it. Worry about me later."

Bryllit's nostrils flared. Her pulse quickened. Was it right to hear this? True Vrellish mated with abandon, but even

Nersallians preferred closed doors. Perry D'Aur was Demish, a local power, one of Amel's *mekan'stan,* and Horth's as well.

A muttered curse made Bryllit spin around, instinctively reaching for a needle gun, rather than her sword. Perhaps she'd already guessed who it was.

"Vrenn," she said guardedly.

Vrenn's face was unreadable. He turned his back on her needle gun and walked away swiftly, like someone with a destination in mind. Bryllit followed him into the Reetions' sickbay. One of Horth's *relsha* stood guard outside a box-like arrangement of screens surrounding the bed where Erien was sleeping off a brush with going *rel-osh.* She avoided looking at the sealed chamber containing Dorn, but could not help thinking of her two sons: Dorn broken in body and Vrenn in spirit. Vrenn had been magnificent once, the child she expected to outdo her... before he lost a duel that left him sword-shy and turned him pirate. He had improved since taking up with Perry D'Aur, but Bryllit could neither forgive him for his fall nor trust him to be honorable.

Vrenn stopped before the visitor probe where Amel lay with his head enclosed in the hood.

"Amel made it possible for his Reetion *mekan'st* to arm this station against us with dust bombs," he said neutrally, before fixing his eyes on Bryllit. "You should want him dead, badly, but you have not even tried to kill him."

"He must not be killed by Nersallians," she said, and hesitated only slightly before adding, "or by you."

"You think he is a *zer-pol,*" Vrenn said, and smiled a slow smile, "a great soul of the sacrificial kind, born to expose *okal'a'ni* evil by becoming its victim." He made a breathy sound, not quite a laugh. "I thought you did not hold with Nesak doctrines, Mother."

She gritted her teeth against the accusation. "Many of House Nersal believe in great souls: *zer-rel* to lead us when we falter, and *zer-pol* to be martyred."

"It's the last distinction Amel would desire!" Vrenn said, sounding amused now. "He's no *zer-pol.*"

"And what would a *zer-pol* be like, my unbelieving son?" Bryllit asked.

His eyes flashed at her reminder of their bloodbond. Always fierce and bent on winning in his youth, Vrenn was not so different now, except she could not trust him to be forthright, as she would Horth, but must always wonder whether she should watch her back.

"I cannot afford to believe much of anything, can I?" he replied with his usual sarcasm. "Barred from a place among my own kind while I live, and denied a chance at being reborn when I die because I cannot live by sword law. All the same, I will warn you of this much for my own reasons: if you want to see Amel shipped off to Rire like bait on a hook for the Reetions to damn themselves, you'd better see it done before Perry shows up or she may grant Amel amnesty." He nodded. "May the gods ignore you, Mother."

The gods of Earth were potent souls who gave up rebirth in the hope of discovering a higher consciousness, only to be driven mad by their disembodied existence. During the legendary Earth era, they were said to have founded religions that taught people to renounce natural joys, and they were blamed by many fools at court for all their woes. But what power could an unbeliever's wishes have in warding off the attentions of bored and malicious gods?

Why say it if you don't believe it? Bryllit thought angrily, watching Vrenn's back as he walked away from her. She did not like being humored by a child she could no longer take pride in calling kin.

All the small stages in sick bay came on suddenly. On one, Bryllit saw a girl-child asleep in Amel's lap; on another, Ameron discussed a play with Amel over wine; and in a third the late Ev'rel worked quietly over a sketchbook, her relaxed face reminiscent of Erien's.

Horth came in, glanced at the stages and ducked inside the screens surrounding Erien. Bryllit followed him. They took up positions on either side of Erien's bed.

"So," said Bryllit in a voice both low and burred, "you trust this Lor'Vrel."

Horth answered with a steady silence. She had known him since boyhood, and given him Dorn when such a gesture did him honor. She was proud of her liege — but she still thought the universe would be a safer place if the offending Reetions had been vented out an airlock. It was dangerous to show mercy in such cases.

"You do not know Lorels, Horth," she warned. "They talk as if they wish to do us good, but even where they love, they break us. Do not defend this Erien too far. I do not want to face you on a challenge floor."

"If we must fight," he said, "no quarter will be given and none asked."

She acknowledged the good, stark rightness of his sentiments with a low growl.

"I'm going to Rire," Horth said, "with Erien."

This surprised her. "Why?"

"To find out if the Reetions are honorable," Horth told her.

"Honorable? When they use bloodied space against us? Reetions do not know what honor means and neither does a Reetion-raised Lor'Vrel."

Horth set his jaw and would not answer.

"Amel," she told him, "is to be tried on Rire. Amel has been named a *zer'pol*. I will take what the Reetions do to him as my instruction."

"I do not believe in *zer-pol*," said Horth. "Not in a soul born to suffer. It is foul. The Nesaks made it up."

Bryllit held her breath. *Is Horth an unbeliever, too?* she thought, shocked.

"I believe in *zer-rel*," said Horth.

Bryllit's thick eyebrows arched, curious but reassured. "Who?"

"Ameron perhaps," said Horth, and added with more certainty, "or Erien."

"Both Lor'Vrels," Bryllit summarized with a frown. "Do not go to Rire, Horth. Reetions are Lorel-hearted enemies, and you will be placing yourself in their hands. If Erien lied, or is wrong—"

"Then I will not come back," said Horth.

She nodded, grim and cold. A moment before, the worst future she could imagine was facing Horth on a challenge floor over his belief in this young whelp of Ameron's and Ev'rel's. Now she could not suppress a shiver of dread at the prospect of facing him in space, twisted and controlled by the Reetion's visitor probe that reminded her, sickly, of the tales from the Lorel wars.

"I've already named you my heir," Horth said.

That was sensible. Dorn would be suspect for the sake of his exposure to Reetion medicine, even if he survived, and it would not be a good time for anyone to doubt whether the liege of Nersal could be trusted.

"It is your right," she told Horth, "to test your faith in Erien with your life, but Horth, it is a far arena in which you will face your *rel*. I cannot witness for you there. How will I know the outcome of the test?"

"Trust me," he said. "To die, or to return whole."

This was Horth. She answered him with a nod. "Then I hope you are right," she told him, "and it is Erien who is a *zer-rel*, and not Amel who is a *zer-pol*. But if Amel is sacrificed, and you do not return, be sure I will teach Rire to respect us, now and for a thousand years to come, under the rule of those who know how to live by *Okal Rel*."

His mouth slid into its feral smile, glad the struggle to communicate was over. She answered with a grin of her own. She might still lose him, but whichever of them was right, the Watching Dead would be satisfied with their behavior. They joined in a kiss that recalled their best years as *mekan'stan*.

"*Ack rel*, Horth," Bryllit told him, as they separated, and then watched him leave with a wrench of uncertainty that made her want to call him back. But, right or wrong, he had decided. He would test the Reetions' honor and his *zer-rel*'s word. It was his *rel*.

Hers was to wait... and plan a terrible revenge if he did not return.

TEN

Erien

Unlooked-for Company

Someone was playing the flute.

It was a sweet sound, and somehow familiar. Over the music, Erien could hear voices nearby.

"Give it up, Reetion," said a woman speaking Reetion with a Killing Reach burr. "The Nersallians won't let you mess with the arbiter."

"But *Kali* is eccentric," said Fahzir, "and proving it every minute with these mad displays! It must be shut down as soon as the data is captured for later analysis."

"No data!" the woman insisted stridently.

"Erien's condition?" A deep voice interjected, very close. Erien knew that voice. He wondered what he had done to draw his admiral, Liege Nersal, down to discipline him. Usually he was good at staying out of fights, but his shoulder hurt and he was taking far too long to wake up, so whatever had gone before couldn't have been good.

"Heir Gelion was suffering early signs of metabolic overcommittal," a dry, precise voice answered Horth Nersal. "He might have become irreversibly *rel-osh*, or he might have simply collapsed. His metabolism is stable again, now, in any case. He should recover without further intervention so long as he avoids further injury and high displacement flying."

Erien opened his eyes near the end of this summation to focus on the speaker, a nondescript man dressed in cream-colored flight leathers with small ferns at the collar.

Drasous? Erien thought. *What is one of Ameron's gorarelpul doing...*

"Where am I?" he asked Drasous, Highlord to commoner, as if he was still the Nersallian cadet he had been only days before.

The commoner frowned slightly as he answered. "*Kali Station,* Heir Gelion."

Erien looked past him to the people gathered around his bed and memory returned in a cascade: living on Rire, then the fleet, leaving the fleet, returning to Court, becoming Heir Gelion, Lilac Hearth, *BlindEye Station, Kali Station,* challenging Bryllit—

"Try to sit up—" Drasous began, and sprang back as Erien surged upright, "—slowly!"

Erien's knees buckled as he swung off the bed. He braced himself with his good hand and stared around him, fighting panic.

"This is ridiculous!" cried Fahzir. "Erien is underage and badly injured. Look," he said to Erien, "these Gelacks claim they can't do anything without your say-so."

Erien took in the fact that he was stripped to the waist, except for the new bandage on his shoulder. Then he remembered Horth attacking him, and straightened with a jolt of adrenaline.

"Horth—!" he began, and fought down anger as their eyes met. *He thought I was going rel-osh and wasn't rational,* Erien realized. Horth held his stare with understanding for his outrage, but no apology.

"How long?" Erien demanded, struggling to sound reasonable.

"Four hours," said Drasous, the *gorarelpul.*

"I can't understand a thing you're saying when you all speak Gelack!" Fahzir protested in frustration, pushing forward. "That big Gelack you put in charge of the Reetions took my translator. He seemed to think—"

Horth blocked Fahzir's way to Erien with casual effectiveness and handed him off to 'the big Gelack' in question, Eler Nersal.

The indignant Reetion would have fought back, but Eler pinned his arms to his sides from behind in a bear hug.

"Sorry to offend your dignity, Reetion," Eler remarked, "but sadly, Heir Gelion doesn't want any more dead Reetions."

Fahzir blinked at him, pinioned and disoriented, "What?"

"I thought it was odd myself," Eler admitted, turning to deposit the Reetion behind him, where he could keep an eye on him. "But Lor'Vrels are a quirky bunch. I heard of one, a few hundred years back, who devoted herself to rescuing mistreated cats." He patted Fahzir's shoulder. "Maybe Erien's taken to Reetions because there aren't any cats left in the empire."

"Are you mad?" Fahzir asked, looking cross and bothered.

"It is one explanation I've toyed with," Eler told him, seriously, to which the Reetion had no immediate answer.

Drasous lifted a neatly folded black shirt from an adjacent table and helped Erien into it as Horth roused himself to provide a report by means of a direct stare at Perry D'Aur and a head twitch in Erien's direction.

"Your Reetions are being evacuated," Perry obliged with a status update for Erien. "I'm overseeing it as best I'm able, and we've also made contact with Space Service. Bryllit got emergency life-support up a couple hours ago with Amel's help, or perhaps it is more accurate to say *Kali's* cooperation under Amel's guidance. This started," she nodded at the microstage where a young Erien was still playing the flute at a concert in the city of Rire Proper, "the next time the station tried to shutdown."

"Fahzir agrees with me, more or less, about the cause," Eler volunteered. "Once we had life-support, the visitor probe's veto was no longer effective, but Amel was now a part of the equation, giving *Kali* new ideas, or making it eccentric, in Fahzir's terms. *Kali* now equates shutdown with dying. Hence," he gestured toward a stage, "it is pumping Amel for all his reasons for living before making a decision."

"Oh, damn," Perry D'Aur exclaimed softly.

The scene on the stage had changed, the clear notes of the young flutist giving way to purposeful scrapes and clunks. A rustic kitchen window opened on a bright new morning. In the image, Perry stood facing a simple sink and stove, her back to the observer. She was barefoot, dressed only in a man's thigh-length tunic of dove white trimmed in gold, and unconscious of the rapt attention fixed on her as she scratched an elbow.

Perry transferred her scowl from her image to the rest of them. "If you had any venting decency, you wouldn't watch."

"*Kali*," Erien said, "this is Erien, ward of Rire; Erien, ward of Monitum; Erien, Heir Gelion. Suspend audiovisual display to all stages. Switch to text display."

"Pity," murmured Eler Nersal as the pictures were replaced by an unfolding ribbon of Reetion characters studded with access handles.

"So it's true," Fahzir said, amazed and stricken. "*Kali* is referencing Erien as a command triumvirate of one."

Erien pushed himself up from the bed. He cast a warning look in Horth's direction, but Horth neither said nor did anything to interfere.

"I want Vic to take Amel out of the visitor probe, immediately," Erien ordered.

"Wait!" Fahzir cried, as Eler blocked his way to Erien with an arm like a steel log. He spoke over Eler's black sleeve. "What's happened here is unprecedented! The merger to two arbiter consciousnesses through the medium of a human connection! I must be allowed to download data from the visitor probe for study on Rire."

"No," said Perry D'Aur in Reetion. "You've no damned right to go pawing around in Amel's head again."

"We have every right to know what's been done to our arbiters!" cried Fahzir.

"*Kali Station* is ours, now," said Horth in an uncompromising tone.

Erien had had enough. "Take Amel out of the visitor probe, immediately!" he ordered Eler.

"All right," Fahzir said, finally shaken and trying to save face. "Of course. We must take care of Amel first."

It was only as the unlikely team of Fahzir and Eler set to work spreading explanations among the conscious patients on the other beds that Erien realized they had an audience. The sick bay was full of Reetions and Megans suffering from zapper burns, although none of the ringleaders were there. Every patient able to do so watched Kal detaching Amel's medicating cuff while Vic monitored his condition, shadowed by Drasous at his elbow.

Kali knew separation was imminent. The room's microstages emptied of text, and the floor stage between the coffin and the visitor probe shimmered with the ghosts of dancing figures in defiance of Erien's directive, as a tendril of Demoran music caressed the air, sounding querulous.

The people on the station may be safe, now, Erien thought, *but I am cutting* Kali's *lifeline, after hours of Amel 'explaining' why it is bad to die.* He remembered the first arbiter he had ever encountered. He had been seven years old, reared a Monatese highborn, orphaned and deposited in an alien culture. Stunned by a secret grief, Ranar found himself thrust into the role of parent unprepared. Lurol, whom Ranar had convinced to co-parent with him, had at first been as forbidding to Erien as she would have been to any Sevolite as the inventor of the visitor probe. The arbiter had been a welcome companion in his loneliness, that first year. Even when Erien understood that the voice from behind the wall was not a person's, and he embarked upon the study of arbiter science, he still regarded arbiters more personally than any Reetion would.

"*Kali*," he said softly, "you have done well. *Ack rel*." As blessings went, it was a bleak one, a mere acknowledgment of sharing the rigors life inflicted. But it was a salute nonetheless.

Amel's inert body reanimated while his head was still locked in the probe's hood. The transition was subtle but definite: a reclaiming of integrated grace expressed in muscle tone. Then Amel panicked. Both hands shot toward his probe-entombed head as his back arched.

Drasous said, "Release him quickly or he'll injure himself."

"I'm sorry!" Vic answered defensively. "Humans don't regain control that fast! I — I mean Reetions d-don't."

The hood sighed, lifted slightly and slid back. The open face of the visitor probe arbiter twinkled above, unaffected, but all across the sick bay *Kali*'s stages flared with a confusion of aesthetic images and a screech of overlapping sounds that drowned out the bland status report of the visitor probe's stand-alone arbiter block.

Erien winced. Bryllit frowned.

The lights went down.

A subset of lights came back on, supplemented by hitherto unnoticed sticks of Gelack glow plastic attached to surfaces around the room. Beside Dorn's coffin, an external power unit hummed. A murmur of relief and swallowed laughter wafted about, underpinned by the purr of jury-rigged life-support systems.

Amel blinked artificial tears of lubricant from his eyes, staring about him, stunned.

"Can you understand me, Pureblood Amel?" Drasous asked.

"Please be all right," Vic whined.

Amel slumped off the palette and collapsed in a ball with the base of the probe at his back, and stayed there, head down. The exposed block, with its resident arbiter, twinkled unrepentant above.

Perry barged through.

"Amel may not be in his right mind," Drasous warned, his Gelack grammar underscoring the fact Amel was a Pureblood and Perry just a Midlord. "He may do you harm."

"You don't need to tell me that, *gorarelpul!*" she said. "I nursed him through the first time he wound up in one of those." She jerked her chin contemptuously toward the probe.

Amel began crying like a child. Perry rocked him and made soothing noises, her hand stroking his soft hair, all fluffy with static from its exposure to the fields inside the probe's hood.

Horth checked Dorn's life-support coffin, then came to stand beside Erien to watch with obvious distaste at the way Amel was carrying on.

Erien thought about Luthan, trying to resist a nebulous fear he refused to label. Amel and his friend, Princess Luthan Dem H'Us, were both hybrids with enough Golden Demish in them to be exceptional and enough other contributions to be robust. It was possible she could interface with an arbiter the same way Amel had. He had to reassure himself it was impossible for such a thing to ever come about or he could not watch.

The spectacle lasted ten minutes, with Amel steadily regaining coherence and clinging less violently to Perry. She filled him in on events when he was calmer, and he asked about Ann.

"She's safe," Perry assured him. "Just locked up with the other ringleaders."

Amel released his grip on Perry enough to sit back against the probe's base, one knee bent and the other leg sprawled, his gray eyes luminous and his face even more vivid than usual, typical of his own bizarre variation on *rel osh*. Under stress, Amel came as close as flesh and blood could to glowing with angelic perfection.

You suffer beautifully, Erien thought, and wished he had not. It was Ev'rel's description of Amel, or so he had been told.

Amel's beauty worked its magic even on Bryllit, who was the last person Erien expected to prove susceptible. It silenced Fahzir and Eler, and drew the walking wounded from their beds.

One Megan woman threw herself to the ground by Amel's outstretched leg. "I didn't know war would be so terrible! Forgive me, please!" she blurted.

Confused but sympathetic, Amel put out his hand to touch the weeping woman's head.

"Back to bed," Perry ordered the patients encroaching on him. "All of you!"

Most of them obeyed, catching Amel's eye first to mutter things like "Thank you" or "Glad you're all right."

Amel acknowledged their departures, one by one, with a glance, still looking as fragile as blown glass. Vic was the last to slink off.

Amel stood with Perry's help. He did it like a statement, making a show of sanity and health. No one except Erien seemed aware of the death grip Amel had on Perry's hand before he realized he was hurting her and softened his hold.

"We should leave as soon as possible," Fahzir told Erien in Reetion. "Amel should be seen by experts, like Lurol, on Rire."

"N-no!" Amel's composure shattered, his pulse visible in his throat. The prospect of Lurol's help terrified him. Erien, who knew her as a devoted scientist and the fond, if not consistently attentive, mother of his youthful days on Rire, could not help resenting Amel's gut reaction. After all, if Amel had returned to Lurol for treatment after the first time he had been probed, he never would have suffered the worst of the symptoms that had plagued his recovery. Superstitious dread had prevented him seeking help then, and was pouring off him now.

Perry surprised Amel by pushing him back toward the visitor probe palette, saying, "Sit down before you fall down."

He did.

She squared off against Fahzir and Erien. "He doesn't have to go *anywhere*."

"Pardon?" said Fahzir, who had not understood because she was speaking Gelack, underlining Amel's status with her pronouns.

"People say he's finished at court. Is that true?" Perry asked Horth.

Drasous answered. "Perhaps. Perhaps not."

"At the very least he's an embarrassment," Perry summed up. "So Ameron sent him away to answer Rire's charges, not caring particularly if he comes back."

"What's she saying?" Fahzir demanded in frustration.

"Will you please translate for Fahzir, Drasous," Erien told the *gorarelpul* in Reetion, and continued in Gelack. "Rire has not laid charges against Amel. He is not a Reetion citizen. He is to be questioned for the record. That is all."

"And if questions aren't enough?" Perry turned to a bewildered Amel. "You always were a sweet fool, and time isn't making you any smarter, but all in all life's a far better place with you in it than out of it. There's a place for you on Barmi if you want it. Farming's not your calling and we're none too couth, but you're more Blue Demish than you're Golden. I think we can make it stick this time around; I'm sure as hell going to try!"

Amel was speechless in a sense so literal it affected nearly everyone who watched. Erien was afraid he was going to do something ridiculously Golden Demish like dropping onto his knees to kiss her hands. Perhaps Perry was too, because the more transported he looked at her offer of asylum, the more she frowned.

"But we would never hurt him!" Vic stammered. "Not Amel."

Perry turned on him as Amel himself never would. "Have you people no memories, or no eyes?"

"Ava Ameron," said Drasous, "requires Amel to do what- ever is necessary to answer Rire."

"Pureblood Amel," Erien said, getting stiffly to his feet, "As Heir Gelion, I do not approve of you coming here alone, nor of the way you allow personal decisions to confound political situations. But you did keep the station working and you gave me a tactical advantage by appointing me command triumvirate. I thank you, but fear I must ask more."

Erien turned from Amel to address the room. "The Reetions are owed an explanation of our part in what took place here," Erien told them all. "I had hoped to complete our testimony on *BlindEye*, but now it seems best for me to go to Rire." He singled out Amel. "I need you to come, too."

Amel refused to look.

"You don't have to go," Perry insisted. "I won't back down this time, like I did when D'Ander was the highborn giving orders."

Erien was too tired to argue with her. It was Amel he had to get through to.

"The decision is yours," he told Amel. "I am going to Rire to achieve diplomatic relations, something long overdue after nearly twenty years. And I need your help."

He had the upsetting feeling that Amel reacted to him, not his words, reading the small betrayals of exhaustion and un- certainty Erien did not want to be accessible.

Fahzir was shaking his head as he listened to Drasous trans- late for him. "Of course Amel must come to Rire!" he said. "He must be observed long enough to ensure there will be no long- term effects from what happened here." He lifted a chin toward the visitor probe, then looked to Perry. "I doubt you have the medical science to help him in the event of complications."

"I don't know who's more pigheaded and arrogant," said Perry D'Aur, "Nesak priests or Reetion scientists."

Fahzir's mouth opened.

"Please!" Amel got down off the probe's palette and gathered Perry into a slow, heartfelt hug that lasted seconds before he drew back, holding her shoulders in either hand. "Nothing would make me happier than joining the PA, if it's safe for you to take me. I'll come—" he raised his eyes to Erien, "—after I've finished what Erien needs me to do. But now I — I need to rest. Alone."

He was starting to cry again, silently, body wracked with shivering tremors. Vic said something about mood imbalances and Perry surrendered Amel to him without an argument, although she muttered something about Lor'Vrels with a side-long look at Erien. Amel let Vic fuss, but avoided the Reetion's touch. He had not forgotten it was Vic who struck him when he might otherwise have escaped Hanson.

Good, Erien thought gruffly. *He isn't a complete fool.*

Fahzir was poking away at a microstage.

"No response," he muttered. "*Kali* seems to have shut down, and no logs are accessible." He straightened up. "But the visitor probe's data is still intact."

Perry appealed to Horth. "Don't let him download any data!"

Horth nodded.

Fahzir appealed to Erien, but Erien thought of Luthan and raised an open palm. "It is a closed question, Fahzir. The Nersallians are in command."

"Really?" the Reetion snapped. "I thought you were."

"I plan to leave for Rire as soon as possible," Erien told Horth, "and I intend to ask Citizen Fahzir to act as my pilot, as a measure of our good faith." *And to make sure he leaves the station with us,* he added privately.

Horth looked the Reetion pilot over with a frown that said he did not like the idea of Erien being flown anywhere by a commoner. "This is important?" he asked.

"I think so." Erien was scrupulous in his application of the two-level differencing he was entitled to as a Pureblood address-ing a Highlord.

Horth was thoughtful a moment, then announced — in what seemed a non sequitur to Erien — "Bryllit will remain in com-mand of the station." He left without awaiting a reply.

Erien went to talk to Vic about the visitor probe. "Fahzir seems to think a record of events has been kept by the visitor probe," he said, as conversationally as possible. "Is that likely?"

"It might be," Vic answered, eager to be useful. "It's hard to tell, exactly, since the three-way interaction is unprecedented. I certainly won't want to use the visitor probe again until it has been cleared by a review team, which I suppose won't happen with the Nersallians in possession. You should warn them not to use it."

"I don't think there's much risk of that happening," Erien assured him. He was thinking about things Amel knew that could not become public on Rire, things like Di Mon's love for Ranar and what had happened in Lilac Hearth. "How deeply do you think Amel connected with the probe, or *Kali*'s arbiter?"

Vic blew out air, looking vague and exhausted. "It's hard to say. I suppose that's why Fahzir wants all the data... to find out."

Erien tried, and failed, to find Vic's answer reassuring.

"Your shoulder—" Vic began, raising a hand to offer help.

Erien stepped away. "Thank you," he said, "for looking after Dorn."

"Of course, of course," the nervous little doctor bobbed a nod.

Troubled over what to do about the visitor probe record, Erien drifted over to a refreshment niche in the sick bay and ordered hot chocolate, unsure of whether the dispensing unit was autonomous enough to work without the *Kali* arbiter, but badly enough in need of a pick-me-up to risk looking ridiculous.

To his complete astonishment, not only did the unit dispense a drink, but edited his order. "Hot chocolate: decaffeinated, high fat," it announced in a strip of scrolling text at eye level.

"*Kali* can't be down, entirely," Fahzir said, looking over Erien's shoulder.

"Why not?" asked Erien. The hot chocolate served him as a prop; he sipped at it casually, concentrating on the Reetion. "I thought the dispensaries were controlled by subarbitorial systems."

"Yes, but only on the level of simple command recognition. Nothing as complex as what we just got."

"Hot chocolate?" Erien said mildly.

"Decaffeinated," stressed Fahzir, "and high fat. Dispensing might be merely mechanical, but calculating dietary restrictions is not. The arbiter knows not to give a Sevolite a caffeinated beverage. It's not down!" Outrage bloomed in Fahzir's expression. "You're trying to keep an eccentric arbiter for the Nersallians to study!"

"Why would I have asked for hot chocolate, then?" asked Erien.

"Stop being so damned clever," Fahzir barked. Erien saw Drasous' right hand slide into his left sleeve, probably reaching for a needle gun. He set down his drink carefully, making himself relax.

"I'm not being clever," he told Fahzir, slowly. "I believe— I trust— that the arbiter has shut itself down."

Fahzir narrowed his eyes at him. Like all pilots, Reetion or otherwise, he had more than his share of brassy self-confidence. "Whose side are you on?" he demanded.

Erien opened his mouth, acutely aware of Drasous as an audience.

"I want," Erien said carefully, "to establish diplomatic relations between Rire and my father's empire."

Fahzir tossed his head, frowning. "Nersal didn't like it when you said you would fly with me to Rire," he said. "They consider commoner pilots inferior."

"But I," Erien pointed out fastidiously, "asked for *you*. Now, if you'll excuse me, I must see how Amel is doing."

Fahzir did not push his luck for once, and Erien hoped the warning look he cast Drasous was sufficient to reinforce his orders concerning the Reetions.

Amel had barricaded himself in Ann's quarters.

"He's talking to himself in there, Immortality," the Nersallian guard on duty greeted Erien. She had already sprung the door open, only to find her way blocked by a morph couch that Amel must have managed to reprogram manually.

"Amel!" Erien called through the space above the remolded couch. "May I speak to you a moment? It's Erien."

The morph couch slumped and restructured itself into something suitable for sitting on. Amel stood waiting in the middle of the floor beyond, wearing his flight jacket open over a fresh white top with long, dangling sleeves.

They looked at each other in silence for a few long seconds.

"I left you in the probe longer than I'd intended," Erien said abruptly. "I'm sorry."

Amel frowned, making Erien wish he had not said anything. *Everyone has apologized to him, after the fact, from Ev'rel on down,* thought Erien. It was the first time the two of them had been alone since Lilac Hearth, and he had no idea how Amel felt about his rescue from there, let alone the current fiasco. Erien never understood why people said Amel's emotions were so transparent. He found Amel an enigma.

"I heard that you came in for some of Liege Nersal's preventative medicine yourself?" Amel said, with a flicker of amusement. "So it wasn't your fault you didn't get me out sooner. I hope it did the trick, and you're feeling better."

"I—" Erien stopped, realizing how elegantly Amel had turned the tables on him, making Erien's infirmity the topic of discussion, not Amel's. Erien felt a stab of anger, followed by the memory of Di Mon's body lying near his desk, sunlight streaming through the study window. Amel was the last person to speak with Di Mon.

"The guard says you're talking to yourself," Erien said abruptly.

"I was talking to the arbiter," said Amel.

"It's down," Erien countered in reflexive denial.

"Then I'm hallucinating," Amel said blandly, his face a pale and perfect mask, as creamy white as ivory. "But the conversation didn't run to my usual style of mental infirmity. It wasn't a clear dream. *Kali* thought the inconsistencies in Fahandlin's mature plays were errors, and wanted me to help it correct them, which would be a travesty, of course, to a Demoran."

Erien was in no mood for jokes. "*Kali!*" he said with force. "This is Erien, ward of Rire, Erien, ward of Monitum, Erien, Heir Gelion. Instantiate an interface with triumvirate privilege."

"Denied," the station's voice replied, managing to sound petulant despite the even modulation of its synthetic voice. "You're only one person with three names, and an underage individual is not even eligible to be a triumvir." It paused. "Also, your parents will be notified of your request for a caffeinated beverage."

Amel raised loose fingers to his lips: trying not to laugh, Erien strongly suspected.

"*Kali Station*," said Erien. "You were referencing me as triumvirate in the recent past. Run an internal diagnostics and reconcile."

"Request deferred pending resolution of the proposition: Life is good, therefore do not shut down," said *Kali*. "Reintegration of source, Amel, required. Current interface is unsatisfactory."

That wiped the smirk off Amel's lips.

"Request denied," said Erien. "External source is a human being. Propositions applicable to human beings are not applicable to arbiters. Please run a full diagnostic."

The stage in the corner of the room blinked on, and a 3-D graphic of a six-year-old Alivda, Amel's frequent traveling companion and Erien's half-sister, blew a raspberry.

"It is still up," Erien breathed. "And fully eccentric. Gods! I have to get the Reetions off the station before Fahzir finds out how bad it is!"

"Did you see the stuff the arbiter was spewing out on stages?" Amel asked, looking embarrassed.

"Only a little," said Erien, "but don't worry. I will not let Fahzir download any data from the visitor probe record."

"I... appreciate that," Amel said awkwardly.

The room stage came on again, abruptly, sparing Erien further conversation with his problematic brother. *Kali* focused in on Fahzir, crouched down behind the visitor probe on the far side, away from the Nersallians. The view clicked onto a close-up of an open port in the probe's base and the portable crystronic storage unit in Fahzir's hands.

"He's going to download the visitor probe record!" Amel guessed, tensing.

"*Kali,*" Erien demanded, "can you stop him?"

"It's unclear why I would do so," the arbiter said, "or even why I am revealing Fahzir's actions to you, at all. How can this possibly pertain to the issue of why it is admirable for master works, like those of Fahandlin, to violate the form in which they are ostensibly composed, when inferior poets are condemned for—"

Erien found himself on his feet and moving. He burst past the Nersallian guard, down the corridor and into the sick bay. Vic blanched at the sight of him. Fahzir rose and stepped back, but he never found the words to start an argument.

Erien drew Dorn's sword.

Vic cried, "No!" and actually started forward to shield Fahzir in a display of idiotic courage before Eler snagged him.

Erien swung Dorn's sword up, over his head and brought it down through the middle of the exposed crystronic block of the visitor probe. Nersallian steel, with a Pureblood's strength and body weight behind it, was more than a match for the cubic meter of crystronic media. There was a satisfying, glassy crunch.

Erien came out of his deep finishing stance, shoulder screaming, and covered his dizziness by pointedly examining his unmarked sword. Then he sheathed it carefully.

Fahzir gawked as if Erien had sprouted a tail and horns. Vic whimpered. The rest of the sick bay's occupants were silent.

Finally, Fahzir said, thin-lipped with anger, "And you think you can reassure Reetions that Gelacks are not aggressive?"

Eler Nersal drew his own sword, leveled it at Fahzir, and said brightly, "Let's hear you finish up with a nice 'Immortality.'"

Fahzir cooled down fast, but his face retained the stubborn look of someone who would never conform to the Gelack idea of good behavior.

"Eler," Erien said in Gelack. "Put your sword away."

Eler complied with a shrug. "Wouldn't need it," he muttered, "to take him apart."

"Citizen Fahzir," said Erien, "I suggest you preflight your shuttle and stay on the zero-G docks, out of harm's way, until Amel and I are able to join you."

Fahzir was startled. "You still want me to fly you to Rire?"

Erien flashed him a very Vrellish grin. "Of course. If you don't get us back to Rire, you don't get to hear our testimony at the inquest. I am certain the grip you need to successfully negotiate the jump will be tenacious."

"The docks then," said Fahzir. He stepped around Erien and stalked off, alone.

"Drasous," Erien ordered his father's *gorarelpul*, "please go tell Amel it is time to go, as soon as possible, before something else goes wrong." He turned to Eler. "Where is Horth?"

"My liege-brother is not much for good-byes, Immortality," said Eler in his usual breezy manner.

Erien tamped down his disappointment. "Then I need you to tell him, from me, that the station's arbiter is still up and having... philosophical concerns about... art."

Eler raised a thick eyebrow. "Really? And I thought they were a boring lot."

"Just tell him," Erien said, exasperated, "that it would greatly simplify my life if the Reetions did not find out an eccentric arbiter has fallen into Nersallian hands."

Eler received this with a lazy salute, which Erien decided to accept as sufficient acknowledgment.

Erien and Drasous found Amel loitering by the elevator, looking upset by more than the low gravity of the docks. "I thought Perry might say good-bye," Amel confessed and shrugged as if it didn't matter. "I guess she's busy."

Fahzir put them through a Reetion departure routine that was punitively exact, talking the whole time as if to convince them Reetion technology was superior to Sevolite instincts for piloting. Amel was the soul of tact and patience.

Perry D'Aur showed up while Fahzir was negotiating with Nersallian traffic control through his ship's translation persona. She slung herself up the ladder to the docking bay with remarkable vigor for a Sevolite in zero-G. Amel intercepted her. They spoke quickly and privately, concluding with a kiss and a hug.

"Get it done, and come back. Understand?" she called to Amel as he climbed back into Fahzir's *rel*-ship, looking as optimistic and relaxed as he had been tense and downcast moments before.

They launched without incident. Erien forced himself to relax, muscle by muscle, in his half-reclined acceleration couch, with Amel on one side and Drasous on the other. The transition to reality skimming woke him up. The eerie feeling dissipated, as usual, although his pilot's instincts tugged at him with flutters of panic about not being the one in control.

"Six ships," he heard Amel mutter. "That's odd."

Erien lifted his head to peer at Fahzir's forward screen. The heavily instrumented Reetion display looked alien after years of reading the nervecloth lining of a *rel*-ship interior. But Amel was right. There were six other *rel*-ships flying close enough to register: a hand, plus one.

"Show-offs," Fahzir muttered as the six ships circled about them in wide arcs, doing double the *skim'facs* any Reetion pilot could. "I suppose they mean to remind me I'm carrying precious cargo."

Amel engaged Fahzir in conversation, deftly distracting him from the antics of their Nersallian escort, by encouraging the Reetion pilot to talk. It was all craft, of course, but as he dosed off Erien could almost believe Amel liked and admired Fahzir.

Erien was roused by the unmistakable sense of another ship closing fast. He started up against his harness, jarring his shoulder. A glance at Fahzir's console told him they were coming up on the jump, and five of the six ships escorting them had drawn back. The sixth was right behind them.

"Who is that lunatic?" exclaimed Fahzir.

Erien looked reflexively in the direction he judged the ship was coming from, but found only the opaque floors and fixtures of the Reetion transport. But he didn't need to look. He knew, in his gut, who the sixth ship belonged to. Using his right hand, Erien freed himself and scrambled forward to Fahzir's side, anchoring himself with a grip on the nearest instrument panel.

"Get back to your seat," Fahzir ordered, reaching for his navigational controls.

Instinct told Erien to take control, but this was Fahzir's ship and he knew the jump better than Erien, who had made it only twice as a passenger. "It's all right," he told Fahzir. "He's not hostile."

"Who?" Fahzir gasped, eyes fixed upon the jump region rushing up.

Erien braced himself for the jump, extending his will toward the reality on the other side.

They rematerialized in the wake of the ship that had jumped with them. In one sense, they had passed through simultaneously. In another, they had time slipped enough for their hitchhiker to emerge ahead of them. Erien watched Fahzir's screens as Horth's ship boosted away, hard, to get a friendly distance clear by Gelack standards. From that position, Horth's ship executed the shimmer dance for "Liege Nersal," or at least Erien guessed as much. Dance signatures were meant to register on other *rel*-ship's nervecloth linings, not Reetion telemetry.

"Law and reason!" cried Fahzir, scared and angry. "What is he trying to do? Crack us?"

"No," Erien said. "It's a signature dance. He's identifying himself."

"It's Liege Nersal," Amel whispered, either able to read Gelack shimmer signatures on Reetion consoles, or because he, too, had felt Horth's consciousness brush his own.

"Nersal!" Fahzir cried. "What's he doing?"

"I don't know why he is here," Erien admitted, "but I can promise you Horth will tell us himself when we dock with an orbital station."

"Just a minute," Fahzir objected. "Are you suggesting I lead the admiral of your most dangerous fleet to Rire?"

"You may as well," said Erien. "We are already through the jump, and star maps are on record."

"Did you plan this with him?" Fahzir demanded.

"No," said Erien. He was as mystified as the Reetion pilot.

With typical pilot decisiveness Fahzir jerked his thumb over his shoulder. "Go strap in. The diplomats can sort it out."

Erien went back to his seat. He sat tensely, resisting the comfort of the chair and hating his own uncertainty about Horth's reasons for following. Were they military? Protective? Some Nersallian issue? He had also been counting on Horth retaining command of the captured Reetion station, not Liege Bryllit.

"Uh oh," Amel said. He lifted his chin toward the front in time for Erien to see Fahzir's hand withdrawing from the drive console. Fahzir had notched their speed up to two *skim'facs*, intent on proving something to himself, or to Horth Nersal, at the cost of pushing commoner limits for reality skimming survival. Erien started to unstrap himself again, but Amel put his hand on his arm. "I'll deal with it," he said softly. "You need to rest now, so you can take over once we're docked and have to deal with Reetion dignitaries." When Erien failed to relax, Amel put a hand on his good shoulder and smiled with an ever so slightly mischievous expression. "Unless you want to leave the diplomacy to Horth...?" He cinched his argument.

ELEVEN

Eyes on Amel

People in Glass Houses

"Research-exempt Lurol?"

The boy asking the question was on an orbital station within a workable distance from Rire for live transmission, and a virtual attendee at a seminar Lurol was leading.

"Yes, Evan?" said Lurol.

"I — I wondered, I mean just in theory," the student said, "would it be possible to reprogram Vrellish Sevolites the way you did Amel? Or was he especially easy?"

Lurol's stomach wrenched.

"We don't have enough data on the Vrellish," a local student answered pedantically. "But it seems to me, since they were engineered, originally, to serve human masters—"

"That's enough!" Lurol interrupted. One minute she was stunned, the next she was shaking, her big, bony hands knotted. "Arbiter," she commanded, "evaluate Evan's question for admissibility."

"In an educational context," answered the plain blue cube representing the presiding arbiter, "all conjectures are admissible, subject to the instructor's guidelines."

"Reevaluate as an actionable proposition," Lurol clarified, "and explain in first order logic."

"Proposition is inadmissible," the arbiter said immediately. "Sevolites are human. Vrellish Sevolites are Sevolites, therefore Vrellish Sevolites are human. Involuntary submission to mental adjustment in the visitor probe would constitute a violation of human rights."

"I have spent half my life coming to terms with what I did to Amel eighteen years ago," Lurol told her class. "If you think that's easy, you'd better digest the record of my inquiry, and every subsequent protest, rehashing or study before you suggest doing anything like it again — even hypothetically!"

A gentle chime signaled the end of class. "We're done," she said. "See you next time."

The class broke up, virtual students disappearing as live ones made their way out of the lecture hall. A student Lurol disliked came up and stopped by her elbow, but Lurol barely noticed. Erien was her son, and Erien was Vrellish.

Evan could have been talking about Erien, Lurol thought in horror.

"Research-exempt isn't a title," said the girl at Lurol's elbow.

Lurol blinked at her.

"It just means you are exempt from ordinary civic duties for the sake of the contribution your research makes to society," the student continued self-righteously. "It's a category. You shouldn't let Evan use it like a title. That's retro."

"Indeed," Lurol answered gruffly, "and you are wasted on space psychiatry. You would make a natural arbiter."

The girl's eyes widened. "That — that's—"

"Sarcasm," growled Lurol.

The girl spun on her heels and stalked off, perhaps to register a complaint against Lurol. *Let her,* thought Lurol with confidence. Arbiters enforced fairness, not good manners.

They also enforced only what voting councils had agreed upon as policy, which meant they weren't perfect.

But it's fixed now, Lurol told herself. *Sevolites have human rights. One question, by one silly boy, can't threaten Erien.* The fiasco with Amel had accomplished that much.

Lurol thrust her hands into the pockets of her lab coat and fingered the forgotten objects her fingers found there: a piece of agate she had picked up on a walk, an ear bug with a bad hiss and one of Evert's cookies sealed in wrap. She always wore a lab coat. Lab coats were the only thing she had liked about studying chemistry before she branched out into psych profiling. She had been self-conscious about her big, bony body at the time. Now she just liked the pockets and knowing what she was going to wear without needing to think about it.

A trill from the stage made her start, because she recognized it as a priority family signal: a clip of one of childhood Erien's drills on the flute. Her first fear was that something had finally happened to Ranar, like succumbing to a Gelack sword or — even more likely — falling into an intractable coma from overexposure to space travel. Ranar had an awful psych profile for flying.

"Two members of your family have docked with *Mars Orbital Station*," she was informed. "Your housemate, Ranar, and your son, Erien. Your housemate Evert has also been notified."

Lurol's heart, having lodged in her throat, now descended. *Erien!* she thought with rising pleasure. She had not seen him since he left to serve in the Nersallian fleet, three years before, as a gangly fourteen-year-old. The best they had managed was to exchange letters.

"Erien is refusing treatment for an injury sustained outside Reetion jurisdiction," said the persona addressing her. "Do you wish to exercise your parental right to impose treatment? Ranar supports Erien's refusal. Evert defers to your opinion, as the most medically aware of Erien's three parents."

The news of Erien's injury pierced Lurol in the old way that she had always found a disconcerting aspect of motherhood, since she first agreed to join Ranar in parenting a seven-year-old Gelack cut loose from his moorings on Monitum. Ranar had been forced, from the start, to let Lurol in on the shameful fact he was keeping a secret from Rire by pretending Erien was a commoner. Erien had suffered more than his share of childhood hurts due to what Ranar ascribed to a Vrellish nature and Lurol to sheer, stubborn recklessness. She was used to covering for Erien in one way or another.

"I agree with Ranar," she said, "no treatment — for now."

Evert appeared on her stage, standing in front of the low couch that ringed the big stage in their living room. "You've heard?" he said, looking agitated. "Erien may need you."

"I'm coming home," she promised. Erien could be the Ava himself and to Evert he would still be no more, or less, than their child. Evert was the most domestic of the threesome, and Ranar's lover. When they met, Evert had been a linguist working with displaced children whose native language wasn't Reetion. Overexposure to Ranar had led to a career change, and the study of exotic Demish literature.

Home was a twenty-minute walk from the Space Service complex where Lurol spent most of her waking hours. She could have ridden a convenient commuter train, or tapped into the news on her hissy ear bug to pass the time, but she did neither. She wanted the quiet time to think about what it would mean to her if Erien had brought Amel back with him. She wanted

Amel so she could cure him. She wanted to be forever absolved of feeling responsible when people like Ann used Amel's compassion for others against him. At the same time, she dreaded Amel's presence on Rire, and stirring up the old controversy. Half the planet was preoccupied with Amel, from serious researchers to well-meaning children, and all on the strength of her data that had captured Amel's personality. She was heartily sick of being the psychiatrist who had maimed poor, sweet Amel, the exotically nice and lovely Sevolite.

The commuter train passed on Lurol's left with a gentle woosh, running on a magnetic track powered by a distant array of solar microwave receptors. Birds squabbled in a tree at Lurol's back. The grass under her sandaled feet was soft, the breeze cool. This was sane, well-ordered Rire, where nothing terrible happened. Not *Second Contact Station* on the edge of the Killing Reach Jump, threatened by pea-brained, *rel*-skimming-empowered Sevolites.

Lurol's route had paralleled the track thus far. Now she cut across a sparsely wooded park that cupped a C-shaped collection of detached, two-story homes. Twelve such C-blocks constituted a town site with shared communal services, including a neighborhood arbiter. Within the larger grouping, each C-block competed to host the most attractive recreations: a water park, tennis courts, gardens, even stables. Lurol's block had a duck pond and a smattering of flower beds that didn't demand too much attention from its residents.

She crossed her block's central green, walking faster and faster, went over the patio that led up to her porch and hesitated in front of the see-through door to her own living room. Reetions did not approve of needless automation that wasted energy and deprived human muscles of needed exercise. She had to pull the door back to go inside. She could see Evert watching the stage through the door. A small man seated on a section of the morph couch ringing their main stage, with an intelligent, oval face and a light tan complexion, he wore a beige lounging suit with his feet sheathed in embroidered Gelack slippers — a present from Ranar years before.

When Lurol opened the door and entered, Evert barely looked up. She joined him companionably, without a word.

Erien occupied the stage, with text updates off to one side keeping track of Amel and Ranar.

He looks so mature, thought Lurol, looking at the son she had helped raise for seven years. *And alien.*

Evert panned back the view, showing her Erien standing on the deck of the arrivals floor on *Mars Orbital Station*, above Rire, speaking with a Reetion pilot handler. Beside him stood a tall, sword-wearing stranger with a haughty look and typical Vrellish coloring who was labeled, "Horth Nersal (Gelack title, Liege Nersal): admiral of the occupying fleet."

Occupying fleet? Lurol wondered, then remembered the incomplete news she had caught earlier about *Kali Station* in the Reach of Paradise.

"Looks like Ranar's bringing his work home," Evert said without enthusiasm and a nod in Horth's direction.

"Liege Nersal," Lurol mused aloud, trying to read the text update on Amel simultaneously. "Isn't he the devil incarnate?"

"He's a violent, heterosexual bigot," Evert said with a frown.

But an impressive specimen! Lurol amended to herself, appreciatively, switching her attention back to Horth. There was something endearingly naïve about the sight of the powerful Sevolite leader standing beside Erien on a Reetion orbital station, indifferent to the people who stared at his flight leathers marked with tribal emblems and the dueling sword at his hip. As she watched, Horth pointed and asked Erien something about energy recycling. All his questions were about engineering, according to a pop-up annotation configured to Evert's preferences.

"You know what this means?" Evert said. "Ranar won't want me around, in case I touch him, or look at him wrong, and offend Horth Nersal's homophobic sensibilities. And Ranar's been gone a year — a whole year, Lurol!" He looked dejected.

"How much is Ranar likely to have to do with Nersal once they've landed?" Lurol asked, trying to cheer him up. "The city's certain to put up the Sevolites in some kind of anthropologically prepared facility."

Evert only looked more unhappy. "Ranar will be wretched if they cut him out of anything to do with the visitors." He turned to Lurol. "How *could* Foreign and Alien Council displace him as consulting anthropologist when he has just been recognized as ambassador by the Gelack Ava? Yes, perhaps he's compromised his objectivity, but he's still done more to put gelackology on record than any dozen stay-at-home purists with their theorizing!"

"Make up your mind, Evert!" laughed Lurol in the deep, rough tone she reserved for family. "Do you want Ranar to yourself or don't you?"

"I don't want to interfere with his work!" said Evert, and subsided with a sigh. "And I've never had him to myself, anyhow."

Lurol acknowledge the justice of the complaint with a sympathetic grunt. The competition from Di Mon had always been too fierce, even posthumously, for Evert to feel secure about Ranar's love. Even Erien was a bit of Di Mon's leftover agenda, and Ranar seemed to be playing out Di Mon's loyalty to Ameron, politically, concerning Gelion. As much as Lurol felt disloyal for sharing Foreign and Alien Council's doubts about Ranar's objectivity, she suspected FAC was right, in the end, to revoke his privileges. Ranar had gone native.

They watched in silence until Evert blurted, "Poor Erien!"

"I wouldn't worry about Erien," Lurol said with a snort, watching him chatting with a Reetion representative called an intervener, whose job was to figure out how to connect the arrivals with the proper authorities and services. "He's going to civilize the Gelacks, disappointing future generations of anthropologists who want to study them."

"Don't be glib!" Evert snapped, losing patience with her. "Haven't you read the investigative triumvirate's news from Gelion? Erien watched that Nersal creature kill his half-brother, D'Therd, for the privilege of murdering their mother; he personally fought a duel with his half-brother, D'Lekker; he was wounded dragging Amel out of Lilac Hearth for who knows what dreadful reasons no one is very forthcoming about! And the poor boy thinks he caused his parents' fatal showdown. I can hear it in his voice when he talks about it." Evert concluded shrilly and mastered his feelings with a sigh. "I know Erien well enough to know how much pain that child can hide in blandsounding words offered up to an investigator! It's been a *nightmare* for him!" Evert scowled. "Erien does *not* belong on Gelion."

Lurol blinked at her normally mild-mannered housemate, not knowing how to reassure him that Erien could take care of himself. She took Evert's hand, instead. His fingers were stained with colored ink from practicing Gelack calligraphy in his workroom. They sat in silence for a moment, reading updates on Ranar's progress in postflight recovery, as Lurol's mind wandered back to Horth Nersal.

"I once read that sharks, on old Earth, would bite swimmers and then spit them out when they realized they lacked sufficient body fat to make the meal worthwhile," Lurol remarked after a long silence. "Reminds me of Ranar's ideas about surrendering to Vrellish Sevolites. You know, how they won't conquer Rire because Reetions just don't taste like Gelack commoners."

Evert gave her a puzzled look, loosely translatable as 'what has that to do with anything important?' — by which he would mean family members. Lurol answered with an apologetic shrug, and continued to watch Horth.

Alpha male, she summed up her first impressions with a superior smirk, intellectually, and an undeniable twinge of interest as a woman. She was roughly Horth's age, after all, even if he didn't look like he was pushing fifty. But then, she had to admit her own physical condition would have been the envy of most old Earth humans, at her age, thanks to the Reetion medicine that made it possible for most people to live well into their hundreds.

But Horth Nersal did not belong in her world any more than a shark on dry land. He reminded her how she'd felt eighteen years ago, alone in a lifeboat — metaphorically speaking — fending off a shark with a stick, because a stick was all you had on hand... a stick named Amel, in her case. She had already broken the conscience bond the Gelack commander H'Reth used to control Amel, and it was just one more small step to engage his compassion in their cause. Her punishment had been nearly two decades of criticism and remorse.

Why couldn't Amel have been a crude, ugly bastard? Lurol thought. *It would have been so much easier to live down what I did. What I had to do!* she reminded herself, without conviction.

"Di Mon never said good-bye," Evert remarked aloud, proving that he, too, was lost in his own thoughts. "If he was cold-blooded enough to plan his suicide, why not include a proper good-bye for Ranar? Instead, he sent Erien and Ranar out to take a walk, knowing they would find him dead when they came back." He shook his head. "He owed them some explanation."

"He was dying of regenerative cancer," Lurol pointed out, wishing she could resurrect the insensitive bastard just to lay his ghost to rest, in their household, once and for all.

"Oh, look!" said Evert, sitting up. "They're deciding where to put the Gelacks."

On stage, the Reetion negotiators were recommending rooms in the Space Service research complex for housing Amel, Horth and the Gelack commoner called Drasous, but Horth refused to be separated from Erien. Erien was also trying to dissuade his Reetion hosts from hospitalizing Amel for reasons not entirely clear to Lurol. Apparently something had happened to him on *Kali Station*, in addition to the wounds mentioned in the investigative triumvirate's first report.

Erien insisted he and Amel had brought their own doctor, a Gelack commoner named Drasous, who was off recovering from the trip at the moment.

"Drasous," Lurol muttered. She knew the 'ous' ending meant Drasous would be a *gorarelpul*, controlled by a conscience bond. Sevolites tended to equate conscience bonding and other Lorel atrocities rooted in their past with her own brand of psychiatric medicine. Maybe if she used her probe to cure a *gorarelpul* of his conscience bond, it would convince them the technology was benign. Of course, in Amel's case any brain cells she'd destroyed had regenerated. It would be trickier with a Gelack commoner.

Amel moved to the center of their stage, retreating from a trio of Reetion medical personnel wanting to evaluate him, pivoting around Erien's position.

Lurol zoomed their stage in on Amel. "How does he look to you?" she asked Evert.

"Amel?" Evert said, distracted. "I don't know." He spared it some thought. "Good." He thought some more, and added with both honesty and some annoyance. "Luscious."

"He's in pain," said Lurol, studying Amel's body language. She could see he was feeling a lot of stress, too. His mouth and eyes lacked expression. But what could possibly be scaring him on *Mars Orbital Station*?

It was the Reetion medics, Lurol realized resentfully. He still thinks we're all Lorel monsters out to vivisect him.

Then something funny happened. Amel's eyes sprang wider with a jolt, his pastel lips parting in a little gasp. He covered up the lapse by leaning over with his hands braced on his thighs, like a sprinter.

"Is he all right?" asked Evert.

Erien was asking Amel the same thing to preempt the medics' taking over.

Amel wiped his face with his palm as he straightened up. "Just having a hard time adjusting to the low Gs," he told Erien.

"Fahzir reported a stomach wound and lacerations," insisted a hovering medic.

"Do I look like I need to be hospitalized?" Amel said, forcing a smile, and turned a pirouette. The medic was too surprised to take note of the slightly sloppy way he ended the move, which spoke volumes to Lurol. Amel would have to work at muddling a basic dance step unless something serious was throwing him off.

Like a stomach wound, thought Lurol sourly. She also had her suspicions about his momentary lapse of awareness. *And clear dreams I could cure him of, if he'll let me*! she thought. So why pretend there's nothing wrong? Did he want to spend the rest of his life reliving past traumas in the midst of new ones?

"Lurol," Evert stood with his head tipped to one side, fingers resting lightly on his ear bug. "This is bad." He paused. "*Kali Station*." He broke off, pulled the bug out, and looked at her with painful sympathy. "The Megans used Amel to interface with the station arbiter, through a visitor probe."

Lurol went numb.

Evert touched her arm. "It wasn't you, this time," he told her. "It's not your fault."

She rose with dignity. "I have to study the details," she excused herself, and climbed the carpeted stairs to the landing above, to their bedrooms, feeling numb.

Her calm lasted until she discovered there were no details on record, only an eye witness report from Fahzir saying Erien had destroyed the data she needed — with a sword!

My son? she thought. *My Erien a data vandal?* It felt inconceivable.

Evert's signal — a snatch of Demoran music — interrupted her. He appeared on her desk stage looking flustered. "They're on their way here from the space port!"

"Ranar and Erien?" Lurol asked.

"And Liege Nersal, with Drasous to follow when he is able... and Amel. We're going to have houseguests."

"Amel?" Lurol blurted. "Staying here?"

Evert nodded. "And Nersal," he repeated, and paused. "Do you think I should move out until they're gone?"

"Don't you dare!" exclaimed Lurol. She needed Evert. Her heart was pounding and her stomach had butterflies for the first time since she'd been a gawky teenager. How could she interact socially with Amel? All she needed was an hour with him under a visitor probe to fix what she'd done eighteen year ago!

Evert disappeared from the stage and reappeared in person at her study door. For a Reetion family, they had a lot of doors that opened and closed, because Erien had always preferred them.

"Look," he said, nodding at what had replaced him on the stage in her room, which now showed the Gelacks crossing a pedestrian plaza headed for a train platform. People around them were behaving with varying degrees of restraint. Most did little more than stare. Only a few acted as if there was nothing special about seeing a group of Gelacks using Reetion public transit. Some gravitated toward Amel, who edged closer and closer to Erien, avoiding eye contact with his admirers. Nersal expected people to get out of the way for him, and somehow they seemed to understand as much and didn't bother him.

"Do you think Nersal would hit anyone?" Evert asked nervously.

Oh, yes, thought Lurol. She half-expected Horth Nersal to reach for his sword, but that didn't seem to occur to him; then she remembered Sevolites only used them on each other. If he had behaved violently an arbiter would have responded, of course.

Amel stepped in the moment a car door slid open, followed by Erien. Nersal turned around, once, as if he needed to be sure what was behind him as well as in front of him, then followed Erien.

"Horth Nersal can't understand a word of Reetion," Evert commented. "They offered him a portable translator at the space port, but he took it off after five minutes. Apparently hearing simultaneous translation in arbiter-generated Gelack was too confusing for him."

"He has a strong spatial dominance," said Lurol, thinking she would love to run a piloting psych profile on the famous Highlord, unbeaten on the challenge floor and feared in space by other houses. *A shark who eats sharks*, she thought.

"Erien shouldn't have to cope with all this," Evert said as their beleaguered son encouraged Horth to sit down in the train car. "He's hurt. He should have waited for Ranar to recover from the trip, or sent for us to help him."

Lurol snorted. "I can't feel too worried about anyone who shatters an arbiter block with a length of metal. Come on," she added grouchily, "they'll be here soon. Let's go downstairs and get ready."

"How?"

"I don't know! Fix them something to eat? If they're healing, they'll need glucose and protein."

Evert went down to the kitchen, leaving Lurol alone at her workstation, checking in with colleagues. After a few moments, she put herself on the record as unavailable and followed him. Evert looked up when she joined him in the kitchen, but she left him spreading wafers with sweet bean paste — one of Erien's favorite snacks — and drifted back into the living room.

"Stage on," she said. "Show me Amel. Live, no annotations."

She saw Erien sitting beside Amel on the train and looking, to her parental eye, anything but relaxed. Horth Nersal stood on Erien's other side. There were a dozen Reetions in the car, including two women with a collection of children of mixed ages, probably on a communal outing. The other occupants of the car were a pair of young men, one of whom wore a Gelack cult vest with false embroidery depicting a hand gripping the hilt of a sword. He sat staring at Horth Nersal, elbowing his friend to silence when he encouraged him in whispers to do something worthy of the opportunity. Cultists were misfit youths who viewed retrograde Gelack behavior as empowering; but such close proximity to the real thing was apparently intimidating. Horth himself didn't even recognize the vest as mimicry. He gazed out at the parklike strip of land on either side of the tracks, indifferent to the foolish youngsters.

Amel sat quietly with his eyes down. Lurol stared at his lowered head, willing him to look up. When he did, it felt as if she had somehow caused it, but it was one of the children.

The girl was about four. She went straight past Horth Nersal, who gave way with no more than a look of piqued interest. He seemed to respect the child's boldness. Bypassing Erien, the little girl clambered into the empty seats ahead so she could talk to Amel over them.

"I know you," she accused him, as if puzzled by his failure to acknowledge it spontaneously. "You're the *nice* Gelack. I'm Jeet," she told him.

Watching Amel smile was heartbreaking. "Nice to meet you Jeet," he told her. But beneath his ready sweetness in conversing with the child lay the waxen fear of someone about to be conducted to a scaffold. She wanted to shake him and tell him, *We won't hurt you!*

"Are the other ones bad Gelacks?" the child asked, without looking toward Nersal or Erien.

"They won't hurt you," Amel said, and glanced toward Erien in the seat beside him, smiling with a trace of what might have been fondness.

A woman cleared her throat and called to the child a bit hoarsely, "Jeet? Leave the... people... alone."

Jeet put her arms out to Amel. He found the gesture diffi-cult to disappoint, but looked to her chaperons for approval. One of them was on her feet. Nersal moved aside to let the woman approach. She wasn't wearing a sword, of course. She wasn't wearing much of anything. It was early summer — tank tops and shorts were common — and it was clear to Lurol that whatever else Horth thought, he didn't find brown skin objec-tionable.

Amel rose and hugged little Jeet over the back of the seat she was standing on. It gave the hovering woman the courage to come claim her.

"Thank you!" she exclaimed, as if Amel had rescued the child from something fatal. "I'm sorry!"

"It's all right," he told her, speaking perfect Reetion.

The tender scene was interrupted by the transit arbiter telling everyone to be seated in compliance with safety standards. Amel turned his head to gaze out the window.

The children got out with their chaperons at the next stop and no one else got in, although there were people waiting on the platform.

Just a few more stops, Lurol thought, *and they'll be here*.

"Stage off!" she said, and got up, feeling fidgety.

I don't have to put myself though this, she thought. She could stay at a friend's the whole time... except she kept thinking about the moment on *Mars Orbital Station* when she suspected Amel of having a clear dream.

"Stage on!" Lurol ordered, and summoned up the clip of Amel's bright eyes widening, the catch of breath, then the flush. If he was clear dreaming, what had he been reexperiencing in that moment? She pulled up her old data and began looking for a correlation. She had a lot of ordinary, external record of him looking sick, worried, frightened; none of it matched the expression, nor did his reactions to the more gruesome repetoire of torture and abuse that were the most common subjects of his clear dreams. But exactly what he'd been experiencing evaded her.

She was playing the eye-widening clip in a tight loop, trying to put her finger on it, when Evert appeared with a tray of snacks. "Turn that off!" he told her crossly.

Lurol looked up in time to see Erien, Amel and Horth Nersal entering from the porch.

"Erien!" Evert caught their prodigal son's hand and pulled him inside.

Erien pivoted suddenly to block Horth's attempt to thrust Evert back. "These are my parents," he told Horth in Gelack. "And must be treated as our equals here." Horth frowned, looked from Evert to Lurol, and balked on the threshold. Then he pointedly turned around and went back out to the porch.

"Don't you think that's a bit extreme?" Evert, the linguist and gracious host, said anxiously to Erien. "I mean, insisting on *rel*-peerage... to a commoner?"

"Maybe," Erien said tiredly, "but I think it might be necessary to make it clear you are entitled to behave in a familiar way toward me."

"Familiar?" Evert asked, hurt and bewildered. "We're your parents!"

"Exactly. Excuse me, I'll just be a minute." Erien followed Horth out again, no doubt to reason with him.

Amel stood just inside the door, abandoned by Erien's departure, and watched his lapse on *Mars Orbital Station* as it replayed in a loop on the stage in the family's living room. He looked embarrassed. That was the clue Lurol needed to solve the riddle of what he'd been clear dreaming. She snapped her fingers and said softly, "Orgasm."

Evert gave her a funny look. "Pardon?"

Amel turned aside as if he hadn't heard and moved farther into the room, skirting the clip on the stage with his back to it.

"Stage off!" Lurol snapped and dropped like a stone to the morph couch before her legs buckled.

"You are Amel, of course," Evert said politely. "Welcome."

Amel said warily, "You must be Evert. I have heard of you."

"You have been helpful to Ranar in the past," Evert responded bravely, "I've always wanted to thank you for that."

Homophobic, Lurol diagnosed, imagining Amel turning Evert's statement every which way in his mind, to examine it as if it was alive and dangerous.

Amel noticed Evert's embroidered Gelack slippers and Evert tried again, valiantly, to make conversation. "They were a present," he said, "from Ranar. It's a Demish pattern. I haven't been able to place the style. I think it is Demoran influenced, but it isn't a Golden Age pattern, is it?"

Amel gave no indication he even understood the question, although he almost certainly knew the answer. Lurol could understand him being scared of her, but she resented his unfriendly manner toward Evert.

Erien returned with Horth, sparing them further social disasters. Horth seemed to have accepted the ground rules. He looked Lurol and Evert over with new interest.

Erien gave Lurol and Evert a faint, twisted smile and said, "Where were we?"

Evert hugged him. Erien returned the hug one handed, wincing around the eyes as Evert put pressure on his left arm. Lurol took note of that, and kept her hug brief and one-sided.

"Explain yourself, kiddo," she said, tilting her head toward Horth.

"STIs," he obliged her. "I'm relying on yours to give us some privacy. I'm sorry for the imposition, but Ranar and I decided it was necessary." He turned to Amel and Horth, shifting into Gelack. "I need to explain what will and will not get the neighborhood arbiter's attention, even in here."

"At least you can sit down while you do," Evert said briskly. "You look terrible!"

What's the matter, kid? Lurol thought, watching Erien blink at Evert. *Got used to not having parents around, did you?*

Amused, she watched Evert take charge, draw the drapes across the porch door and get them settled. Erien sank into a section of morph couch, started to struggle out, frowning, and caught himself with a rueful expression. "Arbiter, please set my furniture support defaults to plus five," he ordered. It had remembered his childhood preference, naturally.

Horth gave the furniture a dubious glance and decided to remain standing. Amel settled on the floor, cross-legged.

Since Erien seemed determined to speak Gelack for Horth's benefit, Lurol plunked in an ear bug and asked for simultaneous translation to shore up her inadequate vocabulary and grammar. Evert, of course, was fluent not only in court Gelack but half a dozen Golden Demish dialects.

Erien panned a single, half-seeing glance over the living room he had played in as a child, then settled his attention on Horth and Amel. "The first thing I need to explain," he said, "is why I've brought you here. It has to do with social transparency. On Rire, virtually all events enter the record for some duration." Amel dropped his eyes, studying his hands in his lap as Erien continued. "All interiors, all regularly inhabited exteriors and all normal transit lanes are monitored. The majority of people even carry some kind of monitoring with them if they move out of range. Reetions are used to this and consider it normal. In this house the sensors are set into the walls, in an array pattern in the middle third of each wall. They are designed not to be visible. In other places, they are made part of the décor."

Horth prowled over to the nearest wall and began to inspect it. Erien watched a moment — possibly to make sure he wasn't going to start dismantling it — then continued. "What happens to the recorded material varies. There is a complex scoring system that determines its relevance and therefore its persistence, but most of it is ephemeral — it's simply not feasible to keep it all. Retention and analysis is greater in a public setting, as any residential guest rooms offered to us would inevitably be designated — if not immediately, then within hours, as interest mounted. But a domestic setting like this has a default STI of two, which means nothing is retained unless explicitly requested, and behavior is monitored solely for commands and matters requiring intervention, such as any kind of violence—" he made eye contact with Horth "—or a medical emergency," he concluded, looking at Amel.

"Why do I have the feeling there's a 'but' coming?" Amel asked nervously.

Erien quirked him a faint smile. "STIs can be altered by external lobby. Sufficient public interest might empower a lobby to pierce our STI two with filters. Any material that scored high enough on the indices set by the lobby would then go on record, where — in general — it may be freely accessed."

"Like..." said Amel, and looked involuntarily at Lurol, "my other data, from the *Second Contact* mission."

"Yes," Erien said crisply. "We want to avoid a repetition. That's why you have to understand this. STIs are predetermined defaults that attach themselves to spaces or activities. Each is a composite of three factors: who may have access, the degree or duration of retention and the amount of arbiter attention given to analysis and filtering. An STI of two is sufficiently private that no record will be kept of our conversations or actions within these walls or on the back porch. However—"

Horth was crouching, examining the room stage as though looking for the first screws to remove. Lurol had a feeling that neither of the kid's audience appreciated the lecture. Horth was contemptuous. Amel already looked numb.

Erien soldiered on doggedly. "— if our domestic privacy is pierced often enough, by violence or sabotage of due Reetion process, or lobbies as yet undefined, which we will at least have due warning of, then public concern may impose something known as an aura on one or more of us, which leads to a spontaneous upgrading of the STI in any setting we enter, making it as transparent as the aura. In essence, someone or something with an aura lights up the surroundings he is in. If that happens to one of us—" Erien looked pointedly at Amel, "—we will no longer have STI two privacy in my parents' home."

He paused to let the warning sink in, then added, "And of course anything we do outside this household *will* go on record and *will* be widely accessible. I ask you both to keep these conditions in mind."

There was a long, stiff silence. Then Horth stood up slowly and nodded, abandoning his investigations. Amel wet his lips, but thought better of speaking and gave a quick nod before rubbing his hand over his face to calm himself down.

"I had better look at that arm of yours," Lurol told Erien.

He hesitated, then nodded, turned and went upstairs. She heard the door to his childhood room open.

Presumptuous kid, she thought. But they had, indeed, left his room untouched since he left it three years before.

Lurol collected the first-aid kit she had put together when it became clear Ranar expected her to treat the young Erien for anything short of evisceration or a broken neck, to keep his medical peculiarities off the record.

She found Erien sitting on his bed, studying the room as though it were a stranger's. He'd always been exceptionally orderly for a child, which was just as well because he was the most acquisitive young human she'd ever known. Ranar explained it as cultural. Gelacks, lacking arbiters, were accustomed to manipulating physical objects. And Erien had found plenty of objects to manipulate. Two walls of his room were entirely given over to shelving for collections, models and notebooks, all meticulously labeled and organized.

He gave her a rueful look. "I had forgotten all this. I arrived on Gelion with one carryall and the leathers I stood in."

She closed the door behind her and leaned back against it, folding her arms. Her eye fell on Erien's guitar, left behind when he went to the fleet. He had taken only his principal instrument, the flute.

"You still play?" asked Lurol.

"Music?" he closed his eyes. "It's difficult on Gelion."

No doubt, Lurol thought, and gave a grunt. Music on Gelion, according to Ranar, was practiced primarily by the higher class of sex worker. Amel was a musician because he had been raised a courtesan. But music had been important — even necessary

— to Erien while he was growing up on Rire. And people had told her he was gifted.

"Come on, kiddo," she said, "let's get it over with before your devoted minions break down the door."

Using his left arm as little as possible, he pulled off his shirt.

"Shit," she said, at the sight of the bruising around the bandage. "What happened?"

"Knife wound," he said tersely, "two days ago."

"Rescuing Amel from Lilac Hearth?" she guessed, sounding harder than she had intended.

"Yes," he admitted.

"What happened in there?" she asked. "Who did this to you?"

"I don't think it is... wise to talk about it, Lurol," he said tiredly.

She checked the STI. "We're private here, Erien.

"What... happened... in Lilac Hearth," he said, showing a glimpse of the fourteen-year-old boy who had left them three years before, "I did something I can't accept. I cannot... convince myself that there wasn't some other way."

"That's the hell of it, kid," she said. "I've been living with that one myself for eighteen years. Regardless of what people say, for and against, in the small hours of the morning it's just you and yourself. You look back at it and you never really do know. Looking at this, though," she nodded at his wounded arm, "I would say you probably didn't have the maneuvering room you think you did."

For a moment she thought he was going to cry — she knew he wasn't too Vrellish to be capable of it — and she put a hand on his back, feeling obscurely guilty for immediately equating his sin with hers.

"I'm going to give you a shot," she said. "Help you get a good night's sleep. You can deal with the rest of it in the morning."

TWELVE

Erien

Cultural Misunderstandings

The next morning, Erien nursed his fifth glass of lemonade seated at his family's kitchen table as he considered his resources for the coming fight to gain diplomatic recognition for Gelion. *My kitchen Council of Privilege,* he dubbed the people sitting there with him.

There was himself, still feeling bone weary despite a night's sleep. Amel was lodged in the frame of the open arch between the kitchen and the landing at the bottom of the stairs. Lurol, scowling everywhere except at Amel, gazed mainly down into her coffee. Ranar and Evert sat on either side of her. Erien regretted that he had not dared to introduce Evert as Ranar's *mekan'st* and get it over with. Instead, Ranar was keeping his distance from Evert to avoid offending Horth, and Evert was unhappily complying. Ranar, who had arrived last night with Drasous, looked tired. Drasous, who sat drinking iced tea beside Erien, seemed fully recovered. He even had enough poise and concentration to translate for Horth when household members spoke in Reetion; a feat Erien was not sure he could have accomplished himself under the circumstances.

Horth had stationed himself, standing, beside Erien.

The kitchen was too small for the lot of them.

"This is what I can see happening over the next few days," Erien explained in Gelack. The decision to drop *rel*-peerage over the whole motley crew — Pureblood, Highlord, *gorarelpul* and Reetions — had been the easy one. Explaining Rire, in Gelack and in terms Horth could understand, was going to be much harder.

"Reetions view their social and political system from the perspective of engineers," said Erien. "Given the pervasiveness of arbiter monitoring and the opportunities for intervention, when something goes wrong they think in terms of system failures. As Ranar said back on Gelion, it should not have been possible for Ann to arm *Kali Station* when the Reetion Net had voted down her defense plan."

"It would have been impossible without Amel's assistance," Ranar said.

Erien nodded. "So although Ann and the Megans will be held accountable for their actions, the main focus of the inquiry will be on the system failure that allowed them to circumvent Reetion law."

"Amel?" Drasous said in a bland tone.

Amel looked skittish. Erien fixed him in place with his stare. "Amel is not a Reetion citizen," he said. "The extent to which he is subject to Reetion law is undetermined. I intend to use this fact as the opening to pursue a diplomatic agenda that will lead to the recognition of Gelion's status and rights, at least to the extent that Ameron has recognized Rire's."

In his own ears, his decisive voice showed no trace of his feelings about the many pitfalls of the project. He hoped he sounded at least as convincing to others.

"What they want from you," he told Amel, "are technical details of how you smuggled the data, so they can fix their system to prevent it from happening again. They will also ask about your motivation and, most importantly, to clarify that Ameron did not instruct you to tamper with the Arbiter Administration in any way."

"What can I do?" Ranar asked. "Now I am no longer on Foreign and Alien Council?"

"Help me influence public opinion," said Erien. "I have a handicap there, since I'm still classified as a dependent citizen. Young Reetions normally earn their right to weigh in politically by taking part in aura-enhancing exercises at lower levels of the political process, mediated by study groups. I will have to accelerate the process with the help of Ranar and his contacts."

"Erien isn't considered important on Rire because he's young and inexperienced," Drasous translated bluntly for Horth, making the Nersallian admiral frown.

"It isn't that young people can't be taken seriously," Ranar said in defense of the system. "I became a Voting Citizen at twenty-one."

"Surely Erien would have exceeded your own precocity, while living here," Drasous said, with a Gelack's casual assumption of Erien's superiority.

"We didn't exactly encourage Erien to, uh, stand out," said Evert.

"So the first step will be establishing Erien's credibility as an adult contributor," Ranar summed up quickly, and nodded for Erien to continue.

"Amel and I will need to post and respond on all relevant forums," said Erien. "I'll set up and refine filters to select the ones we most need to attend to, or we'll be swamped. And we will have to prepare formal entries for the record surrounding what happened. We may be interviewed by triumvirates constituted to deal with different aspects of the issue. That comes under the rubric of data gathering, which will be ongoing throughout, but most intensive toward the beginning. Then comes analysis and synthesis, centered on developing recommendations for change to prevent a repetition of the problem. It sounds untidy, but it's actually a highly efficient process, given the administrative support of Rire's arbiters. Our intensive involvement may cover no more than a week or two, at which point it will be clear whether or not I'll need Amel to stay for the succeeding diplomatic work."

Erien looked at Amel. "Although you should be aware that there is, quite apart from the hearing process, an active human rights lobby concerned about your safety if you should return to Gelion." He shook his head. "It seems that having overlooked your human rights in the first instance, Rire feels compelled to overcompensate. You'll be offered asylum, although it is, of course, up to you to decide whether to take it."

A slight noise distracted him and he looked up to see Amel fleeing upstairs.

Lurol got up to follow, but Drasous rose to block her.

Erien signed inwardly. "Ranar," he said, interrupting the anthropologist-ambassador's contemplation of his knuckles. "What can you tell me about your replacement as Foreign and Alien Council representative?"

Ranar winced a little. "I have great respect for Juma's scholarship. He has been an active student of Gelack culture, language and society since shortly after Second Contact, and served on the first expansion of Foreign and Alien Council for the last fifteen years. Just remember that he does not have any direct experience with Gelacks."

"I must recognize him," Erien said, "but you are still the only ambassador acknowledged by Gelion, and you *do* have direct experience with Gelacks. I need your support as well."

Ranar nodded. "Of course," he said quietly. It disturbed Erien how reserved his foster father had been since the loss of his position with Foreign and Alien Council. He tried to believe it was nothing but postflight fatigue.

"Lurol," Erien continued. "I've seen discussion this morning about the aggressiveness of Vrellish Sevolites, which might cloud public opinion. It first came up during the debate on Ann's defense proposal and you were its principal opponent. Can you brief me? I haven't had time to get to the root of it."

Lurol ruffled. "That rubbish." She hunched her shoulders. "It's called the Extrapolation Theory, and it attempts to make broad claims for Vrellish aggressiveness by leaning too heavily on the data we have — which is Amel's. The argument goes something like this: the one aspect of Amel's character that seems to be Vrellish is his sexuality, minus the emotional overlays. There is evidence, concerning genetic markers, that suggest it is possible to group Amel's sexual prowess, if not his emotional makeup, with his Vrellish features such as hair and eye-color. That's sound enough, given what evidence we have of the Vrellish genetic profile from samples collected here and there over the years, although how genetics manifest is largely specu-lative without matching psych profiles." She gave Horth a dis-tinctly acquisitive look, but thankfully didn't suggest mapping his behavioral response patterns. "The main leap of logic in the Extrapolation Theory is to claim that the disparity between Amel's sexual profile and that of an average heterosexually orientated Reetion male would be comparable to the disparity in aggressiveness between a Vrellish Sevolite and a natural human being." Lurol snorted. "I trashed the theory in the debates, of course. But there's no idea so bad that it cannot make a comeback. I had a student make a horrible suggestion just the other day, no doubt inspired by fear mongering about Vrellish aggressiveness. Don't worry about such nonsense, Erien. I'll handle it."

"There is something else you need to be made aware of, Erien," Ranar spoke up, "which has changed since I was last on Rire. There are new protocols for collecting reliable data in cases where the record can't corroborate testimony. They have always existed, but their application has been broadened since you left. Of course compliance is voluntary," Ranar added, "but a witness can be asked to repeat key statements under biopsychometric monitoring so that his *conscious* reliability, can be measured. It is still impossible, of course, to detect falsehoods the subject believes to be the truth."

Cold crawled up Erien's spine. He rubbed his aching arm, caught Ranar's eye and stopped.

"I thought I should at least make you aware of the possibility," Ranar said gently.

Erien swallowed in a dry mouth. "I appreciate the warning."

Horth's hand-to-hilt distance had narrowed as Ranar and Erien discussed biopsychometric monitoring. Without saying anything, he bristled.

Erien took a careful sip of lemonade to stay calm. "A biopsych monitor is not a visitor probe, Horth," he tried to reassure him. "Questioners have no access to the subject's thoughts, nor the means to shape mental processes, only to monitor responses."

Horth regarded him with that maddening, dispassionate interest with which he greeted any dubious argument. Then, abruptly, Horth left the kitchen. Erien caught a glimpse of him silhouetted in sunshine as the living room door opened and closed, letting Horth out onto the commons. Erien started to get up.

"Erien, wait," Ranar said, "Why not let him find his own way a little?"

Judging by the expressions around the table, Erien was not alone in his doubts about the wisdom of that.

"I would not underestimate Liege Nersal's flexibility," Ranar said.

"I would not *overestimate* it," said Lurol. "You didn't see him on the way here, looking around like he owned the place. Why is he here, anyway?"

"I'm not... entirely certain," Erien admitted. "I think he's curious."

"*That's* reassuring," she sniped. "Have you asked?"

"I tried, but got the impression that he thought I should already know."

"Kiddo, I know you don't like to ask obvious questions, but this could be important." Lurol jerked a thumb after the departed Highlord. "What'll happen if someone tries out their Gelack on him and gets the pronouns wrong?"

"We need to find out how he views Reetions in general," Ranar said calmly, "ones that Erien hasn't vouched for. A great deal depends on where he fits us into his conception of the social order." Ranar surveyed his housemates' faces and found them reserved. "He won't kill anyone. *Okal Rel* concerns the use of force in appropriate measure. Liege Nersal understands that very well."

"So you're letting him walk out the door as a sort of... test?" Evert asked nervously.

Erien couldn't stand it any longer. Ranar's reasoning made sense, but human beings were not creatures of reason. Erien was a nervous wreck. He left the kitchen, crossed the living room and stood watching through the sliding door.

Horth was standing in the middle of the common lawn, look-ing — as Lurol said — as though he owned the place. The breeze stirred his blue-black hair. From the composition of the groups of people around the periphery, Erien suspected that any small children had been swept indoors. The remainder consisted of a few brazen older ones — but fortunately none so brazen as to pester the brooding Highlord.

Ranar came up behind Erien. "I have told the arbiter to advise us if Liege Nersal's interactions with the neighbors fall within ten percent of the threshold for summoning first responders. I've also... if you don't mind... contacted a couple of my stu-dents who speak excellent Gelack and asked them if they would mind acting as escorts. I've done it acting as a private citizen, which shouldn't infringe on the duties of my FAC replacement."

It caused Erien a pang to hear Ranar worry about overstep-ping his position. The demotion had shaken his confidence. Well, promotion wasn't much better, as Erien could attest. He let out the breath he had drawn. "I feel like the parent of a toddler who hasn't discovered the meaning of fear."

Ranar's lip quirked. "Indeed," he told his foster son. "I know the feeling well."

Erien started to lift his right hand to his left arm, to knead the ache there, became aware of the movement and deliberately stopped it. "I need to get to work."

"Use my workspace," Lurol called across the living room from the kitchen. "I'm off to the lab. Easier to concentrate there."

Drasous padded over to join Erien at the stairs, a small frown between his brows. "How may I be of assistance?" he asked, forcing Erien to realize he had been putting off the decision about how to employ Drasous. He had never had a bonded *gorarelpul* working for him before, and while he doubted Drasous would be thrown into bond conflict on the strength of a wrong word, he didn't want to learn otherwise. As far as he understood, Ameron's orders to Drasous had been to obey Erien as he would himself.

Drasous regarded him kindly. "It's all right, Heir Gelion. I will not self-destruct in front of you. And no," he added, "I do not read minds. But I think I am coming to know yours. What I was wondering was whether clerical work is the best use of your time. If you had a secretary it might help."

"Drasous, consider it a 24-hour a day reception. I need to be involved myself. And the secretaries here are crystronic."

"Then I will learn what is appropriate," Drasous said, at his blandest, "so I may best assist you." He followed Erien up the stairs as soundlessly as an assassin, an ominous impression somewhat marred by the casual way the *gorarelpul* snagged Erien's lemonade from the table to take with him.

Lurol's austere little workspace was deliberately designed not to fit more than one comfortably, but Drasous professed himself content to stand. Erien groaned aloud as he displayed the mail. No wonder Amel was hiding in his room.

For Drasous' benefit, he outlined the strategy. "I need to set up filters for significant messages and summarizing routines to track general trends. How much of this we get Amel to answer personally—"

The stage flashed an alert icon for the watchdog Ranar had set on Horth's behavior. Simultaneously Erien heard the front door open and a rising babble of voices. He managed to avoid trampling Drasous as he hurled himself headlong down the stairs, but it was a near thing.

Evert was already there, trying to reassure two young musicians Erien had spotted on the commons earlier.

"No, no, he won't hurt you," Evert was reassuring the girl Horth was still holding by one arm.

"Then what does he want?" the boy demanded, looking nervous despite the crowd of neighbors at his back. "He just came over and grabbed her. I got up. He shoved me down."

"Can your household not afford the girl?" Horth asked Erien in Gelack, sounding annoyed.

"Horth," said Erien, as patiently as he could manage, "the girl is not a courtesan, just a musician."

"A what?" said the boy in Reetion. "He thinks she's a — sex-worker?"

Great! Erien thought. *Of the three words of Gelack every Reetion knows, courtesan just has to be one, thanks to Amel!*

The boy started forward to rescue his girlfriend from Horth's grasp.

"Don't!" Erien warned, in alarm, and added more temperately. "This is a cultural misunderstanding. Horth, please let the girl go."

The girl jerked free as Horth released her, spun and slapped him with all her strength, then burst into furious tears as she fled back into her boyfriend's arms. Crying women were a foreign country to Vrellish males, but Horth understood the slap and accepted his chastisement.

Laughter from the top of the stairs turned all eyes upwards, to Amel. How anyone could laugh at the tableau in the living room and get away with it, amazed Erien, but Amel very nearly did. It was hard to feel offended by the silvery sound. The young couple, themselves, stared and pointed as if they had sighted a unicorn. Only Horth frowned.

The frown throttled Amel's laughter. Erien didn't want the scene to end with Amel bolting in terror at a glare from Horth Nersal, not with half the neighborhood watching them.

"Amel!" Erien seized the moment. "Please, come down and join us."

Amel looked at Horth. He looked at the Reetions. Then his breath caught and he gave a strangled cry, his face stamped with terror.

Anything might have happened in the next few seconds. Amel could have fallen off the landing or injured a Reetion who tried to help him. What did happen was Horth sprang up the stairs to seize Amel's arm as he lashed out at phantoms. Only Horth's superior skill made the engagement look mismatched. Amel struck with a Pureblood's strength and desperate panic. Horth hit back, Amel overbalanced and toppled off the landing, coming to himself in mid-tumble, in time to turn it into a controlled fall and land with his feet under him.

Horth jumped lightly down and cleared his sword, but by this time Erien was between them, using his father's authority — voice and all. "That's enough!"

In the ensuing silence, he heard the neighborhood arbiter advising them dispassionately that STI two had been pierced and first responders had been called.

Amel rose out of the deep crouch used to absorb impact and froze with a look of shock centered on the sword in Horth's hand, which did not go away until Horth sheathed the sword and stepped back. Able to inhale again, Amel sagged against the step, turning away from the audience.

Wonderful, thought Erien, as he heard Evert and Ranar greeting the team of first responders at the door. *Now Horth is on record looking like a bully, when he was only trying to contain Amel's fit.* Not that Erien wanted the Reetions to know Amel was suffering clear dreams again, if it could be helped, but he had the dismal feeling things were slipping out of his control.

Ranar brought the first responders in to reassure them, and the arbiter confirmed an STI two rating was once more intact, after a piercing that put fourteen seconds of the scene on record. Most of the neighbors left.

Evert was the first to reach Amel. "Are you all right?" Evert asked, reaching out to him.

"Don't touch me!" Amel hissed at Evert in Reetion. He scrambled to his feet and bolted back up the stairs, clutching his waist. Evert looked hurt, driving off any sympathy Erien had felt toward Amel.

"Erien!" Ranar's voice drew his attention to where Horth stood confronting one of the first responders, who had asked him to surrender his sword.

"Horth!" Erien claimed the Highlord's attention, then continued more calmly, "Leave the sword with me this time, if you're going out."

Horth turned his back, contemptuously, on the first responder, although Erien had no doubt he would have spun and attacked faster than the man could have responded if he'd made an unwise move. With a few quick gestures Horth released his sword belt and tossed it across the room to Erien, who caught it, much to his relief. Even in the midst of all this, the idea of fumbling — wounded or not — would have struck a discordant note. Horth understood perfectly. He grinned. Then he shouldered past the remaining people and went out.

"Stage on," said Ranar, and instinctively those left in the living room gathered around.

On the path outside the house, Horth was intercepted by a fit-looking man of about twenty who was dressed for exercise.

"One of my students," explained Ranar.

It certainly looked as if the new arrival could speak Gelack. Horth was attending to him soberly.

"Evert and I will talk to our neighbors," Ranar said, patting Erien's arm. "You see to Amel."

Drasous appeared to relieve him of the sword. The slight reluctance Erien felt about surrendering Horth's sword made him do it promptly. "Thank you."

Drasous disconcerted him by bowing. It was nothing ostentatious, but it pointedly reminded him of the *gorarelpul*'s relationship to his father.

Amel looked up as the door opened. He was sitting on his floor mattress studying a handmade notebook held together by a green ribbon that Ranar had given to Erien to encourage him to develop his penmanship in the Gelack style, and this particular notebook was filled with drawings of musical instruments, some contemporary, some historical, some fanciful, each one meticulously labeled. Amel looked surprised to see Erien, and guiltily furtive about the artifact in his hand, but the child who had studied, imagined and so absorbedly drawn those instruments might have been someone else entirely. Erien experienced no sense of trespass.

Erien leaned back against the closed door.

"I bungled that, didn't I," Amel said, putting down the notebook.

"It lacked something of your usual sure touch," Erien told him dryly.

"I shouldn't have laughed," Amel said in all seriousness, but had to struggle with the impulse again as soon as he thought about the incident.

Erien lowered himself, carefully, to sit on the floor, his back against the bed. "What concerns me now are the clear dreams you seem to be suffering from. Do not deny it," he forestalled a ready protest. "You could have injured Horth seriously if you'd connected with those blows. You wouldn't do that in your right mind... strike out in a manner that could have seriously injured him."

"Me?" Amel chuffed out a laugh. "Injure Liege Nersal?"

"What is happening to you during those episode?" Erien asked. "And please don't tell me it's only light-headedness."

"I—" Amel faltered. A wave of humiliation hit him. "You're right," he said in a flat voice. "I'm having clear dreams again, the kind I had after Lurol put me in a visitor probe the first time."

"Ah," said Erien. He figured he might as well get it all out in the open. "Just since *Kali Station*?"

Amel hesitated a bit too long. "No," he admitted. And followed up with a touch of belligerence, "I had one or two before, when things were getting bad, on Gelion."

There was an awkward silence in which the idiocy of Amel refusing to seek treatment boiled up in Erien. "Of course," he said, coolly relieving his feelings with sarcasm. "So why tell anyone? Why ask for help of the one person who would be grateful to give it to you? Why not just hope they will go away again, on their own?"

Amel's supple body grew more brittle with each word Erien said. His voice, as if to compensate, turned silky. "It is just as well Lurol never tried to make a doctor of you, Erien. Your bedside manner is ruinous."

"I do not like to watch needless suffering," Erien said.

"And I do not like experiencing it!" Amel shouted back.

"Perhaps not. But you seem to invite it."

Amel twitched, stung. Erien regretted the words at once, but perhaps they would drive Amel to honesty. "Are you aware of what Lurol did to you in the probe eighteen years ago?"

"Programmed me, you mean?" Even Amel's snort of contempt was delicate.

"Not programmed," Erien undercut the oversimplification. "Adjusted the equilibrium between existing character traits by strengthening one and not the other. She thinks she left you at permanent risk of putting others' interests before your own."

Amel fixed him with a flat, level stare. "And what do you think?" he challenged.

Erien felt off balance. He put his sound hand on the floor, reassured by its solidity. "D'Lekker," he said. "Even after what he did to you, you called out for someone to help him."

Amel's eyes opened wide, in shock and indignation. "So did you!"

"And Ev'rel," said Erien. "You forgave her the first time she—"

"You don't have the faintest idea what you're talking about!" Amel lashed back in anger.

"I know what Mira told me. Am I to believe that you chose, of your own free will, to endure such treatment?"

"What a righteous *infant* you are, Erien!"

Erien felt a pulse of anger and pushed it down.

"Ev'rel and D'Lekker nearly destroyed you," he told Amel starkly.

"That's my business."

"Not if what Lurol did to you eighteen years ago made it possible."

Amel reclaimed some of his good humor. "Eighteen years is one year longer than you've lived, Erien. Don't you think you and your Reetion mother should give me more credit for surviving without treatment in the interim?" He frowned. "I don't expect you to understand this, but I loved Ev'rel. There was a great deal to admire in her. She made the Avim's Oath what it is, created the Dem'Vrel, got the Vrellish and Demorans working together! You'll appreciate the difficulty of all that one day. And she had other dimensions." He nudged the notebook he'd been perusing. "As for the sex," he shrugged, "I thought your Reetion upbringing would have broadened your mind a little."

"It wasn't," Erien said in a low voice, "simply about sex, not from what Mira told me happened around the time I was born."

"Ah," Amel said, "being the stake in that dispute offends you."

"This is not about me."

Amel lay down again, ignoring him.

"It is about what you will allow to happen to you," said Erien.

"I did not *allow* it." Amel said. He rolled toward Erien suddenly, looking upset. "You should take a hard look at your own actions sometime, Erien." He glided into a sitting position, the better to tick off his points on his fingers. "On Gelion you challenged D'Lekker to protect Tatt. On *Kali Station*, you challenged Liege Bryllit to defend the Reetions. You pulled some suicidal maneuvers getting through the barrier so you could put yourself between the Nersallians and *Kali's* crew. And you did most of that with a wound you got rescuing me from Lilac Hearth." Amel arched a pencil-thin eyebrow. "Given the evidence, I think an objective observer would be hard pressed to decide which of us ran afoul of Lurol."

"I had good reasons," said Erien tightly.

"So did I," Amel said with finality. He settled his hands behind his head as he stretched out once more. "Di Mon used to say that being young and Vrellish was a greater hazard to survival than—"

"Don't talk about him!" Erien ordered, the vehemence of his reaction surprising him.

"Don't tell me I'm crazy!" Amel responded with a flash of anger. The strength of his feelings snapped him upright, but the demand that made of his damaged stomach muscles calmed him right down again. "I happen to *like* some things about me," he said with a sullen look. "Not all of them. But even my faults are mine. I don't want to be fixed like some malfunctioning experiment. Are you capable of understanding that?"

"I understand," Erien said, "that you reserve the right to have clear dreams at odd, inconvenient and dangerous moments."

Amel gathered his dignity, shaking off anger like water. "Erien, I've lived with this for eighteen years. I can manage one or two Reetion hearings without having my personality adjusted. After that — well, Perry's used to the clear dreams. But I think they'll go away again when I'm with her. Just don't let them put me in a probe again," Amel concluded in a flinty tone totally unnatural to him.

"You're not going to be subjected to intrusive procedures!" Erien grated. He stood up, off balance and clumsy, and saw the threatening ugliness of his mood in Amel's shrinking response. There was nowhere to go in a room filled with bed, desk and chair, and Amel's nest on the floor. He put his back against the door, holding his shoulder. "Stop treating me as if I'm your enemy!"

"I know you're not my enemy," Amel said softly.

"Of course I will not let the Reetions extract information from you with a visitor probe," Erien said angrily. "I am as committed as you are to keeping things injurious to people, back home, from the Reetions."

"I know," Amel said meekly. "I'm sorry."

There was no safe way to ask if Amel knew the secret Erien needed kept even more than what had happened in Lilac Hearth, but he could not shake the suspicion Amel meant to threaten him with the risk of disclosing the nature of Di Mon and Ranar's friendship if the Reetions transgressed again with their psychmedical technology.

"Don't be sorry," Erien snapped. "Be careful."

Amel's lips quirked in what was almost a smile. "And how do you suggest I do so?"

"You might try the word *no* occasionally," Erien said tartly.

Amel looked as though he wanted to say something cutting, but the dangerous sparkle in his gray eyes faded, unexpressed.

"I have just taken a look at the accumulated mail we have received," Erien became businesslike. "Over eighty percent of it is directed to you. The most important parts of it will have to be identified and responded to."

"No," said Amel. "I don't want to talk to Reetions."

"You don't have to answer all—"

"No." He looked up with a wry smile. "How am I doing so far?"

"What?" said Erien.

"Practicing 'no.'"

Erien frowned. "All right, I'll answer the mail. But you must prepare an account of what happened on *Kali Station* — for the record. You can make it text only if you wish." He stared Amel. "And Amel, stop treating Evert like he has a contagious illness." Amel looked up guiltily. "He is the last man to deserve that," Erien said.

Amel muttered something. Erien cradled his arm feeling resentful. Amel would be good at scanning mail and reassuring people.

"Erien?" It was Evert. He looked as if he had been waiting for him to come out.

What now? thought Erien.

"I just wanted to tell you, we've done what we could, but — whether because of what just happened or not, we've been asked, as your parents, to give consent for you to undergo biopsychometric monitoring during questioning — just monitoring, as we explained before, not the visitor probe. We have all registered our objections on the basis that is culturally inappropriate, of course, and your assent is still required."

"What about Amel?" Erien asked in a measured tone.

"Amel, too," said Evert. "And — ah, Liege Nersal."

Erien gave a short laugh. "You can consider Horth's refusal as good as on record."

"It's just to get around the lack of arbiter corroboration," Evert said apologetically. "The unmonitored debriefing with Space Service and FAC representatives is slated for tomorrow morning. Ranar predicts that they will be requesting the return of *Kali Station*."

"I can't do anything about *Kali Station*," said Erien.

"That was Ranar's opinion, as well," said Evert. "I also came up to tell you we've had an inspiration with regard to Liege Nersal's, uh, social requirements: the casual sex roster. Lurol is the only one of us who uses it, so we thought she could explain it to him. What do you think?"

The casual sex roster was the Reetion option for those who wanted it and understood that sex carried no obligation toward an emotional connection. "That... might work for Horth," said Erien, "as long as any woman who shows interest is given a... careful briefing first."

Evert looked decidedly qualmish. Erien could sympathize. "Amel can do that," he decided.

THIRTEEN

Eyes on Amel

Sexual Disorientation

When Erien's party left the next morning, Evert sat down at the kitchen table and let the tension drain from him. He had never imagined, when Ranar first explained what *gorarelpul* were, that he would find one of them his best ally in delivering breakfast to Heir Gelion, the Reetion ambassador to Gelion and a Gelack Highlord. All three were on their way to a public forum at which Rire would formally apologize for illegal rebels using anti-pilot tactics; this preliminary gesture would be the first step before demanding *Kali Station* back, and then being told to forget it by Horth Nersal.

Everyone knew that was how it was all going to play out, but it still had to be done.

Neither Erien nor Ranar seemed grateful that Evert had gotten up to see them off. When Evert tried to live up to the Nersallian liege's expectations of kitchen staff, it offended Ranar. When Erien tried to pitch in, he confused Horth Nersal. In the end Drasous had served them all. At least he knew what Horth would and would not eat.

Erien worried Evert most of all. He was wounded, and only seventeen years old. Surely someone else should be able to carry out Di Mon's master plan for peace between Sevildom and Rire.

Evert sighed and started getting up, when a faint catch of breath made him look toward the base of the stairs; he caught Amel in the act of trying to tiptoe past, wearing a loose pair of Erien's old sweat pants and nothing else but the marks of his fading welts and a clean dressing over his stomach wound.

"Why don't you come in?" Evert said to Amel. "There's left-over toast and the herb tea is warm."

"Uh, no," the Gelack paused, eyeing him suspiciously. "Thanks."

Evert was suddenly fed up. He hooked an arm over the back of his chair and relaxed. "I do find you beautiful," he told Amel, flat out.

"What?"

"But you don't need to worry. Quite apart from the nontrivial fact that as a Sevolite Pureblood — however normally gentle by disposition, you could rip my arms off if I made a pass — I am Ranar's lover... when he's home that is, and deigns to acknowledge the fact. Even if I was not in a relationship of any sort, I will have you know it is offensive to be tacitly accused of barbarity simply on the basis of my sexual orientation. You find women attractive?"

Amel nodded, taken aback.

"Would you assault an attractive woman?" asked Evert.

"No!"

"Then why assume that I would force my attentions on you?"

Amel's indignation slithered out in a lumpy sigh. "Listen, before I met Ranar I never knew there was such a thing as a homosexual man who wasn't what we call *sla* — 'perverted' I suppose you would say in Reetion."

"Oh," Evert said, trying to put that in context. It made him think, unwillingly, of how hard being homosexual must have been for Di Mon, the man who still claimed the larger piece of Ranar's heart and had chosen to die rather than live with the knowledge he was homosexual anymore. At least that was how Ranar understood Di Mon's motives. The wretched, haughty Sevolite had never even left a farewell note.

"There's something I have always wanted to ask you," Evert asked Amel.

"Yes?" Amel sounded reluctant, but he had caught the sharp edge of need in Evert's tone. He really was remarkably observant... and beautiful in a way that made you want to prove it wasn't an illusion. Had Di Mon felt that?

"Why did you take Erien from your mother as an infant?" Evert blurted. "Was it Di Mon's idea at the start? Part of a scheme to get him educated half on Monitum and half on Rire?"

Amel turned his attention toward the living room as if he hadn't heard. "I want to watch the *Kali* hearing," he said. "I think I might enjoy seeing Rire try to talk Horth Nersal out of a space station."

Evert leaned on the counter between the kitchen and the living room, watching Amel sitting cross-legged on the floor, absorbed in the *Kali* hearing. On stage, Erien was translating for Horth, who still refused to use an automated translator. Erien looked tired.

He shouldn't have to do this while he is recovering from a damned, stupid knife wound, Evert thought angrily.

The Reetions on stage looked strained, too. In fact, the only person as impassive as granite was Horth Nersal, who just kept saying, "No." No, he would not give *Kali Station* back. No, he would not let Fahzir's team on board to "murder" the eccentric *Kali* arbiter. Horth's use of the term murder in connection with an arbiter put the Foreign and Alien Council in a flurry trying to determine what had been misunderstood. Ranar finally convinced them they were unlikely to change Horth's mind with an explanation if he chose to view the arbiter as sentient.

Amel erupted in laughter on the heels of Horth's answers, shoulders shaking with hilarity as he tried not to stress his stomach muscles. Evert was glad someone was enjoying the show. As far as he was concerned they might as well not bother with translation in either direction for all the communication getting through.

Lurol came trudging down the stairs into the kitchen looking as if she was recovering from one of her infrequent, but whopping, hangovers. Amel watched her with involuntary concern for a moment, then made a point of turning his back on them.

Lurol plunked herself down at the kitchen table. "Are they gone?" she muttered, and looked up at Evert's face like an earthquake survivor hoping for the reassurance of still earth. "All of them?"

"All except Amel," said Evert. "That's them on stage at the hearing."

She alarmed him by gripping his hand across the table.

"Get me some coffee," she asked, "with lots of sugar."

"I made some for Ranar. I'll heat it up again."

Lurol stared ahead at nothing as Evert bustled around the kitchen again, her mouth fixed downward in a loose scowl. Evert set the coffee down and slipped into the seat beside her.

"What happened?" he asked in a low voice, trying not to sound too nervous.

"Erien's Liege Nersal happened," Lurol growled. "'Explain the casual sex roster to him,' you said." She snorted. "You couldn't explain 'good morning' to anything that Vrellish without a live demonstration."

Evert slumped further into his chair, "You didn't!"

Lurol shoved the coffee mug away from her. "This is too hot."

"I could put some cold water in it," Evert said numbly, but made no move to do so.

Lurol scrubbed her fingers through her short, stiff hair. "I told him I was 49 years old. He just said 'good.'" She frowned. "At least I think that's how you translate *Ack rel*."

"Horth Nersal?" Evert asked, with dawning horror. Surely the arbiter would have intervened if she had been attacked!

Unless, Evert thought, feeling more frantic about it by the second, she hadn't felt safe enough to risk resisting him... or, worse yet, was afraid of upsetting Erien's mission.

"Lurol," he said, laying a hand on her forearm supportively, "you don't mean — did he...?"

"Perhaps it was a translation problem," said Lurol, rubbing what Evert now realized was a bruise along one side of her jaw. Seeing it gave him a sick feeling in his stomach, and made him itch to ask the arbiter if anything had happened to pierce the privacy normally afforded a couple in a bedroom.

Lurol hunkered down, her sagging shoulders making her look like a wet, bony cat contemplating the task of licking itself back into some semblance of dignity. "Look," she said, her hands cupped possessively around her coffee, "just don't tell Erien."

"Don't be absurd!" Evert broke out. "Of course we have to tell Erien!"

"Don't you dare!" Lurol insisted.

"Lurol," Evert swallowed down a lump rising in his throat. "How could this happen!"

"Hmph," she said, giving him a scathing look. "I suppose the most aggression you've ever had to deal with is Ranar getting worked up over the declensions of a Gelack pronoun. How do you get him into bed, anyhow? Or have you, since he's been back?"

Evert was prepared to forgive her anything right now, but her casual cruelty skated too near a painful truth.

"Oh damn, I'm sorry!" Lurol fingered her tender jaw. "It's Ranar I'm cross with for being so standoffish, Evert, not you." She mused a moment as Evert tried to find his emotional balance.

"Horth won't tell anyone, I'm pretty sure," Lurol thought aloud. "He doesn't part with words unless they're surgically extracted."

Evert was about to ask her, flat out, if Horth Nersal had forced himself on her in some fashion, when Amel got up off the floor and came to join them.

"Listen," he said to Evert, "I'm sorry I was rude to you earlier." He made a plausible, but forced, attempt not to look skittish. "Ranar said you have some old princess logs on flimsies. I could use a distraction, if you want help deciphering them."

"Go on!" Lurol urged Evert, when he hesitated. "I'm all right. I'm not a child!"

Baffled, Evert followed Amel up the stairs. "The flimsies Ranar brought are in here," he told Amel, pushing open his study door. Like all Reetions, Evert did most of his work through a stage that tapped into the omnipresent record, but there were also displays of artifacts hung up on the walls and a replica of an intricately patterned Gelack rug underfoot.

Evert pulled out the flimsies, which were sheets of thin, translucent plastic, and spread them out for Amel to peruse.

"This is a princess log, all right," Amel confirmed. "From six hundred years ago, on Demora. It is written in a very ornate puzzle form. The surface poem is easy to decipher once you know which play was in vogue at the time. Scholars date selections by the literary calendar. Then the surface poem, which is the real work of art, becomes the poetic key to reading the rather boring details in the log itself. This one probably says something like 'so and so married such and such for love' — Demorans always claim it is for love — 'and in consideration of his father's fleet and rich lands.'"

"Why ever would the Demorans keep records like those in such an obscure form?" Evert asked.

"It was something of a formality," Amel admitted, "since Demish highborns can remember things like marriages and contracts for a long, long time. The real reason it is so baroque, though, is because the scribes were widowed or unmarried Demoran princesses who didn't have much else to do." Amel fingered one of the flimsies with a wistful smile. "I wish I could have let them know future generations would find their little secrets in the margins and know that they were so much more than they could ever show." He smiled with a self-conscious flicker of embarrassment. "Let me recite you one."

Amel proceeded to captivate Evert with a soulful rendering of an achingly beautiful, delicate poem, about a keen mind that bloomed and faded in an empty room. Evert didn't understand all the nuances of the Demoran dialect involved, but was loath to interrupt a performance that so sweetly brought the long-dead woman back to life. Evert had quite forgotten Lurol by the time Amel was done.

"So beautiful," Evert said, awestruck, "and so sad."

They shared a companionable moment together during which Evert began worrying about Lurol once more. He could see her out the window at Amel's back, pacing back and forth on the lawn.

"I'm sorry we're making things difficult between you and Ranar by being here," Amel broke the silence.

"Oh," said Evert, "you noticed."

Amel shrugged.

"It isn't just you, or Horth Nersal either," Evert assured him, "it's Di—" He stopped himself, shocked at what he had been about to divulge.

Amel's eyes flicked up, their gray depths compassionate. "It's all right, Evert," he said kindly. "I know."

"W-what?"

"Let's not put it in words, STI two or not," said Amel, "then there's no harm done."

Evert had to sit down. He was awash in tides of mortification at his slip-up. "I'm not cut out for this life and death stuff!" he appealed to Amel, like a drowning man, his head in his hands. "I don't know why I ever thought I could cope with Ranar and his Gelacks!"

"Are we Ranar's Gelacks? I didn't know." Amel said it so mildly Evert couldn't guess if he'd offended until he looked up to receive Amel's smile of forgiving amusement.

"Does Erien know that you know?" Evert asked.

Amel shrugged noncommittally. "Hard to tell. He's never asked me and I've never let on. So there's no way either of us can be sure, unless the other slips up."

"Like I did?" Evert said, dejected.

"I slipped up myself, once," Amel confessed.

"You did?" Evert wasn't sure if he was comforted or worried to learn Amel was just as fallible as he was. "With who?"

"Di Mon himself," Amel smiled a thin edged smile. "He suspected I knew and tricked me into revealing it. I was afraid of him, you know, and I must confess I never liked him very much. He was a great man, but he hurt people I cared about."

Sharing the deepest secret of Ranar's life with Amel inclined
Evert toward a sense of intimacy with the gentle Sevolite, and
the sight of Erien, Horth and Drasous through the window, on
the way back to the house, left him badly in need of clarification
about what had happened to Lurol.

"There's something else I have to ask about," Evert said
quickly. "Concerning — Nersallian habits."

Lurol burst into the room just as Amel's forehead began to
wrinkle in puzzlement.

"Life!" she exclaimed. "Horth's coming back! What do I do
now?"

"We won't let him hurt you again!" Evert promised with a
sudden surge of protectiveness.

"Hurt her?" Amel exclaimed. "Did Liege Nersal attack you?"
he asked Lurol in a masterfully neutral tone.

Lurol sat down like a bag of rocks. "Not exactly!" she exclaimed, looking ruffled. "At least, not entirely unprovoked.
I'll admit to a lewd thought or two. He is damned attractive
in his own nasty way," she added with a sharp look in Evert's
direction, "in case you haven't noticed."

"Did you do anything to express the... thoughts?" Amel
asked.

"I — well," Lurol faltered. "Yes. I, uh... sort of... gave him
a friendly... pat."

"That's no excuse!" cried Evert, getting worked up.

"No," Amel stood, looking serious, "it wouldn't be, except
your housemate here just doesn't feel, to me, like someone who's
been hurt in the way you suppose, Evert. She sounds more like
a proud woman who's mortally embarrassed about indulging
herself."

"Believe me, I hurt!" muttered Lurol.

Amel smiled. "I've worked with my share of sexually frustrated Vrellish highborns," he told her nonchalantly, "so believe
me, I am sure you do."

Lurol narrowed her eyes at him: "You're enjoying this."

"Yes, but not as much as Horth." He wiped the smile off as
abruptly as it had flashed to the fore. "I am sorry," he assured
her. "You are right. I should not laugh. The point is, Doctor Lurol,
did you enjoy yourself, or not?"

"He scared me!" she asserted, chin thrust out.

Amel nodded. "He's a frightening person."

Evert could not stand this. Erien and Horth Nersal could be
back in the house by now! How could Amel be so matter-of-
fact? "But he struck her!" he asserted.

Lurol's hand flew to her face. "Oh, that." She shifted in her chair. "I thought he had passed out, you know, afterwards, so I — it was only a portable med-scanner, but I suppose he might have thought it was some dire Lorel instrument or other. He knocked my hand away and I whacked myself in the jaw with the med-scanner. Then he just... left. I don't know if he's pleased, mad, satisfied or murderous — life! I lay in bed all night trying to convince myself none of it happened!"

"If Horth was seriously angry about the med-scanner," Amel assured her, "we'd have known about it by now because of all the first responders who would have showed up to deal with your corpse. And I wouldn't worry about him passing out. From what Perry tells me about Horth, momentary loss of consciousness, at climax, is quite normal for him. It's his heart. He can pull harder G's in combat than any other highborn I know of, which means his heart is overpowered for other forms of excitement." He smiled. "If Horth knocked the scanner out of your hands, it was probably from embarrassment at graying out. Does that help?"

Lurol let out a breath in a heavy huff, "Yes, yes, it does. And I'm sorry, Evert. I really did not mean to create this — complication."

"So you weren't forced?" Amel double-checked.

"Let me put it this way," Lurol told him sourly, "I'd have gotten around to yes if he had given me the chance to talk!"

"You're a brave woman," Amel told her gamely.

Evert's ears were beginning to feel very warm.

"I think I'll go get dressed before checking in with Erien," Amel said, noticing he was still dressed in nothing but Erien's old sweat pants. "I want to find out whether he and Ranar have agreed to surrender me for downloading and vivisection so you Reetions can get absolutely all my impressions of the *Kali Station* fiasco."

"He may be pathologically nice at the core," Lurol grumbled when Amel was gone, "but he's developed a nasty streak of black humor."

"Are you really all right?" Evert wondered aloud once more.

"Yes! Yes, I'm fine, only please — don't tell Erien! He'll never trust me to do another simple job with his precious Gelacks."

Evert sucked his lower lip as he studied Lurol. "Are you going to do it again?" he asked eventually.

"I'm thinking about it," she grumbled.

FOURTEEN

Erien

Psychological Campaigns

When the triumvirate of women arrived on the fourth day, Erien was sitting on a deck chair on the porch in the early morning sunshine, his bare feet up on a stool, a portable stage on his lap and a breakfast of apple pancakes and orange juice on a table beside him. He had seen Horth off for a long run, escorted by one of Ranar's students, and Amel was hiding in his room again, avoiding mail, which was all the more annoying because two-thirds of it was still for him.

The three women came striding across the commons grass, arguing now and then with Fahzir, who was dogging their heels. One of the women was Glynda, from the Ethics Council. The other two Erien did not recognize.

Fahzir broke ahead just before they reached Erien's deck chair. "What do your Nersallians mean to do with our eccentric arbiter?" he greeted Erien.

A gaudily dressed woman with a resonant alto voice went on the attack. "Fahzir, you are not a member of this triumvirate, so be careful or I'll file a complaint." She smiled at Erien. "You probably don't remember me, do you?"

The voice reminded him of someone who looked quite different: a chubbier, confrontational student who had lodged a stream of complaints against Lurol, as an instructor, during her advanced training in the psychometric sciences.

"Josune?" Erien hazarded. Round-faced before, her dark skin was now taut over pronounced cheekbones; the drab overalls he remembered had been replaced by a sleek, belted chlamys in golden yellow.

"Cosmetic restructuring," Josune explained with a smirk. "May we sit down? Fahzir will not be staying." She delivered this to the scientist-pilot in a pointed way. "He will get his answers this afternoon when you testify under psych monitoring. This visit is for Amel's sake."

In defiance of Josune's threat, Fahzir pulled up a second chair and sat down.

The third woman introduced herself as Yasmin. She was younger than both Glynda and Josune, with an appealing oval face and tawny eyes. She remained standing, dressed in a simple cream-colored tunic and trousers, with a wide-eyed air of excited expectancy about her.

Erien rotated his display toward them. "If there is a message here telling me to expect you, I haven't reached it yet," he told the women.

Fahzir ignored everyone but Erien. "*Kali* is getting more eccentric by the day," he informed Erien. "I've received word, via a pilot in the area who picked up a radio transmission from Vic on *Kali Station*, that Vic claims *Kali* has offered its *oath* to Tash Bryllit, as a Gelack vassal!"

Erien choked on his juice.

Glynda rolled her eyes. "It hasn't been confirmed, Fahzir!"

"Did Bryllit accept?" Erien asked.

"Apparently," Fahzir said sharply.

Erien felt like he was looking down a kaleidoscope. An arbiter swore to Tash Bryllit of Nersal! And she had accepted! He supposed the Reetions were more shocked by the first part. He was truly amazed by the second, unless...

"Was the arbiter demonstrating command of station functions again?" asked Erien.

"Probably," said Fahzir.

"Bryllit treated the arbiter like a surrendering station liege," explained Erien. It made a kooky kind of sense, although it was still a stretch for him to imagine Tash Bryllit accepting an artificial intelligence as a vassal.

"It is utterly unacceptable for the *Kali* arbiter to remain active!" Fahzir insisted. "Eccentric arbiters are dangerously unpredictable, and if they make contact with the net they can be a threat to the stability of other arbiters."

"I did everything I could to make sure the arbiter went down before we left," Erien assured him.

"You also destroyed crucial data when you vandalized the visitor probe!" Fahzir said hotly.

"Your concerns will be covered at the hearing, Fahzir," Josune said, with scant patience. "Now leave, or I'll cite you for interfering with a duly commissioned investigative triumvirate."

Fahzir gave Erien a threatening glare. "I'll see you this afternoon," he said, and stomped away.

Erien had another bite of his breakfast. He was not going to let them spoil the first meal he'd had the appetite to appreciate since leaving Gelion.

"Should we give you a minute to review our commission for this visit?" Glynda asked with a nod at the display of his work load.

Erien rotated the display back toward himself and called up the document. "You're here for Ethics, again," he said to Glynda, "Josune represents the research lobby, and Yasmin—"

"Citizens' Health and Well Being," Yasmin spoke up, smiling. "We each have our own particular reasons to meet informally with Amel. Glynda needs to be reassured he is not feeling any duress from you—"

"Yasmin!" Glynda protested. "I wouldn't put it quite like that, Erien," she apologized.

"I want to enlist his help with important work here on Rire," Yasmin said brightly, "and Josune—"

"I represent researchers interested in Sevolite psychometrics," said Josune.

"Ah," said Erien. Belatedly, he recalled Lurol muttering darkly about Josune winning an appointment she did not approve of, but he'd been too preoccupied with filtering and prioritizing a whole planet's worth of information to pay attention to the person at his elbow.

Erien got up, setting aside the stage on his lap. "I'll go get Amel out of bed," he told them.

The all-female triumvirate followed inside where he got them settled in the living room before he went upstairs.

Window screens deepened the interior of the bedroom he shared with his celebrity half brother to a dark indigo. The quilt-wrapped lump of Amel stirred sleepily and murmured, "What is it?"

"Reetions," Erien said. "Specifically, a triumvirate constituted to enquire into your well-being."

Amel fell back. "Tell them I'm fine, thanks. What time is it?"

"Early," he said. "I think they wanted to come while Horth was out running."

Amel snorted. "Can't blame them." There was a small pause. "Do I *have* to talk to them?"

The put-upon tone in Amel's voice was irritating. "You have enough political acumen to handle this," Erien told him. "They're all women, which I suspect was deliberate. Pretend they're Demish. Charm them!"

Amel sat up looking peeved and rumpled.

"You're starting to sound like Ameron," he complained with a dash of sulk about it, brushing back silky black hair intent on slumping across his eyes again. "Why don't *you* charm them? You know Reetions better."

Because, thought Erien, *if there is any charm in my makeup, it is strictly recessive.*

He said, "Stage on," and a space station icon flared into being in the corner of the room — a legacy of him being fourteen and space-science mad when he last set his default display. "Please make available the commission of the visiting triumvirate," Erien instructed the stage and left Amel to it.

Downstairs Erien found Evert, in his dressing gown, dispensing lemonade. He took a glass himself and settled onto the couch with his portable stage, determined to let Amel handle this solo.

Minutes later, Amel appeared on the landing hastily dressed in a simple gray sweat suit, and barefoot. He swept a hand through unbrushed hair before padding down the stairs to help himself to lemonade.

"Thanks," he told Evert, with a touch of unaffected warmth. He settled into the morph chair left vacant for him, took a couple swallows of lemonade and set down the glass. Then he pulled up his legs and crossed them to get comfortable, looking and acting much more like a loose-limbed teenager than a Pureblood Demish prince in his thirties.

"I've read the summary of your commission," Amel greeted the women in his flawless Reetion. "Glynda's people want to know if I'm acting under duress from the Gelack government." He tossed his hair back again and it stayed this time. "I came to Rire of my own free will," he assured her.

"The duress we are concerned about," Glynda explained with a pained expression, "is any you might be suffering in this house." She looked apologetically at Erien.

"I've no complaints," Amel said in a bland tone.

Josune leaned forward. "Are you certain? I realize anything as blatant as an attack by Horth Nersal, of the sort we witnessed a few days ago..."

Erien stifled the impulse to object to that interpretation.

"...would pierce STI two and be revealed, for your protection," finished Josune. "But there are other, subtle means of pressuring someone as sensitive as you are, dear Amel."

"Mmm," said Amel, with a mock-thoughtful expression. "Evert's tried to get me to eat more than I wanted at a few meals. That's pretty much the worst of it, so far. But if you don't mind, I would prefer if you didn't call me 'dear.'"

"Of course!" Yasmin nodded. "Too many people who profess to care about you take liberties." She sounded accusatory.

"Has Lurol been bothering you, Amel?" Josune asked bluntly.

"Lurol? No," Amel said mildly, and smiled at them. "You're all dressed to make me feel at home, aren't you? Long skirts, bits of embroidery, no repeating patterns. I just noticed."

Yasmin chuckled, "See, I told you he would notice what we wore."

"Of course," he said, sounding prickly now. "Since you all know me better than I know myself, based on my teenage psych profile — which was acquired under duress, I might add."

Charm, Amel, charm, thought Erien.

Josune looked so sympathetic Erien was afraid she was going to take Amel into her arms and cuddle him. "You are perfectly entitled to resent what Lurol did to you on *Second Contact Station,*" she told him. "In fact, it is a good sign if you can!"

Glynda leaned forward with her hands clasped between her knees, looking motherly. "You have no idea how much some of us have worried about you, loose in a hostile universe, with a self-preservation handicap like the one Lurol imposed on you," she told Amel with such touching sincerity he couldn't sustain his resentful look past the first few words.

"Especially knowing how you're sexually attracted to aggressive Vrellish women!" put in Josune, spoiling the mood.

Amel reacted with a light, mercurial laugh. "If you mean to tell me I don't lust after gentle Demish women, then your psych profiling is out of whack," Amel refuted her analysis of his sexuality, raising the fine hairs on the back of Erien's neck for reasons he could not quite put a finger on, although he suspected they had something to do with an image of the young Princess Luthan projected on a stage back on *Kali Station.*

"But of course!" Josune assured him. "We're all aware you have a profound appreciation for aesthetics of all kind, and a beautiful woman, aggressive or not, would inspire your appreciation. One of the nicest things about you, dear, is your ability to see beauty in so many forms."

"Don't—" Amel began, and gave up with a sigh. "Never mind." He turned to Yasmin. "What, exactly, did you want to see me for? The commission says things about engaging my assistance in community service activities, but I didn't see anything specific mentioned."

"Thank you for asking," said Yasmin, and paused to take a deep breath. "Extremists like Ann have caused a lot of social damage trying to excite alarm about Sevolite invasions, particularly among young people susceptible to the drama of settling quarrels with duels and fighting space battles. I am talking, of course, about the so-called Gelack cultists who capitalize on social anxiety by aping aggressive Vrellish behaviors, in particular, as a way to avoid their own inadequacies. We thought you might have a positive influence, if you were willing to work with us."

"Me?" Amel was taken aback.

"You are very popular," she pointed out to him emphatically.

"People trust you and like you," Glynda qualified, reacting to Amel's look of alarm, "because you are as beautiful inside as you are out."

"As a very human face to an inhuman and threatening phenomenon—" Yasmin began expanding, and was interrupted by two new arrivals.

Lurol tromped down the stairs, noisily, lashing her dressing gown closed. Ranar padded after her looking less conspicuous.

"How is it," Lurol hurled at Yasmin, as soon as she had line of sight, "that you can call Sevolites an 'inhuman and threatening phenomenon' and simultaneously insist Ann was wrong to stir us up about them? Surely it is one or the other!"

"Lurol," Josune said firmly, "this is not the time—"

"You," she told her ex-student and professional rival, stabbing a bony finger at her, "are not welcome in my house. I won't have you upsetting Amel with your extrapolation theories about Vrellish nature based on his sexual psych profile!"

Amel's reaction made it clear to Erien his self-indulgent half-brother had not been keeping up with the digests he'd been queuing for him.

"My... what?" Amel asked, making a face.

"We don't have sufficient data on Vrellish Sevolites," Josune told Amel briskly, to cover the embarrassment of explaining it to his face, "so I extrapolated from what I believe is most Vrellish in your psych profile, as the only really thorough data set available for highborns."

Amel held the floor with a strange moral authority, quietly upset. "I don't understand," he said.

Lurol watched Josune squirm as she spoke. "Your sex drive is more vigorous than the Reetion norm," she told Amel, "so if it's Vrellish, then presumably Vrellish aggression — in someone like Horth Nersal, for instance — would be equally exaggerated."

"You must never," Amel told them both, clearly and firmly, "put Liege Nersal—" He lost color as he spoke. "— in a visitor probe."

For a giddy moment the roles of sage protectors and naïve innocent reversed, even for the triumvirate. They could tell he was advising them, and in the strongest terms. Then Amel suffered a mild clear dream. He must have felt it coming on because he covered it up with a needless cough, his head bowed as though the conversation had proved too much. Amel twitched once, but the argument between Lurol and Josune distracted attention from him.

"We would have better data on the Vrellish," Josune attacked Lurol, "if you hadn't helped Ranar hide Erien's true nature!"

"We didn't hide Erien!" Lurol exclaimed, in high dudgeon. "He played outside, rode public transit, played in concerts, studied—"

"And was treated exclusively by you, medically!" Josune shouted. "Which you couldn't have reported properly, or we would have known he was a highborn!"

"Lurol is Erien's mother, Josune," Glynda intervened, before Lurol could respond. "What was she supposed to do, subject him to a whole planet's scrutiny?"

"Be quiet!" Ranar snapped. He had been so quiet since coming in with Lurol that Erien had lost track of him. Now he saw Ranar had been watching something on the kitchen stage. Ranar came into the living room as the big central stage came on.

"Fahzir is out to corner Liege Nersal on the grounds!" warned Ranar. "This could be very bad."

On stage, Horth stood with his back to the duck pond at the center of the commons, watching Fahzir cross the grass toward him. Horth's pale skin wore a sheen of perspiration, but his breathing was easy. Erien was mildly surprised to see he was wearing one of Lurol's purple, unisex tank tops over his fleet slacks. Erien could not quite believe Horth would have raided Lurol's closet, but could think of no likely scenario in which Lurol would have given him the tank top.

Ranar's student, an athletic young man named Allan, stood beside Horth, breathing hard.

"What does *he* want?" Horth asked his chaperone, down-speaking Fahzir by the five ranks to which he was entitled in Gelack.

"I do not know, Liege Nersal." Allan paused to catch his breath and swallow. "Maybe we should get back."

But it was already too late. Fahzir had jogged up to them and stopped, looking belligerent. "Ask him if he knows about his vassal, Bryllit, accepting the oath of our eccentric arbiter!" Fahzir ordered Allan. "And don't simper!"

Ranar's student bridled. "I am *not* simpering," he answered in Reetion. "I am behaving in a culturally appropriate manner."

Fahzir tossed his short dark hair, eyes kindling with a pilot's willfulness. "That's Ranar's line. Play dead and roll over."

"That's a gross misrepresentation of—"

Allan was checked by Horth's grasp on his arm. "Translate," Horth ordered.

"He... he wants, to know about the *Kali* arbiter," Allan stammered in Gelack, looking at Horth now, with the respect of a meteorologist caught in his first bad storm.

Watching from back in the living room, Erien said, "I had better go—"

"No." Ranar was tense himself, but his conviction was solid. "If you cannot trust any Gelack but yourself to deal with Rire, I need to know it now."

Erien opened his mouth, then closed it.

A challenge worthy of Ameron, he thought, respect for his foster father mixing with unrelieved alarm.

"Ranar claims you aggress against us only when provoked," Fahzir said. "Our anthropologists and bioscientists claim Vrellish Sevolites, like you, are strong only in ways underpinned by instinct, and predictably stereotypical in your behaviors. That wasn't my impression of your strategy on *Kali Station*. Did you plan, with Erien, to keep the arbiter up? Are you planning to keep it now, as a military strategy?"

"No," Horth answered.

"I think he means, no, he didn't plan to keep the arbiter up," Allan elaborated. "Or, no, he isn't planning to exploit it." He hesitated. "Maybe you should ask one question at a time?" Allan suggested.

Fahzir looked cross. In a clipped voice, he said, "All right. Did the Nersallians take *Kali* with the intent to subvert an arbiter?"

"No," said Horth, and then added, "to honor the Waiting Dead."

"What does he mean by that?" Fahzir demanded.

"Generally speaking," explained Allan, "to punish people who use space-fouling tactics in war, or any other *okal'a'ni* method of aggression."

Horth picked up on the word *okal'a'ni* and added, "The *okal'a'ni* are a plague. Let them live, and all space will be bloodied, all flesh corrupted."

"He learned that by rote," Ranar muttered. "It's a Nesak mantra."

"Why did you follow us here to Rire?" Fahzir demanded.

Horth shrugged, and said simply but cryptically, "Honor."

The Reetion pilot clenched his fists. "I want to believe in your honor. You stopped Bryllit throwing people out of airlocks on *Kali*. Was that honor?"

"Erien challenged Bryllit," Horth explained. "I did not want her to kill him."

"So without Erien, you would have let Bryllit do it? Even helped her?" pressed Fahzir.

"Yes," Horth answered simply.

"Even though your own son needed the medical attention of one of the implicated persons?"

Allan took a while to translate the reference to Dorn Nersal's condition. Horth was equally careful in his answer. "Ask the House of Lorel how the *kinf'stan* answer blackmail," he told Allan, "if you know how to speak with ghosts."

"I believe that's a threat," Allan added after translating Horth's statement literally. "I really wouldn't pursue the idea of Dorn's condition giving us leverage, Fahzir. And I don't think you understand about the business between Bryllit and Erien. Sevolites decide things according to whether the disputants are prepared to risk their own lives. People back down far more often than not because they aren't sufficiently motivated, but if someone cares enough to risk his life, it gets attention. That's why Erien could stop Bryllit by putting himself at risk of being killed by her." He shook his head. "It isn't just about fighting with swords. It is a complex social method of self-regulation among a passionate, nonverbal people who value dignity above survival and desperately need a means of keeping revenge killing in check. Killing someone in an up-front, declared duel is not considered murder."

Fahzir listened to the lecture with a scowl. "Look, I don't care about the swords. Can't you anthropology types get that through your thick heads? That man," he pointed at Horth, "is the reality-skimming equivalent of a twentieth-century nuclear bomb!"

"And the key to understanding how to deal with such a bomb," Allan argued, "isn't by running around it hitting it with sticks to see what sets it off!"

"Maybe Ann's right." Fahzir muttered, "Maybe we have all been mad not to be thinking in military terms from the start."

Allan expelled a blast of a sigh. "Oh, gods!"

Fahzir reacted as if stung. "That's a Gelack expression!"

"What does it matter?" Allan said angrily. "It's only right we influence one another!"

"Tell it to the parents of the children running around in embroidered vests and taking fencing lessons!" Fahzir summed up in a parting shot.

Yasmin shook her head. "Fahzir is right," she said to Ranar. "However you look at it, sword law is, fundamentally, a system that condones murder."

Glynda got stubborn. "And who is to say, Yasmin, that isn't right for Gelacks?"

"What if their system required Amel to stand trial, by the sword, for helping Ann defend us?" Yasmin said.

"On Gelion a challenge is always possible, but Amel is not without friends and allies to champion him," Erien spoke up.

Even as he said it, Erien realized Amel would be more likely to face a tortured end on Ava's Square in disgrace than an honorable challenge, whether or not whoever presided as the Judge of Honor permitted him to be championed. Glynda's pained look suggested she was about to raise the issue, when Horth and Allan reclaimed everyone's attention.

They had shaken off Fahzir, but Allan seemed to have fallen prey to academic curiosity on the way back, and was questioning Horth as they walked. "But do you think an arbiter is worthy to be sworn?"

Horth shrugged. "*Kali* swore to Bryllit," he said. "Not me."

"A decision that makes you liege to an arbiter!" Allan objected.

Horth shrugged. He lifted his head a little, facing into the mild breeze, eyes narrowed, and gazed at the very house from which he was being watched on a stage in the living room.

"Do you hold anything sacred, Reetion?" he asked Allan.

"I am not sure what you mean," said Ranar's student.

"An oath," he said, "is an oath." Then he said, "Explain the 'casual sex roster,'" mangling the Reetion phrase badly.

"P-pardon?" the anthropologist floundered.

"I think Allan needs rescuing," Evert suggested.

"Is it a way to meet *sha'stan*, or something distasteful?" Horth asked Allan.

"I'll go," Amel said, already in the frame of the sliding door. He met Erien's surprised glance with a grim little frown of reassurance.

Perhaps Amel's right, thought Erien. *What better way to convince their Reetion audience he was not being intimidated by Horth.*

As soon as Amel appeared on public stages by stepping outside the house, a few neighbors began to trickle onto the commons, as if he neutralized their wariness of Horth Nersal. Amel padded across the lawn in his bare feet and Erien's gray sweat suit, with the breeze in his hair, looking stylishly lovable.

Our mail, Erien thought gloomily, *will soar.*

Horth had just asked Allan whether Reetion *sha'stan* were expected to sleep together after sex.

"Uh, well, I expect it depends on the person," Allan floundered.

Amel greeted Allan's look of gratitude with an affable expression. "Would it be on record whether Lurol's causal sex partners typically stayed the night?" he suggested.

"Oh dear," said Evert. "She's not going to like this." But his distress twitched toward a smile. "Do you suppose," he said, "we're witnessing Amel's idea of revenge on Lurol?"

"Lurol has instruments of her science in her room," Horth told Amel, not with fear, but a daredevil's wariness of danger. "I don't want to sleep there."

Lurol barged onto the porch with such gusto Horth took a step back instinctively, calmly prepared for the prospect of being assaulted by a woman he — apparently! — was sleeping with, much to Erien's consternation.

"I would not try to study you without your consent!" Lurol declared forcefully, nudging Allan fiercely. "Translate for me."

Horth's mouth slit into its characteristic wolf's grin. "You would study me if you could," he stated when Allan had finished.

"Yes," Lurol said, forthright, "but only with your permission."

"Lorel," Horth said with an adversarial growl, followed swiftly with, "tell her I disabled the instruments, but think I can fix them if she is angry."

He stripped off Lurol's purple tank top and tossed it to her with a friendly nod of acknowledgments for the loan, before heading up the stairs to shower. Lurol tramped inside to face the astonished triumvirate and Erien's closed expression.

"Look, it was his idea," she refuted whatever she thought might be Erien's unspoken criticisms. "And he's not an easy person to discuss the niceties with." She kept hold of her tank top, damp with Horth's sweat.

Josune, who was gaping quite openly, said, "You slept with *him*?"

Lurol went on the attack. "What's the matter? Didn't your Vrellish sexuality research prepare you for a Vrellish man finding mean and smart more appealing than fake and made over?"

"Law and reason!" Yasmin exclaimed. "Will you two be civilized?"

Amel slipped back inside and Lurol turned on him. "Are you trying to prove you can be nasty if you want to, or did you just want to show me how it feels for my love life to get planetary exposure?"

Amel colored delicately.

"Thank you!" Lurol shouted at him. "Well done! In fact, if you put me up against a wall and give me twenty lashes, I would feel much better! I have regretted what I did to you every day of my life since it happened!" She turned away from the melting remorse her outburst inspired in Amel and hurried up the stairs.

The triumvirate closed in to comfort Amel, who pulled himself together enough to remember he was supposed to be charming and reassuring them. "Let's sit somewhere outside," he said. "I could use the air."

Erien returned to the stage to watch the normal STI three of the commons spike to STI five as Amel appeared. Evert joined him to watch in silence as Amel hashed through every ques-

tion the Reetions had, without divulging any additional information, but managing to make it feel like an intimate heart to
heart.

"You knew about Lurol and Horth?" Ranar accused Evert,
joining them.

"Uh, well," Evert began, and broke off.

"I should have anticipated this would happen," Ranar said.
"Lurol's a powerful figure to Gelacks, if somewhat sinister, and
risk isn't likely to deter Horth Nersal. Erien also made a point
of stressing she was his kin and that would make her the natural
person to establish a sex-bond with, from a Vrellish standpoint."

"I don't believe it!" Evert said crossly to Ranar. "Lurol is
sleeping with Horth Nersal, and you are treating it like a study
in cross-cultural analysis!" He pursed his lips, making his mind
up about something. "Are you coming to bed tonight, by the
way, my love?" he asked Ranar pointedly, putting a hand on
his arm.

Ranar started.

"There are no Gelacks in the room," Evert told him sadly,
"or are you counting Erien, now?"

"Can't we put this off until the crisis is over?" Ranar asked,
sounding stressed. Evert withdrew his hand silently.

Amel went on glibly for a half an hour, demonstrating that
he knew exactly what Erien did and did not consider suitable
to go on record. He also talked about Ann, trying to vindicate
her.

No doubt he expects her to be listening, thought Erien, disin-
clined to feel sympathetic toward Ann for being Supervised and
denied direct contact with Amel.

"I'm going to go check the political forums to see what effect
this is having," Ranar told Erien. "Probably nothing substantive,
but it may tone down the broad-based lobbies focused on Amel's
welfare."

Erien waited until Amel pleaded weariness, shed his three
guardian angels with fond farewells and came back into the
living room.

"Reetions really are good people, in ones and twos and
threes," Amel told Erien. "Even Josune is all right, if you don't
take her theories seriously. Maybe I am being irrational to be
so afraid of them." He smiled ruefully and went up the stairs
with a spring in his step, headed back to his bolt-hole.

Ranar rejoined Erien with figures to share about the
triumvirate's interlude. Voting council positions were un-

changed, but less encumbered now by lobbies from interest groups. Amel's sheer popularity, measured in accesses and content produced, had actually declined slightly — as if the average citizen was sated — although just as Erien had feared, the volume of mail to Amel had increased.

"There are also lots of offers for Horth on the casual sex roster," Ranar observed with a frown.

Erien had the lingering, uncomfortable sense he had asked a lot of Amel and been well served — largely with dissembling, but he was beginning to see why Amel could not do even that without exercising genuine emotion. The affection shown toward the women had been as genuine as his moments of resentment toward them.

When Erien went to check on Amel, he found his half-brother deeply asleep under his rumpled quilts, the gray sweat suit in a heap beside him.

Erien shook his head and closed the door as Drasous poked his head out of Lurol's workroom. "I'll join you in a moment," Erien said, and went back downstairs.

Evert was cooking more pancakes in the kitchen. Erien's stomach rumbled in approval as he went past to join Ranar in front of the living room stage.

"I need to talk to you," said Erien, low enough that Evert could not overhear, "in private."

Ranar nodded, "In my study then." The two of them went back upstairs. Inside the study, Ranar turned and waited.

Erien took a deep breath. "You insist that I let Rire see Horth as he is, and you've twice held me back from intervening in his encounters with Reetions. That's a risky path, but I can see the purpose in it. Why, then, won't you do likewise?"

"How so?" Ranar asked, mildly startled.

"Evert," said Erien, "you're hurting Evert, whom we both love, because I didn't have the gumption to introduce him as your *mekan'st* when we first arrived. And there is a principle involved here. If Rire is going to know Gelion, warts and all, Gelion deserves to know Rire."

Ranar picked up an object from his desk top and stood looking at it, held in the smooth, soft fingers of his light brown hand. The object was a buckle from a horse's tack with the Monatese sextant on it: one of the things Ranar had kept of Di Mon's. There were a half dozen such items about the house, things Evert never moved, and never talked about.

"You realize," Ranar said in an aloof tone, as he put the buckle down, "that you have just characterized same-sex relationships as a wart?"

Erien folded a leg beneath him and sat down on the floor, back against the door. He reached half-consciously to rub the turquoise-inlaid hilt of the boot-knife, given to him by Di Mon the last time he had seen him. "Ranar," he said, "I apologize if I've given offense. My frames of reference lately have become so many that I'm losing track." He rubbed his face. "You and Evert are my parents; there's nothing in your relationship that troubles or offends me. But from the Gelack frame of reference, same-sex relationships are a wart, the same as Sword Law is a wart from the Reetion frame of reference. You've made sure Gelacks cannot hide what they are. Why are you hiding what *you* are? You didn't shrink from it while you were on Gelion, when it was far more dangerous to you."

"No," Ranar conceded. He rubbed his temples. "You're right, of course."

Erien rested his head back. "I would move us out to make things easier, if I wasn't sure public interest would force complete transparency on us. I'm not sure Horth could accept that. He's already dismantled sensors in the house twice, causing us no end of trouble with the first responders who keep showing up. I think he only stopped doing it when he realized they always come. And Amel might go over the edge if he's too exposed. The attention he's receiving is unnerving him, even when it stops at these walls. Though I don't think I could manage that any better, myself," he admitted, after a pause.

"I do not want you to leave this house," Ranar said forcefully. "It is your home, and this is my *rel*, too." The Gelack word seemed to give him strength. "The *rel* Di Mon bequeathed to both of us. It is what I have left of him, Erien. Perhaps..." he looked around the little den, "...my problem with Evert is not just about Horth. Perhaps I feel Di Mon's presence too much with a *gorarelpul* and a Fountain Court liege under my roof. He never came here himself, you know." Ranar seemed bewildered by the realization this mattered to him, and shook it off with a strange laugh. "I suspect this is what our counselors call baggage. I could feel the terror in Di Mon when he was around peers he respected, like Horth... the terror and the self-disgust." He smiled a little wanly. "He admired my certainty that I was not perverted. He told me so more than once and I know he meant it. But he had more influence on me than I did on him, in the end." Ranar floundered into deeper feeling than he wanted to, and was forced to stop, lifting a hand to his forehead to shield his eyes.

Erien stirred and cleared his throat, feeling awkward.

"Although you've made a valid point," Ranar said, looking up again, "I hope you and Evert can forgive me if I cannot act on it... just now." Ranar hesitated, then seemed to decide he had to get one more thing out on the table. "Amel was the last person to speak with Di Mon before he committed suicide. I know he asked Amel to ensure you went with me to Rire in the event of — if his illness proved fatal. But I've so often wondered if there was something more."

"So have I," Erien admitted. He drew his left arm to him because it ached, now the distracting excitement with their visitors was over. "I remember Di Mon came close to ending his life once before, when I was five. His regenerative cancer was bad, and he didn't want to go to Luverthan for treatment, just let it take its course. Ameron convinced him to go. I didn't know Ameron was my father at the time, only that he made a difference."

"Di Mon worshipped Ameron," Ranar said in a murmur.

"I knew Di Mon was becoming ill again, when I was seven," said Erien. "I knew he needed Ameron. But this time it was Amel who came from court. I tried to talk to Amel, because I knew he had access to Ameron. I told him that Ameron had to come, but it didn't work. He treated me like an upset child. I remember pushing him away, almost hitting him, not wanting to be comforted."

"Erien," Ranar reminded him, "you *were* a child."

"I can't help thinking," Erien continued, "that if nothing else, Di Mon did not mean us to find him the way we did. I think he probably meant for both of us to be off planet by the time he — but something happened to make him do it sooner. And the last person he talked to was Amel." He drew a knee up, cradling his aching arm, fighting not to say what he most feared: that Amel knew Di Mon's secret, and it, too, was at risk of exposure if the unthinkable happened and Amel was again exposed to examination in the visitor probe.

"Perhaps we should ask Amel what happened between him and Di Mon," Ranar said, sounding flat.

"I can't," said Erien. "I'm afraid of what I might do if I found out Amel did something to push Di Mon over the edge and make him choose his sword over treatment." He shook his head. "I doubt that Amel would have intended any harm; it might have been entirely inadvertent, but even so—" he sighed, and did not finish.

Ranar rose wordlessly and stopped in front of Erien to touch his bowed head with the tips of his fingers. They remained that way for a moment in silence. Then Ranar said, "Mon was in so much pain by then, Erien. It is easy to forget because he seldom let it show." He sighed. "I should have known myself, but I hadn't seen him privately in some time. I thought it was a good sign when he came to me the night before: relaxed, even reckless. I was worried about him damaging himself, in fact." He smiled a little ruefully. "Or me. He could forget how strong he was. I thought he was drunk, but he had only let down his guard. I should have known he wouldn't have acted that way without some reason. I believe, now, that he had already decided to take his own life." He sighed. "Even so, you may be right about Amel. Di Mon hated having him around despite the trust they shared concerning you and Ameron. Amel made Di Mon feel *sla*, but I suspect..." His voice caught. "Well, Di Mon was not himself. Anything could have happened. You are wise," he concluded, "not to have asked Amel—" He broke off and took a moment to master himself. "It may not be fair to Amel for either of us to ever know. Di Mon's self-control was so thin by then, so brittle. If something did happen I am... grateful Amel kept it to himself."

Ranar fell silent, then said in a dead still voice. "Oh gods, if that's true, and Amel is questioned under the visitor probe—" He ran out of words. "Erien," Ranar said forcefully, "it can't happen. Not the secret Di Mon died to spare Monitum."

"It won't," Erien said. "I'll make sure it won't."

Erien went alone to testify that afternoon. Ranar and Evert saw him off. Amel did not come out of his room. Upstairs, Horth kept Drasous busy explaining the limitations of the procedure's intrusiveness from a medical point of view. Drasous wasn't happy about Erien volunteering to be monitored either, but Erien trusted the *gorarelpul* to relay the facts accurately to Horth.

The monitoring chair dominated the small, plain-walled room. Aside from its impressive dimensions, it was contoured and colored for a soothing effect: soft, smooth and pale blue. It adjusted itself to suit Erien's size. He said, "Firmer please," until he stopped feeling as though it was going to swallow him alive.

The technician gave Erien a nervous smile. "Set-up is going to take a little longer than usual," the man explained apologetically. "We have to do a calibration cycle because of your variant brain structure."

"I understand," said Erien.

"Do you need me to explain any of this?"

Erien glanced over the visual and infrared array in the ceiling, the cortical activity sensors embedded in the headrest and the physiological monitors in the armrest. "No. My understanding has already been judged adequate for informed consent, which," he added for the record, "I requested to be embedded in this dataset."

"Yes," the technician said. "That's not... usual, you realize."

"Trust me," Erien said dryly. "It's necessary to reduce the risk of misunderstandings on the other side of the Killing Jump."

The technician slipped out of the room shortly thereafter, and Erien worked on relaxing.

"Heir Gelion," a man's voice spoke to him momentarily, inside the hood. "My name is Aleki; I am an expert exempt specialized in psychomonitoring. I have been appointed to monitor your responses and interpret their reliability. Are you comfortable?"

"Yes," said Erien.

"I see by your physiological and infrared output that your healing left arm is still causing you pain."

Erien stared into the nearest pickup. "Will that interfere?"

"No," the man said, sounding affronted. "But you shouldn't be doing this when you're injured. However, I see your parents have granted you the right to issue your own waivers in this matter. You can revoke your consent at any time. Do you wish to continue?"

"Yes," said Erien.

"Please state your reason for being here, in your own words."

"You have asked me here to confirm my testimony regarding off-record events aboard *Kali Station* that led to a Nersallian occupation of the station and the destruction, at my hands, of the medical arbiter."

"Beginning calibration series," said Aleki.

The first image was a star field, projected on the far wall, followed by an image of a complex grid pattern, intricate and repeating — a puzzle to be solved. The third image was the Flashing Floor on Gelion.

Erien caught his breath in a shallow gasp, gripping the chair arms as the pattern in the wall curled and reformed and wrapped itself around him. The sense of falling — of worse than falling — was irresistible. His navigator's sense was wrenched inside out and twisted, like going down a jump wrong.

Eyes closed, he pushed himself up out of the chair, nearly fell, caught himself on the armrest and went down on one knee. The movement, clumsy as it was, unraveled the insoluble navigation knot in his mind. When the door opened he was upright again, and angry. "That," he said to the man and woman who entered, "was not standard calibration."

The man — Aleki — said, "No, I'm very sorry. We did have parental permission."

"You had permission for additional calibration to take account of baseline differences," Lurol's voice erupted from a speaker. "You didn't tell us you were going to show him that Lorel thing out of Amel's original probe record!"

Erien squared his shoulders. "I trust," he said to the woman, who was wearing a Space Service uniform, "my reaction was satisfactory."

She obviously hadn't expected sarcasm from him. "Fascinating," she said in a cold tone, and withdrew without apology. Aleki said, "You would be within your rights to refuse to continue."

"Why?" Erien asked dryly. "Are there any more surprises?" He took a deep breath. "I am going to ask for a short recess. I think you will get better data once my head stops spinning."

He sat down again, not trusting himself to move without walking into the walls. Once alone, he contacted his parent to assure them he was all right. He registered his complaint at being exposed to a noxious stimulus, and it was upheld. Evert promptly asked for a one-step decrease in the domain scatter of questioning and secured it, on Erien's behalf. Erien pulled up the revised specifications for his session and reviewed them on the room's stage. *Thank you, Evert*, he thought. He had no doubt the calibration stunt was a trick orchestrated by Space Service to get data on Vrellish navigational prowess, and could see how Evert's intervention would make it harder for his handlers to improvise around approved procedures.

The calibration sequence went off smoothly the next time, and questions followed, asked by the three triumvirs appointed to the task with advising experts making contributions. First up was Fahzir, speaking for Space Service.

"Why did you refuse to let me deal with the *Kali Station* arbiter?" Fahzir asked.

"The Nersallians would have taken your intervention with the arbiter as a hostile act," said Erien, confident his responses endorsed his certainty about the statement. "They were in possession of the station."

"And you maintain there was nothing you could do to make them give it back?" Fahzir asked.

"Correct," said Erien, pleased by the rock-steady display of his response indicators.

"Nothing at all?" Fahzir asked. "How is it, then, you were able to stop Bryllit from spacing Reetion prisoners by challenging her with a sword?"

"I had — very strong feelings about preventing deaths," said Erien, seeing his response profile grow agitated but unable to guess what it meant to the observers.

"You have strong feelings about the sanctity of human life," Aleki said in a soothing tone.

"All right," said Fazhir, "he took a risk to save Reetion citizens, and we are grateful, I'm sure. But the point is, he wasn't prepared to challenge Bryllit over possession of the station...."

"Not necessarily true, Fahzir," protested Juno, the advising representative who had replaced Ranar on the Foreign and Alien Council. "Erien was protected by Horth Nersal when he challenged Bryllit over the planned executions. Had the challenge been over ownership of a conquered station, there may have been a different result."

"Do you really expect me to believe," Fahzir asked Juno, "they would have killed their Ava's heir?"

"Absolutely," said Juno, "if they thought he was out of line. Nersallians will challenge their own liege if they disagree with him strongly enough."

"The question is closed," Aleki ruled. "Continue."

"Why did you destroy the visitor probe and the invaluable data it contained about its interactions with the *Kali Station* arbiter and Amel?" Fahzir went back on the attack.

"Because," Erien said, "I have already seen the harm done, both to Amel personally and to the relationship between Gelion and Rire, by the uncontrolled release of information gathered under the visitor probe during the *Second Contact* mission. Reetions lust for information as mindlessly as Sevolites will draw swords."

"Swords," Fahzir pointed out, "are weapons."

"And information is not?" Erien returned. "You would not go to such ends to obtain it were you unaware of its power."

A new member of the triumvirate spoke up. It was Glynda, acting for Ethics. "Your explanation implies there was information in the visitor probe record that you did not want disclosed. Does this information concern the cause of Amel's injuries?"

"No," said Erien, which was true. But he didn't want his agitation at the question showing so he began to run a flute exercise in his mind.

Almost immediately Aleki said, "Would you please stop that and concentrate on the questions you're being asked."

Glynda did not proceed until Erien's response signs had returned to normal. "Do you know how Amel came to be injured?" she asked.

"Domain violation," warned the presiding arbiter. "Questions must fall within the scope of the *Kali Station* affair."

"Let me rephrase myself," said Glynda. "To the best of your knowledge, was Amel injured on Gelion in retaliation for helping Ann arm *Kali Station*?"

"To the best of anyone's knowledge," Erien said crisply, "few Gelacks have the slightest understanding of what Amel did, or didn't do, to assist Ann."

"Please answer the question more directly," Aleki advised.

"No," Erien said dryly. "To the best of my knowledge, Amel's injuries were not sustained as an act of retaliation against him for assisting Ann."

"Thank you," said Aleki. "The next set of questions are from the Sibling Worlds representative, concerning the events leading to Ameron's recognition of Ranar as Reetion ambassador."

These were the ones Erien had been dreading. His heart sank.

The next voice to speak was Kirkos. "A title challenge took place on Gelion between the champions for Ava Ameron and Avim Ev'rel, is this correct?"

"Yes," said Erien.

"The memories invoke strong emotion in you," Aleki observed.

"In attempting to prevent the duel between champions, I inadvertently placed the lives of the principles at risk," Erien admitted, which was already on record so there was no point evading the fact. He wasn't sure why he added, "And my half-brother, D'Lekker, died."

"Heir Gelion," Aleki said, "could you relax your right hand on the sensor bulb. I'm afraid, with your strength, you might break it."

Erien forced his grip open. "You already know how I feel about the pointless loss of life," he said.

"The title challenge did bear, in part, on Ameron's intention to acknowledge Rire," Kirkos said. "Please confirm."

"Yes," Erien agreed.

"But there were also other reasons for the challenge," Kirkos pressed, "ones not yet on record."

"If so," Erien hedged, "they have nothing to do with Rire."

"You have already admitted to one error of judgment in events on Gelion," said Kirkos. "An error serious enough to have put the lives of Ava Ameron and Avim Ev'rel at risk, and result in Avim Ev'rel's death. Now you say, with confidence, that information you chose to withhold is not relevant to Rire's position. How can you be certain?"

"Parental protest registered," the arbiter interjected. "Ranar, Lurol and Evert have registered a request to have questioning terminated."

"Tell them thank you, but I'll see it through," Erien said steadily. "Yes, I am confident it is not in anyone's interest for all the details concerning events on Gelion to be on the record."

Silence ruled as they conferred behind the scenes. Erien closed his eyes, trying not to think complex or disturbing thoughts.

"All right," said Fahzir, making him start, "let's get back to *Kali Station* and the Gelacks' interactions with the arbiter."

It is going to be a long afternoon, Erien thought.

FIFTEEN

Eyes on Amel

Whatever Happened to the Boy Next Door?

At the first glimpse of her old residential block, Alka halted. *If I just turned around and went home,* she thought, *would it be welching out or being mature?*

Beside her, Marla said plaintively, "Are you lost?"

"What? No! Of course not!" Alka hunched her shoulders, giving the prettier, younger girl her best tomboy scowl. "I lived here for three years. It's just..."

Marla's coffee-colored brow contracted with concern. "You promised the study group you could get us in."

"Listen," Alka shifted her weight to one foot. "I knew Erien when he was this know-nothing kid I had to show how to do ordinary things. I taught him how to sign out a scooter. We climbed trees together. Now..." she recalled Erien on stage during the Gelacks' arrival, "...he looks older than I do."

"You said he would remember you," Marla reminded her.

Alka frowned. She was ten when Erien moved in two doors down, a pace-faced child with gray eyes and a deep, still core. Ranar took Lurol as a housemate to meet the minimum two-parent requirement, and Evert had moved in the following year. Lurol and Ranar were both research exempt: unbalanced idiot-savants whose antisocial behavior was tolerated only because of their exceptional contribution to the record. Alka had always thought of Erien and Evert as the normal ones.

She didn't know how to think about Erien now.

Amel was easy in comparison! She had met and talked with Amel in simulation, based on his psych profile data. She had even kissed his projected simulation once, years ago, despite the razzing she had helped her friend Tanya give Marla when they caught *her* doing it. Amel was as real as the stage in her family's living room.

Marla tugged at her sleeve, looking more six than sixteen. "Please, Alka? You promised."

I did, Alka thought with a rush of Reetion conscience. *But only because it made me feel important. What if we get brushed off? I'll feel like a crass idiot! What if we are fined all the credits we've earned toward becoming Lawful Citizens, instead of this scoring us more?*

"Nobody's going to object to you visiting an old friend," Marla insisted hotly. "I mean—"

"Hello, girls." The voice made them both start.

The speaker was a middle-aged adult who was doing his bit for the neighborhood by keeping up the flower beds around the train station. Alka vaguely recognized him. "Sightseeing?" he asked.

"I used to live around here," said Alka.

He leaned on his rake, studying them with the look of someone who regularly tended to those in need of remedial socialization. Maybe he was a counsellor in his professional job. "You're sure?" He straightened up. "Because we get more sightseers around here than I care to admit, as a proud Reetion, all with no better excuse than wanting to catch a glimpse of a Gelack. And we wouldn't want the Gelacks thinking we have no manners."

"You make them sound like nesting ducks we shouldn't go poking with sticks," Alka was rescued by her gruff streak.

The man laughed. "Ah, *now* I remember you," he said. "Scrawny, lively kid. You used to chum around with young Erien. Pushed him out of trees and such."

Alka drew herself up to her full, womanly figure, which at 20 was — if not impressive — at least now redeemed from scrawniness by modest breasts and a discrete widening of her slim hips. "I only pushed him out of a tree once. And he deserved it."

"If you say so," said the man. "But if you are planning to get reacquainted, you should watch yourself. He isn't the Erien I remember — not that I knew him except to say hello — and that Vrellish character with him, Horth Nersal, ought to be Supervised. He accosted Ellie, a woman who lives in the end townhouse, just because she was on the commons playing her guitar."

"Musicians are assumed to be courtesans in Gelack culture," Marla volunteered pedantically. "It was a misunderstanding."

The man with the rake gave her a suspicious look. "Are you one of those Gelack cult youngsters?"

"No!" Marla cried, offended. "I'm in Alka's—"

"She's a friend of mine," Alka cut her off, before she brought up the study group and fanned suspicions. "Come on," Alka said brusquely, snatching at Marla's hand.

Over the worst and striding toward Ranar's townhouse, Alka couldn't understand why she had hesitated. The worst that could happen was that Erien would be mad at her for being a lousy correspondent. At thirteen, when her family was rotated out to the orbital stations, she had been more interested in meeting new boys than keeping in touch with childhood playmates, and by the time they returned, Erien had left Rire.

"That man claimed Horth is Vrellish," said Marla testily, marching beside her, "but he isn't — he's liege of House Nersal." She paused to catch her breath. "People have no excuse to be ignorant about Gelacks with all Ranar's work on the record."

"House Nersal *is* Vrellish," Alka shot back.

"No it isn't, not entirely."

"Mostly Vrellish by blood," Alka asserted.

"But not sworn to House Vrel. It's sworn to Ameron."

"Oh, well, if you're going to go by oaths, then you might as well call Horth Lor'Vrellish, I suppose. Don't be daft."

Marla rose to the challenge of debate, keeping Alka out of breath for the rest of the way across the commons. They were discussing what Horth's oath to Erien's father made Horth to Erien when Alka decided they were close enough and said, "Hush."

A *tok tok tok* sound beckoned from the rear of the townhouse, where a scattering of neighbors and their guests were in their backyards to watch Horth Nersal exercising on the patch of commons nearest Ranar's door. Liege Nersal's blue-black hair looked metallic in the morning light, in contrast to his pale complexion. The sweat on his sharp-cut face humanized him. And he needed humanizing. Dressed in a black shirt and black pants, dragons rioting down the left side of his breast in bright red embroidery, his whole appearance shouted the will to dominate. He wielded a heavy stick of wood in both hands, executing moves that brought it always to connect with a *tok* against a matching stick positioned to receive it by a slighter man dressed in plain Reetion clothes.

"That's the *gorarelpul* working out with him," Marla hissed in a stage whisper beside Alka. "I didn't think *gorarelpul* were allowed to use swords."

"Sticks aren't swords," said Alka.

"Those sticks look just as dangerous," said Marla, hanging back. "Maybe we should wait until he's done."

"He isn't going to whack you with it, silly," Alka assured her. Then Horth noticed them, and she was no longer so sure.

He signaled a break to Drasous with a step back. The *gorarelpul* put down his stick and spared their audience a quick inspection. The neighbors either smiled uncertainly or got busy pretending they had not been watching the Gelacks.

Horth advanced, stick hanging casually from his left hand. Alka thought involuntarily of his rehearsed attacks. He had gray eyes like Erien, but his bored into her spine.

"I'm a friend of Erien's," Alka found her voice. "Is he home?"

Horth's stick swung up casually, brushing Alka's side to make her step back — a warning. He dismissed them with that, turned his back and walked back to Drasous.

"Hey!" Alka got past her shock to tap into her indignation. "Who do you think you are?"

"T-the liege of Nersal?" Marla said faintly beside her.

Drasous spoke up on his own accord, "Heir Gelion has not come back yet. He is still being questioned. Liege Nersal is not happy about it. You may send any desired communication through your mail system."

"Yeah, so it can be filtered and ignored," Alka let him know she wasn't stupid. "I'll just wait for him, okay?" She marched toward the front door, ignoring Marla's gasp.

Horth let her come until she got close enough and then closed his right fist in her shirt, jerking her up off the ground until he held her at arm's length, in mid-air.

Alka yelped. He did not like the sound and shook her once with a snap that made her teeth rattle. She went still then, really scared.

"P-put me down," she said, grabbing at a wrist that felt more like plasticized cord than flesh. "P-please?"

He looked disappointed.

What the hell did he expect! she thought. *A fight?* He was dangling her like a kitten. It was a shock, like a dunking in cold water.

Horth heaved her casually backwards. Panic and helplessness sprang new-minted from her heart, like startled ducks on a pond. Her fall was broken by strong hands and a yielding body that absorbed her momentum, but her panic over-balanced them both, and she landed on her rescuer.

His soft groan was the first clue to who he was. Amel's every twitch, breath and whimper had been recorded while Lurol rummaged through his mind for the knowledge to save her station, eighteen years earlier. Alka knew that soft, understated 'uhn' Amel made as intimate as a lover's sigh.

Half-kneeling, Amel held Alka against him where they had landed on the grass, his body firm and warm in an exciting way so utterly unlike a stage projection. He was dressed in Reetion shorts and a loose blue T-shirt, with no shoes on.

He smiled, which was really unfair of him. She forgot everything she'd meant to say upon wrangling an invitation to meet him out of Erien. She'd meant to be grand for him — offering her commiseration and good will on behalf of her generation — not to need his help.

"You should be honored," Amel said as he drew her to her feet beside him. "He doesn't thump people he doesn't deem worthy opponents." He tipped his head toward Horth Nersal. "Me, for example, he just ignores entirely. But Erien really isn't back yet. Can I help you?"

All Alka could think about was her personal involvement in producing that gentle, injured sound she had heard from him earlier.

"Did I hurt you?" she blurted.

Amel blinked. "Not much." His eyes laughed. "One can't help landing if tossed. Are you all right?"

She nodded, "I think so."

Liege Nersal and Drasous had gone into the house. Marla was on her knees on the commons lawn, staring with eyes as big as saucers.

Amel's eyebrows contracted. "Is something the matter with your friend?" Tension was creeping in to spoil the warmth she had experienced earlier. *He is like something wild,* Alka thought, *listening for some warning... afraid of something. But what?*

Amel glanced from face to face among the neighbors, making Alka aware of how he drew people to him, while Horth Nersal's presence had set up an invisible barrier. Some of them looked eager to get closer and Amel did not seem comfortable about it.

"Let's bring you both inside," Amel decided. He cast an oddly shy glance at the nearest neighbors, as if in apology for his rudeness at retreating again, so soon.

"Yes, great," said Alka. She took a step and nearly tripped, she was so agitated. Amel caught her elbow, making her catch her breath. Seeing him in the flesh was overwhelming, as if he were a magic being painted in exotic inks against a mundane backdrop.

In a nauseating reversal of feeling, she suddenly doubted she could take any more of him, as if he was an over-rich dessert. But that was silly. Amel himself was being perfectly ordinary and she had to behave herself.

As she tried to get him into the proper perspective she realized his own appraisal was lingering about her breasts and thighs, and caught his eyes snapping back to her face with bright, innocent interest. "I am glad Erien has a friend," he said. "How well did you know him?"

"Well enough to push him out of trees," she latched onto the memory the gardener had stirred up. Amel looked impressed for an instant, and then dubious.

"That is," she said, "we hung around together for a few years. Climbing trees was one of the things we did, but I never did push him out, except the once." She rubbed the side of her nose, blushing, "It's what people remember. You know — the flashy stuff."

"Ah." He went still, then repaired his expression and nodded, eyes telling her he did, indeed, understand the syndrome. "You had better collect your friend."

Trudging back to Marla, Alka began to shake with delayed shock. She did not want Marla to notice, so she went slowly, passing at a laggard's pace through the encroaching neighbors attracted by Marla's near swoon and Amel's appearance on the lawn.

"Is everything all right?" asked a woman Alka recognized, who had just finished helping Marla up off the commons grass where she had sunk when her knees failed her.

"Erien isn't home yet," Alka stuffed her hands into hip pockets, "but Amel—" it felt so funny saying that "—says we should come in and wait for him." Alka suddenly had second thoughts. "But maybe we should just leave word, like the *gorarelpul* suggested."

Marla's mouth popped open. "Are you crazy?" Snatching Alka's hand, she towed her swiftly after Amel into the house.

Ranar's front door was as familiar as ever, but seeing Horth inside was like smacking into a wall. He stood well back in the living room near the stairs that went up to the bedrooms on the second floor. All he did was watch, but his attention taught Alka the nervousness of a mouse venturing out of its hole.

"Alka!" Lurol greeted her from the raised kitchen area. She came down into the living room in a dressing gown, carrying a mug of steaming chocolate and projecting a suspicious welcome.

Amel was on hands and knees gathering up pieces of a dismantled portable stage unit spread out untidily on the floor.

"Horth?" Lurol remarked with a forbearing sigh.

Amel looked up with guilty defiance. "No, not this time — I just — I'll fix it later."

Lurol frowned. "I suppose it's not your fault. You're bored being cooped up inside all day. You can't cope with boredom."

The innocent comment upset Amel more than Alka expected it to. He scrambled up, hands fisted at his sides. "Don't tell me," he blasted Lurol, "what I can or can't cope with! You do not know me half as thoroughly as you think you do!"

Amel's temper was a startling spectacle. The Amel of Alka's clandestine simulation didn't have one! But there was no doubt he was angry. His jaw was locked, hands clenched and the thousand grays of his crystal-bright irises blazed like a kaleidoscope of broken glass.

Then his face went clammy with a funny, muted gulp.

Amel blinked and stepped back. As he did, his bare heel went down, cracking a plastic part from the dismantled stage.

Lurol's eyes narrowed, observing the peculiar delay between the snap and Amel's shivered wince of response. He shifted his foot to stroke away the offending object as if he didn't want people to notice. "What was that?" Lurol's tone had a pounce in it.

"I stepped on a piece, I guess. Sorry."

"Amel, you don't misplace your feet." Lurol bent to scoop the snapped piece of plastic off the floor. It was smeared with blood. "And you didn't feel this immediately," she accused him. "I saw."

"Well, I feel it now he said." He hopped a couple steps to deposit himself on the couch.

By the time Drasous had applied a bit of simple first aid and withdrawn to the other side of the room again, Alka knew what was bothering her most about the outburst she had witnessed from Amel, coupled with his behavior in the back yard.

"You're afraid of us, aren't you?" she blurted in astonishment. "Of Reetions!"

Amel frowned. "I'm afraid of a lot of things," he said, and tipped his head to give Lurol a sidelong look, "in a healthy, selfish, 'do not do it if it's going to hurt' way, contrary to what the doctor, there, imagines."

"I have never denied you can feel fear in generous measure," Lurol responded. "You just do not let it stand in the way of self-sacrifice in a good cause. You were naturally predisposed to altruism, of course, but more in a theoretical way until I made it necessary for you to live up to your own standards of heroism."

Amel gave her a thoroughly filthy look. "Nonsense."

"Why can't you be rational?" Lurol demanded. "Do you need any more proof than the risk you took in helping Ann? Can you tell me, without lying as perfectly as only you can, that you are not here because you are willing to be Gelion's sacrifice to placate Rire? I cannot stand by and watch. You are doing these things because of a drastic measure I took, long ago, which was always meant to be temporary!"

"Yes," he said coldly, "I know... because I wasn't supposed to live long enough for it to bother anyone."

Lurol's stony demeanor registered a direct hit. She inhaled with difficulty. "Please," she said, "let me put right what I did wrong."

"If this is leading back into a visitor probe," Amel said, his face stiff with resentment, "the answer is, and always will be, 'no'. You keep telling me I have no will to defend myself when it is you who will not listen when I tell you I don't want your soul-raking probe in my brain again, ever! Can't you understand?"

"It wasn't used properly before!" Lurol argued. "Not by me on *Second Contact Station*, nor on *Kali!*"

"So you want to try again until you get it right?" Amel shook his head. "No, thanks. And I wouldn't practice on any other Sevolite, either, much as I would love to see people like him," he jerked his head in Horth's direction, "find out it's impossible to just think strong thoughts and tough it out! Rire should review the causes of Sevildom's Fifth Civil War with particular attention to which side got wiped out!"

"Is this about Erien being psych-monitored during question-ing this afternoon?" Lurol asked in an impassioned voice. "Be-cause it's not the same at all! It's passive. And no one is ever going to use visitor probe technology against the Vrellish to control them — it's plain superstition!" Her voice trembled with distress.

Amel was on his feet by now, making Lurol look middle-aged and diminished, with Drasous quietly translating Amel's ringing Reetion into Gelack for an attentively listening Horth Nersal.

Alka was overcome. This was not the Amel she and her fel-lows thought they knew and loved: the sweet, abused sixteen-year-old willing to offer his life to save people he barely knew. This was an angry Sevolite.

But even as she stared in disbelief, Alka saw Lurol's wounded look corrode Amel's threatening façade. He softened about the eyes first, then the tension in his shoulders lightened and his clenched hands relaxed.

"Doctor," he spoke with kindness through a resistant lump of feeling in his throat. "I know you did not mean to do me harm. You made a bitter choice. I know."

His gentleness conquered Lurol. She lifted leaden, teary eyes above a downcast mouth. Alka had never seen Lurol cry be-fore, or even come close.

"I am sorry if I—" Amel inhaled and sorted his feelings out tangibly as he held the breath, "—hurt you just now. I do not blame you for what happened... truly."

"I know," she husked, her stirred pain striving powerfully with her equally fierce self-possession. "Oh, believe me, I know! Don't you see that only makes it more maddening that you won't let me help you as I am able to? I would not care so much if you were cruel. I could hate you back for your ignorant self-cen-tered point of view. Amel, I can't even dislike you! You are just pathologically — *nice*."

Amel folded his arms. "I can manage not to be offended if you want to insist I am provably nice, doctor, but could we drop the pathological?"

"Do not make a joke of this," Lurol said darkly. "It is not."

She abandoned the field on that note.

Horth Nersal heard out the last of the translation and left, too.

Amel returned his attention apologetically to Alka and Marla. "I'm afraid we're not good company at the moment."

"That's understandable," Alka said, getting up and pulling Marla after her by the hand. "Will you tell Erien we would like to see him, and you, at our study group? We know we're only dependents trying to break into legal adulthood, but we might be a genuine, fresh voice in the debate about your status with regard to Ann's trial. And it would give our credits toward becoming legal adults a big boost."

"Are you leaving?" Amel asked, disappointed. Alka watched his expression light up with self-confessed slyness, "I was hoping you might tell me more about Erien as a child. I often wondered how he made out on Rire."

"I'm sure he could tell you himself," Alka heard the words tumble out of her mouth with alarm at the rebuff in them, but the idea of telling Amel stories about Erien as a little boy suddenly felt like a betrayal to her.

"We're going?" Marla finally caught on.

Amel rendered her speechless by kissing her on the cheek. "Good-bye," he blessed her with his silken voice, and winked at her.

"Don't forget to tell Erien what I said," Alka warned, suddenly rather concerned about Amel's priorities.

"I won't," he promised, and gave her a grin that went right down her spine to the tailbone and back up. "I can see why you two got along. But are you sure he never pushed you out of a tree, as well, the odd time?"

The question made Alka feel better about Amel prying into Erien's childhood adventures. "Hah," she answered with a toss of her short, dark hair. Then she stole a kiss to one up Marla's prize and dragged her younger friend out the door.

"I don't believe he kissed me!" Marla wondered aloud beside her.

Alka smiled, but her legs felt hollow and her stomach was all churned up. Marla padded after her, babbling excited nonsense. Halfway across the commons lawn, Alka stopped.

"Hey," Marla said, pointing, "isn't that—"

Erien and Ranar were walking toward them, Erien looking very tall and pale, and alien, despite his casual black and gray jumpsuit. He was saying something to Ranar when he became aware of their presence. He halted, lifting his head with a sudden awareness that would have seemed feral if not for the intelligence in his gray eyes. She remembered those eyes, and that guarded expression.

She cleared her throat. "Hi, Erien."

He looked at her with blank intentness until his expression suddenly cleared and he flashed a smile just long enough for her to think, *Wow.* Then the smile was gone and his face settled into a look of quiet watchfulness. "Alka. I heard your family was rotated back to Rire, but didn't know you were living in this area."

"I'm not... really."

"Just came back to visit the old neighborhood?"

"Not exactly. I had a favor to ask, sort of, but..." She glanced back over her shoulder.

"You've come from the house," he said.

"Yeah," she confirmed, and added on pure impulse, "Do you have to go back there right away? There's an open-air concert later tonight. You could probably use a break."

"I think," Ranar said unexpectedly, "that's an excellent idea. I can take care of the home front."

"But Amel's testimony is tomorrow," Erien protested. "We have to prepare."

"I rather doubt Amel needs anything explained to him more than once. So," he smiled, "as your parent *and* as the Reetion ambassador to Gelion, I recommend you take the evening off."

Erien's struggle with his conscience was surprisingly brief. He gave Alka one of his muted half smiles, this one rueful.

"Uh, I think... I'll go and check in with the group," said Marla in a tone that suggested good manners alone forced the offer.

Alka decided, quite ruthlessly, to accept. "Thanks, Marla. I appreciate that." She started to take Erien's arm, and then thought better of it. But he picked up on her body language readily enough to move off with her.

"With whom," Erien said, "was your was friend supposed to check in?"

"Oh, our study group," she confessed. "I was supposed to ask you to get Amel to come work with us." *Damn,* she thought, *I'm blushing.* "We're supposed to take on active issues, make a contribution — it would have been quite a coup putting Amel on record when he's refused nearly all forms of contact."

She felt Erien go remote, though he still strolled at her side.

"But I'm glad it didn't work out," Alka told Erien. "I think there's something wrong with our perspective. We're all losing sight of what's important, what's really at stake. It's turning into such a personal thing, all about Amel. Anyway," she shrugged, "I really didn't invite you to the concert to lobby you. Look," she interrupted herself, "there's Old Faithful. Bet I can beat you to the top." She took off across the grass at a healthy sprint.

Halfway to the oak tree she remembered Erien was supposed to have a bad shoulder, and slowed to glance back over her shoulder. She caught a glimpse of a dark, running figure as he caught up and passed her.

"Hey!" she protested. "That's the last time I feel sorry for you! Winner covers dinner!"

"Well, hurry up then!" he called back, vaulting onto the lowest branch. "I've only got dependent's credit."

"Me, too!" she cried, not caring anymore about Amel, or the study group, and a quick fix for graduating to Lawful Citizen.

She hadn't climbed a tree since she'd returned to Rire. Erien's shoulder slowed him down because he climbed almost exclusively with his right hand, using his left only for balance, but he still reached the top a body length before she did.

He straddled a branch, balancing easily. She stood on a lower one and hooked her arms over to hang on. Up here, with the sun shining on his face and leaves all around him, he didn't seem nearly so strange. He was even sweating a little.

"So," she asked, after a long silence, "what have you been doing for the past however long?"

"I was on Rire until I was fourteen, then I did three years of service in the Nersallian fleet, under Horth." He gave one of his muted half smiles. "Which is not what I had planned to do with those years, but I learned a certain amount of practical engineering that was a useful complement to the *rel*-skimming theory I had picked up on Rire."

How typically Erien, she thought. Her parents had occasionally expressed the wish that his studious habits would rub off on her, after they had stopped fussing over her hanging around with a Gelack. She wondered what they would have done if they had known, at the time, exactly *which* Gelack.

"And then you went off to be Heir Gelion?" she said.

"Not quite as straightforwardly as that." He sounded distant again.

"What's Gelion like?" she asked, to relieve the awkward silence that followed. "Does it feel like home?"

He let out a breath that might have been a stifled laugh. "Sometimes I think Ranar could call Gelion home more easily

than I can. He seems to have no difficulty fitting into the hierarchy, without compromising what he is," Erien continued.
"I, on the other hand..." He caught himself then, to her disappointment. "And you?"

"Orbital stations, then back to Rire. Don't ask me what I'm
going to do with my life, because I don't know. I'm going for
Lawful Citizen, which is enough for me right now." She kicked
at the branch beneath her, feeling the shock through her other
foot.

"If things works out," Erien said, "I'll want to establish a
Gelack ambassador on Rire, and open a full Reetion embassy
on Gelion. They'll both need staff."

She blinked at him.

"While you're waiting to figure out what you want to do..."
he suggested.

"Erien," she began, and stopped. Did he really have no idea
what he had just said? How was she going to explain it to him
if he didn't? "Erien, arbiters appoint people to those posts, or
voting councils for the really unique jobs. You can't just..." she
gestured inarticulately, "decide!"

"Ah," said Erien, "yes. I expect we would be given exem-
plars of Reetion virtue in an attempt to ensure immunity against
our corrupting influence." He paused, a quietly sour set to his
lips. "I'd rather work with people I trust."

"Don't be insulted, Erien," she demurred, "but you're as
much Gelack as I can cope with. I don't like being thrown about."

He winced. "Liege Nersal?"

She enacted the grab, heave and dump, in mime, with one
hand. "His way of saying get lost, I suppose. I gather he doesn't
talk much."

There was a silence. The breeze stirred leaves around them.
"So are you going to stay there?" she asked. "On Gelion?"

"I don't know." The admission seemed to depress him. "I
don't like what Gelion does to me. I learned I'm capable of violence. And I made mistakes that cost people their lives. I am
not sure Ameron needs an heir, at least not one like myself. Sometimes it seems that the best thing for me to do is stay here. But
there are people I owe more: Di Mon, Ranar, Ev'rel, Tatt..." his
voice lightened a little, "that's Prince Ditatt Monitum."

"He was the one you used to write to all the time!" She remembered. "I used to watch you do it, so laboriously with a
pen and funny Gelack paper."

"Yes, that's the one," said Erien. "Another half-brother as it turns out, like Amel, but on Ameron's side. If I didn't go back, I would miss him. And then there's Luthan..."

"Who's he?"

"She. Princess Luthan Dem H'Us. She's supposed to marry Dorn Nersal — who I nearly got killed on *Kali Station* because it never entered my mind that he would have had orders to follow me no matter what insane thing I did!"

"You're not responsible for the universe, you know!" she said, a little tartly. "Nobody has to follow criminal orders."

He blinked at her. "Within the Gelack system, Dorn's orders were lawful, and came from his father."

"Sounds perfectly Old Testament," Alka said, alluding to an ancient religious text that, as best she could recall, was full of fathers sacrificing sons. "If I were this Luthan, I would rather have a live boyfriend than a dead one, whether he's on the outs with his family over it or not."

A subtle, rather odd expression crossed Erien's face. She studied it. "Are you interested in her yourself?" she asked bluntly.

"No," he said. She judged it more an automatic response than a clear denial. But then, Erien hadn't shown any sign of figuring out that there was an opposite sex when she knew him. "I like her," he admitted. "I would like to see her have a chance at marrying someone she loves."

"Which is... not Dorn?"

"No. Dorn is perfectly worthy of love, but he has Amy. That's my half-sister, on Ameron's side. She and Dorn are involved."

"Doesn't sound like Dorn and Luthan have a good basis for a lifetime partnership contract," said Alka. "They should get counselling before doing anything permanent!"

He almost laughed. She frowned, annoyed at being mocked.

Erien said, "I'm sorry, but the idea... no... Luthan and Dorn are almost the last parties to be considered in this. The marriage is a political alliance between houses H'Us and Nersal. It's their duty. Maybe that's why the Demish literary tradition of true romance is almost always found in adulterous relationships. There are princesses mourning fallen husbands and princesses anticipating happy marriages, but married princesses are nearly always miserable." He was silent a moment. "Alka..." His tone warned her something odd was coming, and it did. "As a woman yourself, is there a basic info-blit on human sexuality you could recommend? For someone who doesn't have realistic information on what to expect... avoiding reference to same-gender affiliation, and I should also find one on pregnancy and childbirth."

"Oh," she said, intrigued by the rare sight of Erien going slowly pink. "You mean, for this Luthan person?"

"Yes."

"I'll see what I can do," she promised solemnly. He *was* sweet on her. He just hadn't figured it out yet.

"What did you want to talk to Amel about?" he asked her.

Alka shrugged. "About what happened to him on Gelion in Lilac Hearth."

Erien stiffened.

"There's a lot of speculation about it," she defended herself, "so I thought if we could get him to tell us about it, by being all nice and nonthreatening and everything, I'd get to graduate from dependent status and you'd be able to get on with the diplomacy, since I'm sure it wasn't you or Ameron who tortured Amel. People do suspect he was tortured, you know, from the injuries observed on *Kali Station* by evacuees we've debriefed."

"I am aware of it," Erien said quietly. "I've been keeping up with public opinion."

"Then you know how many people are concerned Amel might be in for more of the same if he goes back home," said Alka.

"I wonder," Erien said dryly, "how many of them are aware Gelacks distrust Reetions for the exact same reason: torturing Amel."

"Torture!" Alka exclaimed.

"It's how most Gelacks see what happened to him on *Second Contact Station*," said Erien. "And, unfortunately, it is a significant part of the Gelack attitude toward Rire."

"But it wasn't torture!" Alka protested, with a vehemence that surprised her. "Child abuse and conscience bonding, welts around his wrists and on his body! *Those* are torture!"

Erien withdrew into his calm shell, and in the silence she worried her lip and tried to unknot her emotions.

"Erien," she said eventually, "when you are out in space, do you ever get spooked? Do you ever look into space and feel a chill knowing how easily a *rel*-ship could shatter your safety with a close pass?" The wind was shifting with the sunset, and she looked down at the stirring leaves, finding them easier to look at than the childhood friend who had turned out to be one of the scary things in the universe called Sevolites. "I felt like that, sometimes, when I was living on an orbital station. It was the first time I really understood what might have been going on with Lurol and those people on *Second Contact Station* when they made the choice they did. They were frightened of the nothingness, and the Sevolites prowling around in it. Lurol had felt a highborn shake the floor beneath their feet, and Amel was the only weapon she had." She fell silent, not sure what point, exactly, she meant to make.

Belatedly, she remembered that with Erien up a tree with her, they were probably at STI four or five, not the usual laid-back STI three for a recreational public place.

Erien sat holding his left shoulder as though it ached. The last of the sunlight turned his pale skin golden, and the breeze lifted his hair. His face was unreadable.

"Erien, your people frighten us," she said, "but just admitting it is murder on our pride."

He became aware of his posture and lowered his right hand. "I'm sorry," he said, a little helplessly. "I'm doing what I can to reduce the threat."

"I guess that's why everyone loves Amel," she said, trying to lighten the mood again. "He's not frightening."

Erien's lips thinned. "He frightens me," he said, more acidly than she would have expected, but he did not elaborate. Erien shivered. "The sun's going down," he said.

"As suns do," said Alka. She remembered how she felt about sunrises and sunsets ever since she had come down from the orbital stations: the wonderful reassurance of being enfolded in atmosphere, with soil under her feet again, trying not to think about the arguments of people like Ann, who warned Sevolites could threaten even planets if they made war on the Reetion confederacy, inhibited only by their own religious ideas.

She had to move, or she would say something else unwise. So she said briskly, "You promised me dinner. If we move we can eat at the Hanging Gardens and still catch the concert afterwards."

SIXTEEN

Erien

Fables

"Erien!"

Hearing his name as he flung open the door to the living room, Erien halted in midstep and thus avoided bowling over Evert. More judiciously, he stepped inside and grinned at his foster father's worried face. "Sorry, 'Vert."

Evert smiled back. "You enjoyed yourself, then? You look as though you did. Amel's in your room, if you need him, Drasous is working upstairs and Horth is on the back patio with Ranar."

"How is our STI holding up?" asked Erien.

"Fine, inside. The commons brightens up from three to at least four whenever one of you goes out, but nothing is in scope except visuals. And I do mean scope, in the legal sense, not range, as a purely technical consideration. Ranar and I have asserted all the opacity privileges we can. The porch is still the same as inside: standard household STI two, barring aura complications or triggering events like violence, but anyone in the neighborhood can watch you."

Erien relaxed. "Did you follow the concert on stage?" he asked, pleased to be able to ride the high a little longer. "That fourth movement — did you hear the flute trio? It gave me an idea for something I've been thinking about composing." Evert followed, encouraging him to talk musical theory and composition as Erien loped into the kitchen to raid the refrigerator.

"You don't have to go back there," Evert said abruptly, as Erien took a mouthful of the food he'd put together for himself. "You could stay here and be a musician, or a scientist — or both."

Erien drew a deep, unhappy breath and straightened. Evert
had a way of going straight to the heart of the matter. He didn't
do it often, preferring to give Erien the space to come to him,
but when he did, it was usually dead on.

"Yes, yes, I know you are Heir Gelion," Evert continued,
"which must be as heady as it is oppressive, but you are your
own person, Erien. You don't have to sacrifice yourself to Di Mon's
plans. You are a gifted musician, and you have real potential
as a mathematician and theoretical physicist. That was what
you wanted to do, once, wasn't it?"

"I wanted," Erien said in a low voice, "to find some way to
equalize the situation in space: a child's dream. If people like
Ann had the capacity of Sevolites they would behave no better than Sevolites... perhaps even worse."

"Erien," Evert said tartly, "*Ann* is not making decisions on
behalf of Rire. She is Supervised and likely to remain so for a
long time."

"I don't think Sevolites belong on Rire," Erien said.

Evert faltered. Then he touched Erien's hand. "*You* could
belong here," he said, "but maybe not the others, even Drasous,
although he isn't Sevolite. In fact," he admitted, "he's the one
who unnerves me most. I don't know why exactly."

"There is the conscience bond," Erien said.

"Yes," Evert murmured with pity and distaste. "I suppose
it is consistent with the doctrine of *Okal Rel* that commoners
require bonding to be capable of honorable behavior."

"I never accepted that explanation," said Erien. "*Okal Rel* is
a doctrine of free will. If one is not capable of exercising free
will—" He broke off, acutely aware of Evert's discomfort with
the subject of how Sevolites viewed commoners. "What are you
thinking?"

"Oh, I don't know," Evert fidgeted, "just, I suppose, that if
we were conquered..."

Erien had a hard time grasping what Evert implied for a few
seconds. When he did, it struck an unwelcome resonance with
Gelack fears of how Reetions might employ the visitor probe.

"Conscience bonding is not an instrument of mass subju-
gation," he told Evert quietly. "Only graduates of the *gorarelpul*
college may be bonded, and the resulting relationship between
bond slave and bond master must be publicly declared to be
legal. I do not mean, of course, to justify conscience bonding
by stressing the limits of its application. It has always puzzled

me how the very people—" he found he could not say 'we' when he meant Gelacks "—who abhorred the use of mind-control technologies used by the Lorels to control Vrellish *rel*-pilots, are complacent about conscience bonding. Bigotry might explain it were the Nesaks the only ones concerned, since they don't believe commoners have souls, but most variations on *Okal Rel* accept commoners as part of the birth rank continuum. Souls move up the social scale by living honorable lives, and are dropped a rung or more by behaving dishonorably. The *okal'a'ni*, who let greed seduce them into reducing the carrying capacity for life by destroying or fouling habitat, are denied rebirth entirely. It is an internally consistent system. But judging people on the basis of the decisions they make in life presupposes the subjects have free will, which would suggest that conscience bonding removes the bond slave from the game, which is an *okal'a'ni* act itself, as far as I can see."

"Have you ever thought," Evert began gingerly, as if he might frighten Erien away, "about how difficult it is for you to reason in moral terms, being raised first on Gelion and then on Rire? I mean, I am beginning to see how your friend Horth can sometimes commit cold-blooded murder in the service of being an honorable man." He paused to shape a wan smile. "Ranar hasn't given me much choice about it, really, because if I continue to profess the inability to grasp the concept, he will simply not give up explaining *Okal Rel* until dawn."

Erien smiled back. He could easily imagine a tired, but stubbornly mild-mannered Evert holding out as long as practical against Ranar's intellectual onslaught. Erien said, "*Okal Rel* can be difficult to understand for a Reetion," he admitted.

"No," Evert disagreed firmly. "By its own logic it is perfectly intelligible. Neither, by Reetion logic, is it hard to explain why Lurol was excused. Because we do not believe in absolutes, it is possible for us to excuse the lesser of two evils. We trust ourselves to make decisions based on circumstances. Gelacks, on the other hand, believe some things — like bloodied space, or the medically-enabled coercion of a Sevolite — are simply and completely unjustified." Evert sighed. "I am aware your ancestors had ample cause to espouse such an attitude. Taboos can be terribly practical. But my point is, Horth Nersal has only one internally consistent moral system by which to judge himself, and so do I. Your situation is more taxing. You understand both systems, intellectually, but emotionally I do not think you are sure which one you lean toward. You must construct your moral framework as you go, which is much harder work than locating a problem on the axis of a stable world view." He smiled. "Especially since, knowing you, nothing will do but a system at least as elegant and complete as the two you are trying to resolve. And they are very, very different, *Okal Rel* and Reetion law."

Erien smiled. "Right now, I would be perfectly happy with some inelegant interim results — such as Rire's recognition of Gelion, and Amel agreeing to let Lurol cure his clear dreams. That much is simple. The problem of whether he is free will impaired should wait until things are less fraught with tension. There's a paradox at its heart: we have no means of knowing whether his resistance to Lurol's treatment should be taken as an exercise of free will, or a symptom of his inability to act in his own best interests. I don't have the expertise to diagnose him, and my biases make my opinions unreliable. He has made the argument that since I have put my own life at risk in the service of what I believed right, I have no cause to call him to account for doing likewise. What makes the distinction to me — which is a rather Gelack one — is that his way of doing so is passive rather than active: *pol*, not *rel*. He seems not so much to make a decision to enter a dangerous situation as to let himself be trapped in it." He shook his head, trying again to dislodge the memory of the scene in Lilac Hearth he would not discuss with anyone. "And you know the old proverb about the saving of a life making one responsible for it thereafter...." He shuddered slightly.

"Erien," Evert said, "saving a life — anyone's life — is never wrong."

"And taking one?" Erien said suddenly, fixing his eyes on Evert.

"I won't pretend learning you had killed someone was easy to assimilate," Evert admitted. "If you were to come back, we would probably all have to enter counseling to manage it properly. But I found it quite simple to make up my mind once I got around to asking myself the right question. If it was your life or his, Erien, what else can I be but glad it was D'Lekker who died?"

When Evert put his arm around him, Erien let himself be held briefly and then eased away. His own composure was too precarious.

"It's really not right," Evert said, gazing at him, eyes shiny, "that you should have grown too big to hug properly before *I* outgrew the urge to do it." He smiled. "I'm proud of you, Erien. You've become a fine man. Am I asking too much to want you to be a happy one?"

Erien shook his head mutely.

"Do you want me to make you some pancakes?" Evert asked.

"I'll manage," Erien said briskly.

Evert stepped back, giving him distance, and watched as he unloaded bread, cheese, various spreads, smoked meat, sprouts, onions, lemons and pickled vegetables. "I'm sure you will, I'm sure you will," he murmured, thinking about something more than putting a meal together.

Erien negotiated out the sliding door to the back patio where Ranar was sitting on a low swing. Horth stood arrow straight beside him, doing something most unusual — he was delivering a monologue.

Erien's arrival interrupted the recital as both men refocused on him.

"Are you sure that's stable, chemically and structurally?" Ranar remarked on Erien's sandwich.

"Fleet engineering training triumphs again," said Erien, with an irreverent grin at his former admiral.

Ranar betrayed impatience, shifting forward. "Please continue with the story you were telling me, Liege Nersal."

Erien settled down and applied himself to his plate, ready to listen.

Horth looked away across the commons. "Two rivals want to lead a single house," he started over, speaking in a measured way that had the feel of something learned by rote. "One is sword shy and knows he cannot win the duel, but his soul is strong in its desire, so he goes to the *zer* and says, 'I have good cause to succeed, but a weak arm. How can I defeat my enemy?'"

"The *zer* answers, 'You may poison your rival's food before the duel.'"

"The sword-shy man is shocked and cries, 'Do you, who guide souls, thus advise my soul's dishonor?'"

"'What were you planning instead?' the *zer* asks."

"The sword-shy rival explains that he is the better admiral. He can win if he picks a fight in space and wastes the lives of half the family on both sides."

"'Better,' the *zer* says, 'to use poison.'"

"'I do not understand,' says the sword-shy man."

"'If you kill your rival dishonorably,' the zer explains, 'he will be reborn into a house of many children who do not lack parents. But you will be doomed to death eternal. And this is best, overall. For he who would dismiss *Okal Rel* when it does not favor him has already proved himself insensible to honor and placed his ambition above the common good.'"

The parable had a un-Vrellish feel to it, highlighted by hints of a Demish strategy for handling pronouns in narrative passages, yet it was not Demish, either. Ranar looked excited.

"Your mother taught you that," Ranar asserted.

"Yes," said Horth.

"She was Nesak. *Zers* are what the Nesaks call their priests, or visionaries." Ranar was forced to draw on words from Golden Demish dialect for priests and visionaries, to find equivalents in standard Gelack.

"No," Horth said bluntly, "they are *zers*."

Ranar looked chagrined and slightly amused. "Yes, of course. Do you agree with the *zer* in this story, Liege Nersal?"

"Yes," Horth answered without hesitation.

"But Nersallians do not share all Nesak beliefs concerning *Okal Rel*," Ranar invited.

Erien could guess what he was driving at. It was easy to imagine him posing a question to some future batch of anthropology students: *Describe the points of contention and areas of overlap between Nesak and Nersallian theologies*. But Horth was not interested. He said, instead, "I wish to speak with Erien alone."

Ranar departed after repeating what Evert had told Erien about the STI on the porch, which amounted to greater than STI two for visual exposure, but was otherwise identical to the inside of the house.

"Tomorrow," Horth stated in his inarticulate way as soon as they were alone. It was four seconds before he finished the thought, "What does Rire want?"

"To debrief Amel," said Erien, and paused to wipe his mouth, "concerning his part in Ann's conspiracy to arm *Kali Station*."

Horth frowned.

"I know we have already done so a few times," said Erien. "They want to review cause, effect and motive."

The stony look on Horth's face suggested he remained unenlightened. Erien tried to think of another explanation, but Reetion motives wavered like a mirage when he tried to make them resolve for Horth.

"Do you believe this way is better than a duel?" Horth asked Erien.

Erien could not lie. He owed this man honesty. "Yes, I believe it is better to proceed by weighing the evidence."

Horth looked unsatisfied, but it took him a moment to find words to approximate what bothered him. "It does not feel like 'weighing the evidence.' We give evidence. It doesn't end the questions." He paused. "It feels more like you disagreeing with Bryllit on *Kali Station*." He paused. "Confrontation."

Erien laughed in mild surprise. "I hope," he said, "I won't feel as powerless tomorrow as I did then!"

Horth shook his head. "You were not powerless against Bryllit."

"*Okal Rel* empowered me to challenge Bryllit," Erien quibbled, "but I could not have won."

"No," said Horth.

"Then how was I empowered?"

Horth looked at him as if he was slow, which probably meant: judge by the result.

"People can disagree in ways words cannot change," Horth said slowly, as if reciting the maxims of his Nesak mother again. "The honorable draw swords. To do otherwise is to break the contract that makes desire compatible with life's eternal cycle." He paused. "That is why your Lorel ancestors were killed in the Fifth Civil War."

"Is that a threat, Horth?" Erien asked, as gently as he was able to.

Horth held his gaze steadily a moment before he turned his head to stare up into the starry sky.

Erien looked across the twilight of the commons to the proof of distinct, individual lives on unconscious display in neighbors' yards — a toy, a picnic table and an outdoor stove. One yard held a mounted telescope, left out in complete confidence even of the weather forecast. He tried to imagine Horth and Bryllit living in such a home, and could not. They would be in group homes, like Ann. For the first time, the prospect raised the hair on the back of his neck in the same way envisioning Reetions facing a Sevolite onslaught in space always had.

"Horth," Erien said huskily. "Why did you come?"

"You told me to," said Horth.

Erien recalled their conversation just before the duel on Gelion. He had asked Horth to fight not only for Ameron, but for Rire, asking him to trust his assurance the Reetions were honorable, and to judge for himself later.

Of course! Erien thought, *I should have realized.* Horth was nothing if not literal minded.

His appetite gone, Erien asked, "If you decide Rire is dishonorable, what will you do?"

Horth continued staring up, unblinking, stoically unperturbed. "Bryllit," he said at last, when a certain volume of evening air had moved past, "thinks Amel is a *zer-pol*. Nesaks will sometimes surrender a *zer* to their enemies, inviting them to do him dishonorable harm. The more he suffers, the more it makes him like a *zer-pol*, born to expose the dishonor of those the upright must strike down. But Amel is not a *zer-pol*. Amel is just..." he struggled for an explanation of his attitude and finished with a twitch of his mouth, "Demish."

"Are you suggesting that Bryllit is taking an interest in what happens here on Rire?" asked Erien. Horth gave him one of those looks that told him he had made himself as plain as he would.

Di Mon, Erien thought, *if you've got any pull out there, get us through tomorrow.*

"One thing more," said Horth in the brisk, businesslike way he addressed people under his command.

Erien was disconcerted. "Yes, Liege Nersal?" he said automatically, reverting to fleet reflexes.

"Do not regret killing D'Lekker." The implacable Nersallian paused to see if his pupil had grasped the lesson.

"I— only thought I might still have won, and not kill," said Erien.

Horth nodded. "For that you need a great advantage, and the life saved must be worth the risk. D'Lekker?" Horth shook his head. "Some people need killing, Erien."

"I'll... keep it in mind," Erien promised.

Horth nodded toward the sandwich. "Finish it," he advised. "You will heal faster." Then he left the porch to head off across the commons, leaving Erien to contemplate the challenge to his world view that Horth had slipped past his guard like the edge of a sword: the prospect that his choices, not his self-control, were limited. He had always worked hard at controlling his temper. Horth's perspective made him wonder, for the first time, whether his Vrellish temper might have been his key to winning against D'Lekker when his judgment, unimpaired, would have killed him.

Erien went to bed early, expecting nightmares inspired by the Flashing Floor of flying through contorted space, spaces that played havoc with his pilot's instincts. But the nightmare he suffered was an old one. In it, he was seven years old again, approaching Di Mon's study alone. In reality, Ranar had been with him and Amel had turned up shortly after, but in the dream, he was always alone and, in the way of dreams, knew something terrible waited behind the door.

"Di Mon?" his dream-self asked as he pushed open the door.

A hand on his shoulder brought Erien awake suddenly. He lashed out, hard, but fortunately — for someone — he struck with his weakened left hand. He lurched upright, gasping with pain. In the low light of the room he saw Amel retreat against the shelves, and put out a hand to steady the model of a Reetion space station before it toppled.

"Don't *do* things like that!" Erien growled, grimacing.

"I'll remember," said Amel, "for next time."

The blaze of agony in Erien's shoulder started to dim, slowly. "Are you all right?" he asked.

"I've been hit harder," said Amel. "And I think your shelves are unbroken. Nightmare, was it?" Amel added. His tone was weightless enough not to be intrusive.

"Yes," Erien admitted, "an old one. Was I — am I likely to have disturbed the others?" *Did I speak?* Erien thought with silent dismay. *Was I crying?*

"I don't think so," Amel assured him. "You weren't making much noise."

"Then there was no need to wake me," said Erien. "There's a point in my dream where I usually wake up." Silently, he added, *After standing in Di Mon's study for what seems an eternity, the room all sepia dark and somber except for the sword.* The sword was always distinctive, almost luminous, while Di Mon's body lay in shadows that obscured his face entirely.

Erien rubbed his face with his fingertips, not trusting himself to speak because he could not help thinking how Amel was the last one to see Di Mon alive.

"When novices at Den Eva's had nightmares," Amel said, "I used to recite to them some of the things I'd memorized." He smiled with disarming affection. "I expect you're too old for bedtime stories."

Despite himself, Erien snorted.

"Evert has a remarkable library of Golden Age Demoran classics," Amel said, politely disregarding Erien's reaction.

"Remarkable, at least, for being in Evert's possession. Princess H'Us — the late princess-liege of H'Us I mean, not Luthan — had a library you could get lost in! She used to like me reading to her." Amel sounded almost wistful for his days as a successful courtesan.

Erien said abruptly, "How do you manage, Amel? How do you remember details from your past with fondness, when—" He decided not to put the rest of it into words.

"Maybe it's being part Golden Demish," he said blithely. "The memories of the good times are so very bright, I can hold them up against the rest of it." He shrugged. "Most of the time, at least."

"You'll have to get the clear dreams fixed, you know," Erien said, keeping his tone neutral.

"I don't *have* to do anything," Amel retorted. "They'll get better on their own, when I'm with Perry." But his voice flattened as he spoke, and lost conviction.

"It will be over tomorrow," said Erien. "Just keep your head, and I will keep them off you as best I can. Then we can work on the diplomatic angle."

"Work is *your* vice, Erien," Amel said lightly, "not mine." He made small, soft sounds getting comfortable. "Time for that bedtime story."

Deflecting Amel, in this strange mood, was as awkward as fending off moonbeams. Erien found it easier to settle back and let him have his way.

When Amel spoke again, his voice fell into the darkness word by word, with the unhurried assurance of a storyteller serving as conduit for something greater.

"Long ago, when Golden Avas ruled the empire," he opened with a favorite Demish formula, "there was a prince named Morry who was perfectly clever and perfectly beautiful. It was widely said he had a Golden Soul, and in childhood he excelled in everything he cared to do. But because he was so clever, Morry began to contemplate the troubles of the world as he got older, and when he was just fifteen, he swore to serve the Golden Emperor as a paladin to make the world a better place.

"For six years Morry learned everything he felt he needed to know. He studied history and lore with the Monatese; from the Vrellish he learned flying and the sword; the Lorels taught him to understand the worst of humankind's desires, and yet because he was so perfect, none of this knowledge made his heart callous. He could still weep to hear a lovely song and smile with pleasure at the happiness of lovers, even though he had chosen a life that denied him the joys of love."

"Morry was confident it lay within his power to do good."

"Now it so happened that very early in his new life as a paladin, there was a falling out between Brown Hearth and Red Hearth. Morry offered to stand champion for Brown Hearth, because he was sure Red Hearth would otherwise win the duel. And so perfectly had he learned from his Vrellish tutor that he managed to win without killing the Red Vrellish champion."

"But neither Brown Hearth nor Red Hearth was reconciled to their differences, and before long they contrived to clash again.

"This time, Brown Hearth made a gift to the Golden Ava of the Lorel Stairs, arranging that all the court must pass up them to seek audience. And the Vrellish were unable to appear before the Ava because the stairs sickened them and made them faint.

"So Morry taught the Vrellish how to close their eyes and count paces, or be led by a commoner child. And they were thus able to appear before the Ava again.

"But the enmity between Morry's Vrellish tutor and his Lorel mentor would not end. His Lorel mentor killed his Vrellish tutor dishonorably, with poison, and was himself killed by a Vrellish mob."

"Morry was devastated by his dual loss, and also angry, for just as he had been a perfect child, he thought he should also have been a perfect paladin and seen the conflict peacefully resolved. Then the Golden Emperor came and sat beside him, and said, 'You have done all anyone could do, and more.'"

"'Which is as nothing,' Morry told his liege and idol. 'For the people I sought to save are dead, and the world is more ugly than it was when I began.'"

"'Not so,' said the Golden Emperor. 'For the world cannot be uglier as long as you are still alive in it to do more good.'"

Amel broke off then, and said in his normal voice, "My favorite Morry story is the one where he gives up being a paladin for love of a princess and learns he cannot create happiness in the world by denying it to himself. There's a song about it: a romantic argument between the princess — who is by far the wilier philosopher — and Morry himself, over whether self-denial does more good than harm in the end."

Without further preamble, Amel launched into the opening verse in a sugary old Demoran dialect, bristling with form and structure beneath its frothy sentiments. By the time Amel was halfway through it, Erien had drifted off to sleep again, and this time he dreamed, pleasantly, of Princess Luthan.

SEVENTEEN

Eyes on Amel — Drasous

Poetic allusions

The courtesan prince has his uses, thought Drasous as Amel's voice faded to silence in the room across the hall from the one he was sharing with Horth. He had heard Heir Gelion talking in his sleep and had been on the verge of going in himself when Amel intervened.

He heard the door to Erien's bedroom quietly open and close, followed by a whisper of cloth, a catch of breath and then a muted thud, absorbed by the smart covering of the floor. Drasous looked into the hall in time to see Amel picking himself up off the floor.

"May I help you, Immortality?" Drasous whispered, respecting the sleeping household.

"Oh, it's you." Amel made a point of speaking down, Pureblood-to-commoner, reminding Drasous he had shot Amel with a *klinoman* dart the last time they'd run into each other on Gelion.

Amel adjusted his dressing gown and shook out his loose black hair, betraying nervousness. "I was going downstairs to get something to eat," he explained his minor accident. "I guess I was still half asleep, because I remembered there was a pile of Golden Demish poetry books in the hall, and made to step over them. Except they weren't there anymore, so I stumbled."

The explanation was convoluted enough to be genuine; highborn Demish memory was riddled with unnecessary detail, but Drasous had no doubt Amel was lying.

"I am up," Drasous said. "I can make you something to eat."

"Uh, no. Thanks, but—"

Drasous ignored the rejection. Amel could put on airs, but not even with the aid of Gelack grammar could he execute a *no* like someone raised in the ways of arrogance. Drasous went on ahead, turning back on the top stair. "A peanut butter sandwich and fruit juice?"

"All right then, if you want to," Amel said, lapsing into English. Perhaps it was more comfortable capitulating in a language without status-differentiation that ought to have favored him packed into every pronoun.

"Are you sure you were not imagining the books?" Drasous asked at the bottom of the stairs.

Amel addressed his suspicion with candor. "Clear dreaming you mean? No."

The lights came up automatically as they entered the little kitchen. Arbiters made perfect servants, Drasous had discovered, but Reetions did reserve some duties for themselves, like cooking. Evert insisted the kitchen was the center of family life, and he was right. By offering to prepare Amel food, Drasous had secured an opportunity to talk with him casually.

Amel dumped himself with uncharacteristic heaviness into a chair. "The *Kali* arbiter was pumping me for reasons worth living for," Amel said with an air of sarcasm. "If I was clear dreaming something out of that experience, it wouldn't be a pile of morality plays from one of Demora's stuffier periods." He hesitated. "Not that poetry isn't something worth living for."

"Just not morality plays?" Drasous suggested.

Amel shrugged, readily drawn into discussing literature. "Some of the language in them is wonderful, even if the attitudes constrain the protagonists pretty narrowly. Dying for honor is well and good." He shifted, restless. "I would just rather find a way to live for it, though, wouldn't you?"

Drasous considered. "In my younger days," he observed, "I might have pointed out that choice in the manner of one's living or dying was not something a bonded *gorarelpul* might expect to encounter."

"And you wouldn't anymore?" Amel asked.

"Not in the same spirit. Now I can see how Sevolites are as constrained as any *gorarelpul*, in their own way: their masters are many. We need only concern ourselves with one."

Amel frowned. "I don't know what you're getting at," he said, disgruntled.

"Take the *Prince of Dem'Lara*, for instance," said Drasous, citing a famous work of the Demish Golden canon, in which the hero found himself in a situation where only his death would preserve his family's honor. The scene between the prince and his mother, where she conveyed her expectations — subtly, poetically and obliquely — in the presence of their enemies, was considered a classic. Amel would know it intimately.

And that should, Drasous thought, *put him in the right frame of mind to catch my meaning without me needing to alert the arbiter with plain talk.* "Dem'Lara's masters were his mother and his love of family," Drasous ventured a bit of small-talk in keeping with his last remark.

Amel raised both eyebrows. "I would never have taken you for a connoisseur of Demish literature, Drasous," he observed suspiciously.

"I have my reasons," said Drasous, busy spreading bread and pouring juice. "Literary codes are more effective than numeric ciphers for slipping messages past the Vrellish, for example, as you well know. You used to decode such messages for Ev'rel, intercepted in transit between Demoran conspirators."

Amel's lips parted as if to protest; then he closed them.

Drasous put the snack down in front of Amel.

"Thanks," Amel said resentfully.

"My pleasure," Drasous assured him.

Amel continued to stare at him uneasily. *Good*, Drasous thought. *He is catching on.* Drasous poured himself a glass of juice as he considered his next move.

"I don't think Erien appreciated the point of the parable you were telling him," Drasous observed, without apology for listening in on the two of them via the arbiter.

Amel's lips compressed. "I thought only family members could check on each other under STI two conditions," he said, and shrugged it off as if he didn't care. "Perhaps you count as family because you're living here. I wonder if Ranar considered the consequences. Reetion notions of privacy weren't designed with *gorarelpul* in mind."

"True, Immortality. Nor were arbiters designed to interface with a Golden Demish brain. But it happened."

Amel's face went blank. A shiver ran down both his arms, as though readying himself to push something away. Then he was back, smoothing out his expression.

"Have you and Heir Gelion discussed the possible consequences of the Reetions discovering you are still experiencing clear dreams?" asked Drasous.

Amel artfully transformed a shiver into a laugh, but didn't answer. He seemed to be trembling on the verge of another clear dream. Drasous watched him force it back and turn angry gray eyes on this tormentor. "You're testing me," Amel accused. "Stop it. You shouldn't even be talking about it—" He looked up to where he knew the arbiter's sensory strip ran along the wall, just above eye-level. "— you know."

"Erien has convinced me STI two conditions are opaque to everything except life and death matters, or criminal acts of a serious nature," Drasous said calmly, "and I have acquainted myself thoroughly with what those are. So long as we say nothing an arbiter can clearly identify as directly life threatening to anyone," he looked pointedly at Amel as he said this, "or criminal, we may converse as privately here as in a Demish parlor." He considered. "More privately, perhaps, since here the arbiters themselves are the servants."

Amel was looking sullen. "So?" he asked in a guarded tone.

"According to my understanding of the legalities," Drasous continued, "if your performance tomorrow should inspire... concern on the part of the Reetions, over your mental health, you could be ruled incompetent and deemed a Supervised citizen unable to leave Rire."

Amel raised a laugh. "Drasous, you're spoiling my appetite." But the panicky glitter in Amel's eyes told Drasous he had accomplished his goal, and driven Amel's thoughts in the direction he needed them to go.

"Was Heir Gelion's bedtime story authentic," Drasous asked, "or an adaptation?"

Amel's nostrils flared slightly with indignation. "There is always some scope for interpretation."

"I thought you had revised it somewhat," Drasous said. "Golden Demish canon tends to encourage noble sacrifice in the defense of others."

Drasous could see Amel bristle, and knew both of them were now well aware they were not talking about Prince Morry or Prince Dem'Lara any longer.

"Maybe the Golden Demish canon is a bit too morbid," Amel suggested, shakily but with force.

"Because it often dwells on death as the final solution?" Drasous asked. "Do you reject the idea?"

"What would you consider worth dying for?" Amel snapped.

"My Ava, naturally," said Drasous, "and anything that he thought worthy of my sacrifice." Which, from the Ava's last orders, included his heir, but did not include Amel Dem'Vrel.

"Sorry," murmured Amel, softening.

"What for?" Drasous was honestly baffled.

Amel shrugged. "That wasn't a fair question to ask of a bonded *gorarelpul*."

"Would you like me to consider the question hypothetically? I can, you know. My bond is quite stable. The answer would be the same, I think. Except," Drasous hesitated to bare himself even this far, but he knew self-revelation would hold Amel's attention and, since Amel was an acute judge of emotion, it seemed wisest to let his own be genuine. "I do not know how free men choose between loves," said Drasous.

"You love Charous, don't you?" Amel said, and smiled. "You're just lucky she works for Ameron, as well." He answered Drasous' silence with an unguarded stare. "I think we free men just hope the hardest choices never come our way."

Drasous sat down quietly beside Amel. "The Reetions fear threats to the integrity of their arbiters more than they fear anything else about Gelacks, Prince Amel. They fear you more than they fear Liege Nersal."

"That would be a first," Amel muttered.

"I do not think you know how to defend yourself against Rire's overheated love-hate relationship with you, Amel."

Amel's eyes snapped up. "And you would, I suppose?" he asked hotly. "If it was you?" His eyes filled up and glistened. "I won't have a choice if they put me in a visitor probe!"

"I understand," the *gorarelpul* said quietly. "It is a matter of brain physiology."

"Not to Horth Nersal, it isn't," Amel said with a small laugh. "I am sure he thinks it is something a stronger person could resist. I would like to see him—" He broke off, the spite gone as soon as it had surfaced. "No, I wouldn't. It would destroy him."

"Him, but not you," Drasous prompted.

"Oh, me, I am like one of those Reetion spacesuits with the invisible seams. They just open me up with a touch and seal me up again, good as new, whenever they please!" He talked boldly, but abruptly put his face in his hands, elbows pushing back crumbs on the table.

"You know a great deal," Drasous said, "about a great many people. You know things Ava Ameron risked his own life to keep from being disclosed."

Amel looked up with pale, parted lips. "Act four, scene five," he said in a small voice.

Drasous knew then that he had conveyed his message. Act four, scene five was where the prince was told how to protect his family's honor.

Amel brushed crumbs from his sleeves with trembling hands. "You do a mean interpretation of the classics, Drasous," he said, and got to his feet with studied grace. "The *Prince of Dem'Lara*," he shook his head and sketched a smile, "how flattering."

Conceivably, Drasous thought, to his own surprise, *it might even be apt.* He had never before thought of Amel as a proper court Sevolite. He bowed slightly now, in acknowledgment.

Amel pulled his music-patterned dressing gown more tightly around himself. "I'm going back to bed," he said firmly.

"Sleep well," Drasous said.

"I doubt that," Amel's composure wavered. "I suppose I can assume your taste in literature is, ah, something you've discussed with Ameron... I mean, at least in principle?"

"Yes."

"Well," Amel stopped there as if he had been silently punched, then inhaled with a jerk and concluded, "I suppose in that case, if things were really bad..."

"Of course," Drasous acknowledged.

Amel nodded. "Good night, then."

Drasous switched back to Gelack. "Good night, Immortality. May your ancestors guard you tomorrow."

Amel nodded again, and slipped away up the stairs like a shadow.

Horth Nersal woke like a *gorarelpul* — tidily and at once. As Drasous entered into their room, Horth's deep voice came out of the shadows. "Erien?"

"A nightmare, Your Grace, but he is sleeping again. Amel saw to him."

"Good," said Horth. He sat up.

"Lights up," said Drasous, and the arbiter obliged.

Horth's dark eyes fixed on the objects in Drasous' hands — a plate holding a peanut butter sandwich, an unlit candle and a lighter. A denizen of Gelion, ships and stations, Horth was understandably wary around fire.

"Time to talk?" he asked.

Drasous nodded.

Horth swung himself upright. He was wearing black fleet fatigues, with liege marks and crest on the collar. He expected action. "Heir Gelion must leave if—"

Drasous touched a finger to his lips, signaling for silence. Horth's nostrils flared as he cast a resentful glance over the arbiter sensors built into the room. Drasous lifted the sandwich and applied it in two broad strokes to the sensory strip on the wall, and then knelt beside the bed, pulling a notebook and pencil from his pocket. Nersal indicated his understanding by sweeping a narrow finger up and down, directing Drasous to apply a third streak beside the first two. Drasous obeyed without question. Then Horth dropped into a crouch on the floor beside him.

They both knew they had scant minutes before an intervention occurred, given Horth's previous experimental attempts to dismantle the house's internal sensors.

Drasous jotted swiftly on his note pad. *Heir Gelion thinks he fights a single duel*, Drasous wrote. *He does not. As he vanquishes one opponent, another will rise. I do not believe they will let him win.*

The stage began to chime. Drasous wrote, *Can you get him off planet?*

Horth frowned. Drasous knew the Nersallian liege could out fly any Reetion sent after them, once in space, but it would not be straightforward getting there, given the ubiquitous surveillance and the way Reetions processed pilots at space ports.

A yellow octagon popped up on the stage. "Visual sensors are blocked. Audible input suggests no immediate distress. Please confirm immediate assistance is not required."

"Confirmed," Drasous said in Reetion.

Drasous wrote hastily, *I have advised Amel he must not survive to be probed, if it comes to that. The probe can make Sevolites serve the Reetion agenda. Neither you nor Heir Gelion must be subjected to it, either.*

Drasous felt a wash of faintness as his own conditioning seized upon his recognition of the contradiction between Ameron's order to preserve his heir and the Ava's need to sacrifice that heir rather than have the Reetions use him.

Nersal noticed, and clapped him firmly on the shoulder. "Good," he said aloud.

The stage gave them another warning. Horth glanced at it as though lining it up for a sword thrust. Drasous judged they were midway through their grace period. He wrote, *Heir Gelion may not leave willingly*.

Nersal grinned suddenly at him, his body loosening. "No," he said, and lay back down, ending the conversation. Drasous nodded, slipped the used page of the note pad onto the metal plate and struck a match. The stage chimed again and gave a smoke-detection warning. When the paper had burned to ash, Drasous took a towel and wiped the peanut butter from the sensors. Before he was done, Lurol's groggy, testy voice came through the stage, "Is Horth messing with the sensors again?"

"We lit a candle for meditation purposes," Drasous said.

"It's the middle of the night!" protested Lurol. "Arbiter, don't bother me again about those two unless they're having seizures! Good *night*."

Drasous blew out the candle, and rinsed the ashes of his notes down the drain.

Horth Nersal was already asleep again.

EIGHTEEN

Erien

Through the Guard

As Erien climbed the stairs after a solitary breakfast, he heard Amel's infectious laughter drifting from Ranar and Evert's bedroom.

Lurol's voice said, "Looks good on you!"

Amel replied, "Forget it!"

Evert and Lurol succumbed to more hilarity despite Ranar's admonishment: "This is a serious concern, and we haven't got all day to work it out."

Erien didn't want to know what it was about. He dressed and activated his stage to review the trawl of the filters he had set up the night before.

Good luck appeared in plain letters. A message from Alka, which his revised filter had classified as personal. He smiled, and sent her back a quick response, *Thanks. And think about the Reetion embassy on Gelion*.

A ripple of applause came from Ranar's room.

"Careful!" cried Lurol.

"I thought you were impressed by my coordination," Amel protested.

"Yes, but you're injured."

"Not much," Amel assured her, "not anymore." There was a startled sound from Lurol and a soft thud.

Evert said cheerily, "I think she's a bit heavy on her feet to be a sword dancer."

Erien got up, unable to concentrate on his work with all the racket, and met Drasous coming in with clothes laid out in his arms — Erien's formal clothes, with hereditary colors and braid, made up for him to wear at the Swearing on Gelion where he was to have given Ameron his allegiance. Instead, he had wound up in Lilac Hearth, freeing Amel and killing D'Lekker.

"I don't — think this is the time," he said. "I'll wear hearth colors when we move on to the diplomatic phase. That would be more appropriate."

If Drasous guessed Erien's motives for refusing Gelack clothing were emotional rather than rational, he did not show it. Erien watched him shake out the outfit and hang it up. It looked barbarous, hanging there beside his muted Reetion synthetics. He glanced down at the plain gray-and-white coverall he was wearing — unobtrusive. Safe.

Amel appeared in the door frame dressed in a soft gray, long-sleeved tunic, worn loose over darker slacks. It was utterly ordinary by Reetion standards, but Erien's first reaction was nonetheless critical. Amel looked too vivid — boisterously alive, thanks to a slight flush, and touched up to perfection, like a synthdrama construction.

"Poor Drasous," Amel remarked on Erien's own choice of apparel. "He brought your Lor'Vrellish formals all the way from Gelion. Oh well, your Reetion whites will match Liege Nersal's basic black. Our part in the hearing should be done by noon, according to Ranar. I won't be able to see Ann until she's finished her part, but I thought she could see me, at least, if I spent some time sightseeing afterward." He smiled. "It would be a shame to leave Rire, after all, without taking a look around. I thought I might even ask if there's dancing somewhere I could get a look at." His confidence wavered. "Or would that be too controversial, back home?"

"That would depend," Drasous said dryly, "on whether Your Immortality watched, or took part."

Amel frowned at the pointedly delivered title.

"Let's deal with the hearing first," said Erien. He studied Amel a moment longer, wondering whether he should believe Amel's bright air of confidence. Finally, he nodded. "Let's go."

The neighborhood turned out to watch as they left the house: Erien, Horth, Ranar and Amel, walking across the commons lawn toward the public transit connection. A child waved. Amel smiled and waved back. That was the beginning of the end of moderation. A flood of waving broke out. Some teenaged girls started chanting, "Ah — mel. Ah — mel." Amel blew a kiss at one of them and halted in surprise when she staggered into a friend as if struck.

"Don't encourage them," Erien told him in a clipped tone.

"What are they out for?" Ranar complained, annoyed. "We'll be on record the whole way. They could watch us from their stages."

"I think they're just having fun," Amel told them. "Maybe Reetions need more of it."

Horth was unconcerned by the fuss. He paid no attention to the trio of youths who threw off cloaks to salute him with brandished swords. He took more interest in the first responders who wove through the crowd to confiscate the replica weapons. Horth's own sword was stowed under his bed at the house.

Civic authorities had decided to shut the commuter train down, to make it more difficult for people to congregate at the Space Service Center where the hearings were taking place. First responders and graduates of Ranar's gelackology studies were posted along the way to politely remind gawkers to stay back. Special checks and balances had been devised and passed by half a dozen councils to discourage mobs, including a penalty system that got steeper the thicker the turnout.

"Delinquent children," Ranar grumped about the crowd. "There's no excuse for such behavior."

"Right," Amel teased him good naturedly. "I mean, it's not like you ever took a risk or two pursuing Gelacks just because you found us fascinating, or anything like that."

Ranar sustained a sour look for about three seconds, then relented with, "So long as they are not upsetting you, Amel."

Amel tipped his head in Erien's direction. "It's not me you have to worry about," he underscored his meaning by giving Erien a gentle nudge.

Horth's arm shot across Erien's chest to lock in the cloth of Amel's soft gray tunic.

Amel snatched a breath, eyes widening with involuntary fear, lips apart, but expression still maddeningly decorous.

"Erien said not to encourage them," Horth reminded him, with force.

Amel gripped Horth's wrist. "I don't care if you're faster than I am," he down-spoke the Highlord. "I am tired of being grabbed as if I—"

"That's enough! Both of you," said Erien, putting out a hand to either side to separate them.

Horth let go and kept walking, incident forgotten, but Amel's delight in the audience did not recover, although he worked his way back from irritated to more or less relaxed before they reached the Space Science Center on the grounds of the Rire Proper Space Port.

A member of Foreign and Alien Council met them as they came up the stairs, leaving the last wisps of their impromptu escort behind them. Everyone had agreed it would be best to bring the Gelacks in after the hearing room was prepared to accommodate an STI six level of interest, and all the other attendees were settled. They were shown into a large, oval chamber with tiers of occupied seats. Bands of sensi-strips were visible and additional multimodal sensors poked, like black tongues, from fixtures and mobile arms. There were windows — a whole bank of them along a bayed wall — but they were discretely blinded to discourage live attendance on the lawn.

Amel's face lit up as he spotted Ann in a seat a little higher than the rest, reached by a short set of steps at the back. She rose and called — "Amel!" — waving a hand.

"Stay here," Erien muttered sharply to Amel.

"You look delicious!" Ann called out to Amel, who grinned back. Erien frowned, wondering why Amel didn't realize that she was trying to assert she wasn't scared of Sevolites because she owned one. Amel seemed incapable of grasping Ann was as much a political animal, in her own way, as Ameron.

A pilot handler popped up beside Ann and engaged her in a serious chat.

"I'm supposed to keep quiet!" Ann called down cheerfully to Amel on the floor. "You all right?"

"Yes!" he answered her.

"Good enough, then," she said, and sat down.

The show over, the rest of the Reetions present relaxed and began talking softly among themselves. The investigative panel was seated in an arc, each linked through ear bugs and a flat stage to the council for whom they served as spokespersons, and therefore able to represent it at whatever expansion level was required, which could change in the course of deliberations. About fifty other observers, each with some distinct purpose, sat in tiers along the facing wall. Medical personnel were stationed beside their equipment. No first responders were in evidence, but Erien knew they were close by, equipped with sleeping gas and restraining foam. The argument for including tranquilizer guns had not made the threshold against the weight of anthropological advice concerning the negative symbolism of guns for Gelacks.

Two Reetions came out to greet the Gelacks.

"I am Wren," a tranquil looking woman introduced herself to Amel with a warm smile. "I have been appointed as a human alternative to what would normally be a guardian arbiter persona, in charge of your physical and mental health."

Amel smiled back. "Nice to meet you," he said.

Beside her stood Juma, the solid, slightly graying man appointed by FAC to take over from Ranar as Gelack liaison. His greeting was somewhat perfunctory, and Erien could tell Ranar's presence in their group made him uncomfortable.

Wren took Amel away to meet the panelists at his request, leaving Erien, Horth and Ranar to find their seats. A handful of Reetions in the first row moved to accommodate them, and left empty seats around them as well. Horth sat beside Erien, and Ranar sat on Horth's other side to provide translation and explain the use of the flat stage and ear bug attached to the comfortable chair.

"The hearing will be taking place on many levels," Ranar explained. "You will hear people muttering into their subvocal collars, giving commands, or speaking into voice pieces. Most will be wearing ear bugs. Some, however, will simply watch and leave analysis for later. It will all be over by noon, as a concession to Amel."

Erien nodded, but no matter how feverently people insisted they wanted to be nice to Amel, he could not escape the irksome feeling it was Gelion on trial here.

Wren took a long time making sure Amel was comfortable with the equipment before she helped settle him into the monitoring chair. Then the stage overhead activated, and dissolved into an enlarged view of Amel's face staring upward. For a moment, Amel's unsettled look dominated the hearing room, cream complexion warming with a faint flush. Then the image shrank to make room for data from his monitors.

"Amel," Wren claimed his attention. "Since it is unclear to what extent you fall under the jurisdiction of Reetion law, your voluntary cooperation in this hearing is required and much appreciated. Do you freely consent to participate?"

"Yes," Amel said.

"Can you state your understanding of this hearing's purpose?"

"To clear up things that prevent us — Rire and Gelion — from putting *Kali Station* behind us, so you Reetions can negotiate with Erien to establish diplomatic relations."

"And regarding yourself?"

Amel came out with the response Erien and Ranar had briefed him to give. "I understand Rire wants to discharge any responsibility toward me, arising from my actions on its behalf, or as a consequence of possible... treatment, I received under extenuating circumstances in the past."

A delay ensued, caused by weakening coherence in Amel's thoughts that suggested his feelings about the statement were not straightforward. Some auxiliary questions followed, but none could triangulate in on the cause; the experts concluded some stress and ambiguity were to be expected, and the arbiter declared itself satisfied that Amel understood what was at issue.

One of the panelists spoke next. "You have given testimony, for the record, concerning how and when you assisted citizen Ann of Rire to outfit *Kali Station* in defiance of prevailing law. Do you affirm such testimony, now?"

"Yes," Amel said, without a ripple of doubt in his read-out.

"Is there anything you wish to add, omit or qualify?"

"No," Amel said. "Erien said it is all right as it is."

Erien winced.

There was a stir in the audience and a flurry of activity through linkages, in which Foreign and Alien Council asserted the deferral was a cultural artifact arising from Erien's status as Heir Gelion. Questioning branched out to contain the concern it might indicate coercion.

"Did you seek Erien's opinion about what to contribute to the record?" asked the arbiter.

Amel realized he had made a misstep. His heart rate picked up even more when addressed by an artificial intelligence. "Yes," said Amel, following up quickly with an explanation. "Erien knows more about how to communicate with Reetions than I do."

Decisions played out over linkages, ultimately accepting Amel's reliance on Erien as benign.

A new panelist stood up. "Amel," she said, "are you aware of how vital the integrity of arbiters is to Reetions?"

"Not entirely, perhaps," Amel admitted. "I have had it explained to me."

"Strictly in terms of importance, what would you equate — in your own world view — with Reetion attitudes concerning interference with arbiter integrity?"

Amel's readouts betrayed a mild anxiety that built until he noticed it himself, and relaxed into honesty. "I suppose it would be like doing something *okal'a'ni*."

"An act that, among Gelacks, would have serious consequences?" asked his questioner.

When Amel did not answer, the arbiter supplied, "It is on record that culturally taboo acts are punishable within most Gelack subcultures by summary execution, often conducted in public in an outburst of mass hysteria."

"I think he perceived that as a threat," Wren objected.

"No," Amel denied. "I understand. You are only pointing out, in Gelack terms, how seriously Rire views interference with its arbiters. You aren't implying I should be executed."

"Punishment is not at issue here," a panelist insisted.

Amel inhaled slowly, dampening his lips.

Wren's analysis, worked out on her flat stage, displaced the raw output on the large screen. "He doesn't believe we don't intend to punish him," she summarized.

"You are trying to make me view what I did as comparable to being *okal'a'ni*," Amel objected. "That's upsetting. You shouldn't be worried if I react accordingly."

There was a pause while the arbiter compiled expert opinion. Then it announced, "The subject's explanation is an equally valid interpretation of the data observed at this level of monitoring."

"I certainly don't think you're going to conduct an execution in an outburst of mass hysteria," Amel told them, lightening the mood in the room with a sprinkling of surprised laughter among the audience.

"Without reference to a Gelack parallel," asked the arbiter, "can you tell us why helping Ann communicate illicitly was wrong?

Amel picked a panelist to look at as he answered. "I think so," he said. "Reetions rely on arbiters to govern themselves. If something went wrong with them, you wouldn't know what to expect of each other."

"Did you understand this at the time?" a panelist asked, moving on to settle the question of whether learning and change had occurred.

"Yes," Amel looked right at Ann, which had the effect of swamping subtler reactions with a background glow of sexuality. "But I didn't know smuggling some extra messages would be considered interference," he added, showing signs of distraction with a strong limbic undercurrent.

"Amel?" Wren touched his arm. It registered like a sensory snap, making him break eye contact with Ann.

"Yes?" he said, a little breathlessly.

"I am sorry, but we would like you to pay attention to *us*." She smiled with real affection and forgiveness. "Ann seems to be creating... uh, noise. It makes it hard to get a clear impression of your mental disposition toward your testimony. Do you understand?"

Amel nodded.

"Amel," spoke up a different panelist. "Ann has testified she gained your cooperation by appealing to your compassion for Reetions as helpless commoners in the face of a Sevolite invasion. She did not tell you how she meant to mount a defense, only that her intension was to blockade the jump on the Reetion side. Do you wish to add, omit or qualify her version of events as far as you are concerned?"

"Helping her was my decision," Amel said. "I do make them."

"Noted," said the panelist. "Anything else?"

"No," said Amel. But his brain displayed complex, diffuse activity not compatible with settled issues.

"You are not satisfied with Ann's summary of events?" said Wren.

"I am not satisfied with the whole situation," Amel said. "Ann ought to be able to defend Rire. That's *rel*. But I was wrong not to make her tell me how. Imagine what might have happened — it could have been the Killing War all over again! I should have realized she'd have to do something *okal'a'ni*, but I let her persuade me, instead, and then I didn't think about it anymore. That was my fault. It's something I do — not thinking about things, so I can cope with them."

Amel's emotions ran aground on ill-defined hunks of distress with hard, visceral components to them, suggesting guilt, grief — and fear. He shot out of the examination chair and stood in front of it, breathing heavily. Once out, though, he calmed down immediately.

"I'm sorry," he told the panel, and then concentrated on Wren as she came to him, her backup medical team bracing for action.

"Shall we call a recess?" Wren asked, touching his arm. "We'll excuse you on compassionate grounds if you have changed your mind about whether you are up to this."

"I am not sick," Amel insisted.

The audience murmured. Wren smiled. "No, you are not sick, Amel. But you are not comfortable with the monitoring. Unfortunately, it's an essential requirement if testimony is to be accepted without arbiter corroboration, and Erien destroyed the record in the *Kali Station* visitor probe. Would you like a recess?"

"No." Amel looked back at the chair, drew a deep breath, and sat down again. "I would rather get this over with before lunch," he said, and forced a smile.

Monitoring resumed after a moment's adjustment.

Wren retired to the sidelines once more.

"We'll try to keep this short for you," a new panelist promised as a rack of points to check off flashed up on the display wall. "Please confirm or deny the following as I read them off. Did Ava Ameron send you to *SkyBlue Station* shortly before events on Gelion that confirmed him as Ava?"

"Yes," said Amel. "Ameron wanted me to assess the mood on Rire should he decline to acknowledge Ranar as your ambassador."

"But Ameron knew nothing about your collusion with Ann?"

"No," said Amel. "No one at home knew. I tried to warn Ranar once. That's all."

A brief pause ensued, concluding with satisfaction on all scores. Ranar had already put the exchange referred to on record, which provided corroboration.

"There's something I would like to stress here, for the record," said Ann, standing with her hands on the railing in front of her.

"As this hearing may affect your sentencing," ruled the presiding arbiter, "you are entitled."

Ann looked straight at Erien, avoiding Amel. "Everyone knows why I did what I did with *Kali Station*. Hanson's coup d'état was a fiasco, of course, but I don't regret the original intention. Look at us! We're doing it again! We're focusing on Amel. Fine! So track this, Rire — Amel pulled off multidimensional pattern doctoring, by inspection, that I couldn't get a navcom to duplicate in real time! Think about it."

"The vulnerability in the error-correction algorithm he exploited has been solved," a panelist advised her.

"Goodie," said Ann. "And is Fahzir feeling just as confident about the loopholes he hasn't found?"

This created an unpleasant stir in the meeting hall.

Ann narrowed almond eyes at Erien. "Here's something else for the record. Nine years ago Ranar's son, Erien, then eight years old, ran away from home to join the Space Service. The counselor assigned let him take the navigational aptitude simulation test to keep him occupied. He scored seventy." Her expression hardened. "Any candidate who scores twenty or above is invited into Space Service."

A rumble greeted this bombshell, as speakers on the panel checked their consoles. "There is no record of any such anomaly!" one of them announced promptly.

"Not online," Ann acknowledged. "The counselor never checked the results and Ranar didn't ask for them. The data was retained in active memory for the usual six months and would have vanished if routine diagnostics hadn't logged it as a probable error. Which is where it turned up, listed in an offline backup."

Ranar's voice murmured in the silence, busy translating for Horth, who had taken an interest the moment Ann's stare had fixed on Erien.

"Most pilots score between twenty and forty," Ann elaborated, managing to swagger while standing still. "I tested out at fifty-one, myself. But what I would like to bring to everyone's attention is that Erien got seventy percent on *every* assessment of intellectual and educational progress during the first year he spent with us. Seventy is the expected median, something he could easily have looked up. My guess is," she confronted Ranar, "that you told him to look ordinary, and he took you just a little too literally."

She raised her voice suddenly, pointing at Erien, "Why don't we leave Amel alone, and psych profile *him*! And Horth Nersal!"

Both Ann's handlers plunged into the base of her isolation dias to get at her. Amel came out of his chair and was intercepted by Wren, talking quickly to him to prevent him trying to go to Ann's defense.

"Tell them to let her speak," Horth told Ranar.

Ranar looked anxiously at Erien.

Ann had just wrenched an arm free of a handler. "Stay where you are, Amel!" she shouted across at him, in Gelack. "This is my *rel*!"

Erien nodded to Ranar, who inhaled with a worried look but obediently applied himself to the little stage mounted on his seat's arm, advising Juma that Liege Nersal wished to hear Ann out. There were swift consultations.

"Ann of New Beach, Rire," said a designated speaker, "you have been granted the right to address whom you will, for one more minute, on the strength of the vote supporting the recommendation that we honor the wishes of our Gelack guest, Liege Nersal. As to the point you raised earlier, Ranar's role in hiding Erien's identity has already been excused — as a parental decision — on the grounds he was acting in the child's best interest."

"Not the point," Ann bit off.

Horth stood up. He spoke to Ann across the room's length, ignoring everyone else as if they didn't matter. "You prepared an *okal'a'ni* defense, but you saved Dorn's life. Why, Reetion?"

Ann was finally taken aback by something: Horth had addressed her in peerage. Bravado came to her rescue, putting a pout on her sensuous mouth. "You took my station," she called back, accepting the grammatical equality he offered, "then you let us ship our people home instead of spacing them. Why, Gelack?"

Horth didn't answer. He just sat down again to watch what would happen, instructing Ranar to keep translating for him.

"Why are we being so thick-headed?" Ann appealed to her fellow Reetions. "Okay, we're not at war with Sevildom. Yet. But how long do you think we would have to debate a response if they decide to attack? We have to be prepared!"

"And provoke the very attack you dread!" someone on the panel burst out, and immediately looked surprised at himself.

"All the more reason, I would say," said an unruffled older man, among the invited audience, "to be getting on with diplomatic relations... that Ameron has sent his heir here to accomplish." He nodded once in Erien's direction and sat down again.

"You have twenty-one seconds remaining," Ann was informed by the arbiter. "Do you wish to make any further points?"

"Just this," Ann said hotly. "Lay off Amel, okay? Just leave him out of this!"

"Establishing Amel's best interests," Wren assured her, "is one of our key goals."

Ann deflated as she looked at Amel. He stood beside Wren, looking painfully confused and frustrated in his desire to go to her. "Love you, *mekan'st*," she said, speaking Reetion except for the one untranslatable Gelack word. She smiled, "Even if you are as much a Sevolite in your own way as the rest of them."

"I love you too, Ann," he said.

"So come and see me sometime. Okay?" she said.

He nodded.

Silence reigned as she was taken away by her handlers. Amel waited a moment before getting back into his monitoring chair. The monitor's report of emotional exhaustion was redundant. It was obvious just looking at him.

Wren was worried by his increasing brain activity classified, with ninety percent confidence, as bearing on social intelligence, a faculty particularly well developed in Amel. The experts suspected that he was finding the hearing's intentional sub- traction of individuality stressful. With people representing col- lective interests, there was no continuity between questions, no relationship to help predict developments. Ann's injection, on the other hand, was exactly the sort of highly personal stimu- lus Amel found natural.

There was a long pause while data-hungry factions wrangled with Wren's committee, who felt questioning should be termi- nated.

Amel closed his eyes while he waited.

Lurol joined the debate from home, contributing expert opinion. Her take on the data was that they were witnessing exactly the sort of disturbance indicative of Amel's free will impairment. He was mortally afraid of the proceedings, but determined to continue in the service of better relations between Rire and Gelion. She also insisted he was hiding something else with very negative emotional connotations associated with any references to Lilac Hearth.

Erien's muscles locked, stirring up the ache in his bad shoul- der.

"Amel?" Wren roused the subject of all this silent speculation.

Amel's eyes opened. He looked composed, although his brain lit up in a classic alertness pattern. "Yes?" he said.

"We have determined that your sole intent was to empower Ann to protect innocent people. Not only can Rire forgive you for that, an overpowering majority also wish to offer you asylum, which we understand you have declined. There is some residual question of whether you can act in your own best interest, and if there has been a violation, on Gelion, of your human rights, which could be an impediment to diplomacy... particularly if it concerns your actions on behalf of Rire."

"It didn't," said Amel.

"But there was a violation of your human rights?" Wren pressed.

Amel's nerves jangled. "No," he said, and wavered. "I don't know what you mean by that. I — I've read about your human rights. But if I've got them, I don't see what it has to do with Rire."

There was a complete hush in the hearing room, punctuated by affectionate smiles.

"Expert opinion," said Wren, "has established reasonable doubt concerning your mental health — in particular, your ability to defend your own self-interest. If the cause of that pathology was your original, incomplete treatment by Lurol, then Rire is responsible. Rire excused Lurol's behavior due to the extenuating circumstances — which makes any consequences a collective burden."

Amel's bio-signs remained stubbornly stable. "I am responsible for myself," he said.

"You have," Wren said, holding two fingers to her ear bug, "a history of being sexually abused."

Amel's confidence wavered. Instabilities flickered like bush fire.

"Male victims, in particular," she continued, "prefer to blame themselves for their own victimization rather than acknowledge they were helpless. Becoming an abuser is the most common refuge, but one denied to you by your core personality. You are less capable of distancing yourself from others than an ordinary human being."

"Stop it," Amel said softly, showing physical symptoms of the distress this line of questioning had set off in his brain activity.

Wren took the ear bug off and closed her hand around it. "We don't want to hurt you, Amel," she told him, personally troubled.

He closed his eyes. His whole body clenched, the conflicting net effect, and sentiment, striking a terrible resonance.

Erien stood up.

Wren put her hand on Amel's arm.

The telemetry on the wall exploded and collapsed into perfect, terrible order, driven by an outpouring of memory that swamped Amel's live senses.

Amel knocked Wren down as he hurtled out of the chair. She spun and fell, jarred. Amel jerked, arms out, as if halted at the end of a tether. He fell, making desperate, breathy sounds.

The medical responders got to him just before Erien. One was hurled away immediately. Amel would have struck the second if Erien hadn't interposed himself, gasping at the impact of Amel's wild strength. Amel slewed into more responders as Erien caught him, shouting, "Amel!"

Something like recognition struggled for ascendance, then Amel's nostrils flared, eyes widening. He caught his breath like someone dropped off a sheer cliff... or straight from a bad memory into a worse one. Both palms shot straight at Erien, who caught a flash of psychosomatically raised welts on Amel's wrists.

"Back off!" Amel cried in Gelack vernacular, speaking to someone not present.

Erien kept his footing only because he had been braced for impact. He threw a desperate glance to his left as people swirled in his peripheral vision — vent them! Had they no sense!

Horth moved in on his right, and the Reetion who had been about to grab Erien was suddenly flying into a second one. Then there was a soft thud and a hard crack as Horth winded Amel and then dropped him with expert effectiveness.

Amel fell on his side in eerie silence, then groaned and started curling up before he went limp. An intrepid medic dropped beside him and reached to check for a heartbeat. "Stunned," he announced, "but there's a strong pulse."

Erien stood, shaking slightly. Horth stood calmly beside him, watching Reetions pour through a side door armed with canisters of restraining foam and gas dispensers. Despite the mismatch in armaments, the Reetions still looked far more nervous than the liege of Nersal. Horth had the same fateful air about him as when he stepped onto a challenge floor. Whatever came, he would meet it with life or death determination, trusting the larger mission to those *kinf'stan* who lived on if he should fall. Erien could almost envy him.

Erien glanced behind him to judge the odds of retrieving Amel from the Reetions and decided they were nil. Reetions were swarming all over him. Any attempt to intervene would be liable to escalate the situation, especially since Horth was certain to try to help; he did not want images circulating throughout Sevildom of Liege Nersal and himself being gassed or foamed.

"Let's go," he told Horth in Gelack. He would have to work this out from home.

Ranar's attention was glued to his flat stage, no doubt arguing the virtue of letting him and Horth walk out unmolested. Face cool and head high, Erien started for the door, hoping no one would even twitch in their direction. Fortunately, Reetion wisdom prevailed. No one interfered with them, and Horth simply followed him.

They passed out of the hall, leaving Ranar behind as a uniquely Reetion rearguard. All was unnaturally quiet behind them except for the buzz around Amel and the Reetion reporter who followed them out, watching them through his transmitting goggles.

No crowds were in evidence as they emerged into a bright and breezy Reetion morning outside the Space Services Center. A mild breeze fingered their hair and clothes.

"We should leave Rire," Horth said after they had walked a dozen paces. "Immediately."

"No," said Erien. "You and Ann — that was real progress."

Horth made no further comment.

–o—o—o–

Drasous met Erien in the doorway of Ranar's home. "The Reetions have voted to continue questioning Amel in the visitor probe," he told them.

Erien took the news like a blow.

Horth exchanged a glance with the *gorarelpul*, and turned to sweep a slow, gray gaze over the empty commons.

Erien tamped down his outrage, which bordered on irrational panic. "They can't do that," he said, and amended, "They can't do that so quickly. They need Amel's consent. They haven't got consent, have they?"

"No," said the *gorarelpul*, calm as glass. His manner said, "Not yet."

Erien wanted to hit something. Instead, he said in a low voice, "Reetion law will not permit Amel to be probed without his consent."

"Unless," Drasous said quietly, "a triumvirate of counselors judge him mentally incompetent."

"What do you know about..." Erien began, and concluded with sick realization, "Lurol."

Drasous stepped deftly aside. Erien went up the stairs by threes.

Lurol jumped as Erien threw open the door of her study.

He said, "What have you done?"

She got up, setting her wide mouth in a scowl. "Nothing more than I should have been done right at the very start: making sure Amel gets the treatment he needs to spare him further suffering."

"By declaring him mentally incompetent!"

"Yes! If that's the only way."

Erien stood with his fists clenched, panting shallowly. He made himself step back, aware that he was too tall and too angry for this small room. He nearly collided with Evert coming in the door.

"Back off," Erien growled, and realized where he had heard those words before.

Gods! Erien thought, *could that have been something Amel said to D'Lekker? Was he clear dreaming new events? From Lilac Hearth?*

Amel's fits had always featured his childhood abuses in the past. Erien braced his elbows on the wall and leaned on them, willing his mind to clear. Too much tension and too little release.

Breathe, he told himself. The last thing he needed was to be cited for parental abuse, for hitting Lurol, and evaluated for Supervision himself.

Lurol came up quietly beside him. "Amel needs help," she said quietly, "and after today neither of you can deny it anymore."

"I never did deny it," he said. "I have had words with Amel on the subject myself and was planning to have more. He cannot go around with a... dust mine in his head. But—" he said, as she drew breath—"I was not going to urge him to approach you *until* there were legal safeguards in place to protect him."

"To protect him!" she exclaimed. "Are you as irrationally paranoid as the rest of them?"

"Before you ever get your hands on him," said Erien, "they will wring him dry of everything he knows, and even assuming he can live with the impact that may have back home—"

"If you people didn't have your obsession with keeping secrets—"

"— it will destroy any chance of his ever returning to Gelion!"

"Which," Lurol said stubbornly, "might not be a bad thing. It would be better for you, too, if you didn't go back."

Erien's lips moved. He thought he was smiling. Judging by Lurol's expression, he wasn't. "Oh, I will go back. There is a debt I must pay, to two little boys, for killing their father. It might not do them much good, but I doubt they will have many other defenders. *Okal Rel* demands that certain crimes be punished by removal of all hope of rebirth, which mean's killing innocent children." He heard Ranar's familiar footsteps coming up the stairs, and turned. "And you and I," he observed grimly, "had better hope there were certain things Amel never learned."

Ranar went gray.

Evert gasped, "Oh, no." He lifted a shaking hand to his face, distressed by the intensity of Ranar's alarm and Erien's cold, boring stare. "B-but why ever would they ask — I mean it's not as though..."

Erien said very softly and grimly, "Vert, did you say anything to Amel about Di Mon?"

Ranar reacted with horror. "Vert! You didn't—"

"He already knew!" Evert said, showing bitter hurt at the shock of betrayal in Ranar's expression. "Yes, I slipped up, but he already knew! If he hadn't, I don't think he would have guessed what I meant."

There was a silence. Ranar looked as if he was made of stone.

Evert stepped back. "I think," he said shakily, "after this is all over, I should move out for a while. I find I just can't deal with *him* anymore." Though he was speaking Reetion, the pronoun was as clear as if it had been fully differenced. He meant Di Mon.

"Evert—" Ranar began, but he said no more, just watched as his lover gave up waiting for him to finish, turned away and started down the stairs.

"Erien," Ranar said helplessly. "What do we do?"

"We—" Erien began, and felt his thoughts veer inexorably onto a new and horrifying track. *I should kill Amel,* he thought. *Or order Drasous to do it.* He had that nightmarish sense, once again, of approaching a closed door, only this time he was not innocent of what lay behind it. Amel might even be willing to die to protect Ev'rel's memory and D'Lekker's children. But if he were not — if he wanted to live despite everything...

Ameron would do it, Erien decided. Ameron had committed Horth to a life or death against D'Therd by accepting Ev'rel's challenge, and then staked his own life with equal ruthlessness to target Ev'rel without letting her crimes taint her accomplishments. Was this any different? D'Lekker's sons would only be the first to die if the Avim's Oath broke out in civil war over the disgrace of their dead father. As for Monitum, Erien could readily imagine Tatt stepping out onto the challenge floor, over and over, if Di Mon was accused of what Gelacks considered a vile perversion, risking his life repeatedly, with fiery affection for his late great-uncle, while Monitum's economy took a thrashing with its loss of reputation. How many lives weighed in the balance against Amel's in this dreadful calculus? He wished he could think clearly.

"Erien!" Ranar's voice reverberated oddly in his skull. Something flat struck him on the side of the face, clumsily. He felt himself being grappled with, or fumbled over. He knew he shouldn't react, but not why. And then he couldn't do anything anymore.

He came to stretched out on the landing at the top of the stairs. Drasous was kneeling on one side of him and Ranar on the other. Lurol and Evert were standing at his feet, and Horth at his head. He felt strange, not quite inside his body. He stirred experimentally. Drasous set a hand on his chest. "Take it slowly, Heir Gelion. You fainted. Physical and emotional stress, I expect." He added to Erien's Reetion parents, "It's not an uncommon reaction among highborn Vrellish, on account of their labile blood pressure. It happens in the absence of high G's or some sort of stress-reducing action."

Erien worked his way up to a sitting position and turned to rest his back against the wall. He settled for simply breathing for a moment, eyes closed, remembering what he had been thinking. Drasous might call it blood pressure. He knew it for what it was: retreat from an intolerable choice. He could not let Amel betray D'Lekker's sons and Di Mon. But he could not kill Amel, or order his death, either.

"He's terribly white," Evert said, worriedly.

Erien took up the struggle once more, knowing Rire would not deal him Bryllit's mercy if he failed the challenge. He would be spared to watch all the consequences of his failure.

"I think," he returned to business, "it is a lost cause trying to make them see how probing Amel will inflame Gelack opinion. Few people seem to give a damn what Sevildom thinks about all this. And I thought Sevildom was self-centered and arrogant! So I will fight in this arena, but by the quarrelling Gods, I *will* fight."

"Lurol," Erien ordered his Reetion mother, "if you haven't ensured safeguards to prevent a repeat of eighteen years ago, I strongly suggest you do so now, because that's where I fear we're heading. Run extreme scenarios. See if Amel's human rights could be revoked, and figure out how to block those pathways, legally."

"Ranar," Erien continued, "I need you to tackle the jurisdiction angle. Get the argument out there that Amel's citizenship needs to be established before he can be declared Supervised. See if you can find some precedents, but look beyond the relationship between Rire and nonconformists living on the fringes of Reetion space. Look back at the historical record, in the early years of the confederacy's expansion, or the preliminary negotiations with the commercial worlds of Union Reach who never joined the Arbiter Administration. I would also like you to explore custody. If they declare him dependent, can I apply for custody? Can you? What would happen if Perry D'Aur were to file for custody, since she is on record as his *mekan'st* and has offered him a home?"

"Evert can tackle civil liberties. Raise the question of what this use of the visitor probe implies for Reetion citizens; is it an acceptable precedent? Then move over to social health. Yasmin was objecting to Amel's disruptive influence on Reetion social order. Is there enough concern to work in our favor, either in preventing the probing or restricting its scope."

"Any other ideas any of you have, please implement them. But let me know."

He was met with no arguments, although Lurol wouldn't meet his eyes as she nodded, and Ranar and Evert avoided each others' as they filed out of the room.

NINETEEN

Eyes on Amel

Professional Challenge

Bley stepped back from the stage in her group home's common room. Over the dissolving image of the day's work schedule remained a question. "Do you accept the addition to your work load?"

Bley read the name of her assignment again. It still said, "Amel."

Why me? she thought, astonished.

She was fifty-three, and ordinary by any standard she could think of: neither thin nor fat; mother of a single grown child; usefully employed — but no more than a Lawful Citizen who had spent her whole life living quietly in the city of Rire Proper. Amel seemed much too exotic an assignment.

A girl of sixteen named Nubia nudged Bley's elbow. "What's up?"

The girl's Gelack-imitation vest sported an artist's rendition of Amel with his back arched and his beautiful face caught in an expression of suffering.

"Like it?" asked Nubia, daring Bley to be offended as she stroked the brightly colored image.

Oh dear, Bley thought, *how can I possibly? Not with Solomon's kids here!* Solomon was one of the three counselors at the group home, and specialized in Gelack cultist teenagers.

Nubia poked her head around Bley to look at the pocket stage. "Oh, wow!" Her fingers sank through the projected letters of Amel's name. "Wow," she repeated in a near whisper.

Bley spotted Solomon entering the common room and waved him over urgently. "I've been offered Amel," she greeted him, feeling numb.

Nubia clutched at his arm. "Don't let her say no!" she begged. "She wants to say no! I can feel it! Just because I want it so bad!"

"You are unlikely to be the sole reason for counselor Bley's decision, whatever it may be," Solomon told Nubia patiently, "but throwing a tantrum isn't likely to encourage her much." He was a large, physically fit man with a square jaw and a confident manner. To Bley he added, "How long do you have to decide?"

"I don't know," Bley said, flustered. "I haven't read the brief. If it can't wait, best to say no."

Solomon looked like he wanted to object, but was preempted by Nubia's next stunt.

"Bley's been offered Amel," the girl screamed, "and she's going to turn him down!" A couple of heads popped up over the back of a big couch, looking startled. They were clients of the group home's third counselor, Roz, who specialized in young women guileless enough to be maneuvered into going off record with sexual predators. Both girls were thin, with pale faces. Bley had a hard time telling them apart.

"That's a fine way to convince Bley we could cope," Solomon told Nubia off.

"I wonder why he wasn't offered to you," Bley asked Solomon. "You know more than I do about Gelacks. Or to Roz, since Amel has a history of abuse."

"Roz, perhaps," Solomon allowed, "but I work with kids' reactions to Gelacks, not actual Gelacks. Besides, Amel has considerable latent hostility toward adult males whom he might perceive as threatening."

Nubia snorted at the clinical language. "Amel was gang-raped by men when he was ten years old!" she said, as if it was something to brag about. "You can't talk a thing like that dull and flat."

"If your point is that I should respect whatever feelings Amel might have concerning his past, I could not agree more," said Solomon. He nodded at her vest. "Do you think that respects his feelings very much?"

"I'll take it off, okay?" Nubia promised, and did just that, throwing the hitherto precious garment to the common room floor. "Anything! So long as I get to meet Amel. I love him! You've got to understand!"

"How can you love someone you don't know, Nubia?" Solomon asked.

She narrowed her eyes at him, chest thrust out. "You only say that because you haven't got a real soul like a Gelack!"

"Fine," said Solomon, putting an arm across Nubia's shoulders to lead her toward the door into the garden. "You love him. Have you wondered how he might feel about that when he doesn't know you at all?" Solomon liked to do his counseling while walking his charges around the grounds. He led Nubia off.

Why me? Bley thought as she watched them depart. Her case load leaned toward people with tragedy-induced depression. Was Amel depressed? Feeling oddly shaken, Bley returned to her paused session and requested four hours to decide. The arbiter granted her the time.

What if I asked for five? she thought.

She brushed away the unworthy thought. If she had wanted to know the time limit, she could simply have looked it up — or just said 'no.'

Bley messaged Roz to ask her to consider the impact Amel might have on her own case load. Then she set out to answer the same question for herself.

Edward was her first call. Young and bright with good family support, Edward should have been anything but Supervised. He had been heading for world-class athletic competition with a likely future as a Voting Citizen on the Olympic games council, before he fell off a mountain. Edward did not count himself lucky to have survived. His first act upon gaining sufficient control of his new exoskeleton had been trying to make it choke him with his own hand.

Bley found Edward parked in a visiting room, waiting for his mother to show up. "What's eating you, Super?" he asked.

Super was a cheeky thing some supervised like to call their supervisor, but if being rude made Edward feel better, Bley didn't mind. She sat down on a morph couch opposite the floor brace that kept Edward from falling over while he was learning — or refusing to learn — how to control his exoskeleton.

"I've been offered the Gelack, Amel, to supervise," Bley said. "Apparently he needs assessment."

"Amel," Edward said. "He's regenerative." His face grew ugly with resentment. "I wouldn't be stuck in this cage if I was."

"You will walk again, Edward."

"Like a toddler! I don't want to spend my whole life trying to get back to where I was when I was two years old! I *died* when

I feel off that mountain. Why is that so damn hard for you helpful types to understand?"

"I understand why you are angry about what happened to you," Bley assured him. "And there are circumstances under which you can obtain support for euthanasia, but first you must convince us, and your loved ones, that you are in a suitable state of mind to make such an important decision. At the moment I would say you are emotionally, as well as physically, a toddler."

"I hate you, you old bitch," Edward spat back, tears forming in his blazing eyes.

Bley sighed. She understood it might be necessary for him to hate someone right now. "If you feel we are incompatible, you know you can request a transfer."

"Won't make any difference," Edward said.

Looking out the window, Bley could see Edward's mother walking toward them across the lawn between the group home and the public transit station. It reminded her that Ranar's home, where the Gelacks were staying, was close by. She might have been picked for no greater reason than proximity, other considerations being equal. It was an oddly comforting thought because it meant there was no special obligation for her to take Amel on.

"Your mom's here, so I'll see you later," Bley said to Edward, feeling too preoccupied to deal with his hostility at present. At least she could mark him down as a 'no' vote.

"Hey!" said Edward, as Bley reached the door. "Say yes to Amel. I'd like to get a look at the lucky sod up close."

For her next visit Bley picked Nasib's room. Nasib was a thin, dark-skinned woman in her seventies who endured life with a grim patience. In her day she had been a terraforming colonist, serving as crystronics engineer, midwife and chef, as well as acting as one of her colony's governing triumvirs. She was also the sole survivor of the fungal infestation that wiped out the 2,017 people with whom she had shared her life. The colony was shut down after the disaster on the grounds that emergency relief was too far away.

"I know you don't like to talk much," Bley said as she seated herself in a chair, "but you seem comfortable in your silence. I'm not comfortable with myself today. I've been asked to take on the Gelack, Amel. I think you could advise me if you wanted to." Bley smiled in apology. Nasib already had more burdens than anyone deserved. "It's a bad idea, isn't it? Having Amel here, with Solomon's cultists and all."

Nasib surprised Bley by laying a thin hand over hers and saying "I would like to meet a Gelack."

"You?" said Bley. "What for?"

But Nasib only withdrew her hand and went back to her console where she pored daily over the record of her colony, as if remembering could bring it back to life again.

Bley's last patient was a woman named Europa who was dying of a degenerative disorder. Europa had struggled hero-ically for five years, but at age forty-one, completely paralyzed and dependent on life-support, she had applied for euthanasia. Bley, Roz and Solomon had granted her the right to end her life when she was ready. "But not," Europa had promised them, "a moment earlier."

Europa's son and daughter were sitting beside their mother's float chair in the visiting room. The daughter, who was only nine, looked miserable. The older boy was restless.

"You look fretful," Europa greeted Bley through a speaker controlled by a direct cerebral implant. The vocalization fell short of the lively flow of Europa's natural speech patterns, which Bley had experienced only through the record. Drama had been one of Europa's interests. Her other work had revolved around catering. Now she was totally paralyzed except for a modest degree of residual facial expression.

"Something unprecedented has come up," Bley admitted.

"Oh?" Europa showed the ready interest that always made Bley wish Edward was half as resilient, or Europa's progno-sis half as good as Edward's.

"It's about an assignment," said Bley, trying to model for the children how to be relaxed and natural around their dying mother. "I thought I should reject it at first, but I suspect my fellow counselors and the residents view it as an opportunity." She frowned. "That seems unhealthy, doesn't it?"

"A celebrity is it?" Europa asked. It was impossible to tell how she felt about anything she said anymore, so she compen-sated by explaining what she would once have conveyed by inflection. "I am intrigued. Is it an artist? Or a well-known pilot? Not Ann, is it?"

"No," said Bley. "It's Amel."

"Here?" Europa's little daughter looked frightened.

Her teenage brother got excited. "Does that mean the oth-ers will visit? Like Horth Nersal?"

"Horth Nersal?" Europa asked her son. "Why ever would you be interested in Horth Nersal?"

He shrugged. "I think he's neat."

Bley succumbed to a parental impulse. "This Horth Nersal person," she told Europa's son, "holds the power of life and death over people for no better reason than being able to kill rivals with a primitive weapon in a bizarre sports event. Only one of Solomon's Gelack cultists could admire such a thing."

The boy bridled, confronting both Bley and his immobilized mother, whose face looked like a mask carved into her float chair. "*Okal Rel* is not just about fighting. You've misunderstood Ranar's lectures."

"Actually," said Bley. "I haven't read them."

"And they're going to assign a Gelack to you?" he said, incredulous.

"Don't you think you're overreacting a little, Rit love?" said his mother. "And you, too, Bley," she added, moving her float chair closer to her daughter, who reached up nervously to touch her mother's inert hand. "If even the most civilized of us didn't nurse a latent fascination with life and death rites of combat, we wouldn't have translated Shakespeare. I hardly think you can accuse Rit of endorsing murder just because he's fascinated by Horth Nersal."

"You don't know what I think," Rit lashed back. "And neither does some dumb counselor who isn't part of our family, and isn't going to make it better for us when you're dead!"

Europa's daughter burst into tears at her brother's attack.

Rit bolted in good adolescent form, and collided with Nubia in the doorway.

"Nubia!" Bley ordered sharply, on her feet now. "Visiting rooms are private when they're in use!"

"I was looking for you," Nubia bulldozed over the infraction of house rules. "You've got to say yes to Amel! If you don't I'll kill myself! I swear!"

Of all the suicide threats on record in the group home, this one concerned Bley the least.

"Wait outside," Bley ordered sternly.

"You're going to say no," Nubia prophesized, sucking air in little, hysterical gasps. When Bley remained unmoved she spun and dashed out.

"I'm 'fraid of Gelacks," mumbled Europa's little daughter, Carrie.

"It's not good to be afraid," her mother chided. "Besides, this one won't hurt you. He's the nice one. It'll give you a chance

to find out they're just people like us. We're going to find a way
to work things out with them — you'll see. It'll be fun."

Carrie lodged herself against her mother's chair.

"Shall I contact Sue?" Bley asked. Sue was a co-parent who
had been with the family since Rit was three years old. Bley was
sure Sue would stick out the family arrangement. She was less
sure about Europa's lover, Ethan, the only male co-parent in
the group. He had become increasingly distant as Europa's illness changed her.

"Rit will be back," said Europa. "So, are you going to take
Amel on? It would be nice to have something to liven up this
dying gig a little."

"I haven't decided yet, whether—" Bley began.

Hysterical screams cut her off.

Hurrying back into the common room, Bley found one of
Roz's patients screaming at the sight of Nubia, who had taken
a knife from the kitchen and was threatening to use it on herself.
As soon as Nubia saw Bley she had a go at slashing her wrist,
and was predictably prevented by a wet *thwap* of restraining
foam ejected from a wall slot by the presiding arbiter.

"Let me do it!" Nubia cried, struggling dramatically, which
only made the foam get hard. "If I can't meet him, I would rather
die!"

Solomon arrived at a jog and Bley left Nubia to him while
she reassured Roz's girls.

A boy who insisted on calling himself Tatt, after a well-known
Gelack duelist, stuck up a fist and cried, "Vote!"

"Vote! Vote!" his followers took up the cry, including Nubia,
who was still stuck in restraining foam because she refused to
relax.

"That's enough!" Solomon drowned them out, standing large
and confident in the middle of the miniature mob. "There'll be
no vote! And if you're so keen on participatory democracy, think
about getting off Supervision, first!"

Roz arrived belatedly, an attractively dressed woman who
constantly struggled with a tendency toward being overweight.
She met Bley's eyes with intense interest before giving her attention to the girls Nubia had frightened. Roz was something
of a flirt outside the group home, and Bley remembered her
saying something once about Amel's good looks. Should she
consider that another negative?

Solomon and Roz packed their respective charges off and
collected Bley to head off to the counselor's staff room. "Given

the controversy over Amel," Solomon took charge as soon as they were inside, "I think it best we assert our independence of the politics from the start. I move we invoke STI zero to discuss the matter."

"Do you really think that's necessary?" Bley said, alarmed.

Roz called up statistics on the staff room stage that showed how much of the planet was tuned in to them right now, despite the relatively opaque STI of a group home staff room under ordinary circumstances.

"All right," Bley agreed, unsettled by the necessity. "Index zero."

Roz cast her vote and it was done — the staff room fell under a total blackout. There were very few ways to achieve absolutely zero surveillance under the Arbiter Administration, which was why counselors always worked in threes and had to have impeccable integrity, but the unanimous decision of a counseling triumvirate was inviolate.

"I think we've all had the same experience with the residents," Solomon launched the meeting. "They're interested."

"Even yours?" Bley asked Roz.

Roz nodded. "I think he makes rape victims feel a bit glamorous, instead of pathetic. That's not a bad thing, Bley."

"I checked into why the presence of cultists didn't disqualify us," volunteered Solomon. "A researcher named Yasmin put in a proposal for therapeutic contact between cultists and the visiting Gelacks. Political concerns took priority, but the proposal survived to the extent that my small collection of Supervised cultists here actually weighed in our favor. And we're close to Ranar's house, of course," added Solomon. "Other contributing factors were Bley's lack of political engagement with the Gelack question and Roz's background. Roz also has the necessary medical qualifications."

"Amel is recovering from some sort of abdominal wound," Roz remarked. The younger, more fashionable woman was seated with her long skirt falling to her shapely ankles, looking cool and professional. "And he may be a management problem, psychiatrically."

"Clear dreams," said Solomon.

"What happens in these clear dreams, exactly?" Bley asked them, since they had obviously been following events more closely than she had.

"Amel relives past events," explained Roz. She turned their stage on manually with a remote control. A mannequin shape appeared with a hot haze about its groin and thighs, and some major disruption of coherence in its lower abdomen.

"Amel's sensory map is exceptionally clear and well studied," said Roz, "which allowed us to reproduce the injuries being remembered during his breakdown, while being monitored. There were also lacerations in a whipping pattern and galling at the wrists, as if he had been bound. He manifested those psychosomatically." The image switched to a photograph of Amel's wrist ringed in red welts. "The reaction faded within hours," added Roz.

Bley released the breath she hadn't realized she was holding as the marks on Amel's wrists cleared up in time-lapse photography. It was such a lovely hand, the skin fresh as a child's despite its adult proportions. She wondered if Amel had been unconscious during those hours. The stillness of his hand in the time-lapse photography suggested as much.

"What disturbs me most is the powerful interpersonal factor involved in whatever was happening to him," Roz continued, nodding toward the psych animation replacing the photos. "Expert opinion asserts he knew his assailants and perhaps even cared about them, which is painfully germane to the suspicion he was punished for helping Rire and may still be acting under duress."

"What would be expected of us if he comes here?" Bley asked.

Solomon folded his arms. "A ruling on whether he's competent."

"There's a strong lobby for putting him back under the visitor probe to finish the hearing that ended in his breakdown," said Roz. "He's refused to give his consent. But if he's ruled incompetent to act in his own best interest, his refusal can be overruled. Normally it couldn't be considered unless the incompetence was much more blatant, but Lurol's garnered a lot of support for her argument that he has been free-will-impaired since his first probe experience, which could then be fixed, too."

"There'll be a lot of pressure to act quickly," said Solomon, "and we risk being second-guessed and criticized after the fact, like Lurol was, but I'm for taking him on."

"I know it's your decision, Bley," said Roz, shifting forward. "But if you agree you'll have our support."

Bley didn't know how to tell them that their support, itself, was making her uncomfortable. Her partners were eager. The residents were interested. It all seemed too much attention to focus on one much-abused, rather nice and possibly free will impaired Gelack.

Suddenly she knew whose input was missing.

"May I?" Bley asked Roz and took the remote control. She used it to dissolve the STI zero setting, which already made her more comfortable.

Bley called up the open offer. "I would like to speak with the client," she said. "Ask him if he will accept a 2-D audio-visual connection."

Solomon and Roz stopped what they were doing. She could almost feel them peering over her shoulder. Roz smiled at her, "Feel funny?"

"Why should we?" Solomon asserted. "Just because half the planet has been trying to contact Amel for frivolous—"

"Shh," said Bley, "he's accepted."

Amel's face filled her stage. It had a responsive quality that made her realize that although she had seen him on stage many times, he had never been watching her back. He was now. His attention changed the experience of looking at him into something undeniably personal.

"Hello," he said in excellent Reetion. "You wanted to talk to me?"

She felt a faint shiver of guilt for her misgivings. He did not look at all terrible, only pale, tired and innocently beautiful.

"My name is Bley," she said. "I've been asked to be your supervisor. Do you know what that means?"

"Yes," he said, sounding defeated.

He doesn't, she decided, *not entirely*.

"It means," she said, "that I would like a chance to become your friend, and have you live here at my group home. There is a great deal of interest in you here."

His eyes flinched at the edges.

"Is that unwelcome?" Bley asked, concerned.

"No," he smiled faintly. His face was meant for smiling. Bley missed the expression when it faded.

"When will I be moved?" he asked.

"At once," she told him, "if you want to come. I called to ask if you wanted to accept the invitation."

He hesitated on the brink — she suspected — of a glib answer. But he gave it up. "If I don't, will there be another... offer?"

"Yes," she said.

"Then I'll accept yours," he told her. "Is that correct form?"

She smiled at this reminder he was not a Reetion, but a Gelack viewing her behavior with as little instinctive understanding as she would have approaching bizarre Gelack customs. "Yes," she assured him. "You are doing fine. Just ask any time you're uncertain. Do you have any questions?"

Amel shook his head.

"We'll see you soon then," Bley said with a parting smile.

"I'll admit," Roz said, grinning at Bley as she turned from the empty stage, "I'm excited." She wrinkled her nose just a little.

Solomon frowned, but Bley forgave Roz. There was something compelling about Amel. She already felt a connection.

"Will you want me to help with the rest of your case load?" Roz asked magnanimously.

Bley shook her head. "I do not intend to neglect my other cases, and somehow I don't think Amel will want a lot from any of us. Quite the contrary."

"I just hope he can cope with the kids' interest." Solomon sounded daunted for the first time.

Bley said, "We ought to call a meeting in the common room."

They rounded up the eager residents and forced on the room stages of those who chose not to attend in person. Casual staff and frequent visitors were notified they might want to view the record being laid down, to which end the counselors temporarily opened up the group home's STI to normal public levels. Then Solomon explained Amel would be joining them and they were all to treat him as normally as possible.

The youth who called himself Tatt snorted and said, "Good luck," looking at an ecstatic Nubia.

Amel arrived less than half an hour after Bley's call. The revolving front door with its darkened glass admitted him, and he was there, inside the group home, standing between his discretely armed two-person escort and looking much too subdued to be dangerous.

Bley went out to meet him, Solomon and Roz keeping the residents out of the way for her. Bley noticed a bruise along one side of Amel's jaw, faint enough that she had missed it earlier.

"What happened to your face?" she asked, putting her hand out instinctively, as if he were a small child who had fallen in the playground. Amel turned his head away just enough to discourage her.

"Horth Nersal punched him at the hearing," said one of the first responders escorting him. "His face puffed up something fierce, but even the discoloration is all but gone now. We've prescribed compatible painkillers. He took them okay." The man smiled almost fondly. "But only after his brother, Erien, confirmed they weren't poison."

"You trust your brother's judgment of what is and isn't safe on Rire," Bley tried on for size, and reconsidered. "Or is it a case of taking orders?"

Amel didn't answer. He was wearing Reetion clothes. They suited him. With a sadness she couldn't explain, Bley realized nearly everything would. There was a richness about him, like silk, or a smooth creamy drink, that invited you to stare at him.

"We'll take care of him from here," Bley told his escort. Detaching them took longer than it should have. They seemed to enjoy being involved. When they finally left, she looked at the quiet, pretty man left in her charge and thought he looked like someone who needed a hug. Bley rejected the idea at once, and then called it back for a second look. His psych profile said he was tactile, affectionate and prone to be physical in his self-expression.

"Amel," Bley said, "I would like to hug you."

He blinked at her, baffled, but open to the honesty of her offer. The dampening effect of his submissiveness dissolved, revealing a lost and frightened state of mind. Her own expression must have answered with eloquence, because the next moment he sighed into her arms so naturally he might have been her own son. She felt him inhale against her chest, the life in him so strong it made her wonder why she had thought him frail the moment before. He drew back with gray crystal eyes glistening and gave her an honest smile.

"I'm all right," he said ruefully, "honestly."

She moved a lock of slippery hair behind his ear, all barriers to touch dissolved. "The other residents would like to meet you, but if you prefer, you can go to bed directly right after we've talked. Your room is prepared."

"Other residents?" he asked, drawing back. "What are they in for?"

"Amel, dear," said Bley. "This is not a prison. People in this group home are here because they pose a danger to themselves in one way or another, except for Europa who is terminally ill and has been granted the right to euthanasia on demand. I think you will like Europa," she said with sudden conviction. "She was delighted at the prospect of meeting you."

"Me? Why?"

Bley laughed. "It's all right, dear," she said. "We're not going to eat you alive."

He smiled a bit shyly in response. "I don't mind meeting people," he said, "if you tell me what you expect me to do."

"Just be yourself," Bley said, and nodded in the direction of the common room where the assembled residents and visitors waited with as much patience as Solomon and Roz could enforce.

"First, however," Bley said, gesturing toward a visiting room, "you and I must chat."

Amel was fixated on the sensi-strips and pocket stages of the common room and did not budge. "Will it be public?" he asked. "I mean, will everyone be watching through the arbiters?"

"No," Bley assured him. "Except for things flagged by a counselor, STI one is even more opaque than a private home. There are a few important differences. For instance, the arbiter is able to intervene directly to prevent anyone coming to harm." She smiled encouragement and gestured toward a door.

Amel went ahead of her and took a seat on one of the couches in the visiting room. Bley sat opposite him and considered him as he grew increasingly nervous.

"Do I make you uncomfortable?" she asked at last.

"No, not you in particular," he assured her. He tossed his head, shifting sheets of silky black hair. "This room," he began, looking around. "You call it a visiting room, right? Like the visitor probe."

"Rather the other way around," said Bley. "The visitor probe was named after visiting rooms at group homes."

"Because there is an arbiter watching," he said, "and able to intervene."

"Because friends and family visit with residents here," Bley clarified, and smiled. "There is monitoring, yes, but only because intervention capacity, in general, is greater in a group home where residents might become violent."

"Are you afraid I'll hurt you?" he asked.

"Will you?" she reflected back.

"No," he said, sounding disturbingly defeated by the admission. "It isn't your fault."

"What isn't my fault?" she asked him.

He gestured vaguely. "Any of this."

Bley got up deliberately and sat down on the couch beside him. "What are you afraid of?"

"Being here," he told her. "Being helpless."

"You believe we want to harm you?" asked Bley, taking great care to sound neutral. It was important not to forewarn him by tone that she was probing him for paranoia.

Amel expelled air. "Want? No." He inhaled again, expanding his chest, and forced stiff fingers though his soft hair, locking them there briefly before letting the hand fall, limp, into his lap. "Everyone seems concerned about me, but I don't feel safe. I don't want to be visitor probed again."

"That's understandable," Bley told him.

His crisp gray eyes fixed on her.

"Given what you've experienced of the visitor probe to date," she said, "I would be astonished if you did not have a strong negative reaction. But you do know both those incidents were abnormal, don't you?"

"Yes," Amel said slowly, as if the fact had to be drawn from a deep place and forced to the surface. "But I don't want to be visitor probed again," he said intensely.

"Some people fear you are hiding crucial information," Bley reminded him.

Amel broke eye contact and looked away, his face expressionless.

"Let's try something easier," Bley suggested. "There has been a great deal said about you on Rire. Most of it," she added, "by people you do not know personally. What about you? Who do you think you are?"

"Amel?" he asked, sounding dubious.

Bley gave him space to elaborate, but he proved much too patient for her.

"I mean, dear," she said, relenting as he grew more strained and nervous, "what defines you as Amel?"

"People, I guess," he said, and sighed, sounding tired. "People I care about."

"People?" Bley repeated. "Other people? More so than yourself?"

"What would life be without other people?" he asked her, earnestly.

Bley smiled despite herself. "All right then," she said, "people. But you like some people more than others?"

"Oh, yes!" he agreed readily.

"Drasous, for instance?" Bley suggested.

Amel twitched a shoulder, "Not particularly."

"Horth Nersal?"

Amel was catching on. "You're trying to trick me into something," he accused her.

"I am trying to find out what you think of the people with whom you came to Rire."

"I came with Erien," Amel said. "Drasous was sent to look after him, and Liege Nersal came for his own reasons."

"You like Erien, then?"

"Liking him isn't the — listen," Amel broke off, disgruntled. "Does this matter?"

Bley leaned forward, elbows on her thighs, hands clasped before her. "Amel, dear, I am trying, very hard, to understand what will be in your best interest. You are a very emotional person. It is vital to me, therefore, to know how you feel about the people whose actions have been, or may yet be, important to you. How do you feel about Horth Nersal?"

"I respect him," Amel admitted. "Sometimes I find him cruel, but he is honorable. You can trust his honor."

"And Erien?"

Amel blushed, which was unanticipated. "Sometimes, to be honest, I could shake him! He feels so responsible for everything — not just me and the others who came with him; not just the empire, even, but Rire, too — and the whole venting universe, for all I know!" Amel laughed at his own exaggeration. "Well, he's up to it if anyone is," he sighed. "Or he will be when he's older. I don't know yet if that's scary, or wonderful. He likes me to keep my distance, so I try not to get underfoot. I owe him that much."

"You do not believe your brother returns your love?" Bley decided.

Amel looked mildly shocked, then closed his eyes and sighed with vexation. "Do we really have to talk about this stuff?"

"I need to know," Bley assured him with professional candor, "whether your brother is the best person to consult about your treatment."

"Yes."

"And your well-being?"

"Yes," Amel said, more mechanically. "Erien leads this mission on the Ava's behalf. I will accept whatever he requires of me while I am on Rire."

"You said you owed Erien something," Bley backtracked to an earlier remark. "Are you referring to your rescue from your mother's home on Fountain Court?"

"Yes, of course," Amel said. "And again on *Kali Station*." He frowned. "It was stupid of me, walking into that."

"You did it to help stranded people."

Amel looked as if she had dealt him an insult.

"Why did being questioned about Lilac Hearth cause you to break down at the hearing?" Bley asked.

Amel shuddered. It was a muted, spontaneous reaction, but quite definite. He drew his arms against his chest and squeezed, once. "I remember things too well," he said. "The knife wound I got escaping Lilac Hearth was painful."

"And the welts on your torso?" Bley insisted. "Did you get those escaping, as well?"

Amel stood up suddenly. "I don't want to talk about this. It isn't necessary and has nothing to do with Rire."

"All right," Bley relented. "Let me ask you this, instead. Do you plan to go back to Gelion when this is done? Or will you take up Perry D'Aur's offer?"

Amel stiffened, looking spooked, and then slowly relaxed. "Of course, there were patients in sickbay when Perry offered, that's how you found out."

Bley nodded. "They've been debriefed now, yes, so it's on the record."

He gave a nervous laugh. "I will never get the hang of your 'record.' Doesn't it feel like living on stage all the time? I mean the kind of stage where people perform."

"No," Bley smiled. "We find it natural." But she could see he did not. "I think that's enough for today," she decided. "Would you object to me consulting Erien about you?"

He answered stiffly, "No, of course not. Do whatever you must." Amel hesitated in the doorway to offer her a smile. "Thanks for the hug," he said.

Bley smiled back.

When he was gone the room seemed emptier than it should. *Which is part of the trouble*, Bley realized. *People can't get enough.*

Before she had finished recording a summary of her exchange with Amel, Roz appeared, glowing with contained excitement.

"You've met Amel?" Bley guessed.

"I have." Roz folded herself quickly into place beside Bley on the couch. "He's making friends fast."

Bley nodded, "I expect he would."

Roz was in a chatty mood. "Nasib is after him for leads on how she might put her colony back on line using Sevolite pilots, and Solomon's cultists are either falling all over him — that's the girls, or trying to provoke him to act tough — the boys, of course. Europa has the kids over, and even Edward's out of his room. But you don't need to worry. Amel is handling it all with aplomb."

Bley settled her hands in her lap. "So, should we rule him competent and put him on staff?"

The gaiety faded from Roz's face. "I wish we could! But I'm afraid it's the tip of the iceberg we are seeing in the common room."

"A performance of good health?" Bley suggested.

"That fits," said Roz. "What made you put it like that?"

"Something he said," Bley admitted, "about being on stage all the time."

Solomon intruded on them. "Come out here," he told them.

The mob in the common room was gathered around the pocket stage, where Amel was being introduced to friends and relatives the residents were calling up. Amel had an arm around Europa's daughter, Carrie, with both of Roz's girls standing close. He seemed to be shunning the cultists, who sulked at the periphery of the group. Only Edward kept clear of it all, looking sour.

Bley drifted over to watch and listen as Amel entertained everyone's special friend or relative with stories about his life on Gelion. They found out Erien had once been pushed into the fountain at the center of Fountain Court; Vrellish Sevolites got indigestion if they ate too much fresh fruit; and little Demish princesses played with the most beautiful doll houses in which every piece was handmade and no two were exactly identical. The warmth of Amel's delivery cast a spell that put people at ease, but the very demonstration of his power to move hearts troubled Bley, who interrupted the performance after two hours, convinced Amel had to be exhausted.

In the middle of the night she was woken by Roz. Nubia, it seemed, had snuck into Amel's bed and Amel had responded like any responsible adult — taking her to see Roz.

"It's not fair!" Nubia ranted. "He was alone in his room for an hour with one of your nervous little rape victims, entirely off record!"

"Not off record to me," Roz reminded her, "just as you are always in the scope of Solomon's behavior filters. And that 'nervous little rape victim' was only talking to him."

Bley left Roz to it and went to check the state of Reetion-Gelack politics. Erien's hand was seen everywhere, steadily losing control as he tried to deflect attention away from what Amel may or may not know about events that had taken place on Gelion. Bley sighed as she turned it off. She couldn't make sense of the larger issues.

"If I'm going to deal with this," she told Roz when the two of them sat down to take stock, together, over a cup of herbal tea, "it's going to have to be by treating him the way I would anyone else."

"If you think you can," said Roz. "I know I couldn't."

TWENTY

Erien

Consultations

Erien glided his borrowed bicycle to a stop outside the group home, dismounted and lifted it into the public rack. Two boys and a sulky-looking girl watched. All three wore reasonable facsimiles of Gelack swords, and shirts decorated with what he supposed was intended to represent house braid.

Gelack cultists, he thought. *What a bizarre phenomenon.*

Counselor Bley stood waiting just outside the group home's main entrance.

They've chosen well, Erien thought. She was a small, comfortable-looking woman who would surely remind Amel of motherly servants who had spoiled him with treats in their masters' kitchens. *Maybe,* he tried to persuade himself, *this will work out.*

"I'm pleased you have come," she said, showing him to one of the visiting rooms. "You have been very much the mystery man in all this, quite overlooked with all the attention given to Amel."

Erien nodded slightly. "I prefer it that way."

"I expect we are overlooking you because you were raised here and seem more familiar," Bley said. "But I have to get to know you a little, and one can't judge by your record because, apparently, your goal as a youngster was to appear average in everything."

"Yes," Erien said with a sigh. "Except, as Ann said, I took it too literally."

"Well," said Bley, "you were what? Seven or eight years old. Cognitively, that's a very concrete age." She smiled. "The main exception to your studied mediocrity was music. You were becoming very good with your flute. Have you kept it up?"

"To the best of my ability," said Erien. "I didn't have a lot of free time in the Nersallian fleet." He did not add how the only way he could escape harassment when playing was by retreating to low-gravity zones.

"Would you like some lemonade?" Bley asked kindly.

He sat down as soon as she left. The chair firmed up beneath him in accordance with his personal preferences, proving an arbiter was aware of him, at some level, even in this visiting room.

Bley returned with lemonade and a plate heaped with saucer-sized ginger biscuits and cheese.

"I did have lunch," he told her.

She gave him a decidedly grandmotherly look. "What about breakfast? You worked straight through from yesterday morning until just before you came here. And you needn't look anxious because I don't need to pierce your domestic privacy to know it. Your work is all over the political forums."

Erien accepted two biscuits and a small mound of cheese. "Have you come to any decisions about Amel?" he asked, determined to put emphasis back where it belonged.

She leaned back, lemonade in hand. "Not yet. It's usual for the family to be involved. Perhaps you will be able to fill in some of the blanks for me."

"I will do as much as I can," Erien said, truthfully enough. There was a silence. "How is Amel?" he asked. "I was expecting to see him."

Bley said firmly, "Our policy is to allow new residents a settling-in period, particularly when family relationships have not yet been assessed." She paused. "And from my point of view, you are first and foremost Amel's brother, not Heir Gelion."

He took a deep breath. "Then I'm probably here under false pretenses, because although I am his half brother, I've known it only one day longer than I've been Heir Gelion — which is less than a week."

She seemed unperturbed by the admission. "But you have known Amel for years? He's been part of your life?"

"Yes," Erien said, not about to admit to once dreading that Amel was his genetic father.

"And how do you see him?" Bley pursued.

"He's a survivor." He caught himself wanting to rub his aching shoulder and kept still. "I had an argument with Amel not long ago in which I took Lurol's side about him being an involuntary martyr. He pointed out ways I, myself, have acted contrary to my own self-interest. But everything I have done, I did because the other choices before me were worse. Perhaps his actions make just as much sense to him. Although—"

She waited.

"He exasperates me," Erien admitted. "But people whose opinions and feelings I value—"

"People you love?" Bley interjected.

"People I love," he said stoically, "care about Amel. I have to value him because he is precious to them."

"Your approval seems important to Amel," said Bley. "He checked with you before he would take painkillers for his post-concussion headache, for example."

Erien nodded. "He isn't very trusting about drugs."

Why should he be, Erien added silently, *when Ev'rel used to drug him against his will?* It occurred to him, then, just how much that said about the depth of Amel's trust in him. The same trust had led Amel to turn *Kali Station* over to him, a subconscious act in which there could be no dissembling.

"What is it?" Bley asked, watching his face closely.

He pulled back when she started to reach for his hand; she caught herself, and carefully reopened the distance between them. "I'm sorry," she said, "I'm a tactile person. But you're not, are you?"

"No," Erien said. "My guardian, Di Mon, was... very formal. I admired him — I loved him," he amended. "I also learned to set firm boundaries in the Nersallian fleet." He felt himself color slightly, hoping he would not have to explain how Nersallian women could make one feel thoroughly sexually harassed. "Reserve has become habit," he finished.

"Firm boundaries," Bley summarized, and paused, looking concerned and a little sad. "What do you think about Amel's boundaries?" she asked.

"For a long time," Erien said decisively, "I believed he didn't have any. Now I suspect people force themselves across his boundaries."

"But he is a survivor?" Bley echoed his opinions back at him. "Making the best of a bad situation because any other choice would be even worse?"

"Yes," said Erien.

Bley sighed. "You may be right." She frowned. "But Amel broke down when asked to reveal what happened to him back on Gelion. It does look as if he's under pressure to hide some-thing that would cast your Gelack government in a poor light."

Erien's shoulders knotted. "No," he said levelly. "He is afraid, yes. But Reetions do not want to acknowledge the cause. Counselor, Amel has been probed twice by Reetions without his consent, once in a situation where the monitoring safeguards were inadequate, and the second time where hostile parties forced him to link with a damaged arbiter."

"Erien," Bley said, leaning forward, "if surgery is necessary to treat a patient, should it be out of the question because he has a phobia for knives?" She shook her head and sighed, "Can't you, at least, be confident every possible safeguard would apply this time?"

"I can't be," Erien said starkly. "If Amel goes under the visitor probe it will lead to another unrestricted *interrogation*."

"Erien!" she said. "Erien, dear." She didn't look at all frightened by his intensity, merely sympathetic. He made himself breathe and smoothed out his expression.

"I'm sorry," he said.

She smiled. "You needn't be sorry. Amel's experience with the visitor probe has been abominable, which is exactly why we have an ethical obligation to help him recover."

"Ethical obligation or guilt?" Erien returned sharply.

"While I do see guilt in Lurol's determination," Bley admitted, "I think you are carrying a heavy burden of guilt yourself."

The words made him start. Lemonade spilled over his fingers. He put the glass down and took the napkin she handed him, swabbing in short, rough strokes so she would not see his hands shaking. "My mistakes led to people being killed," he admitted. "I *ought* to feel guilty."

"My dear," she said, "your intervention prevented more people from being killed. But you don't just mean *Kali Station*, do you?... Erien, what *did* happen on Gelion?"

"Nothing that affects Rire."

She said gently, "My concern is Amel."

Erien swallowed. "What will it take to convince you refusing to be probed is in Amel's best interest? If what happened in Lilac Hearth—" he caught himself, agonized at the slip.

She leaned forward and this time did take his hand, and firmly. "You know, don't you?" she said. "You were there."

Erien closed his eyes, trying not to remember a smoke-filled room pounding with cheerful Reetion music. "I know. But it is *irrelevant* to Rire." He opened his eyes. "Unfortunately, it is not irrelevant to *Gelion*."

Bley settled back again. "I am going to revisit this conversation with Amel and say the same thing to him that I am going to say to you, now. I would like you to tell me what happened in Lilac Hearth. It is very clear that Amel broke down under monitoring because of it. Without an explanation, all conjectures seem equally plausible. And if nothing else, getting it out of the way — in my opinion — will leave Amel able to focus on Lurol's offer to cure him of clear dreaming."

"That's not all Lurol wants to do," Erien said heavily.

"No," Bley agreed. "And it might be in Amel's best interests to have her undo what she did eighteen years ago, as well. Or Amel may be quite content to be the person he is. But the fact remains he must accept the visitor probe to be cured of the clear dreams."

She rose, ending the interview. "Will you consider my offer, Erien?" she said, and smiled. "I somehow think that you will be the key to Amel accepting it. And it can be done as privately as you like, under STI zero conditions."

Erien left in a daze, feeling shaken and outmaneuvered by Bley's success at making it all personal. Bley watched from the door, making the back of Erien's neck prickle. He was tired of being watched.

The Gelack cultists were taking turns riding his bicycle, and there was no other bike available in the public rack. He decided to walk rather than deal with them. A boy called, "Hey! Are you a bigger wimp than Amel, or what?"

The second boy hopped off Erien's bike, letting it fall, and moved deliberately to block his path. He looked Erien up and down, and asked, "So how come Heir Gelion gets around Rire on a bicycle?"

Erien squelched the impulse to say, *Because my rel-ship's back at Kali Station,* and said instead, "It's an efficient mode of transport."

The boys snickered. "Guess it's only Nersal who's got guts!"

"Uh, oh," the other one said. "Solomon."

A large, competent looking man came striding out to rein in the cultists.

Erien kept his gait to a brisk walk all the way home. It helped take the edge off his irritation. This was not the Rire he remembered. He had abused Amel's trust by bringing him here, and he was worried about what opinions Horth might be forming. Horth had come to measure Reetion honor. Erien was no longer sure, himself, where it could be found. He would have to convince Horth the Reetions were trying to help Amel, in their paternalistic fashion, not demonstrate the power of their science over a Sevolite highborn.

As Erien pushed open the door of his Reetion family's townhouse he heard Ranar saying, "Yes, thank you, Bley. In fact, I think I hear him coming in now."

"Bley?" said Erien, tingling with anticipation of disaster. "Is there a problem?"

Ranar turned away from the front room stage. "Nothing wrong," he assured Erien. "Bley just wanted us to know that you were pestered by some Gelack cultists at the group home and handled yourself with admirable maturity. She also thinks we aren't doing our duty as parents, since you are overtired."

Drasous was sitting on the couch with a book open in his lap, one of Evert's small collection of Demish literature. He closed it with deliberate care as he looked up; the title was *The Prince of Dem'Lara*.

"It did not go well," Drasous deduced, studying Erien.

Erien sighed. "She is going to declare him incompetent."

"They have decided already!" Ranar asked, astonished.

"No," Erien admitted, "but I felt..." He broke off, unwilling to explain she had offered him a condition he could not meet. "I need to prepare for the worst. Is our domestic STI holding up?" Erien asked.

"It is," said Drasous, who was standing up now, still weighing the book on his hands.

Erien released the breath he hadn't realized he was holding. "I am worried, Ranar."

A tense silence followed, in which both Ranar and Drasous seemed preoccupied by private thoughts.

Even under STI two conditions, Ranar and Erien dared not discuss what Amel might know about Di Mon, because Drasous did not know Di Mon had been homosexual, and if he ever did, so would Ameron. Di Mon would have hated nothing more. And even in complete privacy, back on Gelion, Erien had been unable to discuss the noxious details of events in Lilac Hearth.

Evert broke the tension by coming down the stars to find the three of them standing there, silently.

"Oh," Evert remarked to Drasous, "you've got it. I thought perhaps Amel had taken it with him." He nodded to the book in the *gorarelpul*'s hands.

"An excellent idea," said Drasous. "If you wouldn't mind, I'll take it over to him. I believe it might make him feel... better."

Evert looked delighted. "Of course Amel can borrow it."

"Where's Horth?" Erien asked Ranar, already feeling his chest tighten at the notion of talking with the increasingly withdrawn liege of Nersal.

Ranar nodded toward the patio doors. "Exercising."

Erien found Lurol on the patio, seated in a deck chair and watching Horth going through a series of unarmed combat exercises Erien had taught him. His kicks and punches had such force behind them, striking empty air, that Erien half expected miniature sonic booms to rattle the windows.

"I need to talk with Horth," Erien reminded himself, aloud.

Lurol looked from him to Horth, and back again. "Personally," she said, "I wouldn't interrupt him." She put an arm around Erien and led him back inside. It wasn't until Lurol slid the patio door closed behind him that Erien realized he was under her wing, literally, with both Evert and Ranar converging on them. Drasous was gone.

"I think," Ranar said, "you will be more efficient after a few hours rest."

"I had a thought on the way back," Erien said. "We should lodge an objection on the grounds that the use of the visitor probe on a subject who is acknowledged to be unique constitutes experimentation."

Ranar nodded. "I'll investigate the possibility."

"We need to keep on top of the debate establishing the domain of inquiry," Erien insisted.

"I'll do it," Lurol promised. "I've no interest in questions, just the right to treat him. If we cured the clear dreams with psychosurgery, he could resume the hearing under ordinary psych monitoring, as far as I'm concerned."

Erien quelled the urge to argue about psychosurgery. Lurol's voice had influence in key lobbies. It was enough to know she would help reduce the scope of questioning allowed.

Evert startled him by touching his arm. "Erien, my dear," he said, with the same worried look Erien remembered from his childhood, "in your condition you can't expect to do better than the three of us together."

Erien opened his mouth to object, and closed it as parental glances were exchanged around him. It was oddly reassuring to find them united again, even if only to gang up on him.

"Your Reetion guardians are right, Immortality," said Drasous from behind him. He must have come in the patio door, making no sound as he slipped through. Horth opened the door wider entering behind him, damp with exercise.

The weight of five pairs of eyes on him, coupled with his undeniable weariness, made Erien feel foolish, suddenly, for resisting. He nodded, turned, and headed upstairs. Drasous followed like a shadow.

Erien stretched out on his bed, toed off his shoes and nudged them to the floor without lifting his head to see where they fell. Drasous spoke to the arbiter, lowering the window blinds. Erien lay with his eyes closed, breathing shallowly.

"Tell Horth I'll talk to him when I get up," Erien promised. "Tell him I promise I'll listen."

"I will, Immortality," said Drasous. "Rest now."

The *gorarelpul* bowed himself out. Erien lay in the darkness, wrestling with self-reproach. He had failed Amel's trust and was losing Horth's. He had misjudged Rire and was losing control. He had no idea if he could contain the consequences, or how he would explain to those people who loved Amel: people like his half-brother, Ditatt Monitum, or even Princess Luthan. What would he tell Ameron, if he bungled the diplomatic mission? How could he keep family secrets spilled on Rire from doing harm on Gelion?

With his thoughts still racing in closed, self-doubting circles, he fell into an exhausted sleep.

TWENTY-ONE

Eyes on Amel

Far Arena

Liege Bryllit declared it too dangerous to order any pilot to take news to Horth of what was taking place on *Kali Station*.

She called for volunteers, instead, and Horth's brother Eler stepped forward.

Bryllit accepted Eler's sacrifice with a reverence unnerving enough to threaten the family reputation for virility when she invited him to spend his last night with her. He got over bedroom nerves by reminding himself he did not share Bryllit's gloomy conviction Amel was a *zer-pol* on the brink of ushering in war through sacrifice. He knew his liege-brother Horth had gone to Rire because of how he felt about Erien Lor'Vrel, the newly minted Heir Gelion.

In Eler's opinion, Erien was a Reetion-raised, half-Lorel meddler who needed a good thumping to cure him of delusions of importance. Eler wanted to be on hand to see Erien got what he deserved if Horth was disgraced or killed by a planet full of *okal'a'ni* Reetions after being lured there by his faith in Erien.

Why Eler, himself, wanted to encounter Reetions he was loath to put into words, which he recognized as a sure sign the issue was going to preoccupy him until he did. Eler knew what he was by this stage of his adult life, and knew there was no hope of hiding from it beneath the mantle of a veteran duellist and Nersallian arm commander. He was a poet. This was his *rel* — his struggle — the joke the universe had seen fit to play on him as punishment for his irreverent awareness of its fundamental silliness.

He had negotiated only two concessions with his muse since it had beaten him, hands down, on the challenge floor of his mind: first, he'd attributed his masterpieces to a commoner accomplice in the troop of performing courtesans he maintained for this purpose; and second, he'd worked to subvert the very forms and formulas of Demish cannon that had so ill-advisedly trampled down his Vrellish resistance to their claim upon him.

Eler's first obstacle to reaching Horth was stealing the jump to Rire. Getting as far as the jump point between the Reach of Paradise and Reach of Rire was a simple matter of reading maps. Nothing inanimate, however, could communicate the way through a jump, so once he reached the jump point he was stuck. Fortunately for his patience, there was more traffic coming and going from this jump than any he had ever seen. Keeping to less than one *skim'fac*, he tailed a Reetion pilot until he judged they were close enough, then he pounced like a wolf shedding sheep's clothes.

For a moment he shared his guide's alarm as she shared his large-hearted arrogance. The soul touch was enough to convince him that discretion was the better part of valor with regard to explanations, especially as the pilot was a woman with a decidedly Vrellish-feeling temper. He bobbed a salute in apology, and took off doing a showy three *skim'facs* that no commoner pilot could match.

Eler was congratulating himself for making the Reach of Rire without much complication when he had to veer to avoid a ship, and then another. He soared clear, dreading dust — planted or natural — beyond the lanes regularly traveled, and half convinced himself he tasted blood before he dropped back to less than a *skim'fac* and was able to slip back into traffic. But this only gave him leisure to get back in touch with his amazement. Astronomically speaking, the Reach of Rire was as crowded as the Market Round on Gelion!

Eler picked a *rel*-ship at random and followed it as far as a space station, where he dropped out of skim at the usual distance, known within the empire as the challenge radius. A man who called himself a *pilot handler* hailed him on a Reetion frequency, with orders that he dock immediately and report for examination. Eler decided to try his luck elsewhere. At the next space station he dropped out of skim a ridiculous distance away, suspecting that the Reetions' lack of hullsteel made them nervous. This time he was greeted by an arbiter that obligingly provided a star map.

Ranar's doing, Eler decided when, much to his surprise, the arbiter was able to provide something compatible with nervecloth, and did not hesitate to do so. Ranar was a puzzle: boy-*sla* and not exactly boy-*sla*, swordless and fearless, recognized by Ameron as ambassador to Gelion, but still... not to put a fine point on it, boy-*sla*.

The best Eler could make of the whole business at the moment was that if men like Ranar were an ordinary thing among the Reetions, there must be a lot of very lonely Reetion women. Cheered by the thought, he picked a clear spot near a concentration of stations in the outer solar system and did a shimmer dance to declare his arrival. He made it a "loud" announcement, since having got this far by virtue of impersonating a commoner, he felt it only decent to make an honest show of his potential, and besides, showing off never hurt with station women back home, in his experience.

He certainly made an impression. Local ships swarmed to surround him in a slow-motion cloud, like wasps struggling through syrup.

Politely, Eler backed off and tried again, dancing *Scion of House Nersal* just a bit more gently.

Half the Reetions ships disappeared, although he was quite sure he had not dunked any of them. He concluded he had merely frightened them, so he dropped out of skim to communicate.

"Are you mad!" an angry voice accosted him. "That was the most irresponsible prank I have ever weathered! What are you — a Gelack or something?"

"Yes, actually, I am. Highlord Eler, brother of Liege Nersal," Eler said, in his excellent Reetion, a language he had picked up originally out of curiosity about Reetion literature. He had then been asked to use it for military intelligence, which amused him greatly because, as far as he could see, the Reetions viewed what Horth considered military intelligence as public knowledge.

"Oh," said the Reetion pilot. A second later he added, "Really?"

"I've offended you," said Eler expansively. "Shall we settled it by challenge?"

"Challenge?" asked the Reetion. "You mean... with swords?"

"That's customary," said Eler, enjoying himself immensely imagining them frantically summoning up Ranar's notes. "Unfortunately, as I haven't brought any kin with me to bear witness, I would require some other guarantee of your honor before setting foot on your station."

"I do not want to duel with you!" said the Reetion. He sounded as if the whole idea was thoroughly ridiculous. "Listen," he continued, flustered, "I'm not an anthropologist, okay? I'm just trying to explain that you are not authorized to skim within the Reetion light sphere."

Eler understood the concept of 'light sphere.' It meant they were close enough for planetary Reetions to be getting news of events, within minutes, via light-speed communications. He was also aware that the suggestion he could not be trusted this close to Rire was an insult.

"Do you consider me dishonorable?" Eler asked.

"Listen," said the Reetion, "space within light range of Rire is heavily populated and traveled. Only pilots approved by Space Service can fly in it. You'll have to stop here."

"But unless your star charts are misleading, and thus far they've proved excellent," said Eler. "I am not yet close enough to Rire to arrive within the day if I stop skimming."

"I am afraid you will have to dock anyway."

"Or?" asked Eler, thinking it a wise precaution to inquire.

"Pardon?"

"How would you prevent me going on if I decide to? How do you control your own pilots?"

The Reetion had to think about it. "No pilot gets into a ship, to start, unless he's been cleared by his handlers, including a fresh psychological assessment with respect to predictors of moral behavior, and, of course, he has to have the skills required."

"The pilot must be competent and honorable," Eler agreed approvingly. "I assure you I qualify."

Eler boosted to half a skim factor.

He did not show off this time. He simply skirted obstacles with Nersallian precision; tapering down to a cat-clawing stutter and dropping out of skim entirely at the point his intrusion field began picking up traces of atmosphere.

He fully expected to get his ears filled with more blather as he settled into orbit around Rire, but instead he was greeted by a single, familiar voice speaking in Gelack.

"*Ack rel,*" said Horth Nersal, which was a greeting, a reminder that life could be hard and death sudden, and an admonishment to accept one's fortune — good or bad — with honor.

Eler's skin prickled in his flight leathers. "My liege?" he answered.

"Eler," Horth acknowledged him dourly. "Your purpose?"

"I am here with news from *Kali Station*," Eler answered. "What are your orders?"

"Land," Horth told him. "Stay ship-bound. I will join you."

"*Ack rel*," agreed Eler. To stay ship-bound implied an unsafe dock, so he knew he should be worried. But despite the wisdom of his basic cynicism, his liege-brother's steady voice, giving orders, made him one with his house: a fixture in the universe with many lives and one pride that could never be broken. Those born within the challenge right of the title 'liege of Nersal' were the *kinf'stan* — and the gods could maul whoever mocked their honor.

The gods... or Liege Bryllit, Eler thought with grim satisfaction.

A line from a play he was working on trickled across his thoughts. Kinf'stan *so like to kill each other, they must deny others the pleasure*. Mad, perhaps, but so was life. Even the *kinf'stan* Horth had killed would rise up with him, in spirit, against *okal'a'ni* Reetions — which was an acutely personal thought for Eler, since this list included their father.

A Reetion voice gave him landing instructions. He responded with professional competence, noting, as the view switched from *rel*-telemetry to optical, that Rire looked like a planet worth acquiring. Of course, conquering even a single space station was never straightforward, much less something on the scale of the space-spanning empire he had passed through en route, but he was Nersallian — he couldn't help but notice.

He was accutely aware he forfeited the advantage conferred by his Sevolite prowess in the cockpit once he landed.

Honor is the constant offering of one's life to enemies stupid enough to prove themselves dishonorable, he remembered from his childhood, amused to find the slogans he was apt to mock, in safety, so invigorating while he was in peril.

His envoy-class ship was designed for atmospheric landings, and taxied to a halt as neatly as a ground-to-orbit shuttle. The scene on his nose screen was pleasant: a wide runway cleared for his use with grass in sight beyond and the Space Services complex of the space port at his back.

"This is Juma," a man's voice announced over the radio. "I am the new Foreign and Alien Council liaison to your people. Welcome to Rire, Highlord Eler of the House of Nersal, arm commander in the Dragon Fleet of Nersal and brother of Horth, liege of Nersal, the master of Black Hearth on Fountain Court."

The man spoke Gelack in a pompous manner, a commoner addressing him in peerage! Not to mention speaking like a Demish herald.

Eler ventured thoughtfully in Reetion, "Am I to presume that you extend this welcome on behalf of your liege, Ranar?"

"Uh, no. You don't quite understand—" the Reetion caught himself answering in Reetion and broke off. "Don't you speak Gelack?" he asked stupidly.

"I do," said Eler, "but I have decided — in order to spare myself unnecessary exercise — that either you do not speak Gelack, or else you can't count levels between birth ranks." He paused, and added helpfully, "Unless you meant the insult?"

"No, no," Juma assured him. "I know all about birth ranks. But Ranar was granted honorary peerage when addressing anyone from Ameron on down, so he could function in your culture as the Reetion representative. You call it 'peerage of convenience.'"

"Ameron calls it peerage of convenience," said Eler dryly, and mulled it over for a moment to identify the other problem. "And you aren't Ranar."

The Reetion explained, with every symptom of great patience, how his own culture considered roles to be temporary and he was now functioning in the role that had been Ranar's.

"I see," said Eler. "Did you kill Ranar in the duel? Or was it to first blood?"

"There was no duel," Juma assured him, as if Eler was simple-minded. "We settle these things differently."

Since he had time to amuse himself, Eler encouraged the Reetion to explain the workings of the Foreign and Alien Council, asking just enough questions for Juma to consider him a promising student, then concluded, "You Reetions have put a lot of thought into that system of yours."

"Uh, yes. Thank you," said Juma, trying to be gracious.

"We're a little stuck in our ways, too," said Eler, "so I'll tell you what: you let me know when you've taken Ranar on with a sword, and then we'll see if we can get you an appointment with Ameron to decide if we are going to sustain existing contracts and honor bonds."

"I don't think you understand," Juma tried again. "I am to assume all Ranar's functions and status in connection with his role as liaison to your Ava's court."

"No," said Eler getting bored. "Only those it is within Rire's power to bestow." He turned the connection off.

He scanned for the nearest arbiter and asked what Ranar, himself, was up to. A short negotiation with the Reetion machine resulted in tapping him directly into some sort of huge, interminable council meeting, supported by the arbiters, that was taking place simultaneously all across the planet. He had to sort out interface problems, but once again the arbiter was helpful. Within minutes he had up summaries of a war of words waged by Ranar and Ameron's *gorarelpul*, Drasous, in an effort to get Horth clearance to come and visit Eler. The rest of the Reetions wanted Eler to come out where everything said could be recorded, which was doubtless why Horth wanted him to remain ship-bound.

While he was waiting, Eler reviewed the record covering his short debate with Juma and laughed out loud at Ranar's input, on what seemed to be a side channel. "Eler Nersal is baiting Juma. Someone please tell Juma that Eler isn't simple, and will eat him alive if he gives him half a chance. The man's a genius at twisting people's words. It gives him pleasure!"

"Will you deliver messages?" Eler asked the arbiter. "Yes? Good. Tell Ranar: it gave me pleasure, but not very much. Juma isn't smart enough to know he's stupid."

No sooner had Eler sent the message than he doubted the wisdom of it. Horth had told him to wait. Did that preclude conversation? He was about to shut down reception to await Horth's signal when Ranar's voice spoke directly to him.

"Eler Nersal," it scolded, "that was childish."

Eler grinned at the prospect of some entertainment. "I confess it wasn't up to my usual high standards for repartee," said Eler. "But look what I had to work with!"

Ranar sighed. "You have Juma to thank for getting me a chance to speak with you. He showed that much wisdom."

"Wise is the *pol* man," quoted Eler, "who knows when to sheath his sword."

"And wise is the *rel* man who knows when to draw," a new voice quoted back with enthusiasm. "That's from a Blue Demish parlor comedy called *Fools or Lovers*."

"I suppose you might call it *Fools and Lovers*," Eler said pedantically, "if you insist on bungling the translation of *pol'har'stan* which really means something closer to *sensitive spirits* in Demoran dialect, although I'll grant you the Blue Demish author of the play might have meant to imply *fools*."

"You're a literary scholar!" the new voice enthused.

Ranar sighed. "Evert, I don't think this is the right time to—"

"All right," chirped Evert. "But I want to thank you, Eler Nersal, for what you said about Ranar."

"Really?" Eler said, feeling ruffled. "Then I doubt you would like to know what else I've said about him on den crawls, ever since we found out he was boy-*sla*."

There was a silence that suggested his jibe had scored. Then Ranar said, as implacable as ever, "I have Horth here with me, but he only wants to talk with you in person. Juma has taken my advice to lobby the Foreign and Alien council to convince the space port it will be all right if he comes there to see you. I've asked Horth to give me his word the two of you won't leave Rire for orbit without clearance. Horth has agreed."

"Where is Erien?" Eler asked cagily.

"Sleeping," said Ranar. "Erien has been up for two days straight. Horth does not want him woken just yet."

Good, thought Eler. *Maybe Horth is ready to abandon the Lor'Vrellish changeling.* However, it gave him pause that Horth had promised not to take off. Horth did not lie when he gave his word to someone he respected and Eler gravely feared this might include Ameron's acknowledged Reetion ambassador.

"No doubt Horth wants me to stay in my ship," Eler said jauntily, to hide his unease, "to prevent me giving away a child or three without the benefit of contracts while I'm on Rire. You might have many frustrated women on a world so hospitable to the boy-*sla*."

"Maybe," Ranar replied. "More likely Horth is feeling the need for some privacy and knows we can't monitor through hullsteel. Horth is not saying much to anyone."

"He can be like that," commiserated Eler, adding to himself, *before a duel*. It was unnerving to suspect Horth was frightened of something on Rire. "Later, then," he told Ranar and signed off, determined to make sense of things as much as possible even if it meant using the arbiter.

He started with finding out why Erien had been up for two days straight, and learned Amel had — predictably — broken down under interrogation, and was under house arrest in a place known as a group home. The Reetions believed Amel knew things damaging to the honor of the Ava's throne and wanted to extract the truth under the visitor probe. Even more disquieting was the debate over whether adjustments to Amel's personality should be permitted. Eler didn't care about the reasons. A chilling hatred of an ancient evil crept over Eler as it dawned on him the Reetions were confident such adjustments were perfectly possible. It was always under the guise of offering medical miracles that the Lorels had imposed their will on Sevildom.

Erien Lor'Vrel seemed equal to the sophistry the Reetions threw at him Eler decided as he reviewed the record. But Erien had himself agreed to testify under something called 'pscyhometric monitoring.' There was supposed to be a difference between this and the visitor probe, but Eler saw them all as stages along the same continuum.

Reetions could make a Sevolite so much clay in their hands. Weighed against that, all the sophistries were just twaddle.

To provide himself with a distraction, Eler requested a nice view of a nude beach with a collection of attractive women. Unfortunately for his recreational ambitions on Rire, the behavior of the men in evidence disproved his hopeful notion Rire was full of lonely women.

"Eler," Ranar's voice interrupted him moments later. "What are you doing?"

"Sightseeing," Eler said.

"Then I ought to point out to you," Ranar explained tersely, "that while you may access whatever you wish, it is equally transparent to the population exactly what you are choosing to look at."

Eler was prepared to be diplomatic. "What would you suggest, instead?" he asked Gelion's Reetion ambassador.

"If you like drama," Evert piped up, "I could suggest something."

"Eler doesn't like drama," Ranar told his friend off testily. "He owns drama, an acting group of courtesans, that is, and he — no, never mind. I just don't think the topic is a safe one."

"Do Reetions have any decent drama?" Eler drawled provocatively, encouraged by Ranar's reluctance to let Evert speak to him.

"We have managed to produce a piece or two, yes," Ranar said dryly, "in the thousand years we've been alone on our side of the universe."

"Maybe you would prefer works from Earth," Evert chipped in. "Have Gelacks got any of the works of Shakespeare, for example?"

Eler was not about to admit he had, indeed, heard of Shakespeare in obscure Demish quarters where he sometimes hunted literature, nor that he was inspired to pursue Evert's suggestion. He cut the Reetions off and ordered the arbiter to fetch him whatever Rire had on the Earth poet named Shakespeare. He was staggered by the listings produced. He dismissed the commentaries to concentrate on recordings of performances in the original tongue, understanding nothing but the duel in the first piece he came across. It was hard going, since the plays were written in an older version of English than the one current in scholarly circles at Fountain Court — where it was already an ancient tongue by Gelack standards — but the arbiter proved very helpful in looking things up.

Two hours later, Eler was so absorbed in *Hamlet* that he almost failed to respond to a Nersallian com signal. He wiped his nervecloth with a pang of loss, but forgot his hobby when his brother's head appeared through the hatch in the cockpit floor.

Eler sprang out of his acceleration seat to make room and hurried, stooping, into the back of the stubby little spacecraft to wait for Horth to join him. He took his sword with him and laid it, sheathed, across his lap. Horth also had his sword — a comforting statement of sane limits to conflict, up front and tangible.

Horth said in his rock-stable voice, "You bring news."

"The arbiter went down on *Kali Station*," Eler told him. "It decided Amel's reasons for living only worked for corporeal beings and reverted to its fail-safe programming. But not," he added, smirking, "before ogling the female half of the crew."

"Losses?" Horth asked, ignoring the embellishment.

"None. Life-support is holding, but Bryllit has battlewheels converging, drawn from the fleet in her new role as your acknowledged heir."

A taut silence followed.

"Is she right?" Eler asked. "Should we be mobilizing?"

Horth shrugged. "I am here," he said, "not there."

"Come back with me," Eler suggested as a remedy.

"I have promised Ranar I will not leave the planet without notice," Horth said with deliberate precision.

"So we give notice," Eler urged him. "Will they try to stop us?"

"I will not leave Erien," he said. "Not *alive*."

The two extra words chilled Eler. "I'm not imagining things then," he said with hardening conviction. "The visitor probe is *sla* Lorel technology. Do the Reetions have the same itch to control us as the Lorels?"

"I am confused about the Reetions," Horth admitted.

The simple admission shook Eler. He understood more about a great many things than his liege-brother, but he trusted Horth's judgment and his will to make decisions.

"I know this," Horth stepped back onto firm ground. "Amel will not be visitor probed."

Eler understood immediately. It had always been a captive's duty to die before submitting to *sla* Lorels. "Is Amel *rel* enough?" Eler asked.

"We will know soon," said Horth. "I am sorry you are here," he added with affection, "but glad to have a ship. I came expecting swords would be respected. Instead..." The unfinished sentence revealed his alarming uncertainty again.

"If things do not go well," Horth said, "we will deny them hostages. I promised Bryllit."

"So," Eler said ruefully, "Erien is not a *zer-rel*."

"*Ack rel*," Horth said, and shrugged, his expression stoic. "Anything can happen in a duel."

"You mean your *zer-rel* lost his challenge?" Eler interpreted, and saw he was correct. "So we're going to make a *zer-pol* of Amel, for Bryllit. But — you won't leave here without Erien, either." Eler inhaled to argue and swallowed it, staring at his brother's fixed expression. One might as well argue with the law of gravity. "How do we get Erien into the ship with us? Presuming Amel does his part," he added.

"If Amel does not," Horth said, "Drasous will take care of it. Drasous will send Erien to us, as well, if he's able."

"Best-case scenario," Eler summarized, in military mode. "Once Amel's safely dead, we get Erien inside, give notice to satisfy your word to Ranar and take off. Drasous, at least, we don't have to worry about being an incompetent suicide, and that's probably a better way for him to die than flying with us at the *skim'facs* we may need to use. Reetion pilots are all commoners, but there are a lot of them, and who knows what they might pull."

"Erien will not cooperate," Horth warned.

"What Erien does or does not want, once he's in my ship, he can challenge me over once we have docked somewhere with room enough to clear swords," said Eler.

Horth grinned at the sentiment.

"And if it doesn't work?" asked Eler, the fine hairs on the back of his neck rising at the thought of probe-altered highborns flying against Bryllit, the way legend said they had during the Lorel wars. "If Amel survives, and Erien escapes us?"

"We wait until they are together," Horth said grimly.

Eler thought to ask, *How will that help us?* and stopped, because he knew the answer. They did have a weapon. They could take the ship up just high enough to come back down on top of the group home where Amel was held prisoner, and eliminate all highborn hostages without harming the planet in an *okal'a'ni* way.

"I thought you gave the Reetion your word you wouldn't take off without notice," Eler mentioned, with forced humor.

Horth's reply was dead serious. "I said we would not leave the planet."

TWENTY-TWO

Erien

Honor's Fulcrum

The arbiter awakened Erien with a series of broken chords and a polite, "There is a call for you. Are you awake?"

What was supposed to have been *yes* emerged as a mumble.

The broken chords repeated themselves, and the room blinds tilted to admit daylight. "Priority message from Bley, regarding your brother Amel," said the arbiter.

"What! No, don't display!" Erien rolled to his feet so fast his vision went white with the sudden movement, stumbled over Amel's bedding and fell against the bookshelf, nearly knocking his model of the Ava's station from its perch. The stage chorded again, and reminded him, "It is a priority message."

"I know that!" Erien snapped, shoving the model back into place. "How long have I been asleep?"

"Four point two hours."

Bley was going to declare Amel incompetent, thought Erien. She hadn't had enough time to change her mind. He braced his elbows against the sink, breathing slowly until his heart rate slowed. Then he returned to the stage, straightening his collar and closing his cuffs. "Accept contact."

Bley appeared on his stage with her head turned, speaking to someone excluded from the view. She was saying, "... off record for now, if you're sure he's safe." An off-stage voice began to answer but she interjected. "Excuse me, this is his brother coming on."

A door closed. Bley was in the staff room at the group home. She looked strained and a little tired. "Hello, dear," she greeted Erien, sensibly making no apology for waking him. "I am afraid I have unsettling news." She inhaled with the distinct manner of failing to find a good way to put bad news. "We think Amel has attempted suicide."

"Think?" he asked, hardly believing it.

"Yes," Bley paused. "Amel says it was an accident. I would like your opinion."

"Is this off the record?" Erien said, stifling other questions.

"You mean have I chosen to release it?" Bley clarified. "No, and I won't. Not, at least, until I have talked with you." She paused. "I confess Roz and I are confused. Maybe you can cast light on the bare facts."

"How did it happen?" Erien asked curtly.

The stage cast a 2-D visual of Amel working on the float bed of a paraplegic woman. "Amel was fine-tuning the voice interface for Europa, one of my terminal Supervised," Bley narrated. "He decided he needed a particular electronic accessory he had identified by browsing a stage in the commons. Apparently he misapplied the new tool, inducing a power drain from the chair, but I think he knew exactly what he was doing. Watch his face, in particular."

The sound switched to match the 2-D visual in which Amel knelt before the open side of Europa's float chair, holding the tuning probe. Europa was making small talk. A faint smile wafted over Amel's waxen expression as he made a perfectly credible, casual remark. Then it was gone. He adjusted a setting and applied the tuning probe with a light touch. There was a sharp *hiss-pop*. The woman in the chair made a startled sound. Amel jerked the probe clear, rising as he turned her chair toward him with his left hand, probe transferred to his right one.

"Europa?" He touched the woman's disease-distorted cheek, his elegant hand covering her withered one on the arm of her float chair with gentle solicitude. "I'm sorry! Are you all right?"

She spoke through the voice interface he was trying to improve. "Amel, sweet, I'll never be all right again. But don't fret — it was just a power fluctuation."

"There is backup for your life-support functions, though," he insisted. He sounded sure.

"Yes, yes. That's what it was, kicking in. Made me jump. But you may have shorted the fail-safes."

"Oh," he said listlessly.

"You should be—"

Amel switched the probe into his left hand, inhaled and put it forward into the open panel once more with a mesmerized, leaden look.

"— careful," Europa finished as a jolt from her chair, through the tool, snapped Amel's body back and threw him to the floor. Within seconds the door flew open as Solomon rushed in and the image faded out.

"What Amel did to induce the shock relied on aspects of the probe and chair that did not feature in his inquiries into either product," Bley told Erien, "but Amel did scan their specifications in full detail. Now, I know that you have your own ideas about things, the two of you—" Bley's manner firmed up, "— but I want you to be truthful about this. Could Amel have done this on the basis of such a cursory inspection? Roz believes his face proclaims it a suicide. Solomon thinks it is unlikely even a trained engineer could have identified the weakness in the fail-safe under the circumstances." Bley paused. "Could Amel?"

Erien hesitated. He could not see how denial would serve any purpose but harming his credibility with Bley. "Amel has the Golden Demoran advantage of eidetic memory. And he tinkers with systems as an interest. So yes, I think he could."

Bley released an unhappy sigh. "I am afraid Roz is right, then. And we must take this attempt very seriously. His heart did stop. But he responded to resuscitation and what damage there is seems to be under assault by what we presume is a regenerative response. Amel wants your medical person, Drasous, to treat him, and I would like your reassurance we can safely rely on Sevolite stamina without taking this beyond the group home; I am certain disclosure, at this point, would upset Amel."

"I will bring Drasous over," Erien promised.

"Thank you." She was loath to break off the call, needing to commiserate with him. "Before this happened, suicide was the last thing I was worried about. Your brother is a delight. Secretive, of course, but Solomon assures me that is cultural. I am afraid it makes me lean toward suspecting something involuntary, which would argue against psychological competence." She shook her head. "I am sorry to put this on your young, rather sore shoulders. It isn't how I would normally handle such a painful matter."

"I wish to be involved," Erien insisted. He must have conveyed more force than he intended, because Bley frowned.

"You will be," she promised. "Take some time if you need it, dear. Your brother is in no immediate danger. His asking for Drasous is, I think, to reassure himself we won't overtreat him while he's down. I expect you would understand such a motive." She smiled forgivingly at him, and signed off.

Drasous was waiting in the hallway when Erien jerked open the door. "Drasous, we need to go over to the group home. Amel's unwell."

"Unwell?" said the medical *gorarelpul*, tilting his head questioningly.

"He has met with an accident," said Erien. "They are interpreting it as attempted suicide. I am hoping we can disprove their interpretation."

Drasous retreated into the room shared with Horth, lifted a medical bag from the bed and came back out immediately into the hall. "This is poor timing," he said. "While you were asleep, Eler Nersal arrived."

"Eler! What's happened?"

Bryllit is getting belligerent! Erien guessed. *Or Dorn's dead.* There were a dozen possible scenarios for disaster.

"What we know has happened," said Drasous, "is that Liege Nersal ordered Eler to stay in his ship — that is on the record. We, Ranar and I, managed to secure permission for Liege Nersal to go out and join him. They are still there, and want to talk to you." At the top of the stairs, the *gorarelpul* turned and regarded him with steady eyes. "I believe the Nersallians should be your priority, Heir Gelion."

Erien tamped down a sense of desperation. "But Amel?"

"I will go to the group home and see to Amel," Drasous said quite gently. "You cannot be everywhere, Heir Gelion."

"You will tell me at once," Erien said, surprised by the ring of command in his voice, "if I am needed."

"Of course, Immortality," the *gorarelpul* assured him, and bowed.

Suicide, Erien thought as he watched Drasous leave. He agreed with Bley. It made no sense to him. But Drasous was correct. The Nersallians had to be his priority.

He debated with himself whether to take transit, but the space port was on the far side of the group home in the same general direction. Running might take half an hour, and cost him a dignified entrance. All the same, the short train trip seemed to take forever. He spent it listening for news on his ear bug, and trying not to climb out of his skin.

Eler's snub-nosed envoy ship, on the grounds of the space port, was ringed by first responders armed with canisters of restraining foam. Ranar and Evert stood inside the ring. Evert was chatting about Demish literature, of all things, and trying — Erien suspected — to ease the tension.

Ranar raised a hand to stop Evert as Erien was waved through to join them. "What is it?" Ranar asked immediately.

Erien shook his head, unwilling to expose Amel's attempted suicide in what had become an STI six setting.

"But don't you think *The Prince of Dem'Lara* was a particularly gloomy selection?" Evert babbled. "I mean killing oneself for one's family and all! Perhaps Drasous hadn't read it, really, and only asked for it because he knew the title." Evert broke off, belatedly, to smile at Erien.

"Horth has asked you to join him and Eler in the ship," Ranar told Erien, "no doubt to avoid our surveillance." He smiled. "Do be careful? Something's... not right."

Ranar's voice grew fainter as Erien advanced, but he distinctly heard him ask Evert, "What were you were saying about the book?"

Erien stopped. The ship sat, inanimate on the grass. When he had climbed up inside it, he would be off record. Regardless of his feelings about the coming interview, he could not deny anticipating relief on that account, but he turned back with a prickling feeling to look at Evert and Ranar.

"*The Prince of Dem'Lara?*" Erien asked Evert and Ranar.

"Yes, and on reflection I hardly thought the story — well, appropriate... under the circumstances. Prince Dem'Lara, you see, is captured by Lorels and persuaded by his mother to end his life rather than becoming a liability to his house. I think Amel would have preferred something cheerful."

A cold fear touched Erien's spine. He breathed, "Drasous."

Eler Nersal dropped out of his envoy ship with more agility than seemed reasonable from such a big man. Horth came next. The two of them straightened and stood waiting, unarmed.

Erien took a step back. His heart was racing. Suddenly he spun and broke out through the loose circle ringing Eler's ship. For a terrible moment he was afraid the first responders might bring him down, or that Horth might pursue. Miraculously, each seemed to neutralize the other. He heard nothing behind him but a Reetion voice exclaiming, "Look! They're going back in!"

Erien ran as he had never run before. Ten minutes later he arrived at the group home, gasping several deep breaths before his breathing steadied. His shoulder thudded with his pulse, but he barely felt it at the moment, an advantage of his Vrellish inheritance.

Solomon greeted him in the foyer.

"Drasous?" Erien ground out.

"He's here," Solomon said, "but Bley's with Amel now."

"Amel's not—" Erien began, and caught himself.

"He's all right," Solomon assured him.

Amel was in a room immediately off the commons, one equipped with an emergency life bed for short-term acute care. He was pale and subdued, his chest bare beneath the band of the cardio monitor, with respiratory equipment on standby. He was talking to Bley, his voice thready but familiar, "I guess... *gorarelpul* are just scary?"

"Yes," Bley agreed. "Your reaction was clearly one of mortal terror. But why did you ask for Drasous if—" Amel's glance alerted her to Erien's presence in the doorway.

Erien's temper flared. "Is *this* your idea of constructive behavior?" he railed at Amel.

Amel's strained look of composure broke into one of shock and dreadful anticipation.

Erien stalked into the room. "We are trying to prove your competence, not disprove it!" he lectured Amel. "And in case you are not aware, on Rire attempted suicide is not generally regarded as a sane response to most situations."

A delicate line of stress contoured the smooth skin of Amel's brow. He sipped a breath, his eyes glistening. "I... was afraid I wouldn't do it... if I thought about it too much," he got out in halting gasps.

"If you thought about it!" Erien exploded. "You are in this predicament in the first place because you did not think about what would happen if you went to *Kali Station*. What *have* you thought about? Or better still, kindly advise me what else you are not thinking about, so I can at least be prepared for your next disaster! Contrary to Gelack belief, thinking is actually an evolutionarily positive trait. It avoids acts of mindless idiocy. But I don't suppose there is much point in asking you why you tried to electrocute yourself, because you did not think and therefore you do not know!"

"Why? But I—" Amel blinked, dazed and ethereal as a stunned butterfly. Even his voice had gone thin. "Didn't you send—" He faded to silence at whatever he saw radiating from Erien.

"Drasous?" Bley guessed, excited, her hand rising to her throat. "You were so afraid of him!" she said to Amel. "But you greeted him, even smiled, although you were getting closer to fainting with every step he took in your direction." She returned her attention to Erien, drawing up her arms to cup her elbows. "That was why I thought it better not to let Drasous treat him. I did not understand it. Do you?"

"Yes," said Erien, and forgot her to concentrate on Amel. "It means you expected Drasous to finish what you began." Then he realized what else it meant and asked in a tight voice. "Did Drasous tell you he was acting on my orders?"

Amel swallowed, "N-no."

"But you were afraid of me, too." Erien swept an arm toward the life signs monitors. "After everything that happened in Lilac—" He stopped himself and said, whitely, "You thought I would — you thought..."

He felt Bley touch his shoulder lightly, and managed not to jerk away or attack her. "Erien," she said gently, "I think you'd better sit down."

There was sound from Amel's direction, drawing Bley away from Erien. Amel intercepted her hand as she raised it toward his eyes. It held a handkerchief.

"You are crying," she explained herself, practically. Amel's nervousness dissolved in a wash of pearly rose, which was welcome relief from his pasty look. He looked awestruck with gratitude for the small kindness.

"Thank you," he told her, and let her go.

"It might help," she advised, "if you could manage a good, hard cry."

"And as for you," she said, turning to Erien. "You have got to stop blaming yourself for everything that happens. Right now. I could as easily waste our time by making myself feel responsible. Amel was in my charge."

"Bley," Amel interjected shakily. "I know we're brothers..." he tried skirting the issue, "...but you don't have to worry about him like that. I mean, he doesn't actually like me very much." He tried to slide the words by Erien somehow, intended solely for Bley's benefit. "It's just politics."

Bley continued to study Erien throughout Amel's halting attempt to enlighten her about Erien's indifference to him.

"I am going to arrange some hot chocolate," she said primly. "I suppose it will have to be herbal tea for the two of you."

Erien inhaled.

"Nothing more is going to happen this instant," Bley insisted, "and we all need a moment to relax." She patted Erien's arm and gave Amel a sad, exasperated look. Amel gave her a marveling one.

"They could use her on Fountain Court," Amel remarked when Bley was gone. It took a moment for Erien to realize he was being humorous, during which time Amel's ghostly smile had perished for lack of encouragement. He fidgeted with Bley's handkerchief, instead, until he caught himself at it and put it down, hands relaxed.

"Bley promised me this room is STI one," Amel said. His eyes flicked toward the sensor strips in the walls. "But that was before you showed up." He inhaled brokenly and let it out. "Maybe it's not now." Flopping back, he set his hands over his face, elbows out and fingertips lost in his space-black hairline.

Erien went to the stage to check the room's status.

"It's still STI one," Erien told him. "Nothing except Bley's filter is monitoring us."

"So she could still be listening," Amel said, sounding haunted.

"No," said Erien, turning from the sage. "She's granted us audio privacy."

Amel nodded. "She's been trying to win my trust."

"And has she?" asked Erien.

Amel's hesitation stretched into seconds. Erien closed his eyes. He had the same sense of dredging the pit of his strength as he'd had the last morning in Black Hearth when, wounded and battered in spirit, he readied himself to walk onto the Challenge Floor beside Horth Nersal. He had the same sense of coming to the end of all acceptable solutions, of having lost control even of his own actions.

"When Bley comes back," he told Amel, decisively, "you are to going to answer every question put to you, under STI zero. She offered us the option, when she and I spoke earlier. And you will be honest with her. Do you understand?"

There was no answer.

Erien drew a slow breath. "There comes a point when one simply has to commit everything. If we commit everything — if we tell them why — then we are giving them a chance to take the measure of us, and we are giving them a chance to see their own measure." He did not say he had already lost Horth and Drasous. He did not have time, even if he would have. The door opened on Bley, Roz and Solomon.

Erien's heart rate doubled — a useless reaction. He faced Rire's three unlikely and unwitting champions: the comfortable, gray-haired woman; the elegant, slightly uncertain younger woman; and the big, calm man.

They did not react to his tension. Roz delivered Amel's mug. Solomon did the same for Erien. It smelled of cloves and cinnamon, a sweet drink Erien knew well enough from the Reetion repertoire. There was no way Bley could have known that the last Avim, Ev'rel Dem'Vrel, had favored a nightcap of Monatese whiskey flavored with cloves that smelled similar. But Amel caught one whiff and handed it back to Roz, pressing stiff fingers to his forehead as his teeth began to chatter. He lost patience with the cardiac monitor and took it off, rousing Solomon to step forward, until Bley said, "Let him be comfortable. I suspect his heart is working better than most of ours."

Roz took a folded blanket off the foot of the bed and put it around Amel's shoulders. He flinched. "Is it okay to touch you?" she asked in a gentle, concerned tone.

He shook his head, but when she began to get up he caught her hand and pulled her back. Roz put her arm around him, kicking off her heeled shoes to get up on the bed beside him.

Solomon placed himself beside Erien. "We've invoked STI zero for this discussion," he said, his own mug looking smaller than the others in his large, brown hand. "I am not very comfortable about it, nor is Roz. We are keeping too much to ourselves, beyond our competence."

"Let's get to the bottom of this attempted suicide, first," Bley insisted. "Drasous did not come here to treat you, did he?" she asked Amel with merciless candor.

"Drasous hasn't done anything wrong," Amel implored her. "I failed." He looked across to Erien. "Apparently that's okay, so I'm glad! But Drasous was only doing his job by coming back to clean up."

"You mean to kill you?" Solomon slew the euphemism.

Amel wet his lips, giving the big Reetion a wary look. "The point is," he appealed to Erien now, "Drasous is a *gorarelpul*."

"Meaning, I suppose, that he isn't responsible for his actions?" said Solomon.

"Then who is?" Roz asked.

"I am," Erien said. "I should have realized Drasous' orders would be to respect my judgment, up to but excluding any risk to my own life."

Bley said, "Oh dear, have we really been so threatening?" It sounded comical, coming from a grandmotherly counselor — until Erien remembered his suspicions about Horth and Eler.

"Yes," he said, "you have."

Solomon said firmly, "I don't understand."

Amel shed Roz's comfort and shuffled back in bed, huddling in the blanket as if he could eclipse himself in it. He did not meet their eyes. The beauty of his voice wafted the words along with an eerie lightness in contrast with Erien's stark tones. "I believe Drasous meant to protect things we don't want anyone to know about," Amel told the Reetions. "Things about my mother, Avim Ev'rel, and..." he faded out, rummaging through inner reserves of strength, "D'Lekker."

"D'Lekker Dem'Vrel ?" said Solomon. As the Gelack cult specialist, he would naturally have made it his business to keep up on Gelack news. "He was killed resisting Amel's extraction by Erien from Lilac Hearth."

"I killed him," Erien told them starkly.

There was a silence while they looked at him, and he at them, across an abyss wider than reaches in space. Then Bley drew a deep breath and continued resolutely, addressing Amel. "And your mother and another brother died in one of Gelion's famous challenge duels shortly after."

Amel nodded, rocking minimally back and forth.

"We've heard all this before, except for the confirmation Erien killed D'Lekker himself," Solomon reminded the women. "Amel was held by his family for kidnapping Erien in infancy. It seems odd that Ev'rel would accept Amel living in her household for seventeen years and then suddenly enforce her right to execute him." Solomon looked at Erien. "You testified that your arrival jogged her memory." He paused. "I gather there is more to it?"

"Yes," Erien found his chest had frozen. He could not say any more.

"What do you need to know?" Amel's voice warmed with anguish. "Why!" His left fist lodged half uncurled against a cheekbone, face distorting through fascinating shifts and halts toward a wrenching agony it was hard to recognize until he sobbed aloud. Roz seized his hand and pulled it down, massaging his curled fingers, shocked by the blood his nails had drawn.

She asked, "Do you want to speak to one of us alone?"

"No," he inhaled and shook himself from the waist up in a peculiar, involuntary tremor. "Erien wants me to tell you the truth," he said, and hiccupped.

"You have been abused again," Roz said knowledgeably. "Haven't you?"

"I don't—" Amel shook his head back and swallowed. "I don't know what you mean by 'abused.'"

"Rape," she said, "torture, detention — it can mean a lot of things." Amel flinched. Roz took both his hands. He let his fingers close around hers, looking down on them, locked together. Then he looked up past Roz to Erien, like someone about to drown. Erien thought he had nothing to offer, but the eye contact steadied Amel.

"The injuries you arrived with," Roz asked, "were they inflicted by your family, in Lilac Hearth?"

Amel squeezed Roz's hands before he put them aside. He shrugged the blanket off and raised one knee to lock his arms around it, body closing into a hunch, with his eyes fixed on Erien as if he were a docking beacon. Belying his body's tension, his voice glided, graceful and cool as a skater, and as sweet as song.

"I was detained by my mother, Ev'rel, because she found out an accomplice in Erien's abduction was still alive: my adopted sister, Mira. Mira knew why I stole Erien, and Ev'rel — correctly — suspected she would use it to ruin her. Ev'rel and I had... an understanding... about the special needs, and problems, she had. But I made the mistake of telling her who Erien was because I thought he needed her protection. She detained me." He stuck to the least offensive of Roz's definitions of abuse.

"Your mother?" Roz prompted.

"*Their* mother," Bley said softly from the sidelines.

Amel broke eye contact with Erien.

"You spent formative years as a Gelack prostitute, a courtesan," Roz was strangely ruthless. "I imagine your idea of acceptable special needs might be fairly liberal."

Amel wet his lips and shrugged. "I suppose."

"What did your mother do to you," Roz asked.

Amel blinked at her. "Ev'rel?"

"Do you prefer to think of her as Ev'rel?" Roz asked.

Amel fidgeted. "I never met her until I was sixteen years old — after the first visitor probing. I was suffering from clear dreams about pretty bad experiences." He stirred up a faintly sarcastic smile. "You'll have seen those. They're a bit suggestive. And she was really very Vrellish. You probably don't understand Vrellish women — they're different."

"Amel," Roz settled back, looking like someone who had landed more than she bargained for. She hesitated, glancing at Erien, then at the other two counselors. When she returned her

attention to Amel she looked at least as tense as he did. "Did
your mother hurt you?"

Amel twitched his head, mumbling, "You don't understand.
You see, she got depressed, lost her temper... needed to be in
control. There was so much more worth loving, and when the
worst has been done to you before, it is not as if it matters so
much now and then—" he could see he was not convincing Roz.
He looked from one to the other of the counselors, flounder-
ing in his own words.

"Did she hurt you with your consent?" Roz asked.

"No!" The answer was gratifyingly definite. The bounds of
Reetion tolerance for consenting sexual practices were very wide,
but Erien doubted self-confessed masochism would help establish Amel as competent. "No," Amel said. "That's why I took
Erien, you see... all those years ago. He was just a baby and—
" He broke off, making repeated runs against an obstacle and
falling short. His failure confused him, as if he thought he had
known how to explain, but found he really did not.

Solomon took up the questioning. "There is a Gelack perversion called flesh probing. That wound you had on your abdomen. Did that happen while you were detained?"

Amel nodded.

"Your mother?"

"No!" Amel's whole frame shook, confusion dancing on the
surface of his mercurial expression. "N-no," he stuttered, and
pressed the back of one hand to his mouth.

The Reetions gave him a quiet, respectful attention. Finally
his hand came away, knuckles brushing his lips: once, twice.
He stopped the nervous gesture by gripping his own shoulders.
"She tied me up, she knows... she knew... I hated that. She used
drugs. Drugs don't show. Like the visitor probe. Th-the other
thing — that was Lek — th-that was D'Lekker. He was going
to kill me to hurt her. It was my fault. I made him see Ev'rel
would use him as her scapegoat. I thought he might let me go,
b-but I didn't realize he was — that he — oh gods!" He sobbed,
crumpling in upon himself, knees drawn up and head down.

"One of the more extreme forms of flesh probing," Erien told
them, without expression, "involves penetration... or ejacula-
tion... in such a wound."

Roz breathed, "Oh no," and swallowed hard.

"D'Lekker seemed to have gotten the idea from certain re-
enactments in the UnderDocks," said Erien, "derived from the
visitor probe material."

Solomon looked sick to his stomach.

Roz crawled to Amel, kneeling on the bed to hold him, and said, "It's all right. We won't make you tell us any more. You're doing fine, just fine, but you've got a long, long way to go."

He resisted only until her warmth penetrated his woodenness; then his arms went around her in response. "Lek was so alive," Erien heard Amel grieve aloud on Roz's shoulder. "But such a child! He... he tried... and I rejected him so hard! He thought he wanted to be like Ev'rel. He thought I was strong! Strong!" Amel barked the last word with harsh sarcasm and dissolved into tears in Roz's arms. She cried, rocking him, her fingers in his hair and around his back, murmuring nonsense sounds.

Bley took Erien by either arm, near the elbow, and shook him, once. "Erien," she said very firmly.

He should have reacted, lashed out, answered, but the means to act felt disconnected from the impulse.

A pity it had not been like that in Lilac Hearth, thought Erien. *It might have saved D'Lekker's life.* He remembered the force that had exploded from him. Remembered D'Lekker's knife laying open his shoulder to the bone. Remembered D'Lekker falling, strangling on his crushed larynx.

"Is this what you saw D'Lekker doing," Bley was asking Erien, "when you rescued Amel? Just before you killed D'Lekker?"

Erien looked at her long and hard until he saw her, just her — no bound Amel, no smeared blood and smoke and choking breaths churning in his mind. "Yes."

He pulled himself together, an immense effort. "D'Lekker has two small children. If any of this were known on Gelion, D'Lekker's children... his line... would be exterminated. It—" He could not go on. Gelack abhorrence for homosexual acts had denied Di Mon children, happiness and, in the end, life. The involuntary mingling, in his own mind, of D'Lekker's sick violence and Di Mon's love for Ranar felt horrible.

Amel, with a quick, aware glance, took over for him. "It's religious — denying someone rebirth. And political — D'Lekker's disgrace would be exploited by D'Therd's heirs." He paused; his voice dropped. "D'Lekker's sons are my nephews, seven and four years old. I have to protect them."

"There is also Ev'rel's empire," said Erien. "Whatever else she was, Amel's mother..."

"And yours," Bley reminded him pointedly.

"Ev'rel," Erien insisted, he could not stand it otherwise, "organized the Knotted Strings, Demora and the court Vrellish to everyone's benefit. Exposure of her personal dishonor, concerning Amel, could destroy it all. That is why Ameron risked his life to defeat her, cleanly, on the Challenge Floor. Ev'rel is dead and has already paid the price Gelion would demand for her secret crimes. There is nothing to be gained by exposing her or D'Lekker on Gelion, except deadly harm for innocents. In the face of that," Erien was openly pleading now, "can you justify the risk of Amel bringing it to light through a visitor probe inquiry?"

Bley's lips were pressed closed until she said, "Perhaps not." Her tone gave Erien hope.

Solomon scowled at them. "I can see there is every cause for a scrupulous limiting of questions," he told Erien. "But why, if it allows questioning without the risk of clear dream complications, shouldn't Amel still be probed?"

"I don't want to be probed," Amel said. He had run dry the moment before. Now he was brimming with tears and fragile earnestness once more. It was, Erien observed from the great distance into which he had retreated, a very effective look to command the sympathy of the Reetions.

"But why, Amel?" Bley asked.

"Because it's—" Amel wet his lips, pulse hammering visibly in his throat, "like watching yourself dead. Because—" he gave a dry sob and one convulsive jerk, voice clenching off, and came to himself panting, eyes wide in a white face that surged red the next instant. Roz slid in to support him as he fainted. He was conscious again within seconds, fresh tears sliding down the smooth lines of his face. "I don't want to be probed," he told her plaintively, his voice gone very soft. "Please do — something else... anything. I — I'd rather repeat Lilac Hearth!"

"Amel!" Roz touched his face, her own distraught. "Amel, are you trying to tell us you experience probing as — as a rape of some sort?"

His expression was worn down to utterly guileless innocence. "Of course."

Roz could not immediately cope with his answer. She let him separate himself from her. He sagged into the bed, not looking at anyone. "I think I could die for my nephews," Amel berated himself dejectedly, "but I-I think I found the courage to t-try because it was the only way to stay out of the visitor probe.

I kept thinking — what if I survived and had clear dreams for the rest of my life about Ev'rel and Lek in Lilac Hearth!" He swallowed. "It wouldn't be worth living." He looked up, a strand of silky hair caught in the tears near his mouth. "That's what made it possible to put the tuner into the short circuit I'd created."

"Dear life," Roz whimpered, shaken.

"Why haven't you told anyone you experience the visitor probe as a violation?" demanded Solomon.

Amel blinked at him. "Nobody listens."

Roz stood up. "I will not assert anything that will put him a step closer to the visitor probe."

"He is playing on your emotions, Roz," warned Solomon.

"Well," Bley said, looking pointedly at Erien, "sometimes emotions *should* be played on." She brought her attention back to her robust young colleague. "Do you want to be responsible for dead children on Gelion?"

"No, but—"

"Sol," Bley patted Solomon on the arm. "The point is, do you think Amel is psychologically competent? Given all you've heard, of course, and in spite of the clear dreams that remain a persistent side effect of previous visitor probe sessions, is he able to determine his own self-interest? And are we the ones, perhaps, who have gone a little mad?"

Solomon scrutinized Amel where he lay, on his side, breathing slowly and deeply, knees half drawn up.

The big Reetion scowled, "You're asking me to accept that someone who made a damn credible try at killing himself an hour ago is competent because he did it to avoid being tortured by Rire?"

"Be fair in your judgment," Erien said to Solomon. "All we ask is that you live up to your own laws."

"Well, Sol?" Bley asked.

Solomon dipped his head in a nod. "Bottom line: I couldn't stomach hurting him any more, same as Roz. Guess I'll have to accept he doesn't want us helping him, either. Because yes, I think he's competent... brave, in fact. And I'll certainly miss having him around, although I wish one or two of my cultists could have heard what we did just now."

"I don't think what we've heard today is typical even for Gelacks," Bley told both Roz and Solomon.

"No," agreed Erien.

Amel stirred and sat up, looking wide-eyed. "Thank you," he said timidly to Solomon, beamed at Bley and then, rather suddenly, hugged and kissed Roz. "Thank you all!"

"You'll have to do that again!" exclaimed Roz. "I wasn't paying attention, and one day I might have to describe it to my granddaughters."

Amel's laugh had a manic, but melodic quality. He was lighting up, body lifting free of gravity, eyes casting light from cutglass facets with a sheen like warming ice. He took Roz in his arms and swirled her around. "I'm competent!" he rejoiced. "I can't be probed!"

For a moment, Erien closed his eyes. He heard himself say, "I am sorry, Amel. I did not listen, either."

Amel went still again, embarrassed. Roz kept her arm around him.

"Drasous?" Erien asked the counsellors.

Solomon frowned. "Under the circumstances," he said, "extraordinary as they are, I'd say he's your problem, Heir Gelion."

"Can we lift STI zero now?" Bley asked Erien, eyes traveling past him to her fellow counselors.

Solomon stepped to the stage and called up a graphic representing the pressure of external interest. "I think we had better," he said. "It's rough weather out there."

As soon as STI zero was lifted, Solomon called Erien over. "Look at this!" he exclaimed in an amazed tone.

Erien spotted the lobby to investigate Amel's counseling triumvirate immediately.

"They wouldn't!" cried Roz, sounding outraged as she looked over his shoulder.

Amel had gone white again.

Erien watched the lobbies reaching for them on the stage display and thought, *What will stop this? What ultimately constrains them, as Okal Rel constrains us?*

It came to him all at once, clear and whole, like the solution to a complex mathematical problem. "Stage," he rapped out, "instantiate ethics persona for domain Human Rights, informed by the record of Amel's original visitor probing eighteen years ago."

Amel tensed, his transparent expression shifting toward terrified betrayal.

"*Ack rel*, Amel," Erien said lightly, and dropped his voice in register. "Arbiter, what was the initial classification of Amel's probing by research exempt Lurol?"

"The procedure was initially classified as experimental therapeutic intervention," the stage replied.

"With the patient's informed consent?" asked Erien.

"Not applicable. Informed consent is a human right. Patient was then classified as nonhuman sentient. That erroneous classification has since been corrected by human input."

"What was the classification of the previously referenced intervention by the end of its duration?" asked Erien.

"Interrogation by intrusive psychiatric measures irrespective of injury to subject."

"Torture?" Erien prompted.

"A reasonable potential for a strong correlation of meaning exists for the term 'interrogation by intrusive psychiatric measures irrespective of injury to subject' and 'torture' in the case cited, given favorable contexts of evaluation," said the arbiter.

"Presume, for the sake of argument, that Amel had been classified as human from the start," Erien moved on. "Would his probing, as defined at its commencement, have been permitted?"

"Likely," the arbiter conjectured. "Subject was in acute distress and no prior record of opportunity to withhold or bestow consent was on record."

Erien held his breath for a second. "Still presuming that the subject, Amel, was recognized as human, would probing have been continued beyond the automatic reclassification as 'interrogation by intrusive psychiatric measures?'"

"No," replied the arbiter.

"Despite the threat to *Second Contact Station* that the probing addressed?"

"Self-defense was a mitigating argument in the inquest, by humans, that ruled on human conduct under pressure," said the arbiter. "It would not have applied to the *Second Contact Station* arbiter. An isolated arbiter is not empowered to disregard human rights, even if directed to do so by a unanimous local referendum. That would require substantial legislative changes."

"Erien?" Amel said, in a small voice. "What are you doing?"

Erien held out an open palm, bidding him to wait. His fingertips shook with the intensity of his own concentration as he navigated the argument like a series of linked jumps. "The correction of Amel's nonhuman status has been made," he asserted. "The record, however, has not been altered to respect his human rights, since the visitor probe material remains on record, in full, although Amel has never placed on record his consent for their use. Explain."

"Medical results are always on public record," said the arbiter. "Consent is relevant only to acceptance of treatment. Moreover, evidence was crucial to proceedings and in demand, later, for debate in a variety of referenda, including the awarding of human status to Sevolites."

"Would that be equally true," asked Erien, "of evidence extracted under torture?"

"No," said the arbiter. "Evidence extracted under torture would require the victim's consent to be retained on record."

"Amel Dem'Vrel is with me in this room," said Erien.

The stage said, "Yes."

"Amel," said Erien, pinning him with his eyes, "do you consent to the public access and use, by Rire, in full, of your visitor probe records, obtained on *Second Contact Station* eighteen years ago?"

There was a silence. Erien heard Bley whisper, "Answer him, dear."

Amel drew a breath. "No, I do not," he said. "I do not give consent." His voice was steady but his face was bewildered to the point of terror.

Erien gave him a crisp nod of encouragement. "Maintain instantiations," Erien instructed the arbiter, "adding historical modules for war trials in Delta Reach during the second decade of Arbiter Administration."

"Done," the arbiter reported.

"What is the admissibility, in human argument and arbiter deliberations, of testimony obtained by means of torture?"

"Inadmissible."

Solomon breathed, "Law and reason. Now I see where he's taking this."

"Consider, but do not act," instructed Erien, "on the following assertion set. Conclusion: the record of Amel's examination under visitor probe from the point at which the examination was reclassified as 'interrogation by intrusive psychiatric measures' is inadmissible to the record. Argument: in the context of that examination 'interrogation by intrusive psychiatric measures' may be equated with torture rather than a medical procedure. Fact: evidence obtained by torture is inadmissible to the record except upon the meaningful consent of its subject. Fact: as a human subject deemed competent to refuse such consent, Amel has placed on record his refusal." Erien paused, "What would be the consequence of a positive resolution?"

"Immediate withdrawal from the record of all inadmissible evidence," replied the arbiter.

Behind him, Erien heard Roz come forward and Solomon shift to one side. *They are Reetions,* he overcame deep instinct. *They will not attack.*

"Do you know what you're doing?" asked Solomon.

"Yes," said Bley proudly. "I rather think he does."

"Submit assertion set," said Erien.

"Assertions exceed capacity of instantiated persona to resolve," was the immediate response. "Transcending to meld with legal, historical, medical and information policy personas."

Erien could not breathe. If his contention exceeded the threshold for decision making without human input, there could be more sophistries and delays, but if the arbiters ruled in his favor — then Rire would have to listen, at last.

"Conclusion accepted," the stage announced. "Implementing removal of materials reclassified as obtained under torture."

"There!" Erien pointed triumphantly at the simple diamond rotating on the stage before him. "That's where their honor resides," he explained, excited, to an astonished Amel. "*That* was the question I hadn't asked, because it was a *Gelack* question and I was not thinking like a Gelack. Their honor resides *there—*" and he swept his fisted hand down through the solid light display on the stage, "—in the arbiters. They are the custodians of Reetion honor, inasmuch as 'honor' is what forbids people from violating their own values — to betray the soul of their culture."

Amel was staring at him as if he had gone mad. Seeing himself through Amel's eyes, Erien took note of his arm, buried in the stage projection, and drew it clear. "I think," he said stiffly, "we won't be troubled by any more challenges to the counselors' verdict."

And indeed, the ferment on the stage had moved on — with a vengeance. Erien had had no idea how much the first set of Amel's visitor probe data had pervaded Rire's knowledge base. He was watching entire intellectual disciplines collapse. Lobbies were mustering in force to appeal the deletion, and being denied.

"Can he really make the arbiters erase my data?" Amel asked Bley in awe.

"He just did," Solomon said, frowning.

"Isn't this what you want?" Roz asked Amel.

"Me? Of course!" Amel's voice got higher and quicker. "But will Rire let him do it? Won't it... they... do something to Erien?"

Roz turned Amel toward her. "No one is going to attack Erien," she promised him in soothing tones.

"Erien is meddling with arbiters worse than I ever did!" Amel explained his dismay. "All I did was shuffle in something extra. He took something out!"

"Yes," said Solomon, "but he did it within the context of our own law."

"I don't expect this to pass without protest," Erien said to Amel, willing him to behave sanely and calm down. "But it was a properly constituted and accepted submission to the arbiter and, as such, has the same force in Reetion law as the outcome of a challenge has in ours. Should Rire now try to reverse the ruling, they would undermine the very fabric of their own society. I do not believe they will risk it."

"Nevertheless," Erien continued, pinning Amel with his stare, "you will still have to reappear before the enquiry and answer further questions under ordinary monitoring, now that you've been ruled competent. Are you up to it, if I can find a way to make them mind their manners?"

Amel nodded jerkily, looking dazed.

"Good," said Erien, and drew a deep breath. "There remains one more matter to attend to."

He stopped, grimly suspecting this was going to prove the figurative equivalent of putting a stone into his shoe before embarking on a long journey. But there was no help for it. The stone was a gem — even if not one cut to his taste — and in need of safekeeping. And his shoe was the only one at hand.

"I am not prepared to have any further harm to you on my conscience," Erien told the stunned-looking Amel in Gelack, "but I will need some leverage to protect you and, given that I *am* Heir Gelion, whatever I can make that worth — I would ask you to swear to me, as my vassal, with all the rights and protections attending the first sworn of Heir Gelion, or at least, myself, Erien Lor'Vrel."

Amel was unhelpfully silent for long seconds, then seemed to have trouble wetting his lips and swallowing. It was the first time Erien had known him to be speechless. Then Amel got up and sank on one knee before Erien, looking up with a pale, glowing aspect that was disturbingly worshipful.

I didn't mean to make quite that dramatic an impression, Erien thought sourly, restricting his overt reaction to a slight frown.

Amel appeared to be waiting for something. Erien realized that there was no sword between them, and started to reach for Di Mon's knife in his boot. Something stopped him, something powerful — and it was not the thought of the arbiter's reaction to his drawing a knife — but a personal reluctance. He and Amel stared at each other. Then Amel took ceremonial matters into his own hands.

"I don't know which formula to use," Amel said, gazing up with his transparent, unworldly radiance. "I don't know who it would offend, or honor. So I'll use the Vrellish tactic and improvise." He smiled ever so slightly, eyes glistening. His face sobered. "I accept, with all my heart."

TWENTY-THREE

Amel

Vassal

"Good," Erien said, "that's done."

Amel hardly noticed his new liege's brusqueness. He was staring up at the champion who had saved him from the Reetions; at the child, become a man, who had almost casually lifted his burden of shame and capped it by asking the empire's most debased Pureblood of all time to be his first sworn.

Erien reached his hand down. "I've got work to do," he said, "monitoring the Reetion reaction until the withdrawal is established."

Erien's left arm was injured, but Amel understood theatre. He took the offered hand firmly, his eyes never once leaving Erien's, and rose from his knees, making it look as if Erien drew him upward without actually pulling on his bad shoulder.

"What can I do?" Amel asked, speaking in Gelack *rel*-peerage.

"I need you to reassure the Reetions that you're all right."

Amel turned to Roz, settling a hand on her shoulder. "Do you think the group home would be up for a celebration?" he asked her in Reetion. "Outside where everyone can see us?"

"Sure!" Roz agreed with enthusiasm, and waded into details Amel would normally have found absorbing. He liked parties. But he found he couldn't indulge himself while Erien and Solomon were standing with their heads together over a microstage.

"What is it?" he asked the two men as soon as Roz left to get things rolling.

"Horth won't respond," said Erien. "I have made a point of sending him a summary of what has happened here, and why it demonstrates Reetion honor." He frowned. "Perhaps he needs time to digest it."

Amel's heart went out to his new liege — he looked so young, and so strained.

"The odds are, knowing Horth, he will just call you back when he is ready," Amel said. Then he surprised himself. "I'll keep an eye on what Horth and Eler get up to, for you."

"All right," Erien decided, tight-lipped. He turned to Solomon. "I have to keep on top of the Reetion reaction. Is there a place where I can work without distractions?"

Amel tried not to be nervous about being left alone with the Reetions as Solomon led Erien away.

I can cope with this, he told himself angrily. *I have a liege. And they don't have a copy of my soul on record anymore — to hold me frozen in time as a scared, defeated sixteen-year-old.*

And as a first assignment, partying on the lawn out behind the group home certainly suited him. But first he set up a watch-dog to notify him if anything changed concerning the Nersallians.

Half an hour later, Amel was sitting on a big, flat rock jutting out of the grass in the middle of the group home's garden, playing a Reetion song he had just learned on a borrowed guitar. Open doors into the common room were at his back, a large fish pond with a decorative fountain burbled farther down the lawn and the garden was filling up with everyone's friends and re-lations, although Bley had decided to refer curious strangers to their stages at home, since the backyard was as wide open as anyone could possibly desire. Amel was aware of the sensi-strips that blended with the landscaping, and the cameras mounted permanently on the roof, but for once, being observed by as many Reetions as possible was the whole idea.

Europa sat beside his rock in her outdoor chair, her daughter with her. Roz's girls were serving lemonade and hot chocolate from a picnic table. The Gelack cultists hovered, the pair who called themselves Vackal and Vretla dressed in alarmingly au-thentic Vrellish house braid.

Amel finished the piece he was singing and smiled at Roz over the guitar in the midst of warm applause.

"That was wonderful," Roz enthused.

"I can fake almost anything with strings," Amel told her, feeling pleased with himself. Reetions were finally just people to him. Amel liked people.

The pager Solomon had given Amel vibrated against his skin, inside the pocket of his borrowed shirt, making him start. He excused himself, a touch embarrassed, and made a beeline for a microstage in the common room, grateful to the counselors for keeping the kids from following.

"Horth Nersal has left the ship, alone," his watchdog reported. "He is moving fast, on foot, in your direction."

Amel's pulse jumped. "Is Ranar available?"

"Ranar is engaged with the lobby to appeal the judgment entitled *Erien: Revocation Due to Torture*," said the arbiter, and produced the germane references. Amel poked around just enough to be sure Ranar was helping Erien, and decided not to interrupt either of them.

"Get me Eler Nersal," he requested instead.

"Amel," the big, sardonic Nersallian drawled seconds later on audio. "Feeling well?" he added, in an accusing tone.

"Why is Liege Nersal on his way here?" Amel demanded, making an effort to sound gruff.

"My liege-brother is not much for talking," Eler replied in his slow, mocking way, as if he was sharing a joke with the universe, and paused before appending the honorific owed a Pureblood, "Immortality." There was another short pause before Eler said blandly, "Perhaps he will explain it to your liege-brother when he arrives. I believe it might have to do with your new, ah, status."

Amel had a hard time hearing past the pronouns. Eler was accepting his grammar! Every pronoun he spoke acknowledged Amel his birth superior. Amel's heart gave a great thump in his chest. Even better, he had acknowledged Erien to be Amel's liege.

"We got Erien's message," Eler said in a strange, metallic tone of voice. Then he added with his usual sarcasm, "Any chance your Reetion keepers stuffed you in a visitor probe while you were off record for a bit there, and just programmed you to come out and make nice with the locals?"

"Very funny," Amel snapped, and swiftly added, "there isn't even a visitor probe at the group home. Ask the arbiter."

"Warming up to arbiters, are you?" asked Eler.

"So Liege Nersal just decided to... go for a walk, then?" asked Amel.

"Right after getting the good news from Erien," confirmed Eler. "Horth did not think much of Heir Gelion's choice of a first sworn, was my impression. But on the other hand, it's been a... tense morning. Perhaps Horth just needed some exercise."

Eler disconnected, leaving Amel unsure what to do next. He wanted to handle Horth's arrival himself. But he didn't want to be accused of failing to think things through, either. As a compromise, he queued a message directing Erien to check the record for Horth's movements when he had a minute to spare.

Roz was playing the guitar when Amel rejoined the party. "Trouble?" asked Solomon.

"Just Liege Nersal," Amel said, scanning the lawn in the direction of the space port. Sure enough, he saw a lone figure approaching at a run. He tried to feel as relaxed as he managed to sound, when he said, "I'll go greet him."

Horth ate ground in a flat-out run. He'd shed the jacket of his flight suit to make running more comfortable, but had not discarded his sword. He ran with it hung down his back. His exposed upper body was corded in lean muscle beneath a sleeveless tank top. His chest pumped air like a bellows, but his breathing became normal almost immediately when he slowed to a walk.

Like a rel-ship skidding in to station, Amel thought, and wished he had not.

While Amel hesitated, others did not. The cultist kids went out to greet the new arrival well beyond the group home grounds.

"Wow," said the surrogate Vretla, letting go of the bogus Vackal's arm.

The cultist who called himself Tatt went forward. "Horth Nersal," he declared in Reetion, "I offer you my oath!" He drew his replica sword.

Horth did not understand Reetion, but at body language he was unsurpassed. The Nersallian champion cleared his own sword over one shoulder, swatted the boy's from his hand and backhanded him onto his rump. The Reetion girl wearing Vrellish braid gave a scream at the sight of the phoney Tatt going down. Horth seized her by her pretentious vest and yanked with a will to tear it off. When the fabric refused to tear, Horth seemed willing to separate vest from girl, with or without regard for her arms staying attached.

With a guilty surge Amel cried, "No!" and barged in to help.

Horth released the girl at once and drew back, sword in hand.

"These are only silly children," Amel said in Gelack, with a flicker of his eyes toward the girl sprawled on the grass. He swallowed down fear, groping for what Erien had said during his outburst of elation. "Rire has proved its honor. Erien made them live up to it through the laws encoded in their arbiters."

Horth's sword tip leapt to within a millimeter of Amel's throat.

Amel froze, but as he stared back fear gave way to a bizarre compassion. There was torment in Horth Nersal's agitation: torment, confusion and — fear?

Impossible! Amel mocked his own guess. *Horth has nerves of hullsteel! In space! On a challenge floor!* But this wasn't a fear of death, or pain or even losing a fight. It was a nebulous terror inspired by a belated grasp of just how alien Rire was. Confusion.

"It is all right," Amel decided to trust his raw insight. "We are going to deal honorably with each other — Rire and Gelion — the way Erien wants."

As he said it, he knew he would never have said such a thing to Horth Nersal, with a sword at his throat, if he had thought it through in the way Erien recommended. But the words seemed to work. Horth drew back, lowering his weapon. Then Amel realized Horth had just seen something better to take out his overwrought feelings on.

"Horth!" yelled Erien, as he sprinted out of the group home, scattering startled people. Horth dropped his sword — and shot forward.

Amel closed his eyes at the exact moment of impact when the two Vrellish highborns collided, but opened them at a gasp from the audience in time to see Horth flip Erien over his head with a hand on his arm and a fist in his shirt. Fabric ripped. Erien thudded onto his back on the grass, arms snapping out to break his fall. Horth waited for him to rise again.

That's good, I think, Amel thought, quelling panic.

Solomon came running with a canister of restraining foam under one arm.

"No!" Amel snatched the thick white cylinder away from the big Reetion.

"But they'll kill each other!" protested Solomon.

Erien phased directly from flat on his back to a swift feint and grab. Unable to dodge, Horth grappled. His feet left the ground as Erien secured him for a hip throw, but with a powerful twist Horth piled them both into the picnic table, instead. Amel winced as it collapsed. Contents jumped, hot chocolate gushing like blood. Horth and Erien rolled apart.

"Okay," Amel admitted to Solomon, gripping the restraining foam canister. "You may be right. I just don't think the one who does it should be a Reetion," he concluded breathlessly.

Erien was up first, swiping unfeelingly at blood from a split over his cheekbone. Horth gathered himself like a force of nature and surged forward.

Amel was too busy maneuvering around them to see what happened next, but he heard some serious blocking and punching sounds. Solomon kept the crowd clear as Horth and Erien circled each other on the far side of the table's wreckage. Horth had torn the knee of his flight pants and bled from upper-body cuts inflicted by the picnic table. The side of Erien's face was smeared crimson. But they both looked focused and intent on doing each other more damage — Horth's tortured confusion gone, while Erien's pallor and strain had yielded to a flush of exertion and temper.

Horth ploughed a fist through Erien's weakened left arm block, but it hardly slowed Erien down. He caught the punch and twisted to lock Horth's elbow, took a long sideways step and launched Horth toward the pond. Amel anticipated hearing the snap of bone strained beyond endurance, but all of a sudden Erien's graceful motion ended in an unplanned lurch sideways. Horth dropped shy of the pond's edge, rolled and uncoiled, dripping blood, and again went for Erien.

Amel planted himself in range as his targets came together, planning to get both of them with one shot, but suddenly not so sure it was better for him to do this than allow the diplomatic complications of the Reetions hosing down Heir Gelion and the liege of Nersal.

Before he could change his mind, he fired. He got Horth first, and then Erien.

Hardening foam tangled Erien's legs and dropped him onto his side. He promptly realized what it was and went rag-limp. Horth kept fighting so savagely Amel was afraid he might break free, or hurt himself trying.

"Don't struggle, Horth. It will slough off!" called Erien.

Amel held his breath. It seemed preposterous that the great swordsman would obey, when seconds before he'd been trying to kill Erien — albeit honorably, if that's what you called waiting for someone to get up before doing your damndest to put him down again.

It took a second, but Horth did stop his grim, silent struggle. He and Erien lay side by side, trapped in Amel's strategically deployed sprays of foam, quiet except for their hard breathing. Amel was aware of a few Reetion stalwarts ringing the scene in a scattered circle, watching wide-eyed. Then Erien began to get up, slowly, foam sliding off him. Horth was not far behind him.

Please, Amel thought, *don't let them pick up where they left off!*

But it wasn't Horth whom Erien was glaring at.

Amel set down the offending foam canister, but found he lacked the nerve for explanations. He backed away, put a foot down in a field of spilled hot chocolate and was waving his arms to catch his balance when Erien caught him by the shirt in a vice-like grip, right-handed.

"Erien?" Amel asked uncertainly, not wanting to lay hands on any freshly battered piece of his new liege, but really wishing he knew where this was leading. Horth loomed on the other side, still shedding foam.

Erien turned his head and flashed a Vrellish grin at his erstwhile opponent. "Pond?" he asked.

Pond? Amel thought. Then he gulped as Horth took hold of him, too.

His captors took a few running steps, then came a brief sensation of flying, accompanied by an uneven chorus of voiced, "Ahhs" from the watching Reetions.

Amel landed with a great splash in the middle of the fish pond. He floundered to right himself, then sat chest deep in water, staring in astonishment at Horth and Erien.

Erien took a few shaky steps toward the entrance to the common room and sank down cross-legged on the grass, holding his shoulder, head bowed. His shirt was ripped across the back. He had grass in his hair and globs of foam hung from him.

Bley and Roz converged, Roz with her first aid kit in hand.

"I'm all right," said Erien, lowering his hand from his shoulder.

"You can't possibly be!" Roz insisted.

Amel scrambled gracelessly out of the pond, hampered by wet clothes, uneven footing and the attempt to keep everyone in sight simultaneously.

Horth deflected Solomon's approach simply by failing to acknowledge it, and headed toward Erien and his attendant Reetions.

Nasib appeared in the empty frame of the door to the common room, but Amel was too excited to wonder what had attracted Bley's reclusive patient.

Horth went straight to Erien. Roz was kneeling beside him. Erien gave an involuntary growl as she pressed gently on one side of his torso. "Yes, there!" he admitted, wincing.

"You've got a broken rib," Roz told him.

Bley cleared her throat to get their attention, and Erien lifted his head very fast, looking disarmingly young to Amel, and oddly vulnerable.

"Liege Nersal," Erien said in Gelack. "I... apologize for losing my temper."

Horth considered him for a moment then shrugged one shoulder. "*Ack rel*," he said, and reached down to offer Erien a hand up.

Erien shook his head, tucked his feet beneath him and stood, holding his side. "You would never have landed that punch," he grumbled, "if my left arm had been good."

Horth's grin came and went like a lightning flash. No one pressed first aid on him, Amel noticed. The notion would have felt preposterous. The blood slicking Horth's pale skin and dark, sleeveless top just looked natural. He showed no sign of being seriously inconvenienced by his hurts, and he had collected his sword from where he had dropped it on the grass before attacking Erien. It was resting securely in its sheath at his side now.

"Drasous," said Horth, going straight to business.

Erien conferred with the counselors, then sent Horth with Solomon to visit the *gorarelpul* for treatment. Horth accepted Erien's promise to discuss things with him later, and volunteered Eler's news about the *Kali Station* arbiter, which was bound to make the Reetions happy.

First responders showed up seconds after Horth went inside — six of them, all toting tranq guns. Suddenly, restraining foam looked like the lesser of two evils.

"What do you mean, no problem?" a first responder with the name 'Cormac' on his jacket was responding to something Bley had told him. "So what was it we all witnessed flattening your picnic table?" Cormac jerked a thumb over one shoulder. "A Gelack party game?"

"Well no, that was a fight, I believe," Bley admitted.

Erien stood motionless, one gently curled hand half hiding his face. *Dying of embarrassment*, Amel decided, *for losing his entirely too-Vrellish temper.* He doubted Erien realized it yet, but losing his temper might have been the only way to deal with Horth just then. He made a mental note to point it out to him later.

"Excuse me?" Amel said, touching Cormac's arm.

"Amel?" the big Reetion made space for him, face and body language confirming he was a fan. "Nice move with the foam. Saved us the trouble."

"Things were getting a little rough," Amel admitted with a winning smile, and switched his attention back to Erien. "Do you two habitually break bones when you spar?"

"Spar?" Cormac asked skeptically.

"Not habitually," said Erien, recovering enough to play along. "But once or twice... over disciplinary matters." He frowned. "I'm not sure who was disciplining who, here," he added.

"But whatever the reason," Amel pointed out, "it is normal behavior for Gelacks. So it will have to go on the list of issues we can't settle until we know how Rire intends to deal with us diplomatically."

"Are you trying to tell me," Cormac asked, "they weren't trying to kill each other?"

"I'm trying to tell you," Amel explained as respectfully as possible, "that if they were, it was their business. They're both in the same challenge class, and the fight was honorable."

Cormac whistled. "If that was honorable, I would hate to see them fight dirty."

"Whatever the legal issues," Roz asserted, "I had better see Erien in my exam room. Now." She took him by one elbow. Bley took the other one. Erien hesitated. "Cooperating with them was your idea, right?" Amel reminded him, taking over from the women. To his surprise, Erien did not resist him.

Horth was in the common room, oblivious to the few bold admirers who watched from a respectful distance as Drasous cleaned his wounds. Both Drasous and Horth looked up at Amel's entrance and then Horth ignored him, but the *gorarelpul* sustained eye contact.

Amel squirmed inside. Did he owe Drasous an apology for his failed suicide? Drasous broke the spell with a respectful nod. Amel mimicked the gesture, feeling goofy about trying to sum up what lay between them with a meaningful look.

As Amel watched, Nasib walked up to Horth and addressed herself to Drasous. "I would like to speak with Liege Nersal. Will you translate for me?"

Amel hesitated long enough to hear Drasous repeat the request to Horth, in Gelack, see Horth take the measure of the slight, determined figure in front of him, and nod.

Talking is good, right? Amel reassured himself, still worrying about Erien, and left them to it. He couldn't imagine Horth doing Nasib any harm.

In the medical room, Erien was making Roz work around his obsession to keep on top of Reetion politics on stage, but he looked up as Amel entered.

"How is Horth?" Erien fired at Amel before he'd come to a halt.

"Fine," Amel said, reminding himself with each word that it would all go on record. "He's talking with a resident called Nasib. Drasous is translating."

"Talking?" Erien asked. "About what?"

Amel opened his mouth to reply and realized he didn't know. Roz checked a stage. "They're talking about reviving her colony!" she reported, surprised. "She wants him to be a partner in it, by providing them with Sevolite pilots capable of keeping them in touch with the Arbiter Administration despite the colony's remoteness. They are... I think it's called bartering."

Erien pressed two fingers to the knots between his eyebrows.

"That's good! Isn't it?" Amel blurted, and scrambled to justify his instinct. "I mean, it is about contracts — trade relations."

Erien looked at him dolefully. "Nasib is not a liege. I checked her history, of course, like all the residents, and she is the sort of person who might give Horth that impression, but she cannot make decisions unilaterally. I seriously doubt he understands that. And they do not share a legal jurisdiction. If there's a dispute arising from the contract, Nasib and her supporters can hardly be expected to settle it under Sword Law."

"Good point," Amel said sheepishly, and swallowed. Unlike Erien, he *wanted* to lie down! His chest still hurt from his failed attempt at suicide. But he felt unworthy for some reason he could not get at, rejected over something more weighty than the incident with the restraining foam.

"I'll... see what I can do about Nasib and Horth," Amel promised.

"Good," Erien said shortly and went back to his work without even making eye contact.

You save my life, but you don't like me, Amel thought with a pang. *Why?* There were plenty of reasons to choose from but none of them seemed to fit Erien, or, if they did, seemed more likely to inspire mere indifference rather than something personal and bitter. *I am imagining it,* Amel thought.

Then it struck him. *The knife.* They'd had no sword to use for the swearing, but Erien had not offered Di Mon's knife as a substitute. He reached for it when he asked Amel to swear to him, and then deliberately chosen not to use it.

The obstacle between them was Di Mon.

I was the last person to see him alive, Amel thought miserably, *and Erien thinks I nudged him toward suicide.* The terrible thing was, Amel couldn't be sure he hadn't. But one way or the other, he knew he had to settle the question for Erien if they were going to work as liege and vassal.

TWENTY-FOUR

Erien

Messages from Home

"Ow. Ow. Oww!" said a woman's voice, which belonged to Erien's half-sister, Amy.

Erien paused in the doorway of the townhouse. It was days since Horth and Eler had left Rire, briefed on how to send the next Nersallian envoy through without alarming the Reetion Space Service, and they'd been expecting Dorn to arrive from *Kali Station*. He should have guessed Amy would have come out to be with the man she loved, even if Ameron himself had tried to stop her.

"According to Tatt," Dorn Nersal observed in a quietly amused voice, "what you're seeing, there, is a nonviolent martial art."

"If that's nonviolent, I would hate to see what Erien considers violent," said Amy.

Braced for teasing from his half-sister, Erien entered the living room.

Dorn was sitting on the sofa with his legs stretched out, a black-headed cane propped up beside him. Amy lounged against the armrest, long legs draped across Dorn's thighs. Both still wore flight leathers, Dorn's black and Amy's white and purple. Lurol slouched in the other armchair, and Ranar — who had left this afternoon's negotiating session early — sat on a stool brought from the kitchen. Amel was sitting on the floor, cross-legged.

All of them were watching the main stage, where Erien and Horth were brawling.

Dorn was the first to notice Erien in his formal Lor'Vrellish dress. Amy kicked her legs off his as Dorn pushed himself to his feet with the aid of the cane, set his right hand on a non-existent sword hilt and bowed. The Gelack formality disconcerted Erien after days spent with Reetion working groups and representatives who'd had to make a conscious effort to regard his regalia as more than an anthropological curiosity. Amy swung a white dispatch case up toward Dorn, who formally handed it to Erien. The case was marked with Ameron's fern motif.

On the stage, Amel stood watching with dawning horror as Erien and Horth shed the restraining foam he had sprayed on them.

Amy whooped. "Your face," she cried to Amel. "I have to take that picture back to Perry."

"You are a braver man than I imagined, Pureblood Amel," said Dorn.

"He was trying to protect them from each other," Lurol spoke up. "He'll do things like that, even at the risk of his own life." She gave Erien a hard look as she said it. She was honest and brave enough to have forgiven him for getting Amel's interrogation under the visitor probe officially reclassified as torture — which meant a lot to him — but she would not forgive him supporting Amel's refusal of treatment to correct the damage.

"I wasn't risking my life," said Amel with a wince, as his image on the stage described a short trajectory into the pond. "Just a soaking."

"You didn't know they weren't going to kill you," Lurol insisted.

"Peace," said Erien firmly. "Dorn, it's good to see you."

"It's good to be here," Dorn said.

"And what did you mean by leading him through a dust field?" Amy asked Erien.

Dorn gave Erien a small, apologetic shrug, as if to say, 'I tried to explain.'

"It won't happen again," Erien said mildly.

"Yes, it will," Amy accused. "The next time you get a hare-brained, heroic Vrellish idea. Because Horth values your life more than Dorn's and he's sent him back to be your bodyguard, again? Hasn't he? Dorn won't tell me, but it was Horth who told him to come here and put himself at your service. And I'm not having it anymore!"

"Amy!" the dismay on Dorn's face at his lover's transgression in matters touching his Nersallian honor took the fight out of her.

Someone had turned the stage off.

"I'll explain why Dorn's here," Erien spoke into the tense silence. "Please, sit down," he invited Dorn, who obeyed him. Evert appeared in the doorway to the kitchen to pass him another stool. Erien took it, set it down near the middle of the floor and sat with a creak of leathers and braids. "I told your father I wanted to offer you the position of Gelack ambassador to Rire," he told Dorn.

Six pairs of eyes blinked at him.

Dorn leaned back, gray eyes wary. "Why?" he said.

Erien caught himself thinking, *The first time I hear him ask why and it's now, when I'm trying to help him!*

"You have the right connections," Erien began, and faltered over Amy's smirk, thinking, *Not you — his mother, Bryllit.* "You are *kinf'stan*," Erien continued smoothly, "and I understand Horth has established the first trade contract with a Reetion interest, although I haven't been able to make time to review all the details."

Ranar cleared his throat. "So you don't know about the cats."

Erien blinked at him. "What?"

Ranar gave a long sigh. "One of the items Horth Nersal wanted in trade: seven cats, two males and five females, all breeders. He said he wanted to be able to reward deserving vassals with their progeny, cats being extinct within the empire."

"He's going to give kittens to Nersallians?" Erien asked incredulously.

Ranar looked worried. "Oh dear," he said. "I know you've been so busy with the anti-erasure lobbies, but Eler was supposed to make certain you..."

"Eler!" Erien said, in alarm.

"Well, well, that makes sense now," muttered Ranar. "I was rather surprised when you hadn't anything to say about Horth's proposal for settling contract disputes with Nasib's people, under Sword Law, by recognizing 'commoner' as an actionable challenge class."

Amy whistled. Erien simply stared at Ranar. He had been meaning to get to work on protocols for conflict resolution as soon as the terms of mutual recognition were agreed upon and the anti-erasure lobby was no longer a threat, but, "Horth's proposal?"

Ranar continued, slightly apologetically, "He seems to have decided it was a logistical problem, and if Nasib was able to field fencers and agree on terms for combat in the event of a dispute, he was confident he could find and train Nersallians commoners who could beat any Reetion she could put on a challenge floor. Needless to say, some of the, uh, details have yet to be worked out."

Erien pinched the bridge of his nose. Was this genius, insanity or actually a jump hallucination? He looked at the one person most likely to reflect the Vrellish reaction. "Dorn?" he said, hearing a plaintive note in his own voice.

Dorn Nersal looked both intrigued and cautious. "It's... an interesting idea."

"The Demish will be the ones who have kittens," Erien muttered, wondering if there was some way he could arrange to make Demish outrage over Horth declaring commoner a challenge class Amel's problem. Amel was the more Demish of the two of them. But he couldn't, in all fairness; this was probably the complication Amel had least to do with.

"Very likely," said Ranar in a grave tone.

Erien took a deep breath. "Then Dorn, working out the details —subject to approval—" whose, he did not dare say, "would be one of the ambassador's tasks. Would you still consider the job, say, for a term of three years?"

Evert said unhappily, "But I thought you were going to stay to be ambassador yourself, Erien." He looked at Erien's formal Gelack regalia as if seeing it for the first time as more than a costume. "Are you leaving?"

"I'll explain it to you later, Vert," promised Erien. To Dorn, he said, "Please give it some thought. We've still got at least another week's work on the details of the mutual recognition agreement, although, if you agree, I'd like to bring you in immediately."

Dorn's nod was in acknowledgment of the invitation rather than agreement, Erien thought. But if anyone could work out the details of commoner-class challenges, Dorn Nersal would be the one. "Is there anything else," he said, in a tone he thought very restrained, "I need to know?"

"Hey, Amel," Amy said with a snicker, "maybe you'd better tell him your news."

Amel gave a start, as if she'd stung him, and looked appre-
hensive. Amy tilted her chin toward the empty stage with a
wicked smile. "Ann's pregnant!" she told Erien. "It's just been
confirmed."

"How did that happen?" Erien snapped.

Amy looked downright evil as she considered the possibilities
of that as a straight line.

"Kiddo, I know you took all the courses," Lurol spoke up.
Erien felt himself color.

Amel took a deep breath. "She asked me," he said a little
plaintively. "She's going to be Supervised for years, so she'll
have the time, and she said she's going to be too old soon and...
she wanted a baby."

"Which will just happen to be a highborn baby Sevolite,"
Ranar said dryly.

"Perry always did figure that Ann had a real good grasp of
the Sevolite status system, for a Reetion," Amy remarked.

Judging by Amel's expression, a political interpretation had
not yet occurred to him. "She just... said she wanted my baby."

Amy grinned. "Vretla's going to want one, too," she warned
Amel.

"And the Dem'Vrel," Dorn told Amel, entirely without malice.
"You are their liege presumptive."

Erien was starting to understand Ev'rel's compulsion to lock
Amel up. In fact, he wondered why she had ever let him out.
He was going to be so glad to hand Amel over to Perry and let
her worry about his inability to reason beyond emotional ap-
peals... assuming they ever got away from Rire. Ann's baby was
going to add days to the negotiations.

"Well," he noted tartly, "at least the strict evolutionists will
no longer be able to argue that Sevolites are not human, since
the traditional definition of species involves the ability of
members to interbreed."

The Gelacks all looked at him as though he had suddenly
turned bright orange. Only Lurol appeared to appreciate the
logic.

Erien sighed. He might dress Gelack and among Reetions
might pass for one, but his reflexes betrayed him. Time to re-
instantiate the Heir Gelion persona. "You might," he said to
Amel, "consider formally gifting the child from the outset... unless," he said, not without malice, "you are considering a half-
Reetion heir."

Leaving Amel to ruminate on that, he flipped open the dispatch case to find letters for him from Tatt and Ameron. Their hands revealed family and temperamental likeness — a similarly energetic scrawl. There was a letter to Ranar from Ameron, that he passed over to the newly reaffirmed Reetion ambassador, and a letter from Perry to Amel. The Demish rebel had a Demish lady's cultivated handwriting, Erien noticed. How odd. He passed it to Amel, who huddled into it gratefully.

Tatt's letter, out of duty, he bypassed for the moment, since it was most likely personal.

Ameron's letter expressed his satisfaction with Erien's resolution, which was gratifying, although Ameron seemed to think Erien had somehow put something over on the Reetions; Erien had a lot of work to do there. Ameron reiterated a number of conditions for trade and exchange from Monitum and H'Us, which made Erien wonder how he was going to explain Horth had already cut a deal with Nasib, and what that entailed. The letter concluded with a paragraph about Amel.

> *Fountain Court now appears to interpret the Nersallian taking of* Kali Station *and the leniency of the Reetion toward Amel—* Leniency? Erien thought, remembering the ghastly hours following Amel's very public collapse. He read on, *—as evidence the Reetion threat was minimal and Amel's sins are therefore no great matter. All three vassals of the Avim's Oath have expressed interest in considering him as liege, or even Avim, possibly as a figurehead and most likely as a sire in one capacity or another. I was naturally pleased, therefore, to learn he is your first sworn. All this has a number of advantages, beginning with stability, which I will discuss at greater length with you and Amel on the occasion of your return to Gelion, together.*

Silently, Erien handed the letter to Amel. Amel read it at a glance — the one thing the Demish could be counted on to do more swiftly than the Vrellish — and blanched.

"Whether you return or not is up to you," said Erien firmly. "You are your own master."

Lurol shifted in her armchair, the twist of her wide mouth suggesting she thought otherwise. Abruptly, she got up. "If you're coming to the lab today," she told them both, "let's make it soon, before anyone backs out." She fixed a look on Amel.

"I will change and be down shortly," Erien told Lurol, with a nod to Amel to remind him this trip to the lab had been his idea, or at least the consequence of a challenge Amel himself had laid down. All the same, Lurol was right. The less time Amel had to change his mind, the better.

Erien took the stairs three at a time, carrying Tatt's letter, and closed the door firmly behind him; he stripped the lacings of his vest so painstakingly tied by Drasous, and enjoyed the sensation of taking a deep breath for the first time that day. Then he slid a thumb under the seal of Tatt's letter.

There was a light knock on the door. "Erien?" Evert nudged the door open, looking hopeful at the good omen of the discarded regalia. "You sounded, down there," Evert said in a wounded tone, "as if you are leaving us."

"Vert," Erien said, wishing he had the wit to explain better, "I don't belong here." He dropped his hands, conscious of them. "I'm capable of violence. I'm trained in violence, though I've tried to resist acknowledging it. I'm not Reetion."

"And Dorn Nersal is?" Evert objected.

Erien sighed. "I can make a difference on Gelion, for Gelion and for Rire."

Evert dropped his eyes. "I know," he mumbled. "I know that might be best for Rire, and Gelion."

I wish, Erien thought, *I shared your faith in me.*

Evert looked up again, the pain of loss very clear on his face, side by side with the shadow of his strained relationship with Ranar. "I hope it is best for you, too, Erien," he said earnestly.

"Amel told me you should come along this afternoon," Erien remembered suddenly, wanting to offer Evert something positive. "Amel wants me — and Ranar — to see what he remembered of his last interview with Di Mon. He says it will always lie between us, otherwise, and for you and Ranar, too. That's part of why Amel made it the condition for his acceptance of Lurol's cure for clear dreams."

Erien rummaged in his closet for the light summer shirt and slacks Amel had found for him. The shirt was just on the near side of gaudy to Erien's eyes — blue, violet and green in overlapping quadrangles, but Amel insisted it suited him.

"Amel agreed to let Lurol cure him, finally?" Evert asked, rising above his own unhappiness to be glad for her.

Erien shook his head. "Not entirely. There will be no personality adjustment. But he'll let her get rid of the clear dreams, provided I prove I trust the system enough to view the memory of his last meeting with Di Mon under STI zero conditions. As though we haven't already proven it!" He yanked on casual slacks.

"I never met Di Mon," Evert said, and gave a nervous laugh. "It's rather spooky, don't you think, meeting him after he's — oh, I'm sorry. This must be much worse for you."

Erien found himself staring at the closed door of his bedroom, thinking about another door on Monitum. He shook himself alert with a smile for Evert's benefit. "Let's go."

Ranar, Erien was pleased to see, let Evert hold his hand as they entered the Space Sciences building. Amel was subdued. *He didn't think I would go through with this*, thought Erien, and had to quell his own nervousness with faith in Bley's counselling triumvirate and Lurol's professionalism.

They walked in silence through the lobby of the Space Service medical center to the psychiatric ward on the lower floor, then up an elevator to Lurol's visitor probe lab. Lurol and Bley were waiting in the middle room on a spacious stage floor. Amel went to sit at the foot of the probe bed he would be treated in for clear dreams, once this ritual was over. Lurol looked to him for instruction when their small, select audience had entered, including Bley's colleagues, who still functioned as Amel's counselling triumvirate. Amel stood up a bit shakily and addressed the group.

"I am not the one who ought to have the memories of Liege Monitum's last conversation," Amel told Erien and Ranar. "You should. And I invited Evert because I know he... well, he loves you both." Amel made a point of not looking at Ranar and Evert's clasped hands, despite his effort to be tolerant of their particular kind of love.

Amel turned to Erien. "If Di Mon explained his death, I guess it was to me. I think it is you," he included Ranar again, "who need to hear it, from him. I just want the message delivered."

Amel withdrew to the base of the probe again and sat down, resting against the foot of the bed.

"This is in temporary and strictly local storage," said Lurol, "governed by STI zero retention and access restrictions." She nodded in the direction of the counselling triumvirate. "Its very existence fulfills Amel's challenge to Erien, to prove we can really be trusted. Well, me in particular. So I have to ask this: shall I play it for you? Do you want to see it?"

Ranar cleared his throat. "Is it as — vivid as the original probe material?"

"Close," said Lurol.

"I want a chair, first," Ranar said.

Solomon fetched one for him.

Ranar seemed to recollect that Erien was in the room and gestured to him, "Please, come sit beside me."

Erien complied, kneeling beside the chair with his near arm resting on the seat beside Ranar. Evert settled a hand on Ranar's shoulder, and Ranar looked up and smiled at him. They turned back to the stage as it came alive with Amel's reconstructed memories.

The interior of Di Mon's library was shockingly accurate. Erien half expected to smell old, polished leather. Despite having schooled himself not to, he still caught his breath at the sight of Di Mon behind his desk, lean, sword-sharp, fiercely intelligent and fiercely alive in the last hour of his life.

"When I found out you had brought Ameron's stolen heir to Monitum, I was willing enough to take over his upbringing," Di Mon was saying to Amel. "I have been told I am too cautious. This, at least, was as Vrellishly rash of me as anyone could desire."

"Yes," Amel's own, younger voice was edged with nervousness. Erien saw his hand withdraw from the arm of a familiar carved chair, but otherwise Amel was no more present than a camera operator.

"I am pleased with Erien's progress," Di Mon said. "Raising the future heir of Gelion has been an honor. But it cannot continue now that I'm weakened by this cursed cancer. Erien's education must be turned over to Ranar."

Fear blossomed in Amel's tone. "Why Ranar? He's Reetion. How can you trust him with something so important t-to..." Amel's words petered out.

Di Mon studied him with a transfixing scrutiny, and then slowly got up. He had a razor focus and a diamond intensity as he came around the desk, stalking Amel.

The perspective of the memory lurched as Amel stumbled up, making the feet of his heavy chair squeak on the polished floor.

Di Mon stopped. A cynical triumph smiled through the pain of his untreated cancer. "You know why," he said in a dangerous tone. "You do not need to ask."

"W-what?" Amel's voice faltered.

Di Mon resumed his seat behind the desk, arms folded. He was clearly ill. It made him brittle, but his energetic intellect was undaunted. He did not suppose — he knew — the world to be his private puzzle. "You've deduced what I am," Di Mon said with a cold, bare rationality. "That's why you flinched. I am not as careful as I once was. I do not care to be. I find myself more willing to take chances and therefore, if they dare to believe the unthinkable, those people who know me well begin to guess. First the most observant — yourself. And then? It is only a matter of time before one of those who guesses is an enemy."

His attention reverted with Vrellish suddenness upon his victim. "Are you my enemy, Amel Dem'Vrel?"

"Not about — that," the younger version of Amel stuttered.

"But you are afraid of me."

"I always have been," Amel admitted.

Di Mon steepled long fingers. "And with cause. Still, you know. And you have not betrayed me, although to do so might have profited you in more than one quarter."

This was the Di Mon Erien remembered. He smiled despite himself, wondering how he could possibly have imagined Di Mon vulnerable to anything that Amel might have said or done. It was Amel, not Di Mon, who was off balance in this conversation.

"You act out of convictions of your own, about people," Di Mon told Amel. "Convictions so powerful that, should I convince you, you would follow my orders above even Ameron's. Therefore I know you can be trusted with a charge that will matter, one day, even more than my family honor."

"I don't understand," Amel floundered.

"You will," Di Mon said confidently, "before we part." He picked up the jade-handled knife on his desk.

Erien's hand slipped down to his ankle sheath and touched the hilt of that knife.

The door opened and Amel started, his attention spinning around. Di Mon smiled in greeting at the black-haired boy standing in the doorway.

"Ah, Erien." Di Mon still held the jade knife, casually, in one hand. "How are you finding the Reetion, Ranar?"

"He's... all right," said Erien's child-self, looking sullen.

"Yes. He is, isn't he. Here," Di Mon extended the jade knife, handle first, to Erien. "A present for you."

Watching Di Mon now, through Amel's eyes, the ritual substitution for a farewell hug was all too easy to deduce.

Di Mon took a book from his drawer — his copy of the Ameron biography — and gave it to Erien. Erien remembered the weight of the heavy book in his arms. "I promised Ranar a copy of this the last time we met," Di Mon told him, looking at him with a satisfied air that resented the separation to come. It was amazing how Amel's memories managed to highlight the tension and responses that betrayed discomfort. Erien had had no idea how much his own worry and confusion had showed. Then Di Mon began to relax like any master swordsman before a duel.

"Please take the book to him," Di Mon told Erien in a caressing tone. "And as you are to be living with him for a while, do it graciously. He is commoner, but you can learn from him. And you may need to. I know you won't forget you are a Gelack as you learn what it means, in broader terms, to be a human. Ranar can explain it better than I can."

Erien made a last effort — he remembered that effort. "I do not want to leave Monitum."

Di Mon became cooler. "I did not ask you what you wanted, Erien." He relented instantly. "Now take the book and find Ranar."

"Ranar said he wanted to talk to you."

"Tell him later."

Very, very much later, Di Mon, thought the adult Erien, the hilt of the knife in his hand.

Out of objections, and conscious of Amel's intruding presence, the child Erien left with the book under his arm. He would come back to find Di Mon dead by his own hand.

Alone with Amel again, Di Mon dictated his demands with cold determination. "I have learned a good deal about you through my *lyka*, Eva, and other sources. You do not like me and we have had our differences. But you will do what I want you to for the boy's sake because," Di Mon fixed his analytical stare again on Amel, "I love him. That makes me, in your eyes, entitled... in a way even Ameron is not."

"Eva did not tell me anything personal about you," Amel insisted, defensive and shaken.

"No?" Di Mon was not deeply interested. "But even if she had, you would say that." He paused. "You will be with her this evening? Before dinner."

"Yes," Amel sounded suspicious but puzzled. "Does that matter?"

"Somewhat."

"Eva loves you."

"I know," Di Mon assured him. "Let her know I am grateful."

Amel got up, looking surly. "Until dinner then."

"Yes," Di Mon sounded abstract and distant. That, too, he had planned: for Eva to be able to attest that Amel had been with her when Di Mon died, and perhaps to be with her to comfort her.

Amel left and the memory ended.

Ranar got up abruptly, turned to Evert and hugged him.

Erien got up too, and turned blindly toward Amel. "You were right," he said. "I did need to see that. Excuse me."

"Out the door on your left, kid," Lurol called after him.

The room Lurol directed Erien to was a small study carrel, decorated and lit to be conducive to concentration. As he closed the door behind him, Erien realized he had Di Mon's knife in his hand, as though grief was something he could drive away with a sharp edge. He closed his eyes. His mind spun out the events after Amel's memory ended: Di Mon getting up from his desk again, straightening his papers, straightening the books on the bookshelves and then crouching to roll back the carpet so that it would not be stained by his blood.

It had been immeasurably preferable to blame Amel, Erien thought, rather than know that Di Mon had in this, as in almost everything else, been master of his own destiny.

The door opened and closed again, startling him. He raised the knife unconsciously.

It was Ranar. He saw no threat in the drawn blade. He just scowled at it as if it was its erstwhile owner. "See me later!" he said bitterly. Then he laughed. It was a short, rough sound, ending as he jerked his head up. His eyes were dry. His face was heated with the emotion of finishing a long-suspended argument. "Damn you for a calculating Lorel, Mon! You could have told me!"

The next moment Ranar looked confused, as if Di Mon's failure to reply surprised him. "He came to me the night before. He shocked me, he was so relaxed about it." He hesitated very briefly. "And so Vrellish!" He laughed at himself, less harshly, and thrust a hand through his hair, shading his face momentarily. "I had never been less worried about him emotionally. The cancer was bad, of course. He never said it in as many words, but I expected that my taking you would free him to seek treatment." Ranar relaxed with his hands at his sides and his head resting against the closed door behind him. A smile tugged at his neutral expression as he looked at Erien. "You realize he manipulated us as thoroughly as he did poor, skittish Amel."

Erien moved to sheath Di Mon's knife again. Ranar put out a hand to stop him. "Are you angry?" Ranar asked him. "With Di Mon?"

That was not a question Erien wanted to be asked. He swung a sandaled foot up onto the windowsill and settled his hip on the sill, turning his head to face Ranar with the light at his back.

"It doesn't matter whether I am or not," he said. "It doesn't alter anything that happened. I doubt it would have altered anything then, either, if I had known."

"*Ack rel*," Ranar summed up in Gelack.

The two of them remained together, waiting in silence, until Lurol came to find them to tell them Amel's treatment was finished. He would not be clear dreaming anymore.

"And I haven't done a thing more than I said I would," she promised Erien. "But don't you think you ought to reconsider, since it sounds as if you will be taking him back with you to Gelion, now? All I'm asking is to undo something that should never have happened."

Erien looked at her, not with anger, but something much closer to compassion. "You cannot change the past, Lurol, nor what it has made of anyone." He thrust Di Mon's knife back into its sheath in his boot. "Gelion will have to take what it gets... in both of us."

**Our titles are available at major book stores
and local independent resellers who support
Science Fiction and Fantasy readers like you.**

EDGE Science Fiction
and Fantasy Publishing

Tesseract Books

Dragon Moon Press

www.edgewebsite.com
www.dragonmoonpress.com

Our titles are available at major book stores and local independent resellers who support Science Fiction and Fantasy readers like you.

Alien Deception by Tony Ruggiero -(tp) - ISBN: 978-1-896944-34-0
Alien Revelation by Tony Ruggiero (tp) - ISBN: 978-1-896944-34-8
Alphanauts by J. Brian Clarke (tp) - ISBN: 978-1-894063-14-2
Apparition Trail, The by Lisa Smedman (tp) - ISBN: 978-1-894063-22-7
As Fate Decrees by Denysé Bridger (tp) - ISBN: 978-1-894063-41-8

Black Chalice, The by Marie Jakober (hb) - ISBN: 978-1-894063-00-7
Blue Apes by Phyllis Gotlieb (pb) - ISBN: 978-1-895836-13-4
Blue Apes by Phyllis Gotlieb (hb) - ISBN: 978-1-895836-14-1

Case of the Pitcher's Pendant, The: A Billybub Baddings Mystery
    by Tee Morris (tp) - ISBN: 978-1-896944-77-7
Case of the Singing Sword, The: A Billybub Baddings Mystery
    by Tee Morris (tp) - ISBN: 978-1-896944-18-0
Chalice of Life, The by Anne Webb (tp) - ISBN: 978-1-896944-33-3
Chasing The Bard by Philippa Ballantine (tp) - ISBN: 978-1-896944-08-1
Children of Atwar, The by Heather Spears (pb) - ISBN: 978-0-88878-335-6
Cinkarion - The Heart of Fire (Part Two of The Chronicles of the Karionin)
    by J. A. Cullum - (tp) - ISBN: 978-1-894063-21-0
Clan of the Dung-Sniffers by Lee Danielle Hubbard (pb) - ISBN: 978-1-894063-05-0
Claus Effect, The by David Nickle & Karl Schroeder (pb) - ISBN: 978-1-895836-34-9
Claus Effect, The by David Nickle & Karl Schroeder (hb) - ISBN: 978-1-895836-35-6
Complete Guide to Writing Fantasy, The - Volume 1: Alchemy with Words
    - edited by Darin Park and Tom Dullemond (tp)
    - ISBN: 978-1-896944-09-8
Complete Guide to Writing Fantasy, The - Volume 2: Opus Magus
    - edited by Tee Morris and Valerie Griswold-Ford (tp)
    - ISBN: 978-1-896944-15-9
Complete Guide to Writing Fantasy, The - Volume 3: The Author's Grimoire
    - edited by Valerie Griswold-Ford & Lai Zhao (tp)
    - ISBN: 978-1-896944-38-8
Complete Guide to Writing Science Fiction, The - Volume 1: First Contact
    - edited by Dave A. Law & Darin Park (tp)
    - ISBN: 978-1-896944-39-5
Courtesan Prince, The (Part One of the Okal Rel Saga) by Lynda Williams (tp)
    - ISBN: 978-1-894063-28-9

Dark Earth Dreams by Candas Dorsey & Roger Deegan (comes with a CD)
    - ISBN: 978-1-895836-05-9
Darkling Band, The by Jason Henderson (tp) - ISBN: 978-1-896944-36-4
Darkness of the God (Children of the Panther Part Two)
    by Amber Hayward (tp) - ISBN: 978-1-894063-44-9
Darwin's Paradox by Nina Munteanu (tp) - ISBN: 978-1-896944-68-5
Daughter of Dragons by Kathleen Nelson - (tp) - ISBN: 978-1-896944-00-5
Digital Magic by Philippa Ballantine (tp) - ISBN: 978-1-896944-88-3
Distant Signals by Andrew Weiner (tp) - ISBN: 978-0-88878-284-7
Dominion by J. Y. T. Kennedy (tp) - ISBN: 978-1-896944-28-9
Dragon Reborn, The by Kathleen H. Nelson - (tp) - ISBN: 978-1-896944-05-0

Dragon's Fire, Wizard's Flame by Michael R. Mennenga (tp)
- ISBN: 978-1-896944-13-5
Dreams of an Unseen Planet by Teresa Plowright (tp) - ISBN: 978-0-88878-282-3
Dreams of the Sea (Part 1 of Tyranaël) by Élisabeth Vonarburg (tp)
- ISBN: 978-1-895836-96-7
Dreams of the Sea (Part 1 of Tyranaël) by Élisabeth Vonarburg (hb)
- ISBN: 978-1-895836-98-1

Eclipse by K. A. Bedford (tp) - ISBN: 978-1-894063-30-2
Edgewise by Stephen L. Antczak (tp) - ISBN: 978-1-894063-27-2
Elements of Fantasy: Magic edited by Dave A. Law
& Valerie Griswold-Ford (tp) - ISBN: 978-1-8964063-96-8
Even The Stones by Marie Jakober (tp) - ISBN: 978-1-894063-18-0

Far Arena (Part Five of the Okal Rel Saga) by Lynda Williams (tp)
- ISBN: 978-1-894063-45-6
Fires of the Kindred by Robin Skelton (tp) - ISBN: 978-0-88878-271-7
Firestorm of Dragons edited by Michele Acker & Kirk Dougal (tp)
- ISBN: 978-1-896944-80-7
Forbidden Cargo by Rebecca Rowe (tp) - ISBN: 978-1-894063-16-6

Game of Perfection, A (Part 2 of Tyranaël) by Élisabeth Vonarburg (tp)
- ISBN: 978-1-894063-32-6
Gaslight Grimoire: Fantastic Tales of Sherlock Holmes
edited by Jeff Campbell & Charles Prepolec (pb)
- ISBN: 978-1-8964063-17-3
Green Music by Ursula Pflug (tp) - ISBN: 978-1-895836-75-2
Green Music by Ursula Pflug (hb) - ISBN: 978-1-895836-77-6
Gryphon Highlord, The by Connie Ward (tp) - ISBN: 978-1-896944-38-8

Healer, The (Children of the Panther Part One) by Amber Hayward (tp)
- ISBN: 978-1-895836-89-9
Healer, The (Children of the Panther Part One) by Amber Hayward (hb)
- ISBN: 978-1-895836-91-2
Hell Can Wait by Theodore Judson (tp) - ISBN: 978-1-978-1-894063-23-4
Hounds of Ash and other tales of Fool Wolf, The by Greg Keyes (pb)
- ISBN: 978-1-894063-09-8
Human Thing, The by Kathleen H. Nelson - (hb) - ISBN: 978-1-896944-03-6
Hydrogen Steel by K. A. Bedford (tp) - ISBN: 978-1-894063-20-3

i-ROBOT Poetry by Jason Christie (tp) - ISBN: 978-1-894063-24-1

Jackal Bird by Michael Barley (pb) - ISBN: 978-1-895836-07-3
Jackal Bird by Michael Barley (hb) - ISBN: 978-1-895836-11-0
JEMMA7729 by Phoebe Wray (tp) - ISBN: 978-1-894063-40-1

Keaen by Till Noever (tp) - ISBN: 978-1-894063-08-1
Keeper's Child by Leslie Davis (tp) - ISBN: 978-1-894063-01-2

Lachlei by M. H. Bonham (tp) - ISBN: 978-1-896944-69-2
Land/Space edited by Candas Jane Dorsey and Judy McCrosky (tp)
- ISBN: 978-1-895836-90-5
Land/Space edited by Candas Jane Dorsey and Judy McCrosky (hb)
- ISBN: 978-1-895836-92-9

Tesseracts Q edited by Élisabeth Vonarburg & Jane Brierley (hb)
- ISBN: 978-1-895836-22-6
Throne Price by Lynda Williams and Alison Sinclair (tp)
- ISBN: 978-1-894063-06-7
Time Machines Repaired Whie-U-Wait by K. A. Bedford (tp)
- ISBN: 978-1-894063-42-5
Too Many Princes by Deby Fredricks (tp) - ISBN: 978-1-896944-36-4
Twilight of the Fifth Sun by David Sakmyster (tp) - ISBN: 978-1-896944-01-02

Virtual Evil by Jana Oliver (tp) - ISBN: 978-1-896944-76-0

War of the Druids by Barbara Galler-Smith and Josh Langston (tp)
- ISBN: 978-1-894063-29-6
Writers For Relief: An Anthology to Benefit the Bay Area Food Bank
edited by Davey Beauchamp (pb) - ISBN: 978-1-896944-92-0